A REPORT of MURDER

A REPORT of MURDER

F.L. EVERETT

bookouture

Published by Bookouture in 2023

An imprint of Storyfire Ltd.
Carmelite House
50 Victoria Embankment
London EC4Y 0DZ

www.bookouture.com

ISBN: 978-1-83525-494-3
eBook ISBN: 978-1-83790-500-3

For Eve, my lifelong Annie, but wiser.

To send light into the darkness of men's hearts – such is the duty of the artist.

— ROBERT SCHUMANN

CHAPTER ONE

MANCHESTER, DECEMBER 1940

Failure is a wet coat, dragging behind you. I wasn't sure if I'd read that somewhere, or if I just thought it and meant to write it down. I was twenty-four and I had already failed.

The war had been rumbling on for well over a year, and I'd done nothing heroic. All my notions of dragging people from burning buildings, or sounding the alarm as bombers roared overhead, had dissolved when it became clear that my long hours at the *Manchester Chronicle* meant I barely had time to knit a scratchy scarf for Our Brave Boys. I'd volunteered a couple of times at the WVS shop in town, which sold moth-eaten old clothes and battered cricket stumps to raise funds, but arranging yellowing lace doilies in the window under the beady eye of Mrs Bailey didn't feel much of a wartime sacrifice.

I'd failed at having a sweetheart. Half the girls I knew were already married, or primed for an engagement ring when their uniformed boys came home on leave.

When I met Ricky, before the war, I was dazzled by his little sports car and the way he flourished my coat for me when we left Lyons Corner House. It turned out he lived in

Mobberley with Jane, his wife of seven years, and their two small children. I only found out because the waitress had seen him with his family at church, and she told me while my so-called boyfriend was buying cigarettes.

Worst of all, I had failed at work. Five years on the *Manchester Chronicle* and I was no closer to being a real reporter than when I'd arrived at nineteen, full of visions of myself in a stylish suit and pillbox hat, frantically scribbling notes while the victim of a terrible crime sobbed nearby. That little fantasy was soon knocked out of me. I could probably teach a packed Corn Exchange how to make the perfect cup of tea for twenty different people, I could take dictation without a pause, I could run the telephone switchboard like a symphony conductor, or soothe someone who had fallen down a chute and wanted to expose the Coal Board on the front page. I could write copy better and faster than half the reporters, and extract succinct headlines from the people who wrote in with their rambling stories. But no one would give me a chance. And much as I liked working at the *Chronicle* and though it was infinitely better than working all hours as an auxiliary nurse, like my best friend Annie, I didn't know how much longer I could stand feeling overlooked and underpaid.

It all came to a head when Tom Harwood announced he was joining up. During what the papers were calling 'the phoney war', when nothing actually happened for months, he'd been swanking around the office as usual, full of wildly exaggerated tales regarding the gripping life of a crime reporter. He'd done a bit of basic training, but apparently being a journalist was a protected occupation, or so he claimed, despite several of the others leaving to go and fight.

Now, however, it seemed he'd 'had enough of watching buddies zip off to the front line' – he always talked like a cheap detective novel – and had made up his mind to join the Royal

Air Force. I suspected it was as much the allure of the uniform as anything more noble, seeing as the minute he mentioned it, Gloria from the typing pool turned pink with delight and admiration. He'd always been enormously pleased with himself, and though obviously I didn't want his plane bursting into flames, I did rather hope his new 'AF buddies' might take him down a peg or two.

From where I was sitting, Mr Harwood's crime-reporting job looked remarkably easy. He'd stroll in, cigarette clamped between his lips, throw his hat on the mahogany stand and settle back with a cup of tea delivered by head secretary Pat – or if I was unlucky, me. Then he'd regale us with snippets of information about Manchester's criminal underworld, albeit nothing we couldn't get from reading that day's paper. The rest of the morning would be taken up with him nagging the switchboard girls, Sally and Olive, to ring up his 'contacts' at Willert Street Police Station.

Since the war began, he'd been unbearable, nodding and winking about 'the black market', hinting about his 'contacts in intelligence.'

No wonder I was thrilled when it transpired he was finally going.

'I'd love to be considered to take over your position,' I told him. 'Just while the war's on, of course. Perhaps you could mention to Mr Gorringe...'

Tom had looked at me as if I'd said, 'I'd love to play Cleopatra in the middle of St Ann's Square.' Eventually, he said, 'I think Desmond Barry's getting it,' and that was that.

It wasn't that I hated my job. I loved the clattering and dinging of typewriters, and the constant murmur of copy-taking. I liked the people – the *Chronicle* was one of the city's bigger newspapers, and it had a large office, filled with busy, ambitious types, most of whom were good fun. I got on particularly well with Ethel Cooper on the letters desk, who was ten years my senior and unmarried. She spent her weekends trekking up Kinder Scout with like-minded folk in Fair Isle jumpers and bobble hats, and owned a cat called Silas Marner.

'I don't want a husband,' she once told me. 'I want a wife – someone to have my tea ready when I get in, and bring me the newspaper while I sit by the fire.'

Sometimes, we ate lunch together, but often she would say, 'I'm just nipping to the Kardomah,' which was a new café on Market Street, with refrigerated cakes and blue neon lighting. I'd only been once – it was beyond my budget – but before the war, Ethel had occasionally treated me to a coffee and a kunzle cake. It was a sponge in a chocolate shell, with a coffee cream topping. I still thought about those glorious cakes when I contemplated my meagre lunches.

I enjoyed chatting to the other secretaries, and Marge, who did a bit of everything – copy-taking, answering phones, writing captions for pictures. Marge had always been jolly, full of jokes and fun, but since her husband, Vince, had joined up, she'd been much quieter.

'I've not heard from him in a fortnight,' she'd say, dabbing tears away with her lace hanky, and there was often a huddle of ghoulish sympathisers round her desk, speculating on 'what might have happened.' I didn't think that did Marge any good, but people liked drama; the war had proved that.

I didn't even dislike being a secretary, despite five long years of answering idiotic enquiries. 'My budgerigar's flown away, can you put something on the front page to help find him?' was one such classic, often quoted by the reporters. 'Not much news today. Use the budgie for the splash,' they'd say.

I had always longed, though, to be a proper journalist;

someone who roved the city, chatting to contacts, uncovering crimes and writing about them. I knew I was capable; I didn't need to be mollycoddled because I was female. I just needed a chance.

Annie couldn't fathom why, but I'd wanted to be a crime reporter since I was ten. Long, grim nights in the children's home were only survivable because I used to smuggle in mystery books from the school library and lie awake until one or two in the morning, or until I finished them. My bed was nearest to the window and the thin curtains let in just enough light from the street lamp outside, if I strained my eyes, to make out the words.

By the time I was eleven, I'd abandoned children's books and was borrowing *Sherlock Holmes* from Miss Mellor, my English teacher, and speed-reading Margery Allinghams from the public library till dawn. I didn't want to be a detective – it seemed impossible, and besides, I didn't want to be killed. I only wanted to write about crime, find out why they'd done it and what they'd felt as they thrust in the knife. I wanted to understand how people survived after something terrible happened to them or to somebody they loved. I had so many questions burning inside me, I was certain I could find out more than any man.

Now Tom was going, a tiny window of possibility had opened up. If I could impress Mr Gorringe, who thought women were mostly useful for 'keeping a pleasant atmosphere in the office', as I'd once heard him say to his secretary, I could become one of the *Chronicle*'s crime reporters, at least while the war was on. I knew how unlikely it was, but life was unlikely, I told myself. It was unlikely that I'd ever find my parents, but I still hoped that one day, I might receive a letter from one of them explaining why they'd left me on the orphanage steps as a baby. So getting promoted to the crime desk seemed possible too. At least I had a job in the right place, and so many things had been upended thanks to the war, why shouldn't a woman be a crime reporter? Annie had worked on the returns counter at Marshall & Snelgrove's department store, and now she spent her days rushing up and down the wards at Manchester Royal, tending to injured soldiers back from the front.

'I hate it, Edie,' she said. 'I'm supposed to be a ministering angel, according to Matron, but I feel dizzy when I see a grazed knee.'

She was always exhausted and bedraggled when she came home to our tiny shared flat, and I felt it was only fair to let her have the hot water for her bath, which generally left me with a sketchy, freezing wash from the ewer on my dressing table. It was bearable in summer, but in winter, one splash from that bowl felt like a breathless plunge into the icy boating lake at Platt Fields. No wonder Annie dreamed of handsome soldiers, who would spirit her away from our first-floor flat at Violet Bank Terrace in Fallowfield. The violets were long gone, a distant echo of some long-ago Edwardian fancy, and Annie and I called it 'Violent Bank Terrace' to reflect our generally troubled finances.

'Joan Willis is engaged,' she'd say gloomily, flicking through the Births, Marriages and Deaths columns in the *Chronicle*. 'She's known him five minutes; she wouldn't have looked twice without the uniform. I knew Billy Peake's brother and he was a right so-and-so.'

'I suppose they want to hurry up because... well...'

'He may not come back? In that case, at least marry someone handsome and have fun while you can,' grumbled Annie.

Her own sort-of fiancé Pete was now in the army, and so far, handsome doctors had been in short supply. 'They're always moaning about the carbolic soap, or fast asleep,' she said. 'Fat lot of good that is.'

The day after Tom announced he was leaving, I sat in the grandly named luncheon room – in reality, a spare office with a window looking onto a soot-blackened wall – eating sandwiches made with my cheese ration and some grey, lumpy bread of Annie's making, and I dared to allow myself a little dream. I imagined myself researching and writing up an exclusive crime story and leaving it on Mr Gorringe's desk. He'd read it and be so impressed he'd call me into his office and offer me Tom's job on the spot. All I needed was a tip-off.

'All alright?' asked Ethel, as I wandered back past her large desk. She had curled her hair tightly and drawn on her pencil-thin eyebrows, so they looked like little brackets.

'Yes,' I said. 'Same as usual. Don't suppose you know of any crimes, do you?'

'Only the price of lipstick,' she said, winding a fresh sheet of paper into her typewriter. 'Don't suppose you've any tips to make woollen stockings look like nylons at parties this Christmas?'

'If I'm invited to any parties, I'll let you know,' I said. So far, my social life was me, Annie and our downstairs landlord banging on the ceiling if we dared to put the wireless on.

Back at my desk, in between answering letters, I was enjoying a further daydream about moving to London, reporting on the Blitz, fellow reporters crying, 'here she is!' as I staggered in, covered in dust and soot, with a ragged notebook held triumphantly aloft...

I sensed a change in the atmosphere and a waft of Woodland Fern, and looked up to see Janet Paulson standing beside my desk, buttoned into her brown tweed suit like an overstuffed hassock.

She was the editor's secretary, and didn't we all know it. Some of the girls and I called her 'Parrot Paulson' behind her back because of her tendency to repeat little remarks the boss had made.

'Could you come into the office, please?' she said. 'The editor would like a word.'

I'd read the expression 'my stomach dropped' in books, and thought it was a wild exaggeration. But it appears that's exactly how it feels when your world is about to end. I saw myself as a child, as a miserable adolescent, passing my school certificate, filled with hope arriving at the *Chronicle*, then the steady stream of disappointments and failed attempts at promotion.

I couldn't imagine that Mr Gorringe was about to do anything but give me the sack, as in half a decade, he had never once asked to see me personally. The most I'd ever had was a nod of acknowledgement, and even then, he may only have been adjusting his collar.

I'd be out on my ear with no references and nothing to show for the past five years but a pile of unused reporters' notebooks. I should have befriended Norma, the domestic matters editor, and politely suggested that I could write about knitting or 'baking with scraps', and perhaps one day, I'd have been in her chair, sifting through letters about 'the amusing thing that happened to me on a trip to Chester', or why the *Chronicle* needed to serve its crocheting readers more effectively.

As I walked the ten or so miles through other peoples' desks to Mr Gorringe's wood-panelled office, I found myself noticing small things, the way I imagined someone who has just had a diagnosis of terminal illness appreciates sunlight anew, knowing that soon, it will all be swallowed by darkness. I felt sudden tenderness towards the posed, studio picture of sub-editor Mr Chandler's children that I'd always silently mocked (they really were odd-looking, with big, milk-bottle glasses that made them look like little flies) and I felt nothing but endeared by Pat's 'indoor shoes' bag that she always kept by her desk, ostentatiously showing her concern for the *Chronicle*'s tired parquet floors.

'Mr Gorringe won't be a moment, if you'll just take a seat.'

I tried to read Janet's face, but as ever, it was blank as a china doll, her rolled hair immaculate. I slid into a chair and briefly closed my eyes to try and imprint this moment, the last before it was all whisked away, with its ordinary sounds of typing and people murmuring, and the smell of ink and Camp coffee mingling with Mr Gorringe's pipe tobacco whenever he took his general-inspecting-the-troops stroll through the newsroom. God, how I'd miss it.

'Miss York.' Mr Gorringe ushered me through to his inner sanctum. It was all brown. Wooden panels, nicotine-stained portraits of the city's Victorian councillors and previous editors, oak desk, brown pipe rack, brown leather chairs, one of which I sank into.

He looked at me over his tortoiseshell spectacles. He may have been handsome once, but years of lunchtime pints at the Nag's Head and incessant worry over front-page headlines and incorrect grammar usage had aged him.

'Well,' he said, in his distinctive Manchester-by-way-of-Oxford accent, 'I've been hearing certain things, Miss York.' I thanked heaven Janet had gone downstairs, or the whole office would know I was about to be sacked.

'Certain things?'

I had a sudden stab of sympathy for Parrot Paulson. There was something about the editor's manner that made having original thoughts difficult.

'I have, in fact, summoned you to discuss whether you would indeed care for a promotion of sorts. Not to the crime desk, I fear – that is rather a step for anyone, let alone a young woman.'

I wondered how on earth he knew, and it occurred to me that Tom must have said something mocking before he left. For a moment, I imagined his aeroplane spiralling into the North Sea, trailing black smoke, then I felt a stab of guilt.

'...but to what is indubitably a journalistic position,' said Mr Gorringe.

I was so surprised, I laughed. He regarded me patiently.

'I'm so sorry,' I said. 'I thought you were going to give me the sack.'

'I cannot imagine why you thought that,' he said. 'You have offered me no cause of which I am aware.'

He really did talk like a grammar primer. It was hard to square this exacting, prep-school Mr Gorringe with the editor who signed off headlines like BUBBLY BLONDE BARMAID IN CROWN COURT BABY BATTLE.

'The role in question is newly created,' he said. 'I shall be frank, I initially thought of offering it to Linda, it being her field, but she was uncertain as to whether she would possess the necessary journalistic rigour. And she is in the WVS, I believe, and is rather short of time.'

I had no idea where this was going. Linda was on BMDs, or 'hatched, matched, dispatched' as Tom referred to the announcements pages.

'What I have decided this paper needs,' he went on, 'is an obituarist.'

Of all the things I'd expected him to say, it wasn't that. I had seen the obituaries in *The Times*, and the *Daily Telegraph* – they were solemn, dense, eulogies to great men and the occasional woman who had achieved marvellous things. Manchester had its wonders, but I wasn't sure if nobles and statesmen were amongst them these days.

'That sounds wonderful,' I said. By then, if he'd asked me to write an obituary of his ginger cat, Pawlock, I'd have stayed up all night to craft it.

'My thinking is this,' he said, steepling his fingers. Through the frosted glass of the door, I could see that Janet had returned to her desk, and was craning her neck to find out what was happening on the other side of the door. 'We are at war,' Mr Gorringe said, like a Pathé newsreel.

My leather chair creaked disrespectfully, and I murmured 'yes' to cover it up.

'Of course, military casualties are a tragic but necessary result of such a situation,' he said, moving his spotless blotter slightly to the left. 'We could fill the paper several times over with stories of doomed nobility,' he went on. 'However, that will, I suspect, do little for morale when so many of our readers have brothers, sons, husbands battling at the front and indeed, behind it.'

I nodded. A piece of coal clinked from the small fireplace in his office and rolled into the grate. Mr Gorringe sighed.

'That is why,' he concluded, 'I have decided to attempt something new. I want the *Chronicle* to celebrate our city and its readers, to reassure them that no matter what Hitler might attempt, our people will prevail.' He pushed his glasses up his nose and a gust of acrid smoke billowed into the room as wind found its way through the chimney.

'As a result,' he said, 'I think it would be seemly to have a column devoted to obituaries for civilians. People still are born, are they not, and still pass onward to the Elysian fields?'

I nodded again, feeling I should break into a hymn after this lengthy sermon.

'Manchester is full of notable individuals,' he added. 'Retired headmasters, great scientists from the university, inventors, writers, and perhaps even those who have eschewed fame altogether, in order to live a blameless and charitable life in the shadows.'

I felt very sorry for Mrs Gorringe if this was how he talked at home.

'Therefore,' he said, 'I propose that you, Miss York, should be our obituarist. You appear to have a *way* with people, so I cannot foresee any difficulty in the sensitive interviewing of relations. Eight hundred words main piece, and a further two or three two-hundred-word paragraphs, to run weekly. Of course, if a photograph exists of the individual, all the better. Please do request one.'

I must have been gaping in shock as he added, 'Is that acceptable to you?'

'Yes!' I said again. 'Yes, it's marvellous.'

He looked slightly askance at my wild enthusiasm.

'Good. So, a piece on the life, the achievements, why we should remember them fondly, and most importantly, how they contributed to the life of the city. They don't need to be famous, or even well known in their fields. The main criterion is that they have enjoyed a good, full and interesting life, lived for the most part in Manchester. *Sic itur ad astra*, Miss York: thus, one journeys to the stars.'

I couldn't quite take in what he was saying. 'So I won't be doing my current job any more?'

'No, I rather think this will fill your time adequately,' he said. 'I'm told that you enjoy research, and have a pleasant telephone manner. I assume you're able to string a sentence together, though if I sense that you're struggling, I shall ask one of the reporters to rewrite...'

I bristled.

'But one hopes that won't be necessary.' He took off his glasses and polished them on his sleeve.

I needed a cup of hot, sweet tea for shock, and a lie-down on our enormously uncomfortable horsehair couch. A terrifying thought suddenly occurred to me. 'Is there a particular way you should like me to find these people?' I blurted. I had no idea how to go about this, despite all my crime reporter bluster.

He looked up wearily. 'The usual routes, I should think,' he said. 'The deaths column, the police, your own contacts, funeral homes, the council offices – use your brain, Miss York, I'm told it's a considerable organ.'

I wanted to shout 'by whom?', but it was impossible. I'd spent the interview blushing and stammering like a terrified nine-year-old, and he was clearly expecting me to leave. 'I shan't let you down,' I said.

'Good,' said Mr Gorringe again. 'First copy with me next week then. I shall look forward to reading it.'

I bobbed my head as if he were royalty, just stopping short of walking out backwards, and as I left, he added, 'Oh yes, and speak to Miss Paulson about a pay rise. Nothing huge, but she'll talk to accounts.'

I nodded furiously, feeble, girlish tears welling. I didn't know if they were of relief or gratitude, or simply shock at dodging the bullet I'd been sure had 'Edie York' engraved on its case.

Outside, Miss Paulson looked up from her typewriter.

'Somebody's doing well for themselves,' she said.

I returned to my desk, light-headed with shock, and wondered who would now do all the work I normally did. It didn't matter, I reminded myself. I was now a reporter, of a sort – an obituarist, a person with a title. I was finally allowed to write, to interview... if it weren't for the war, I knew, some useless lump like Toby O'Dowd would be doing it. He was a junior reporter who, like Tom, had claimed initially to be in a reserved occupation. I was very unconvinced that his news-in-brief stories – RATS SPOTTED BEHIND LAMBERT'S FISH SUPPERS IN CHEETHAM HILL or BEER SHORTAGE ADDS TO RATIONING WOE – were enough to keep him carefully preserved behind the front lines. But as Annie said, 'some men are just cowards and that's all there is to it.'

Back in September, someone in the War Office had finally decided Toby needed to shift himself for king and country, and off he went, to march at half-speed no doubt, while complaining about his flat feet.

'Telling off, was it?' asked Pat, readying herself to luxuriate in my misfortune.

I shook my head. 'No, actually I've been promoted.' I ruined the elegant effect by grinning with delight.

'What to? Chief time-waster?'

'Obituarist.' I told her what my new job entailed, and she shook her head.

'Interviewing dead people,' she muttered. 'I've never heard the like. I suppose Muggins over here will be doing all the extra work you're not doing then.'

I carefully rolled a new sheet of paper into my typewriter. 'I don't know,' I said. And the glorious thing was, I no longer had to know.

It was another bleak, lightless winter morning, and the blackout felt like a muffling glove over my frozen face. Annie and I staggered to the bus stop together, holding onto the railings of houses to guide us.

'You're so lucky, Edie,' she said, as we waited, bouncing up and down on our worn-out soles to keep warm. 'You can go to a lovely warm office and write about people. I have to go and patch them up, and believe me, I'd swap.'

'I know,' I said. 'But honestly, it's not that wonderful, I have to—'

'It sounds it,' she said crossly. 'You get cups of tea from a trolley and a coal fire and nobody's dying or losing limbs. It sounds heavenly, actually.'

In a fit of guilt, I said, 'Do you think I should volunteer to be an auxiliary nurse too?' As soon as I'd said it. I desperately hoped she'd say no.

'No,' she said. 'You couldn't do the hours, what with your job. And you hate blood. But you could volunteer for something. I know you did the WVS shop,' she added quickly, as I drew breath to argue. 'But we haven't won yet, have we? I think we should all do everything we possibly can to get rid.'

'Of what?'

'Hitler,' she hissed, as our bus arrived with a squeal of brakes and clouds of exhaust. 'Him.'

I forgot about the guilt when I arrived at the office, horribly aware that my one half-decent suit, a bottle-green gaberdine wool, was falling apart and my hat was more squashed owl's nest than chic pillbox. If I was going to be out and about interviewing grieving relations, I'd need to try and find something better to wear. I wondered if I could unpick one of Annie's old coats, given that I had no money. Perhaps I could steam the hat over a pudding bowl.

I was hanging my things up on the rickety office coat stand when I looked up and saw Desmond Barry, the crime reporter who had taken over from Tom, heaving towards me like a galleon in full sail, wreathed in pipe smoke thick as sea mist.

He had come out of retirement in Leeds – Des's days of glory had been in the Great War and just after, with his stories about gangs in Headingley stealing hospital equipment, and men pretending to be crippled soldiers to earn more money begging. He was a nice old thing, and seemed as unlikely a crime reporter as I did. So far, he had pottered about the office, whistling 'Roses of Picardy' through his teeth, and blowing noxious pipe smoke over the typing pool.

'Here,' he wheezed like an accordion. 'My dear, I need a small favour.'

I paused, still holding my hat halfway to the peg. I imagined rushing to a crime scene on his behalf, securing the interviews, producing reams of perfect copy, perhaps unmasking the killer...

'It's just a little thing for News in Pictures. Albert's down with the influenza, so he can't do it, and I'm meeting an informant in the Rising Sun at noon. I've asked everyone else and they're all busy with this and that...'

I felt rather insulted. Clearly, I was the very last, and worst option, whatever it was.

'So,' he went on, 'as I believe you've been promoted – and congrats, dear, all the best with the stiffs – I thought a quick trip out of the office wouldn't do any harm.'

'Where to?'

I wondered how he ever got any crime reporting done, but as he seemed to spend his time largely at the pub or the dog track, he'd probably gathered a decent network over the years.

'Well, now that the Home Guard have got their uniforms, and a proper structure at last – honestly, what a shambles it was, old timers with their rusty medals and youngsters with bloody colanders on their heads...' He wheezed indulgently. I waited. I was vaguely aware that back in November, new rules had come in, and the ragtag men of the Home Guard, who couldn't fight in the army because they were too ill, too old, or needed elsewhere, were no longer being left to their own devices but tidied up into battalions and regiments, wearing proper kit. Pat's husband Billy was in their local troop, and according to her, spent his on-duty nights smoking and playing poker in the scout hut overlooking Winter Hill. 'Looking for enemy parachutists,' she'd scoffed. 'Looking for ten bob on a royal flush, more like.'

Des puffed a stream of stale smoke at me, and finally said, 'So the Local Defence Volunteers Withington Company is on a training mission in Platt Fields and we said we'd send someone down with a snapper. Can you go?'

'I think so,' I said, baffled. 'But go and do what?'

'Well, the usual, dear!' Des said. 'You know the drill, surely – have a chat with the sergeant, find out whether they've seen anything alarming on the night watch, get some bits of colourful biography from the new recruits. It's only a couple of paragraphs and a picture – you know, an old boy looking down his rifle sights at a passing dog, bit of humour, that sort of thing.'

It occurred to me that what he was offering just about amounted to a journalistic assignment. Two days ago, I'd have leapt at the chance. But now, I said, 'I promised Mr Gorringe I'd start looking for obituaries today.'

'Well, where better?' boomed Des. 'One of them's bound to know someone who's died. Ask! Rule one of journalism, dear, ask questions!'

I couldn't imagine approaching a marching battalion of men and saying, 'Are any of you recently bereaved?', but I could see Des wasn't giving in, if I was standing between him and his lunchtime pint.

'All right,' I said. 'I'll do my best.'

'Marvellous,' said Des, cumbersomely patting me on the shoulder like a dancing bear. 'I'll ask Ernie to pop down with you, and take some pics. Half past eleven, by the bandstand, apparently. Sergeant's name is Leslie.'

'First or second name?' I asked, but he was already stumping back to his desk.

Ernie was the 'snapper' who had been on the *Chronicle* since long before the Great War. He looked at least eighty, and his camera, too, seemed to date from another era. It was the size of a suitcase and almost as big as he was. He had already parked his ancient and rusting car outside when I went down to the lobby, clutching my notebook.

'In you get, miss,' he said, holding the door open for me. 'Don't get many pretty young ladies on me jobs, I don't mind telling you.'

I smiled politely, and arranged my coat over my knees. He was older than Annie's Grandad Norman, and I didn't want him getting any ideas.

On the way, crawling past sandbag-filled doorways, boarded-up windows and heaps of rubble left from the summer's bombing raids, my nerves clanged like church bells. For all my fine talk, I'd never had a chance at writing a real news story – and while this was clearly just a bit of cheery propaganda to keep up the readers' spirits in between news of bombs and rationing, I was desperate to do it justice.

By the time we arrived, a light drizzle was misting the air.

'I'll park her up,' said Ernie, patting the steering wheel and accidentally honking the horn with his elbow, making me jump. 'You go and do the how-do's and have your chats while I nip for half a pint in the Wheelwright's, and I'll be over in a jiffy to do the honours.'

I had assumed Ernie would be coming with me to greet the mysterious Sergeant Leslie, and my stomach swooped with sudden nerves.

'Go on,' he said, seeing my face. 'You'll be fine, lovely-looking lass like you. They'll be eating outta your hand like starving cab horses.'

I sighed and decided the men of the Home Guard were probably the lesser of two evils.

At the bandstand, what appeared to be hundreds of men in the drab sand-colour of the Local Defence Volunteers, now known as the Home Guard, were milling about, smoking and joking with each other. I scanned the crowd, looking for someone with military bearing, and was greatly relieved to see a tall man with a bristling grey moustache beckoning me over.

'You must be Miss York,' he said. 'Sergeant George Leslie. Decorated officer in the last war, proud to serve once again.'

I wondered if he talked like this at home. *'Medals won, three. Successful campaigns, six. Pass the salt, darling.'*

'Mr Barry said you'd like to speak to some of my lads?' he said, striding along so I had to scuttle to keep up, like a beetle after a pigeon. I was unnerved to see that they all had guns – a motley collection of air rifles, pistols and... was that a bayonet?

'Ah yes,' said Sergeant Leslie, seeing my expression. 'All unloaded, of course. Until we're issued with standard weaponry, my men have sensibly provided their own. I believe that bayonet was the property of Mr Curtis's uncle, and indeed, was once responsible for killing three Germans in a collapsed dugout at Ypres.'

I nodded, trying and failing to think of an intelligent question about the use of bayonets in modern domestic warfare.

'Right-ho. We're all assembled, so perhaps you should like a brief parley with the men and then we might begin our training exercise in earnest.'

That reminded me – Ernest was still in the pub, and I very much doubted he'd limited himself to half a pint. He was called Ernest Holloway, but the wags in the office called him 'Ernie Hollow-legs.'

I agreed that I would, and he beckoned over a little gaggle of men who seemed to be all shapes and ages. 'This is some of our B Platoon,' said Sergeant Leslie. 'Lads, please speak to Miss York and answer her questions.'

'I'll tell her anything she wants to know,' said a rakish young man with his new cap pushed back to reveal gleaming Brylcreemed curls. 'Time of the latest showing at the Plaza Picturehouse? Best cocktail to get you tight?' The others laughed, and I cleared my throat, irritated.

'Perhaps you could tell me how you first came to join the Home Guard?' I asked the one who looked most reputable. He was in his early fifties, I guessed, tall and slim, with a kind, crumpled face and round spectacles.

'Edward Turnbull,' he said, shaking my hand. 'Ah, well,' he began quietly. 'You see, I rather felt that we must all do our bit. I'm a teacher by profession, and my wife is... she's not... Anyway, I heard about the local battalion, and turned up back in May, when it all got going, and here I am. Hoping we won't be needed, but ready if we are!' He smiled.

'Do you mean if there's an invasion?' I asked, and he looked uncomfortable.

'Yes. Yes, I suppose so,' he murmured.

'We'll show the Hun what-for if there is!' shouted a ginger-haired lad of about seventeen to his right. 'Road blocks, grenades, Molotov cocktails, bullets – you name it, Jerry'll get it, signed, sealed and delivered by Colin Brian Pocock! That's me,' he added helpfully.

He seemed wildly overexcited, and I wasn't sure he should be out of school, let alone waving a rifle about. 'Simmer down,' said Sergeant Leslie, in quelling tones. 'Miss York wants facts, not idle boasting, Pocock.'

He blushed and subsided. I asked a few more questions, about training regimes and the difference the new uniform had made to morale – to my eyes, it resembled potato sacking sewn into a baggy approximation of a siren suit, but they seemed pleased that the government had 'finally done something for us', and grumbled cheerfully about cold nights on lookout duty without proper coats.

I soon had enough for Des's 'brief paragraphs' and after the training exercise, I thought, I might ask Sergeant Leslie if anyone had a suggestion for my obituary page's first subject. It would be awkward, but I had no other leads, and mild embarrassment was nothing compared to facing the weary disappointment of Mr Gorringe.

'Right!' Sergeant Leslie suddenly roared, and I jumped. Brylcreem laughed, and I glared at him.

'Ready yourselves, B Battalion!' he bellowed, and men tossed their cigarette ends on the ground and ran to their pre-agreed positions. I was furious with Ernie. Surely he should be here photographing all this, not lurking with the crossword and a pint of mild, chatting up the barmaid. I was certain he wouldn't have dared sneak off if he'd been with a proper reporter, and I determined to have a word with him when he finally emerged.

Sergeant Leslie turned to me and indicated a copse towards the boating lake. 'If you were to stand over by those trees, Miss York, you should have a fair view of events. But I warn you, there will be smoke to obscure movement, and our men will be feigning genuine warfare.'

I almost laughed at the idea of all these dads and lads playing at war, when the real thing was all around us. I couldn't imagine any German soldiers parachuting into Platt Fields, with its curlicued wrought-iron bandstand and pets' corner. I did as Sergeant Leslie said, with my pencil poised to take notes as the exercise unfolded. It was getting on for lunchtime, and I was looking forward to my jam butties and an apple back at the office.

It began with a roared command. A young recruit belted at top speed across the park and threw something, which hit the ground and exploded into plumes of grey smoke. For an instant, I thought it really was some sort of explosion and ducked, before remembering Sergeant Leslie's warning – it was only a smoke bomb. I could see shadows running beyond it, a flash of movement in the trees opposite, and then the crack of a gun going off.

This was all far more convincing than I had expected, and I

was now mentally crafting my opening paragraph. 'A suburban park in mid-December, raindrops splashing gently into the boating pond – and yet all is far from calm...' would be a nice opening line, I thought, when I heard urgent shouting from the knots of men across the green. Remembering the horror of hockey at school, I assumed I was getting in the way of the exercise, and prepared myself for profuse apologies, but they weren't looking at me.

As the clouds of smoke dispersed in the damp air, I could see a group of men gathered in a huddle, shouting instructions. They sounded shocked, and I wondered whether somebody had fallen over in the skirmish and hurt their ankle.

'He's not breathing!' yelled Colin Pocock, and at that, I ran towards them, horrified yet simultaneously aware that this was my chance – a real story, and I was the only journalist here. The broad cluster of backs parted slightly, as Sergeant Leslie shouted, 'Run and telephone for an ambulance, Butler, don't stand there gawping!' and a man in his thirties, white-faced, sprinted past me towards the box at the park gate.

I elbowed my way into the crush and looked down. A man lay on the damp ground, his hat knocked off and glasses askew. His eyes were half-open, and a trickle of blood ran from his neck into the mud. A middle-aged man was crouching beside him, pressing his hands to the wound, silent and focussed, as others exclaimed in horror. More soldiers were running over, realising that the exercise had been halted, and a nanny with a pram stood unmoving by the lake, entranced as a cinema-goer watching the big picture.

'What happened?' they asked each other. 'I heard a gun, how the hell...' 'What on earth...' 'Who is it?' A cacophony of voices swirled above me. I gazed down at the unmoving body, and as somebody stepped back and daylight illuminated his face, I realised with a jolt of shock that it was Edward Turnbull.

I unwound the rayon scarf from my neck – I wasn't the sort

of girl who could afford real silk – and offered it to the silent, crouched soldier. 'Can you use this to help with the bleeding?' I asked him, and as he glanced up at me, I saw the emptiness in his eyes. He shook his head.

'Too late,' he said shortly.

'Oh, come on, pal!' someone exclaimed. 'Don't give up on the geezer, keep trying!'

'I served until I was injured out last year,' he said bleakly. 'I know what death looks like.'

He was right, it was obvious. Whoever Edward Turnbull had been, he was no longer. His sunken face was grey, his eyes glassy. I felt tears rise in my throat, and turned away, but there was no time for silent contemplation, as an ambulance had arrived and was trundling across the grass towards us. The men now stood in quiet groups, holding their hats in their hands, gazing at the ground, as the soft rain fell, soaking through the new uniforms.

I stood back as they loaded Turnbull onto a stretcher, and Sergeant Leslie spoke, with anguished gestures, to the ambulance men. 'Are you all right?' I asked, finding Pocock beside me, hatless and damp.

'No, I'm not,' he said, his cheeks flaring pink. 'They're all saying it were an accident, some idiot firing his rifle by mistake. But I saw someone in those trees, miss, and he were watching us.' He indicated the trees where I'd seen movement and assumed it was a pretend ambush, grown men playing cops and robbers.

'Then the gun went off,' said Colin, 'and when I looked back, he'd gone.'

'Are you saying it was deliberate?' I asked, but as he moved to reply, I felt a wiry hand on my arm, and turned to find Sergeant Leslie looming over me.

'A dreadful business,' he said. 'I can only apologise to you, Miss York, and I assure you, there shall be a full inquiry. I believe your photographer has come to collect you...'

I looked over to see Ernest, pointing his giant camera at the departing ambulance. *A bit late, Ernie,* I thought bitterly.

'Do you think it was an accident?' I asked quickly.

Leslie looked appalled. 'By God, of course it was a ruddy accident!' he shouted. 'And when I find out which one of these snivelling fools was responsible for ending a good man's life,' he spat, 'believe you me, they will know about it. Untrained idiots, waving guns at each other, after I'd specifically made clear... And how or why they were carrying live ammunition, I shall never know.'

I scanned the shocked, milling crowd for Pocock, but he was now nowhere to be seen. Did someone really shoot mild Edward Turnbull, I wondered – by accident or design? Or had he taken the opportunity to end his own life, something I did not dare suggest to furious, distraught Sergeant Leslie? I had seen Turnbull's gun lying beside him, and such a neat, decisive wound... I shuddered.

'Come on, lass,' said Ernest, appearing beside me. 'I'll stand you a cup of tea with two sugars. Must've been a nasty sight.'

The crowd was breaking up, wandering unhappily towards the gate, and there was nobody left who looked as though they'd want to talk to me.

Still, I certainly had a story, I reminded myself. Just not the one I'd set out to write.

Back at the office, news had already come in on the wires. Within seconds I had a jostling crowd round my desk, including Pat, Gloria, and half the typing pool. Ernie was holding court nearer the fire, surrounded by actual reporters. 'Dead as a doornail,' I heard him say. 'Terrible sight. Of course, the police wouldn't allow me near the body with me camera, try as I might... he had a scream frozen on his face, blood everywhere, it were dreadful...'

Thankfully, Des was still with his informant in the local pub, no doubt knee-deep in Best Mild and a meat pie, so was unable to report this tissue of lies as fact in the evening paper.

'But how did it happen?' Gloria asked me, leaning in as if she was at the pictures, waiting for the detective to reveal the killer. 'I mean, you must have seen something!'

'I didn't,' I said for the ninth time. 'There was all the smoke, and it was chaos.'

'But did he look murdered or just dead?' asked Pat.

I had no idea how to answer that. 'He'd been shot,' I said. 'It was horrible and upsetting, and I'm quite sure it was an accident.'

Even as I said it, I wondered if I was sure at all. The efficient shot had killed instantly; it didn't seem the work of a clumsy recruit messing about with a farm rifle.

When Des returned, somewhat flushed and with a rolling gait as if he were on board a frigate, he was immediately beckoned over by Ernie. 'Des!' I shouted across the office. Parrot Paulson glared at me. 'This is not a football pitch, Miss York, it is a place of work,' she said, and Pat snorted.

Thankfully, Des changed direction and swayed over to me. I told him what had happened, and he looked delighted. 'Dreadful... terrible,' he said sorrowfully. 'But what a story! Think he topped himself?'

'I don't know,' I said. 'He seemed fine when I spoke to him – maybe a bit distracted, but not upset.'

I remembered that Turnbull had been going to say something about his wife, then stopped. I opened my mouth to tell Des, and closed it again.

'Don't suppose Ern took any snaps?'

'No,' I said. 'He was otherwise engaged.'

Des nodded. 'Well, I appreciate your efforts, Miss York,' he said. 'I'm afraid this now comes under the mantle of possible crime, so I'll write it up. It'll be in tonight's late edition. I'll keep your name out of it, of course.'

'Why?' I'd already had the biggest story of the day taken from me, I didn't see why I should be erased altogether.

'Because you're a nice young woman!' said Des, surprised. 'You don't want your name associated with sudden death!'

'I'm the obituarist, Des,' I said, but he wasn't listening.

When I came back from a very late visit to the luncheon room, and fifteen minutes' silent contemplation of the pigeon-infested back alleys of Deansgate, I felt rather shaky despite the curling jam sandwiches and cup of tea I'd had. I assumed it was delayed shock.

'Something for you on your desk,' Pat muttered without looking up.

There was a clipping laid on my blotter, with a printed slip reading 'Compliments of the editor's office'. Mr Gorringe had written: *Mrs Novak's father was a great supporter of the* Chronicle *in the business community. It would be a kind gesture to cover her husband's death. F.G.*

I picked up the clipping, which was from last week's births, marriages and deaths column. Mr Gorringe had circled the relevant announcement.

10 December, 1940, Withington:
NOVAK, Joseph
Suddenly, at home: Beloved husband and businessman. Survived by his wife, Pamela. No flowers. Please send any donations to The Jewish Refugees Fund, PO Box 324.

I assumed he wanted me to follow it up, and I could see

why. Before the war began, in the early thirties, Manchester had welcomed a tide of European refugees fleeing the rise of the Nazi party, and despite a nasty anti-Semitic response from some quarters (including Mr Benson, our landlord, who had a sign in the window reading NO DOGS, NO IRISH, NO BLACKS, NO JEWISH – he'd taken it down since the war began), most had settled down, and found jobs and homes here.

I thought how sad it was that Mr Novak had probably only been here a few years, had managed to find professional work and marry – and now it was all over. He probably didn't even know he was dying. I wondered what the cause of the 'suddenly' had been.

Glad to have a distraction, I stumped up to the library on the fourth floor, a silent, clock-ticking land of obscure systems and tightly packed manila clippings folders, to borrow the L–N phone book. I found myself coldly assessed by Mrs Borrowdale, the widowed gatekeeper of all filing cabinets.

'After more on the Turnbull story, are you?' she asked. 'Let him rot, I say.'

'I beg your pardon?'

'He's been up already,' she said. She seemed to be sucking something, either toffee or teeth. 'Mr Barry. Took his own life, they say,' she hissed.

'Who?'

'Turnbull! That feller in the Home Guard! Bringing shame on the regiment. And on us all,' she added darkly. 'The disgrace his poor family must be feeling. I'd be surprised if they dared to have a funeral.'

I knew her husband had been killed in the last war, and she liked to talk at length about his noble exploits. 'No medal for us,' she'd add bitterly. 'Just because my Eric wasn't an officer. Likes of us get nothing for our bravery.'

I wondered when she'd started using the royal 'we'.

'I was there when it happened,' I told her. 'It's impossible to know if it was self-inflicted, but I doubt it was.'

She shook her head. It was now sleeting outside, and in the grey light, she looked like an illustration from a book of cautionary tales.

I had a sudden memory of the orphanage where I grew up. Perhaps Turnbull couldn't bear his life now, and took what Mr Pugh had once called 'the coward's way out'. I remembered him saying it, while we all sat, rigid with shock and grief, haunted by the image of our friend Kenneth dangling in the woods like a rabbit strung on a fence.

I felt glad that Mr Turnbull's family wouldn't be treated to Mrs Borrowdale's views, even if the Church agreed with her.

The late edition landed just before five, as people were ramming hats on and gathering up briefcases. Des had made the front page – MYSTERY DEATH ON PARK TRAINING MISSION – and I was quoted as a 'bystander' which annoyed me no end.

Edward Turnbull, aged 52, from Burnage, a respected teacher at Burnage Girls' Grammar and member of the Home Guard, died this morning in an LDV training mission. He was shot by a single bullet, according to DI Brennan, the investigating officer. As yet, none of Turnbull's fellow soldiers have come forward with new information, though enquiries are ongoing...

His family were 'shocked and distraught' and his wife, Winifred Turnbull, declined to comment. I bet she did, with judgemental ghouls like Mrs Borrowdale hovering about.

There was no further explanation, just a quote from the school's headmaster claiming that Turnbull had been 'a dedicated teacher, who will be much missed by his grateful pupils'.

Des was hedging his bets on what had really happened, of

course, but I couldn't see him wasting shoe leather trekking off to Burnage to find out.

I couldn't have Turnbull as an obituary due to the unresolved nature of his passing, and the Borrowdales of the world. But perhaps I could find out more, and if there was some foul play – perhaps it was murder, not suicide or accident – I could prove to Mr Gorringe that I was perfectly capable of being a crime reporter, at least while the war was on. My plan crystallised. I decided that first thing tomorrow, I'd head off to find Mrs Turnbull and – sensitively – ask her what she knew.

CHAPTER TWO

I set the alarm clock for half past six the following morning. I'd forgotten to muffle it as I usually did – Annie always got up after me, and normally I'd stuff it under the pillow when it started its piercing trill.

'Edie!' she shouted through the wall. 'For God's sake!'

I suspected she'd been up late, writing to Pete. They'd 'stepped out' as Annie called it before he was called up, and had got engaged in a rush the night before he left, but even then she'd been rather half-hearted about it. 'He's just rather... ordinary,' she had said.

'But Annie, *we're* ordinary.'

'Not like Pete. He just wants a boring, simple life where we have two dear little children and he smokes a pipe and I warm his tartan slippers by the fire...'

'I thought you wanted to get married,' I'd said. She had shrugged.

'Only to someone I'm in love with,' she had said sadly.

She seemed to be finding Pete far easier company now he wasn't here, saving up all her best stories from the hospital for him, and labouring over endearments – 'You can write properly,

Edie. How can I say "I miss you dearly" without sounding like a Victorian sampler?'

Now he was in uniform, Pete apparently seemed a more enticing prospect, and it wasn't for me to suggest that was because she hadn't seen him for months.

I had a good wash in the freezing basin, a cup of tea made with the last of the milk and hurried to put on my coat. As I was gathering up my unused notebook, Annie appeared, wrapped in her flowered dressing gown and shivering ostentatiously.

'Where are you off to at the crack of dawn?' she demanded. 'It's Saturday!'

'I'm going to interview somebody in Burnage,' I said grandly. I wasn't going to admit that nobody had asked me to do any such thing.

'But Edie, I had a plan!' Annie said plaintively. 'I thought, seeing as you were keen on volunteering more, I'd introduce you to Mrs Pelham who runs the WVS canteen on Daisy Bank road, and you could offer to help out...'

'I'm sorry, love, I've got to go or I'll miss the bus.' My gloved hand was on the door handle. Annie said, 'I just think you could do a bit more. What with...'

'Fine!' I said. 'I'm doing a very patriotic job at work, raising spirits, but if you think that's not enough, sign me up.'

I was ashamed of myself for being so petty. I knew it was because, deep down, I suspected that she was right. I wasn't a 'joiner-inner' as Pat called it; I had learnt to be happiest alone during my interminable childhood, and it was a hard habit to break. This wasn't some awful, jolly, fête-organising committee to wriggle out of, though, I reminded myself, it was a war, and it was time I tried harder. I turned back.

'You're right,' I said. 'I'll be back by dinner time, and we'll go and see her then.'

'Good,' said Annie. 'And later on, I thought we might try

that Christmas dance at the church hall. What do you say? There could be a few handsome soldiers knocking about.'

I laughed. 'Worth a try,' I said, though the idea of getting dolled up and traipsing out in the blackout to listen to some old-timer bashing out 'Run, Rabbit, Run' on the upright wasn't my idea of a wonderful evening. She seemed cheered, though.

'Don't forget your gas mask again,' she shouted, as I started down the stairs. She threw the battered cardboard box at me, and I slung it over my shoulder. It wasn't as if I'd ever needed it.

I stopped by the newsagent's and dug in my bag for the address, even though I'd already memorised it from the article. The Turnbulls lived on Vale Street, a bus ride and then quite a walk away. By the time I arrived on the corner, I was steaming like a cab horse in the freezing morning. My shoes were on the verge of collapse too. I'd had my brown lace-ups for three years and I couldn't see myself affording new ones, even with my tiny pay rise, while my 'good' navy woollen coat was no longer very good at all, no matter how often I brushed it and re-sewed its buttons.

Part of me wished I was just going to Boots lending library to change my book as usual. I'd enjoyed Dashiell Hammett last week but I wanted *One, Two, Buckle My Shoe*, the new Agatha Christie. My nerves about marching up to the Turnbulls' house of bereavement were matched, too, by my tension about seeing Mrs Pelham to discuss her military WVS arrangements later. The idea of having to summon cheery greetings for the dispossessed, while negotiating a spitting tea urn, made me feel helpless with inadequacy.

As I neared the Turnbull household, I realised I needed to concentrate on the first, equally alarming part of the day. The street was bleak, with wintry front gardens studded by dark, glossy laurel bushes, but every house had some attempt at decoration in the window: a few Christmas cards, or a little tree with a glass bauble or two. One even had a string of fairy-lights over the mantelpiece when I gazed in. The Turnbulls', however, had a shuttered darkness about the place. There was nothing in the window but a dusty majolica vase, shoved up against the net curtain. I pushed open the green wooden gate and inched slowly up the icy path, feeling I was going to the gallows and cursing my own stupid ambitions.

I had a list of questions I was going to ask, and I'd decided how to introduce myself; I'd simply say 'I work for the *Manchester Chronicle*' and ask if Mrs Turnbull would be willing to have a chat. I put my notebook in the pocket of my bag, so I knew where it was and wouldn't be fumbling and looking unprofessional if she let me in.

Of course I was nervous, I told myself. I had never done a 'door knock' before, and I knew that sometimes there was a huge dog throwing itself against the letterbox, or somebody would swear at you and slam the door in your face. One *Chronicle* reporter, Christopher Weeks, had actually been chased by a man wielding an iron frying pan. We were all falling about when he told us, because it sounded so much like a Saturday morning cartoon, but really, an iron pan is a decent murder weapon – one clang in the right direction, and it'd be lights out. Perhaps that was part of the reason why Chris ended up transferring to Scotland. He'd sent us all a postcard of a gloomy-looking loch, reading: *Plenty of whisky, but not much to report – in any sense!*

'Come on,' I said crossly to myself. 'Just ring the bloody bell.'

Just as I was saying it, the door opened, and I said 'bell' loudly into the face of a tall, thin woman who looked to be in her late forties. She was wearing a limp tartan frock and a shawl, and her eyes were rabbit-pink.

'I'm so sorry to bother you,' I said. 'Would you be Mrs Turnbull?'

I was about to produce my notebook and explain, when a

hefty man in a suit and tie appeared in the small, square hall behind her. He was in his fifties, I guessed, and stood like a Beefeater on guard between the banister and the door.

'Come inside, Winnie, love,' said the man, and she backed away gratefully, as if I'd pointed a gun at her chest.

'Now, what is it?'

He had a Lancashire accent and pale, beady eyes like a seagull. 'Is it about the house? Because if it is, we've already explained that I'll be taking over the mortgage, but as it stands, we've not...'

'No, no,' I said, finally extracting my notebook, and thrusting it out as if it were a police badge. 'I'm with the *Manchester Chronicle*. I just wondered whether I could have a word with Mrs Turnbull about... yesterday's tragedy. I'm so sorry...'

I tailed off under the force of his contempt.

'What is it she wants, Dennis?' called Winifred, fretfully, from further inside.

'Hang on, Winnie,' he called. 'You want a "quote", do you?' said Dennis. He said 'quote' as if it was a made-up word. 'All right, you can have one.'

I held my pencil and waited expectantly. It was unlikely I was going to be asked in at this stage, so I'd take whatever I could.

'Edward Turnbull was a wonderful brother-in-law to me, and we will never get over his untimely death,' said Dennis. 'Now sling your hook, go on.'

'It's only that... we'd like to know what might have happened,' I persisted. 'I'm a reporter,' I lied.

'You're a girl,' said Dennis. 'I doubt it, missy. Now off you go.'

'I was there when it happened,' I said desperately. 'I saw him. It was very quick and he wasn't in any pain.'

Mrs Turnbull reappeared in the doorway.

'You were there?' she repeated. 'Did you see who did it?'

'Of course she didn't, Winnie,' snapped Dennis. 'Now be off with you. The cheek of you people...'

'No, wait,' said Winnie. She extended a trembling hand. 'Are you going to say anything awful about Ed?' she asked. 'Because you have to understand, if he did it himself, he wasn't in his rightful mind. He...'

'Winnie...' warned Dennis.

'Please, let me say it aloud,' she said. She turned to me. 'I know that if it wasn't an accident, what Edward did was wrong, and he can't have a proper Christian burial. It's brought shame on us, I know, but—'

I reached out my gloved hand to her. 'Oh no, that's not true,' I said inadequately. 'I'm sure he was a wonderful man.'

'He was.'

'What do you want with us?' Dennis demanded. 'We don't want publicity. If you hadn't noticed, there's a war on, shouldn't you be reporting on that? And you're letting the heat out, Winifred.'

'Yes, you're right,' she said. I could see she had been very pretty once, but now her face was grey with grief and her wispy hair was escaping its bun.

'Look, come in,' she said, ignoring Dennis's glare. He reluctantly stood back to let me in, and I made a great production of wiping my feet on the mat to appease him.

Inside, the house smelled of gas and old cooking and was as icily cold as it had been on the step. She showed me through to the front parlour, where a green moquette three-piece suite guarded a small, round table, and the remains of a fire smouldered in the grate. The walls were papered with a bamboo pattern, and there were a few photographs framed on the upright piano.

Good, I thought. *We can print one of Edward when I write the story*. Now I'd been admitted, I was hoping for a tale of criminal passions and dark dealings to emerge.

Mrs Turnbull perched opposite me. 'Would you like a cup of tea, Miss...'

'York. No, no, I mustn't take your tea ration,' I said hastily. Dennis shifted back in his chair, relieved. I was dying for some hot tea – I was cold to the core – but I suspected he would have poured it over my hat if I'd asked.

'What would you like to know?' she asked.

'I... well, I'm interested to know what you think happened to Mr Turnbull – to... well...'

So far, I was failing hopelessly as a crime reporter. I was more like a nervous curate on a parish visit.

'I know exactly what it was,' Mrs Turnbull said. She clasped her hands, and I saw her gold wedding ring flash in the light. She was so thin, it was a wonder it had stayed on. 'It was my fault.'

'Winifred! That's nonsense!' snapped Dennis.

'No, it's true. You see, it was the war...'

'Do you mind if I write this down?' I asked.

'You're a reporter, apparently,' said Dennis. 'Isn't that what you lot do?' He poked the dying fire irritably.

I was starting to hate him as much as he clearly loathed me.

'It was... he fought in the last war,' Winifred said. She cleared her throat, fighting back tears. I felt wretched that I was forcing her to relive this, but having got this far, it would have been ridiculous to call a halt, or so I told myself. I tried to think myself into the role of a hard-boiled private eye, and sat forward. My knees banged painfully into the table.

'He was very... well, he wasn't quite the same afterwards,' she said. 'His nerves, you know. He found life much harder.'

'Had he been injured?'

'Weak chest from gas,' she said. 'He was very lucky to come back. Most of his pals didn't. We were newly married and

Sylvia was only little and he found her quite tiring. I tried to keep her quiet, but you know, children...'

She trailed off. Dennis gazed angrily into the embers.

'Do you have any other children?' I asked.

'No, just the one. I don't think Edward would have wanted... Anyway,' Winifred said quickly, 'Sylvia is working as a nanny now, living with a very well-to-do family in London. But you see, that was part of the problem.'

'Her being a nanny?'

I was thoroughly confused.

'No, I'm getting muddled, I'm so sorry. Perhaps we will have tea. The help isn't here, you see, it being Saturday...'

She looked helplessly at Dennis, who remained seated.

'I'll just get it,' she whispered.

The mantel clock's hands pecked round, dropping seconds and minutes into the void. Dennis was breathing heavily. I felt I'd crept into the cage of a dangerous, sleeping animal.

'Are you staying here at the moment?' I asked eventually.

'No,' he said shortly. 'I'm here when she needs me.'

'You're nearby then?'

'You can keep your nose out,' he hissed. 'My job is to protect my sister from parasites like you, and I'll do that, by God.'

I reeled at his venom, as Winifred returned, carrying a wobbling tray.

'I've no cake, I'm afraid,' she said, crashing it onto the low table. 'I haven't really felt up to baking. Edward always liked my ginger sponge.' A tear tracked down her cheek. I wondered if I'd ever felt worse about my job or myself.

'Look here, I can leave,' I began, but she was seated again and offering cups and saucers. It took her several historical eras to balance the strainer and pour the tea and milk. I felt dreadful about the tea ration. Annie guarded ours like an Alsatian, pouncing if I ever had an unsanctioned cup. She was a great believer in 'watering the pot', and I was getting used to a drink that was more the memory of a distant tealeaf than the real thing.

'So, Mr Turnbull...' I said eventually, once we were all seated with a rattling cup each. I felt as though we were about to perform a seance.

'Yes.' Winifred drew a shuddering breath. 'It was all because of me. And Sylvia. You see, Edward was so worried, and he hated the idea of war so much, after what happened before, seeing his brothers and his friends killed, and...'

'In the line of patriotic duty,' muttered Dennis reprovingly.

'Well yes, of course, but he found it all very hard. He was a teacher, you know, he felt things terribly deeply, and he loved languages and he hated to see Europe so at odds...'

'At odds' was an interesting way to describe what was happening, I thought.

'So, when all this started' – she gestured vaguely outside, as if the war was crouching there, in the bare-twigged garden – 'he wanted to send Sylvia and me away.'

'Where to?' I asked.

'America. I know,' she added, seeing my surprise. 'I didn't agree, I wanted to stay here and do my bit, but he was so scared. We were all he had, and he used to say...' She faltered, and fished out a balled handkerchief from her sleeve.

'He used to say that he couldn't go on if anything happened to us.'

I nodded. Dennis looked disgusted at this talk of emotion.

'I have cousins over there, you see, and he hoped we could stay with them. But, of course, sailing is dangerous now, so it would have meant an aeroplane, and it was so much money...'

'Did Sylvia want to go?' I asked.

'No,' said Winifred sadly. She hadn't touched her tea. I drank some of mine, to encourage her. 'She loves her job. Edward wrote to her, he begged, but she said the parents had a lovely house in Kensington and they didn't want the children evacuated. So they weren't going to watch their nanny run off to safety.'

I felt Sylvia had a point.

'But he wouldn't listen,' she went on. 'He was quite obsessed with keeping us safe, but he couldn't afford to send us. He'd been given a painting before the war that he believed might be worth something.'

'Who gave it to him?'

Winifred shook her head. 'A foreign man called Joseph,' she said. 'He'd given it to him as a thank you gift years ago, and said if we ever needed money, we must sell it – but I never really thought it was worth much, it was just a little daub. It had vanished long since, I don't know where it went,' she added. 'Maybe I had one of my clear-outs while Edward was away, or it went off in a charity bundle, but when the war started, Edward decided he was going to try and find it, and sell it to buy our air tickets...' She sighed. 'But he couldn't find it anywhere – so recently, he decided he'd go to the man who'd given it to him, and explain that it was lost and ask if he could loan us the money until the painting was found. He'd become a very successful businessman and Edward wrote to him, then just last week he found out he'd died, the death notice was in the paper. So the money wasn't ever coming, and that was when he lost hope,' she said, gazing into her cooling tea. 'He was convinced that if we stayed here, Sylvia and I were going to die. He was obsessed with the idea.'

As I nodded, it struck me. Joseph, who had died so recently, shortly before Edward Turnbull... and who lived within a mile of his home. The giver of the painting must surely have been Joseph Novak, I realised. And Jewish – perhaps that was what Mrs Turnbull had meant by 'foreign'; some people had strange attitudes. I could ask what linked Edward and Joseph, and discover why the painting had been given and then lost – and perhaps it would somehow shed light on Edward's death.

I was about to ask what the painting had been like, and why Edward believed it was worth something when Winifred didn't and most crucially, why this 'foreign man' had been giving her shy husband paintings, but she began to cry; great choking sobs wrenched from deep inside her.

'I think you've heard enough, don't you?' said Dennis, banging his empty teacup down. Winifred was holding the damp handkerchief to her face, her shoulders shaking.

I stood up, realising I hadn't even taken my coat off.

'I'm so sorry,' I said. 'When is the funeral?'

'None of your ruddy business,' said Dennis. 'Ask the funeral home down the road if you're that eager.'

Winifred waved a vague hand, in possible objection to his tone, but it was too late. I whispered my thanks for the tea and left. The door clicked shut behind me, and back on the step, I saw it had started to snow and I'd left my hat on the couch. Hardened reporter that I was, I had absolutely no desire to ring the bell again, and I set off, hatless, to find the funeral parlour, flakes settling in my hair.

I trudged up the main road, aware that Annie was going to be furious when I failed to turn up for our appointment with Mrs Pelham. But this was my career, I reasoned. I could go and sign up for tea-making duties later on, surely.

Much to my dismay, I had to stop at the Bull to ask for directions. Several men in caps were drinking their lunchtime pints. They all swivelled towards me as I poked my head in, the air a fug of pipe smoke and spilled ale and damp wool. I edged through the public bar and nodded at the barman. He had a wooden leg, and I wondered why he'd want to work somewhere that required constant hobbling up and down.

'I can't serve you, love,' he called, as if I didn't know that women weren't welcome.

'I just need directions,' I said.

'Direct yourself over here, dearie!' called one of the men near the door, and they all guffawed.

It turned out that Whiting's funeral parlour was a good half mile away.

'Not sure it'd even be open,' he added, 'being Saturday.'

But surely people died at the weekends too and couldn't be expected to lie about, clogging up the sitting room till Monday morning. I thanked him, and as I went out, I realised I'd been holding my breath to keep the smell out of my nostrils. I lit a cig to take the spilled-beer taste away, and huddled under the awning of the closed furniture shop, cold, wet and irritable.

Why was I bothering? It wasn't as if some funeral director was going to tell me who Edward Turnbull's mysterious dead benefactor was. It was a perfectly ordinary, tragic story of fear and sadness – and if he hadn't taken his own life, it was just a horrible accident that nobody would admit to causing. I'd grown up in the long shadow of the Great War, in a city of lonely, widowed wives and bereaved mothers and crippled, hollow-eyed men. I'd always assumed my own father had been killed and that's why my mother decided I'd be better off left on the broad stone step of St Saviour's in a laundry basket. It was nothing special.

All I'd done was cost myself money I couldn't afford, upset two complete strangers and my best friend, and waste an entire morning. I flicked the end of my cigarette at a poster in the chemist's window (HITLER WILL SEND NO WARNING – SO ALWAYS CARRY YOUR GAS MASK), and trudged on towards the funeral home. The way things were going, I thought, I might ask them if I could check myself in.

On the front door of Whiting and Son, there was a small cardboard sign: RING ONCE AND WAIT.

I wondered why. It wasn't as if peals of ringing bells were

going to disturb these customers. Perhaps it was to stop grief-stricken relatives leaning desperately on the bell, pounding on the frosted glass panels, shouting, 'bring my Cedric back!'

The blackout curtains were open and a light was on upstairs, so I hoped someone might be in.

I rang, once, and waited. My feet were damp and numb – the snow had finally won over the cardboard I'd stuffed between my paper-thin shoe soles and the lining, and my hatless head felt encircled by a metal band of cold.

The door was eventually opened by a young man with bright red hair and freckles. He had light blue eyes and frost-white skin.

'Can I help you?' he asked.

'I don't know,' I said. 'I'm a reporter and I wondered if I could have a quick word.'

He looked alarmed. 'What about?'

I drew a breath, and tried to wiggle the cardboard back into place with my toes – discreetly, I hoped.

'Shoes hurting?' he asked.

I smiled, embarrassed. 'A bit,' I said. 'How can you tell?'

'You'd be amazed what women do to their feet,' he said. 'I've seen it all. My dad wouldn't let me do faces at first. So I started at the other end, learnt the trade from the ground up.' He laughed at his joke, and I realised he was talking about embalming.

I had a terrible vision of old, gnarled feet sticking off the end of a gurney, while this man painted some sort of formaldehyde onto them, as if he were varnishing a chair.

He was still looking at me, his expression quite open and friendly.

'I'm Arnold Whiting,' he said. 'I'm the "and son". And you are...?'

'I'm Edie York,' I said. 'I know you're probably closed, but I'm researching a story for the *Chronicle* and I'd love to chat to you for a moment, about a recently deceased individual.' That was too much; now I sounded like Inspector Japp in an Hercule Poirot novel.

Arnold gave a professional smile. 'We don't normally know much,' he said. 'The police and the hospital deal with all the immediate cause-of-death business. We just prepare the body and arrange the funeral. You'd be better off talking to the city morgue or the police.'

He was right, of course. But the truth was, I didn't know any policemen. Tom had kept all those useful details to himself. I knew I wasn't going to turn up at Newton Street nick and be welcomed with a cup of tea and a sticky bun, though, so Arnold was currently my best hope.

'I wouldn't have come if it wasn't important,' I said.

Arnold shrugged. Clearly, everyone he dealt with thought their family death was the most important thing that had ever happened.

'Come in then,' he said. 'You can give your feet a rest.'

It was ridiculous to feel a sense of terror stepping into the dimly lit hallway after him. It wasn't as if there'd be dead bodies lined up along the walls, or unquiet spirits massing outside the chapel of rest. But I was suddenly reminded of the dim lighting in the corridor that led to Mr Pugh's office, back when we were little.

'You're all right,' Arnold said, noting my hesitation. 'Some people get a bit funny about it. But to be honest, we live over the shop and I've never heard a ghost in my life. There's none so quiet as the dead.'

It sounded like something his dad must have said, and I wondered what it had been like for Arnold, growing up, doing his homework, having liver and onions for tea, knowing that beneath his feet, an ever-changing procession of corpses were resting on their final journey. *Good Lord, Edie,* I thought. *Don't go into the entertainment business.*

He led me upstairs, through a door into a small, brightly lit kitchen. It all seemed perfectly normal, apart from the lingering scent of formaldehyde, which reminded me of the chemistry labs at school. I assumed it must be coming from him. If he was married, I thought, it must have been strange for his wife, getting into bed with the smell of a preserved specimen every night.

'Tea?' he said, turning to put the kettle on. I nodded and slipped my shoes off under the Formica table. I felt less guilty about Mr Whiting's tea ration for some reason.

'Do you run the... parlour?' I asked ludicrously.

He smiled. 'For now. Dad died a while back, so it's just me and a couple of assistants at the moment. Mum greets the clients, but... we do the rest,' he said delicately.

'You didn't have to join up?'

'Reserved occupation. But even if it weren't, I had rheumatic fever when I was twelve, so' – he tapped his chest – 'lungs.'

I nodded.

'So, Miss York,' he said, assembling flowered teacups and saucers efficiently. 'I seem to be telling you the story of my life. What can I do for you?'

'Call me Edie,' I said. 'I'm just trying to find out a bit more about Edward Turnbull, who lived on Vale Road. I could do with knowing when the funeral will be...'

I was about to explain further, but Arnold winced. He could only have been in his late twenties, but he suddenly looked much older.

'Ah, Ed, that's a sad business,' he said, pouring water into the pot.

'It's just, I was going to write an obituary...' I began. The lies were lining up nicely. 'But his widow didn't want to talk about it much, so I'm rather stuck. Perhaps you could just explain...' I flipped open my notebook and turned over a few sheets, as if I'd filled reams already, and Arnold was just helping me fill in a few gaps.

'We knew Edward a bit, you see,' he said. 'It's always tricky, when you know them.'

'Of course.' I nodded sympathetically. What luck!

'I believe he was given a painting and was hoping for some money...' I began.

Arnold shook his head. 'I don't know about that,' he said. 'Seems odd. Was it something to do with lessons?'

'Lessons?'

'He taught languages at the girls' grammar. So maybe it was to do with that.'

My mind flew immediately to blackmail. Had Edward been dallying with a pupil? Had he been threatened with exposure? What a story that would be, I thought. Though the idea of further devastating Winifred was less enjoyable.

'I'm sorry, I don't know much,' he continued. 'But as far as I know, the Turnbulls were very happy. Winnie's first husband died in the last war, did she say?'

'No – I thought she was married to Edward during that time?'

He shook his head. 'She doesn't like to mention it because some folk thought it was unseemly how quickly she married Edward after her first husband died. He isn't Sylvia's dad, though.' Arnold stirred his tea thoughtfully. 'Not sure he and Sylvia always got along – I knew her a bit growing up, she used to say she couldn't wait to leave home.'

Arnold was unwittingly adding a great deal of fuel to my crime reporter's fire. 'Do you know why?'

'No. But she was off at sixteen, hardly ever comes back.'

'So this plan for evacuating her and Winifred to America...'

'She'd never have gone along with it. Tell you one thing, Sylvia's not a coward. She'd have thought it nonsense.'

I sipped my tea. Out of politeness, I hadn't asked for sugar.

'Do you think Mr Turnbull's death was really because of the airfares?' I asked Arnold.

'I don't know,' he said. 'Sorry not to be of more help. But the funeral will be after Christmas, at All Saints, I imagine. The coroner's hanging onto the body for now because they're not sure if foul play was involved.' He sighed. 'Impossible to imagine anyone wanting to harm Ed. I'm certain it was an accident – he'd never have done that to Winnie, he adored her.'

'So you don't think it was a suicide?'

'Lord, no,' said Arnold. 'I mean, if you were going to do... that, you wouldn't do it there, would you? You'd go somewhere private, leave a note. Besides, Ed was shy, he wasn't the type for a grand gesture.'

'You don't think...' I didn't know this man, I reminded myself. It would be wrong to speculate.

'Think...?' he encouraged.

'That someone shot him deliberately?'

Arnold sat up, clearly taken aback.

'Gosh,' he said, 'I can't imagine... Why would they want to shoot poor old Ed?'

'I don't know,' I said. 'This man who gave him a painting... maybe he was some sort of criminal?'

Arnold snorted with laughter. 'The idea of Edward Turnbull being tied up with a criminal!' he said, shaking his head. 'He was the mildest man in Manchester, he wouldn't even bet on the Derby 'cos he felt sorry for the horses. Nobody would harm Ed. No, it was just a horrible accident, and I hope they find the careless bugger that did it,' he added angrily. ''Scuse my French, Miss York.'

I sat for a moment, the pain in my feet almost forgotten but for a dull throb. This had definitely been worth the walk, the awful reception at Edward's house, and the loss of a full Saturday morning, even if I would have to do without my Agatha Christie.

In a rush of gratitude, I said, 'My friend and I are going to our local dance tonight. Would you like to come? You could bring someone, a girlfriend, if you like,' I added hastily, in case he'd got the wrong idea.

'I'd love to,' he said eagerly. 'I was going to meet a pal for a drink, shall I bring him along?'

Thinking of Annie, I said, 'Oh yes, do!' and we parted with arrangements to meet at the church hall at seven.

All the way back, I wondered why I'd done it. He wasn't my type at all, and he'd already told me all he knew.

CHAPTER THREE

As I'd expected, Annie was highly irritated when I finally got home.

'I had to walk all the way to see Mrs Pelham and tell her you weren't here, and all the way back!' she snapped, kneading pastry for the pie she was making. Its main filling seemed to be carrots, judging by the withered offerings on the kitchen table.

'I'm so sorry, honestly I am, the bus was late and the interviews went on...'

'I suppose helping our soldiers and homeless people is neither here nor there to you,' she said, her narrow shoulders stiff as she pressed and rolled.

'It is,' I said helplessly. 'I will go and see her, I promise.'

'Yes, well, it won't be today,' Annie said. 'Her lad's coming home on leave for two days and she'll be with him.'

'I'm sorry.'

'I just hope it was worth it,' she said, in a tone that suggested it very much wasn't.

'It was, actually.' I reached up to unpin my hat, then remembered it was still on the Turnbulls' couch. 'Oh, and we might have partners for the dance tonight.'

Annie whipped round, umbrage forgotten. 'Who?'

I didn't want to say 'a strange mortician I met two hours ago' so I said, 'A lad I met through work. About our age, he seems nice. Mr Whiting – Arnold.'

'Well, that's you sorted out, what about me?'

'He's bringing a friend.'

'A soldier?' Her face glowed with delight.

'I don't know,' I admitted. 'He didn't say.'

'Well, let's hope it's not some weedy feller in civvies with a conscientious objector armband,' she said. Thankfully, she seemed to have forgotten about Mrs Pelham for now.

'I'll steam my red crêpe over the kettle,' she added. 'It's the last-chance Christmas dance, and I'm bringing my own mistletoe.'

A few hours later, I was sitting on Annie's bed in my slip. I only had one decent dress, an olive-coloured artificial silk thing with a square neckline, and I'd let her wear it to a dance with Pete on his last leave. I hadn't seen it since.

'How did you end up asking this Arnold out?' she asked, rummaging in the back of her wardrobe for it. 'Isn't that a bit forward, even for you?'

'I didn't!' I shrieked. 'I felt sorry for him and he'd been helpful, it just came out. It's not that sort of asking out. Just as friends. He's not my type. Or yours, I imagine.'

'His friend might be, though!' she said, finally producing my crumpled dress from a nest of her nursing aprons. She threw it to me.

I examined the dress for stains. It smelled thickly scented under the arms, and I knew as soon as I was warm, I'd reek like the Worth Perfumes factory.

I sighed. 'Can I borrow your brown heels?'

'Oh, go on then.' Annie dug them from under the dressing

table where she'd kicked them off. 'I wish you weren't the same shoe size as me.'

'I wish you weren't the same dress size as me. I'm going to have to steam this one too.'

She shrugged theatrically. 'If you don't like him, I don't know why you're so bothered about dressing up. And anyway, your main competition is dead people, so I'd say you're already ahead.'

'And that's what my love life has come to,' I said. 'Am I more attractive than a corpse?'

'Not first thing in the morning,' said Annie. 'Bags me first bath. I'll hang up the dress, don't worry.'

She whisked it out of my hand and left. I hunched back against her brass bedstead and wondered why I was making the effort, but I had to go now; I didn't like to think of Arnold's pale, freckly face falling in embarrassment as he realised I hadn't bothered to turn up.

I got off the rumpled bed and went to Annie's dressing table. I could hear her splashing about in the six inches of water Mr Benson allowed, singing, 'When You Wish Upon a Star'.

I took her little block of well-worn mascara and licked my finger, then rubbed on the matted brush and swept it over my eyelashes. I still had the stub of a red lipstick I'd bought before the war, called Cinema Scarlet, and a scattering of face powder left in the jar. One of my eyes now looked top-heavy.

It reminded me of when Suki and I were seven, and had found some scissors in the bathroom at the orphanage. We'd taken turns to give each other 'hairdos', panicking and giggling as we realised we'd gone wrong, cutting more hair off to try and even things up. I could still feel the sting of the slaps on our legs when we were discovered, our hair standing in uneven tufts like abandoned dolls.

I should smarten myself up a bit, I thought. One of the articles I'd read in *Home Notes* magazine had advised: *Dress for the wartime job – or husband – you dream about! It's no use hoping for a respected secretarial position or a handsome fellow, unless you're willing to look the part.*

'Your turn!' shouted Annie, scuttling across the freezing hall clutching a ball of clothes. 'Ooh, I like your eyes. You should do them like that all the time.'

'Maybe I will,' I said, gathering up her shoes, and crossing to the clammy bathroom, which now smelled overpoweringly of Yardley's English Rose bath salts. And perhaps I'd do my hair properly as well, I thought, just in case, against all the odds, Arnold's friend turned out to be acceptable.

After a slice of Annie's indeterminate vegetable pie, featuring boiled carrots we could have used as bullets in the event of a sudden invasion, we set off to the local church hall, three streets away. The blackout was far worse when it was freezing; you couldn't see icy puddles and were liable to take a sudden lurch into a garden wall. We crept along, clinging to one another and trying to follow the white lines newly painted on the kerbs.

'I hope there's not a bloody air raid,' grumbled Annie. 'We'll break our ankles running to the shelter.' My feeble torch only illuminated a foot ahead of us, and occasionally a shape would loom up far too close, mutter an apology and shuffle off.

By the time we arrived, the hall was heaving. It still carried the lingering scent of tea and toast, with an undercurrent of old clothing bundles, but now there was silver tinsel swagged along the walls above the blackout blinds and a band on the little stage, thumping out a jazzy foxtrot. According to the hand-drawn poster, this was Leslie Parker and his Orchestra. The orchestra consisted of three glum older men in suits and tartan bow ties. I recognised the one irritably parping a trumpet as Mr Carradine, who'd taught me mathematics at school and had a bad leg. I remembered him saying, 'Edie, I pray for your sake that you shall never take a job requiring you to add up.'

'Come on,' shouted Annie, dragging me off towards the makeshift bar through a crush of uniformed types on leave and girls in their best home-made frocks. 'Where's this friend of yours?' she bellowed in my ear.

Part of me hoped that Arnold hadn't bothered to turn up. Even if he did, I thought, what would we talk about? I'd pump him for more information, he wouldn't know anything, and the best I could then hope for would be a blow by blow account of an embalming. But as I scanned the backs of Brylcreemed and pin-curled heads, I spotted a tuft of vivid fox-red hovering in the corner. I pointed and Annie veered towards the trestle table of drinks, gesticulating wildly, as I made my way over.

'Ow, do you mind?' I shouted, as the burning tip of a man's cigarette brushed my arm.

'Not if you don't,' he shouted back, and I looked up, crossly, to see that he was standing beside Arnold.

'You came!' I said idiotically.

'Of course.' Arnold reached out to shake my hand, and thought better of it. 'This is the pal I mentioned, Edie,' he said, 'Louis Brennan.'

'Lewis?'

'Lou-ee. Like a French person.' He didn't sound French. He had a faint Manchester accent, a bit like mine. 'But you can call me Lou. Everyone else does.'

He was wearing a civvy wool, pinstriped suit with a smart trilby pushed back on his head. He had a wiry black moustache and was good-looking if you liked that sort of thing – obvious, and flashy, I told myself. I could imagine him in a bad oil painting, clutching a swooning maiden in an unravelling bodice. I wondered if Annie would be instantly besotted.

'So, Edie...' He pushed his hand into the small of my back, which – it occurred to me – was probably as damp as everything else in here, and propelled me towards the bar.

'Yes?' I said, trying to edge away in the crush of people.

Arnold was smiling benignly at us, and I didn't want to offend him.

'I'd like to hear all about you,' he said. 'Whiting here tells me you marched up to his front door, invited yourself in, and then demanded that he come to this dance. Interesting, I thought to myself. A lady who knows what she wants.'

I was speechless for a moment. 'I did not do those things!' I blurted, like a six-year-old accused of stealing wax crayons. I turned to see Arnold laughing wearily.

'He's always like this,' he said. 'Of course that's not what I said.'

I smiled grudgingly and reached past a uniformed couple who were kissing as if they were performing a dental check-up, to tap Annie's shoulder. She craned round. 'You must be Arnold!' she shouted, noting the redhead of my description.

'And this is Lou,' I added, gesturing vaguely at him.

She twinkled at them both, and Arnold offered her a cigarette. She held his hand still as he lit it, to steady the flame – though as we were indoors, there was really no need.

I adored Annie. I'd known and loved her since we first sat next to each other at St Saviour's Church Primary, but she was as loyal as a farm cat when it came to men. I was no great fan of Pete's, but he was off God knew where, risking his life for king and country, while his future wife gazed adoringly at this blue-eyed stranger. To my surprise, it seemed the suavely handsome Lou wasn't where her interests lay – though in a certain light, if I squinted, Arnold did have a very slight look of James Cagney, who was currently Annie's great pin-up. She had been to see *Angels with Dirty Faces* four times.

Lou was gathering up lemonades, and beers for Arnold and himself, and shouldering his way out of the huddle. Arnold had found a little table, and the band were still playing jaunty dance tunes. I had never felt less like dancing – my feet were still throbbing from my trek earlier in the day and now I was thinking about the likelihood of chilblains.

Lou threw himself into a chair beside me, with Annie on his other side.

'How do you know Arnold?' I asked him, to make conversation.

He smirked, tossing a cigarette into his mouth without offering me one. He had well-shaped lips, annoyingly. I bet he'd kissed thousands of girls with those lips, all melting into his pin-striped arms and gazing into his narrow, dark blue eyes as if he were Clark Gable. 'Oh, that would be telling. I have to be careful what I say to these reporters.'

'I'll just ask Arnold then,' I said, turning, but he was fumbling in his pocket for tobacco.

'What do you do?' asked Annie.

'I'll give you both three guesses each, and the loser buys me another drink,' said Lou.

'The winner gets a dance with me,' Arnold added.

I glanced at Annie to roll my eyes, but she was giggling and batting Arnold's arm like some silent film star miming 'coquette'.

'Miner,' I said.

Lou looked at me, slowly shaking his head. I sipped my drink.

'Band leader,' said Annie.

He smiled. 'Not quite.'

'Butcher's boy,' I offered.

'I'd be the butcher by now, love. I'm all of twenty-nine.'

'Butcher then.'

'You've used up all your guesses. And the answer's no,' he said. 'I don't see myself slicing up offal, somehow.'

'That was two guesses,' I argued. 'Then you're a morgue person, like Arnold.'

'A morgue person,' he repeated. 'You reporters, you're sticklers for accuracy.'

Annie cackled, the traitor.

He shook his head again. I couldn't imagine how someone as seemingly serene and cloistered as Arnold would get along with this louche irritant.

'Two more guesses for me then,' Annie said. 'I think you're something terribly glamorous. An actor!'

'Alas, poor Yorick,' said Lou, holding his glass in the air as if it were a skull. 'But wrong.'

'He's a private detective who spies on unfaithful wives,' I said pointedly.

'Edie!' Annie glared at me, apparently deeply hurt. Sometimes, she was quite insufferable.

Lou laughed. 'Not that far off.'

I had no desire to let him know I was curious, so I turned away towards Arnold, who was now talking to a man in RAF uniform after rolling him a ciggie.

'Always a Burnage boy...' I heard Arnold say. Numbingly dull as their conversation was, I was about to join in when I heard Lou say, 'Manchester City Police,' and Annie saying, 'Crikey! I'd better stay on the straight and narrow then.'

I whipped round. 'You're a policeman?'

'Detective Inspector, actually.' He fingered his top pocket as if he was about to produce his papers. I suddenly remembered I'd left my ID card on my dressing table, along with my gas mask.

'You don't look like one.'

'What does a police inspector look like?' he asked. 'Navy blue serge, and a permanent bend in the knees? You don't look like a reporter.'

'What's that supposed to mean?' I felt myself flush.

'I mean, you don't have a grubby raincoat and a hat with a Press ticket in it,' he said, draining his glass. 'I don't wear a uniform, as it happens.' He couldn't disguise the pride in his voice.

My mild disgust at his boasting was halted by a realisation. If he knew Arnold, that meant he had dealings with the local morgues and funeral homes on a regular basis. And that, therefore, he might be able to help me find out more about Edward Turnbull's benefactor. I knew that the story was probably going nowhere. Joseph Novak probably hadn't really intended them to sell the picture, he'd just handed over a worthless painting – but why had he given it to Turnbull in the first place? Or maybe Edward Turnbull had turned up at his door one day, begging for money, and the shock had made him collapse. Then Edward had done away with himself out of guilt... I had a sudden memory of hearing Albert Wells, Tom's predecessor who retired, saying, 'You can't make it up, no matter how much you'd like the facts to fit your story.' I couldn't remember who he'd said it to – perhaps a trainee who had skipped off to one of the nationals, shaking the provincial dust from his trouser hems. But I'd always thought it was worth remembering, knowing my tendency to fit stories to theories.

I'd done it about a year ago, when we'd had a front-page splash on an actress who had been found dead at the bottom of the stairs, with a smashed bottle of whisky next to her. At work, we'd all agreed she'd been drinking and tried to come downstairs to answer the door – perhaps to her lover – and had tripped in her excitement and broken her neck. I'd imagined a beautifully lit Hollywood scene, played out in some antebellum mansion, the shadow of the wrought-iron balcony cast over her porcelain face as she lay on the black and white tiles.

It turned out she'd been attacked by a man who had become obsessed by her, who lived in Miles Platting. He'd travelled to her house on the bus, she'd answered the door holding the unopened whisky, and he'd strangled her then and there.

'So, who do you deal with?' Lou asked me.

'Deal with?' I was still thinking about the actress, and how shocked she must have been when she answered the door thinking it was a fan, and it had turned out to be someone else altogether, someone who wanted to fasten his dirty hands round her neck and squeeze the life out of her.

'As in, your contacts. Bootle Street? Newton Street? I tend to work out of Willert Street mainly.'

'A reporter never reveals her sources,' I said primly.

'I probably drink with all your sources,' he said, 'and believe me, I wouldn't trust a single one of 'em. It's funny,' he added, looking into my eyes, 'I didn't hear anything about a girl crime reporter. Last I knew, some bloke from Leeds was being lined up. Shame Tom's gone, though. He's a damn good man.'

I didn't want to reduce my status to 'lady obituarist' or invite awkward questions from Arnold about my amateurish sleuthing. The band were striking up a jive, and I grabbed Annie's hand. 'Come and dance!' I said.

Unsurprisingly, she gaped at my change of personality, but to her credit, she stood up.

'Since when are you a crime reporter?' Annie shrieked in my ear. She jabbed her elbow in my ribs. 'I don't recall us celebrating.'

'I'm not,' I began. I couldn't possibly explain the full story in the midst of this heaving mass of people, all now throwing themselves round the pocket-handkerchief dance floor like marionettes, legs kicking, bodies whirling. I took a glancing blow from a buff-clad knee, and a girl in a dress I was sure was made from curtains cannoned into me as she twirled.

'I'll tell you later,' I bellowed, and she shrugged. I noticed that Lou was now up and dancing, and as Annie whirled happily into him, he caught her. He was an annoyingly good dancer.

Like the gentleman he was, Arnold clasped me in an awkward, leaning grip, as though we were dancing on either side of a pothole, and we attempted to move, though it was clear we both hoped the tune would be over soon.

'Having fun?' I asked, craning towards him. He no longer smelled of formaldehyde, so he must have had a bath.

'Yes, it's super,' he said. 'Your friend seems nice.'

'So does yours,' I lied politely.

'Look, Arnold,' I said, as we sat down again, 'do you think Lou might be able to help me?'

'Help you...?' He gulped his drink.

'Help me track down the bloke I mentioned. The one who gave Edward Turnbull the painting.'

Arnold shrugged. 'Maybe. I don't know, I'm afraid. We met on a job of his once, and since then, we haven't really talked about work. We tend to go to the football together, the odd drink...'

'But don't you ask him about his cases?'

'Not really.' Arnold swirled the beer in his glass. 'He's quite a closed book.'

'Aren't you interested?'

'Not really, no,' he said again. 'I mean, murder and armed robbery and all that... it's depressing, isn't it?'

I pondered briefly that someone who spent his life preparing the dead for their final journey to the flames would find police work depressing.

Annie and Lou danced back to the table, breathless.

'Lou,' I said. 'May I have a word? It's about work.'

Annie slid in beside Arnold. 'Don't mind us,' she said, smiling up at him. 'We can entertain ourselves.'

Lou shrugged. 'Certainly you may,' he said to me. He jerked his head towards a small corner with a peeling poster reading YOUR OWN VEGETABLES ALL THE YEAR ROUND... IF YOU DIG FOR VICTORY NOW and two empty wooden chairs. I felt the slogan was quite appropriate, given my fact-finding mission.

Lou settled into the chair and rested his drink on his knee. 'If you're about to warn me off your chum, don't bother,' he said. 'I know she's taken, and besides, she's not my type.'

That surprised me – Annie was usually everyone's type. 'Actually,' I said haughtily, 'It's about my job. I'm researching a story, and' – I paused – 'none of my contacts can help with this so far.' That was hardly surprising, given that my contacts were Pat and her biscuit tin and Mrs Borrowdale.

'I just thought maybe, with you being a DI, you might be able to point me in the right direction.'

He looked at me with that irritating, appraising look, as if I were a horse he was sizing up for purchase.

'What direction is that?'

I sipped my drink and realised there was nothing left in the glass. Another couple banged into my chair and apologised, laughing. I was getting a headache. 'Well, I need to find out more about Edward Turnbull, the man who died yesterday. I was there, I was meant to be reporting on the training. You were quoted in the paper, and I've discovered there's a bit of an odd story attached to it and thought you might know more...'

'I'm not a medium,' he said. 'Madame Louis, seances a speciality. Don't trip over the ectoplasm, dear.'

'I thought you might have been investigating – somebody told me he'd been given a painting and needed some money...'

Lou was shaking his head. 'I'm getting nothing,' he said. 'Though I can tell somebody with an "A" name has disappointed you recently, and your grandfather says his chest is much better now he's on the other side.'

I refused to laugh. 'I just thought you might be able to tell me a bit more,' I said, like a sulking child.

'Even if I could, I'm not sure I would,' said Lou. 'I imagine the family are distraught. Unlikely they want their suicide all over the paper.'

'Was it a suicide?' I said beadily. 'I thought it was an accident. Or maybe even...'

'Look, Miss York, as you're aware, I'm sure, there's a war on. There's plenty to worry over, without digging about in other people's sad business. Perhaps you should be reporting on what the WVS is up to, or looking into conditions for evacuees. There's a whole lot just arrived from the Channel Islands – that might make an interesting tale. '*SEASIDE TO MOSS SIDE*,' he suggested, spreading his hands to indicate a newspaper. '*The heartwarming tale of the community that welcomed little foreigners...*'

'That's not the sort of reporting...' I began.

'No,' said Lou, standing up. 'Apparently, the only sort of reporting you do is obituaries. That should keep you busy these days.'

Annie didn't need to worry about an air raid, I thought, because I was going to kill her first.

On Monday, I had decided, it was time to start my obituary of Joseph Novak. I put thoughts of Edward Turnbull aside – considering I was getting nowhere at speed – and prepared to set off to Burnage again to track his widow down. Nobody had answered when I rang the listed number, so my brilliant plan was simply to ask at the shops, and if nobody knew where they lived, I was going to be very stuck indeed.

I had to bag this one, though – Mr Gorringe himself had suggested it and he was hardly going to let me loose on crime if I couldn't even find the wife of a recently deceased businessman.

It was novel, after years of having to apply for a passport if I wanted to go out for a lunchtime pie, to be waved off from the office as though my absence was not only normal but expected.

'Will you be moving desks?' Pat asked, as she sat typing up a list of invitees to the editor's New Year cocktail party. *Capt. and*

Mrs P.W. Quinn, The Rowans, Bowden – still alive? was scribbled at the top of her notepad.

I knew she was only asking because hers faced the sooty window, and she guarded her plum spot as if it were some Biblical promised land by a sparkling river and fertile fields.

'No, I don't think so,' I said. 'I'll be spending quite a bit of time out of the office now,' I added, unable to keep the pride from my voice, but Pat merely sniffed and continued to type.

I was nervous about appearing on Pamela Novak's doorstep uninvited. I wondered whether to take flowers, but I was already encumbered with my handbag, and my notebook shoved into the pocket of my green suit. I'd forgotten my gas mask again, but in my bag, for once, I had my ID card and ration book – I'd promised Annie I'd buy something from the fish van at dinner time, but given that every housewife in Manchester would have swiped anything edible by then, I didn't fancy my chances. It also contained my purse, and a squashed packet of leftover mutton sandwiches that Annie had thrown at me as I left. She was obviously still feeling guilty.

As I sat on the bus rattling out of the city, we passed the remains of buildings, wooden poles still reaching vainly upwards, piles of bricks and broken frames where once there'd been offices and people, all engaged in what they'd thought was unchanging routine. I thought about how long it took to create a building, and how, in one night last summer, it had been instantly undone, like a film reel spooling backwards, tiles and glass flying outwards, flames bursting from desks and chairs. Already, we were used to this new life – the air-raid shelters, the endless queuing, the government telling us what we could and couldn't eat and wear and buy. Nobody I knew really believed that we'd die. It all felt like a ridiculous inconvenience, a silly experiment that had got out of hand. Yet at the same time, I wanted nothing more than for us to win the war and return to normal. *I must go and see Mrs Pelham,* I reminded myself. Perhaps if I got back in time from work.

As we bumped and rattled towards Withington, and the conductor flirted optimistically with a smart young woman in a fur coat, I wondered what Mrs Novak would be like.

I pictured a glamorous older woman in a Chanel suit, with pearl strings clasped round her crêpey neck and diamonds twinkling like sugar plums on her fingers.

Was she like Winifred, I wondered, wan and grieving – or was she what Pat would call 'a do-er,' bustling round town calling on Joseph's friends, or visiting relatives in Southport or Llandudno, to take her mind off the tragedy?

Once I was off the bus, a mizzling rain began to fall and I stopped at a parade of shops to ask where the Novaks might live.

After several blank looks, a shrug and a 'can't you see we're busy, dear?' I struck lucky.

'Oh, I heard about him passing on. It's them big houses up near the park,' said a woman in a pink overall at the General Grocers'. 'Mrs Novak's daily shops here sometimes, always trying to get extra for that bloody dog,' she added. 'As if rations aren't for everyone. Don't have a dog if you can't feed it, I say. My Bobby's got a white rat. Friendly little thing, really, and more than happy with scraps.'

A few people in the queue shifted and cleared their throats as she leaned on the bacon slicer confidingly. It was nice to be out of the rain, breathing the scent of sawdust and dried meats.

'Sad what happened,' she went on, holding up a hand to quell the restive housewives like a traffic policeman. 'It's fifteen Alfreton Avenue. I remember from the bill, you see, because of all the Fs. About half a mile, past the military training ground, turn left at Wallace Way, and keep going,' she said. 'But mind out for that dog.'

'Training ground?' I said.

'In the park. They pop in here, you know, the soldiers,' she added proudly, as a woman in a flowered headscarf muttered, 'Now look here...'

'I'm coming!' she snapped. 'Best of luck, dear,' she threw over her shoulder, as the angry woman thrust her ration book forward like a shield and strode to the counter. I heard her say, 'I'll have my usual, please, Mrs Woodcock. When you're ready.'

Outside, the road sloped upwards. I set off towards the park, wondering if there were now soldiers in the orangery, marching up and down where ornate Victorian plant pots had once stood. All I could see as I passed the high fence were rows of gloomy-looking prefabs, where I assumed the soldiers stayed until they were ready to go and fight. What did they teach them? I wondered. It occurred to me that Pete would have gone there too, and I felt a stab of pity for him. Arnold had walked Annie home ahead of me and Lou the other night, and I'd heard a lot of giggling.

So far, my attempts at being a crime reporter had resulted in nothing but mild humiliation and some very long, damp walks.

When I finally located it, soaked through and with my notebook a damp brick, number fifteen, the unimaginatively named Green Lawns, was largely as I'd imagined, but bigger. It was a huge Edwardian detached, with gables and long windows, and a brick-paved path leading to the front door. There were clipped shrubs round the porch, neat as the pom-poms on a child's hat, and serried, empty flowerbeds ready for spring. Nobody was digging for victory here, but a new Anderson shelter dominated the front garden, its corrugated metal like an alien visitation next to the venerable old lines of the house.

I tried not to think about the dog and rang the bell, a polished brass circle. It boomed out in the hall as if I'd activated

Big Ben. Simultaneously, there was a burst of frantic barking, great resonating huffs and roars, coming from somewhere alarmingly close.

I stepped onto the path again, glancing back, judging the distance I'd have to run to the gate when this *Baskervilles*-sized hound was unleashed. The door opened and the barking became a wall of noise.

'Major!' called a female voice. 'Major! Get down!' There was a scrabbling of claws and a black and brown snout poked urgently through the gap, snarling and drooling. I saw a flash of amber eye and the glint of wet teeth, and then he was hauled back in, and a door slammed shut, from where more muffled barks and shrill instructions emerged.

Eventually, the door opened again. She was nothing like Winifred and even less like the woman of my imagination. She was short, only five feet or so, and wore steel-rimmed glasses and a shapeless sage-green frock. She was plump, and her mousy hair was greying. I wondered if this would be my life now – calling on grieving widows and asking them difficult questions.

'Good morning. I'm sorry to call on you unexpectedly...' I began.

'I tend to stay in bed late in the mornings,' she said. 'Since my husband passed on.'

'Of course. I'm so sorry,' I said. 'That's why I'm here. I'm from the *Manchester Chronicle*...'

'Oh no, thank you,' she said. 'Sorry, but nothing doing.'

'It's nothing sinister,' I said. 'I'm the obituary writer. We're starting a new page, we cover the existences of significant citizens...' That was a stupid phrase to use when I was talking fast; I was buzzing like a bee by the end of it.

'You think Joseph was a "significant citizen", do you?' she asked. Her face was expressionless.

'Yes, of course!' I said. 'It doesn't have to be a big, important job – we're equally interested in dustmen or sweeps, people who help in their neighbourhoods...'

'He wasn't a dustman or a sweep,' she said.

'No, they were just my silly examples... What was he, in fact?'

I longed to escape. Haranguing a devastated widow wasn't coming as easily to me as I'd hoped.

'A businessman,' she said, as if she were being charged for every word she spoke. 'I already put that in the deaths column in your newspaper.' The dog was still agitating in the background.

'A very successful one, I'd guess,' I said, sweeping my gaze around the garden and into the hall, of which I could only see a small slice of mahogany staircase and a shadowy sideboard, empty of flowers. I tried a different route. 'I believe my editor knew your father, he said that he—'

'Look, Miss...'

'York.'

'Miss York, my father is long dead, and I don't want to discuss Joseph with a stranger. He died, it was a dreadful shock, I'm on my own, and the last thing I need is reporters groping about. He was a good husband, I'm very sad, that's all there is to it.'

I nodded. 'How long had you been married?'

'None of your business.'

'Are your children...?' I began.

'No children. I think that's enough. I need to let the dog out, so if you'll excuse me...'

That was a threat, if ever I heard one.

'Is there anyone else I might speak to?' I asked, backing away.

'I doubt it,' she said. 'We kept to ourselves.'

'Why was that?'

'Good Lord, you don't give up, do you?' she said. 'Joseph

was a refugee and English was his second language. It was hard for him to go out gadding because people speak too fast.'

She put her hand on the latch. 'Now, goodbye.'

The door clicked shut.

Once again, that grimly familiar feeling of failure was creeping over me. I'd forgotten about the fish van, too, and my mutton sandwiches had leaked grease onto my ID card.

The sensible thing would be to abandon the idea of Joseph Novak altogether, and find a nice old lady who'd left all her money to the cats' home to write about. Then I could go and throw myself into the icy depths of the River Medlock, rather than face Mr Gorringe.

CHAPTER FOUR

Back in town, cold, damp and tired, I walked up Deansgate, past piled-up rubble that looked as if it had always been there and little heaps of sandbags lying in doorways like seals on a rock.

'Where's your gas mask, miss?' a passing ARP warden asked.

'I've only nipped out for a ciggie,' I lied. 'It's just in there.' I nodded vaguely at the nearest building.

'No use to you in there, is it?' He looked down at me. 'Take it with you everywhere. And the blackout's on in two hours, so don't go forgetting that either.'

'I know,' I said irritably. 'I won't.' He sighed heavily at the arrogant stupidity of youth, and stamped off in his big boots. Something about him reminded me of Lou – the air of condescension perhaps. I was so nervous about failing at my first task, I was struggling to think straight. A gas mask was really the least of my worries. If I lost my job, I'd have to do war work full-time, learn to drive an ambulance and spend my days tending to the injured or stay up all night flashing a torch into bombed buildings to look for weeping children whose parents had been killed by falling masonry.

I wasn't the gung-ho sort, though – 'a head hen' as Annie called the peremptory matrons and volunteers at the hospital, who were never happier than when carrying a clipboard and telling someone they were in the wrong place. I loved the *Chronicle* and my boring desk with no view, and even Pat and her sarcastic grumbling. I felt safe there, in a way I'd never felt at the home. Of course, now nobody was safe, but I'd survived so far. I just had to avoid getting sacked.

Back at the office, Des was holding court, and the most junior messenger boy, Bobo (his surname was Bobbett, and 'he rides his little bike like a circus clown' according to Tom Harwood), was hanging on his every word. 'Of course, it could well have been murder, but the police don't want us press men to know these things,' he was saying, tapping his nose as Bobo gazed, wide-eyed. 'Strictly hush-hush and it's our job to... oh, good afternoon, dear,' he said, spotting me. 'Just giving our Bobo the low-down on the shooting yesterday.'

'Do we know it was murder?' I asked.

'Well' – he glanced around, as if snipers were lurking under Parrot Paulson's desk, and leaned forward in a miasma of tobacco and Old Spice aftershave – 'let's just say, nobody's yet come forward from the platoon. Which is suspicious, hmm?'

'Would you?' I asked. 'If you'd accidentally shot your friend and knew you'd go to prison?'

'Thing is,' said Des, in a half-whisper, 'they weren't supposed to have ammo. And according to DI Brennan, who I happened to bump into in the Nag's Head, it wasn't a rifle bullet.'

'What was it then?' I asked. Bobo was almost trembling with his efforts not to seem interested.

'You didn't hear it from me, but apparently it was a Webley,' murmured Des. 'Proper pistol, that. Do a lot of damage. They're making enquiries, of course, but if anyone did have one, it'll be at the bottom of the Mersey by now.'

I knew about Webleys from my detective stories. They were used by the real army, and the use of a bullet from a Webley surely ruled out the suicide theory. Winifred could stop dwelling in her misplaced shame now, I thought. I wondered if I should tell her. Though 'good news, your husband was murdered, after all,' perhaps wasn't what she wanted to hear either.

'Anyway,' Des said, stretching, 'be off you with you, Bobo, get back to your messages, you cheeky little tyke. And good luck to you, dear.' He heaved himself upright again and went on his way, pausing to have a good gaze at Gloria, with her tight pink jumper and victory-rolled hair.

Gloria's hair was a miracle of gravity-defying curls. I asked her how she did it once, and she showed me her 'rat' – a little roll of padded cloth she used to keep it all in place. 'They're ever so easy to make,' she had said. 'I sleep in mine, saves the bother in the morning.'

I couldn't imagine having the will to roll my hair and sleep like a corpse all night to avoid dislodging it. Mine was lucky if it saw a brush and a couple of hairpins most days.

I spent the afternoon under the beady gaze of Mrs Borrowdale, researching potential obituaries from the recent deaths columns – a man who had been a champion swimmer despite losing his leg in the Great War sounded a good possibility, and I was pleased to stumble on a 'much missed' nonagenarian academic who had discovered a rare plant in 1903. Though even if I wrote a glowing obituary of the King of Siam in rhyming couplets, it wouldn't please Mr Gorringe if I failed at the very first task he'd set.

It was odd, I reflected, that so few were for people who had died in the current war, other than a scattering of *dear sons* and *beloved husbands* back in June. We had all got used to a life without bombs since the brief air raids in the summer, and as Annie continually reminded me, I seldom remembered my gas mask. All the little annoyances loomed far larger in our lives: the queuing; the endless stretching and tucking of blackout curtains; the sudden disappearance of foods we liked, and their replacement with ration books and ersatz imitations. I had never tasted anything quite so foul as chicory coffee.

Of course, there had been bombing raids – the horror of the London Blitz, and that week, Liverpool had taken a battering too, though we weren't allowed to say so, in case the Germans didn't know where they'd hit. INDUSTRIAL CITY IS BOMBED OVERNIGHT, our bald headline read, with the copy going on to say how very little was damaged and how cheerful the citizens were, helping each other out of shelters, and whistling their way to work like the dwarves in *Snow White*, through a million shining diamonds of broken glass. Sometimes, I didn't know if we were a newspaper or a propaganda sheet, but all the others did it too. *A cheerful WVS worker adjusts her hat after a night of bombing*, read the *Chronicle's* photo caption, showing a pretty girl with lipstick on, tipping her helmet flirtatiously at the camera. I supposed it made people feel better, but it wasn't my idea of news.

All the recipes and cartoons and snippets of entertainment seemed a weak response to the bombardment of Britain in my book, but when I said this to Annie, she snapped, 'Oh, don't be so earnest, Edie. People need a good laugh,' and I thought she was probably right.

There had been a few false alarms, and we'd rush down to the cage-like Morrison shelter in the cellar of our building, then the all-clear would sound and we'd gather up our knitting and magazines and stagger back up to bed. It was beginning to feel like a dare – the planes would go overhead, the siren would sound, we'd all run about in a flap, then it would be a case of 'ha, fooled you!' and we'd return to our lives, like a giant game of musical statues. The last time, we had taken down a freshly-brewed pot of tea and some fish paste sandwiches we'd been about to eat, and it felt rather like a strange picnic.

We were lucky to have the cellar, of course. Most people we knew were required to drop everything and rush off to the public shelters, and I'd heard some very unsavoury things about those – the necessity of relieving oneself in overflowing buckets and men trying it on with girls in the crowds being just two of them. Annie's mum had told her horrifying tales of slum kids giving everyone in the shelter fleas, and spoke grimly of one terrible night when a man brought in a recorder and played folk songs for several hours 'to cheer everyone up'. Her mum said she'd been forced to wad up a bit of knitting wool and stuff it in her ears.

Beyond the general worry and annoyance of the war, though, I hadn't given a great deal of thought to us actually being bombed. It was hard to imagine our little kitchen with its metal teapot and jolly, patterned tins lying in a chaos of beams and plaster, or think of my small, tidy bedroom with the single bed blown into sticks and my meagre cosmetics scattered across Fallowfield.

It was almost Christmas too, and some ludicrous part of me felt that even the Germans wouldn't ruin people's brief festivities with an air raid. Besides, what was the point of the blackout if it didn't mean they couldn't find us? All those ARP wardens beetling about, checking up on us – surely it counted for something?

I was still thinking about this as I finally trudged off before tea to see Mrs Pelham about volunteering. I arrived as a stream of people was pouring out of the church because they'd moved Weekday Evensong earlier, thanks to the blackout. I wondered if I should pretend I'd been there too, but I decided I'd only get found out, and judged a liar as well as a heathen.

She was exactly as I'd imagined. Stout, with a helmet of

iron-grey curled hair and leather brogues. I found her whisking round the church hall with a cloth, polishing the urns as if they were battle guns. 'Oh yes, you're Miss York,' she said doubtfully, consulting a notebook.

'I believe I was meant to see you on Saturday.'

I tried not to sigh. 'I'm afraid my work at the newspaper...' I began. She pursed her lips as though I'd said 'cabaret'.

'When we volunteer here, our duty to the country comes first,' she said. 'As I'm sure you're aware. I expect you have a sweetheart away fighting, do you?'

I shook my head, thinking of Annie's Pete.

'No, I don't have a young man,' I said.

'Well! No wonder – a girl your age, too busy working to court, in your slacks.' She looked down at the sensible trousers I'd changed into, thinking I'd look willing and hearty. 'You'll want to hurry up, before you're left gathering dust. My Connie's just turned nineteen and expecting her second. And she runs the paper collection in Ladybarn.'

I had nothing to say in reply.

'I'll put you down for a stint on Christmas Day, shall I?' she went on. 'Should be quiet, you can learn the ropes.'

My heart sank. I had hoped to spend the day reading – I'd decided to allow myself a new detective novel, and Annie and I had agreed to pool our rations and try and get a decent bit of meat to roast. I'd imagined us peeling potatoes together and singing Christmas carols along with the wireless.

'Four... o'... clock,' said Mrs Pelham, licking her pencil and writing busily in her notebook.

'There. I shall expect you on the dot, and please bring well-scrubbed hands and your own pinny.'

'Merry Christmas,' I said, and she looked at me beadily.

'Let's hope so, dear.'

It was dark when I emerged from the hall just after six, having been talked through the tea urns and the larder, and I hadn't a torch. It wasn't far to home, but once again, I felt that life had turned into an awful sort of parlour game; a blind man's buff which required me to find my way back without slipping on an icy puddle or crashing into someone.

There was a weak sliver of moon, like a water ring on a polished table, and I could just make out the white edge of the kerb. A girl flew past on a bicycle, shrieking, 'watch out!' and I jumped back. 'Stay on the road!' I shouted, heart pounding.

As her wheels whirred away, the sharp, eerie wail of the air-raid siren sliced the air. Fear bloomed in my chest, and I began to run, leaping over the shine of puddles. The siren rose and fell, and I sprinted and slithered through the icy dark, counting the garden gates, until, at last, I reached our own. I unlocked the front door and banged straight into Mr Benson, our landlord, carrying a large torch, his gas mask and a packet of Gold Flake tobacco. 'Get down there,' he said, pointing to the cellar door. 'And where's your ruddy gas mask?'

'Where's Annie?' I gasped, tugging the damp-swollen door open.

'Work,' he said. 'Heard her leave earlier. Come on, girly, do you want us bombed?' He reached over me in a blast of damp wool and BO, and shoved the door, so I almost fell downstairs.

'My gas mask is upstairs,' I said, turning round, but he hurried me further down.

'No time now,' he said. 'You'll have to take your chances.'

As usual, the cellar smelled of coal dust and damp. There was a folding canvas chair the mice had been at and a couple of blankets that Annie and I had left in the Morrison shelter.

'I hope it's over soon,' Mr Benson grumbled. 'I had a nice bit of coley laid out for me tea.'

I hoped he wasn't about to jump on me, but as he was well over 70 and had a gammy leg, I fancied my chances if he did. I also noted that Annie had left a stray knitting needle by the shelter, and thought I could lunge at him with it.

He settled into the chair, and I padded the blankets into a cushion and perched on an old coal scuttle. 'I'll have forty winks,' he said. 'Wake me when the all-clear goes.'

I was relieved that I didn't have to make conversation, but less so that I had nothing to read to distract me from my worry about Annie. She'd be at the hospital, tending to patients as bombs fell outside, while I lazed about with our snoring landlord. For the first time, I felt real shame.

I must be better, I told myself. Find patriotic stories for the *Chronicle* that would stir peoples' blood and help them through it all, and make tea alongside Mrs Pelham, showing willingness and good grace. I said a little prayer for Annie and her mum. I was not religious – I hadn't been to church since the enervating misery of Sunday school at the home – *but when there's enemy planes droning overhead*, I thought, *it can't do any harm*.

The time dragged on. I thought about risking a dash upstairs for my book, and cursed my past stupidity for failing to leave at least an out-of-date magazine down here. I thought about Mr Novak, and tried to plot a way to find out more, but without any help from Lou, or a dramatic conversion to open-hearted friendliness from Mrs Novak, I'd have to go into work tomorrow and give Mr Gorringe an unwanted Christmas present – the news that my very first column had failed.

By nine thirty, I was starving, and Mr Benson was still snoring. I was also freezing. I'd draped one of the blankets over him and wrapped myself in the other, but it felt like tissue paper in the face of the biting, underground chill. I longed to go and get my book, a bite to eat, a cup of tea, the stone hot water bottle I used on cold nights... and just as I was making up my mind to risk my life for a Shippam's paste sandwich and a pacy novel, I heard the glorious note of the distant all-clear, as welcome as the opening phrase of 'Ode to Joy'.

I woke Mr Benson, and he shook his head like a dog after a bath. 'Bloody coley's ruined now,' he said, creaking to his feet.

He blew out the candle and switched his torch on to guide us upstairs.

'Better survey the damage, eh?'

I followed, heart thudding. If Annie was all right, I thought, I'd always be nice to her, I'd let her borrow my precious drops of Après L'Ondée perfume whenever she liked instead of guarding it jealously, and I'd shut up about her flirting with men, no matter what she did with them...

We had reached the hall, and Mr Benson cautiously switched the light on. Everything seemed to be as we'd left it. He opened the front door, surveying the street. There was nothing, no fires, everything was peaceful, though a few people were straggling by, from the public shelter. 'Any news?' he called, and one turned. 'Town's taken a few hits,' a man shouted back. 'They're tackling the fires, no news on casualties.'

I felt faint. Annie worked in town. 'Are the hospitals...' I began, but they'd gone. 'I'll be seeing you,' said Mr Benson. 'Go and rescue me tea.'

He disappeared through the door to his flat, and I went slowly up to ours. As I filled the kettle, wondering if the gas would be working, I heard the click of the front door downstairs, followed by quick feet on the stairs.

'Bloody hell,' Annie gasped, collapsing through the door. 'What a shift that was! We had to get all the ones who can still walk down to the basement, then we were up and down with the porters, trying to move the bed-bound ones in a lift the size of a flipping sardine tin, I'm shattered...'

She looked at me. 'What's up?'

'I thought you might be dead,' I said, my voice wobbling.

'Oh, give over!' She laughed. 'There were no bombs near us, it was all round Trafford Park and the factories. One or two in the centre, I heard, but nothing really serious, and I saw lots of fire wardens on the way back. I got a lift with David.'

'Who?'

'Just a doctor,' she said breezily. Perhaps Arnold wasn't so appealing, after all. 'That tea won't make itself, dear,' she added, pulling off her lace-up shoes and replacing them with grubby pink knitted slippers.

'Won't they need you in case there's any casualties?' I asked, as the gas came on with a cheering pop.

'No, I'm on all day and evening tomorrow,' she said. 'Merry Christmas, Annie, here's a series of wounds to dress. At least we can have a nice rest on Christmas Day.'

I told her about Mrs Pelham's plans for me.

'Oh, for heaven's sake,' she said, disappointed. 'Trust you. I suppose I'll have to ask Monsieur Brennan if he's busy. I'm sure he could drop in for a mince pie.'

'We don't have any...' I began, and she reached down to her bag and flourished a cardboard box at me.

'Oh, we do,' she said. 'Gift from a grateful patient. Perhaps you'd care for one? With brandy!' she added gleefully.

For the second time that evening, I wanted to hug her.

CHAPTER FIVE

By morning, I felt less jolly. There were no buses into town when I arrived at the stop. A glum woman in a brown coat and matching headscarf over curlers said, 'Town's in ruins, I heard.'

That wasn't what Annie had told me, but I wondered if she had secret information. I was contemplating the forty-five-minute walk to work, unsure whether the office would still be standing, when a car drew up.

'Jump in,' shouted the driver. I peered in to see Lou Brennan, gazing irritably up at me. 'Come along, York, I don't bite. There's no trams or buses running yet, so I'm your best bet.'

'All right for some,' sniffed the woman as I climbed in.

'Perhaps we could give her a...' I began, but Lou had already pulled out into the road and driven off.

'That poor woman,' I said.

'No, she's not,' said Lou, once again lighting a cigarette without offering me one. I was saving some Player's Weights I'd found in the newsagent to supplement Annie's present. 'I know her type. Ghouls at the feast. They love things going wrong. Unexpected deaths, sudden explosions, they gather like harpies.'

I thought he was being rather unfair. 'Is it true, though?' I asked. 'Is town ruined?'

'No,' he said shortly. 'Most incendiaries hit the factories. One or two fires, a lot of broken glass, but it's still standing. I was at work all night, just had an hour's kip.'

'At the police station?'

'No, you great sausage,' said Lou, to my annoyance. 'I'm a part-time fire warden. If I can't go and fight, at least I can do my bit here.'

'Why is it that you can't go and fight?'

He looked furious. 'Injury,' he said, and I didn't dare ask anything further.

He dropped me off at St Peter's Square, opposite Central Library. Smoke rose in the distance. 'You'll have to walk from here,' he said. 'There's glass and nails all over, I'm not risking my tyres.'

He was right. Once I emerged from Library Passage, I could see fire engines and flocks of helmeted ARP wardens like armoured birds. There were hoses being unwound to tackle sullen little fires and plenty of people standing about gawping on their way to work. Albert Square had taken a hit, and as I inched down to Deansgate, I could see why the trams weren't running – the overhead wires were drooping and tangled like knitting a cat had been at.

Some of the glass had already been brushed into the gutter, and I was careful to step around the jagged pieces. Windows had been blown out in a couple of tall office buildings, and people were carrying sandbags to and fro to lay in doorways. I heard a fire warden shout, 'Portland Street's going up,' as I passed, and saw men running with a ladder.

Outside the Wood Street Mission, a straggling queue of battered, dusty people waited for shelter after their homes had been bombed. 'What happened?' I asked a woman with wild hair and her jersey on inside-out. She was carrying a wailing, soot-streaked child.

'Cooke Street,' she said. 'My house is gone. Thank God we're still here, we were at the shelter. I never thought they'd hit my house... all the kiddies' Christmas presents are gone too,' she added. 'But we're not!' She smiled bravely, and I felt tears prick at my eyes. Cooke Street was down near Oxford Road, I remembered, not far from Annie's hospital. A uniformed man shepherded the woman inside the building, saying, 'Let's get the little one a bite to eat,' and she disappeared after him.

Despite it all, I felt excited. This was real life, and we were all part of something. All trying to defeat the same enemy. I composed headlines as I walked and crunched along – BRAVE CITY DEFIES BLITZ perhaps, or CHIN UP! TIRELESS WORKERS RESTORE OUR CITY TO FORMER GLORY. I wasn't sure about 'former glory', and was trying to think of something better when I saw a dark figure trudging ahead of me, neat as a pin with his bowler hat and briefcase, and a rolled umbrella. He looked uncomfortably familiar, and I suddenly realised that I was following Mr Gorringe, a symbol of British pluck in an apocalypse all by himself.

It struck me that the first thing I had to do was tell him that Mr Novak was a no-go. What a Christmas. Last year, there had been no bombs, and Annie and I both had a few days off. We'd gone to her mum's for Christmas Day and stayed the night. It had been wonderful, teasing from her brothers, and little presents for us all, carol singing and a roast dinner. This year, her brothers were away fighting, and Annie's shifts meant she couldn't get away. And here we were, as bombs rained down and my career stalled before it had even begun.

'As you will appreciate, Miss York, we have rather more pressing concerns this morning,' Mr Gorringe said, when I presented myself in his office.

'I just wanted to...' I began, and he flapped a hand.

'I have an urgent government meeting awaiting my attendance. If it's about the obituary, write it up and I shall concern myself with it later.'

'It's just that...'

He stood, and gathered up a buff cardboard folder.

Miss Paulson somehow divined by telepathy that he'd finished, and swung open his office door. I was pleased to see she had a bit of cobweb in her hair, presumably from the shelter where she'd been last night.

'Dreadful, isn't it?' she said, as he swept out.

'Shocking,' I agreed.

I imagined there would be many exchanges like this over the course of the day. What else could we say? I had thought myself fairly safe, and now I didn't. I assumed everyone else felt the same way.

In the absence of a glowing tribute from Mrs Novak, I thought I'd better press on with the nonagenarian botanist academic, so I'd at least have a small offering to lay at Mr Gorringe's feet.

I telephoned her daughter, Dorothy, who sounded delighted to speak to me. She lived nearby in Fallowfield.

'My mother worked at the University till she retired, so it was near,' said Dorothy. She insisted she was happy to talk to me on the telephone. 'My dear, I'm so sorry I can't ask you for tea, but we've a houseful of guests for the funeral and there's simply no space to think, would you mind terribly?'

At one point there was a crossed line and somebody irritably saying, 'Abdul? Adbul, is that you?' into my ear, then he went away again and we resumed. I took copious notes, one-handed, and learnt that Professor Ada Morley-Pratt had spent time exploring the Amazon with her father, also a keen botanist, and had philanthropically donated her entire botanical library to the university on her death. 'And she was a wonderful mother,' Dorothy added. 'She never interfered, she let us do whatever we liked, and as long as we were quiet, we could sit under her desk while she worked.'

It occurred to me that 'wonderful' and 'neglectful' could be two sides of the same coin here, but there was going to be a university laboratory named after her, and a reprint of her most famous monograph, *A Study of the Patagonian Marsh Orchid in its Natural Habitat with Particular Reference to Native Soil Types*. I doubted I'd be able to squeeze that in, but I expressed delight and amazement.

Admittedly, it wasn't the editor's requested hat-tip to Mr Novak's helpful father-in-law, but I reasoned that with parts of Manchester in flames and vital war factories bombed to smithereens, the editor would barely notice the change of personnel. As people began to drift away early to get home before the blackout, offering lifts and wry comments, I dropped the finished copy in the tray outside Mr Gorringe's office. I hoped he'd be far too busy to think about it very much.

To my horror, as I struggled into my coat, contemplating the long walk home in the dark, he appeared like a pantomime genie, springing from behind his office door, and plucked it up. I watched him scan it, with a puzzled frown.

'Miss York,' he called.

I looked up, trying to arrange my face into 'interested and helpful' rather than 'terrified'.

'This is not the obituary I asked you to write,' he said quietly. My heart thudded. I longed to be outside, taking the full force of an incendiary. In the distance, sirens wailed.

'I know,' I gabbled. 'Mrs Novak wouldn't speak to me, I'm afraid, and so I discovered another interesting Mancunian who died recently, and I thought...'

'Miss York,' he said. 'This is the first piece you have been asked to write. I may run this one, given the circumstances, but I would greatly appreciate you using your as-yet untapped reporter's skills to provide the piece I originally commissioned.

Imminently. The board are all keen to see Mrs Novak's father's support for the *Chronicle* recognised.'

I nodded. 'Of course,' I said. He rammed his hat onto his head and nodded goodbye.

'It is at least well written,' he said over his shoulder, as he strode to the door. 'Keep it up.'

From despair to joy, I thought, as a great, foolish smile spread across my face.

It was only as I picked and staggered my way home, past burning buildings and filthy civil defence workers that I faced the truth. If I couldn't find out more about Joseph Novak, my career would be over before it had begun.

As I walked down the centre of the road on my long way home, I passed a group of workers standing over a series of bundled sheets and wondered why they were gazing at bedding, until, with a pure thrill of horror, I realised they were covered bodies.

For some reason, I hadn't let myself think about people dying. All the sirens and fires, the glass and beams, and the eyes of the woman I'd met, so clean and wide in her filthy face, were alarming enough. The idea that people were trapped, in pain, mortally wounded – it didn't seem real. I knew it would soon sink in, that this assault on my home, my city, would make me terribly angry, but for now, I was numb. I wanted only to get home, have a cup of tea and some stew, and escape into a book.

I'd drawn the blackout curtains and was listening to the wireless and wondering how Annie was getting on when I heard it again, an eerie, drawn-out howl, like the wind through bare trees. As I stood up, there came another sound – a violent banging and ringing of the doorbell downstairs.

I wondered if Annie had left work early and forgotten her key, or if Mr Benson had locked himself out, and flew down the stairs. Another night with Mr B down in the dank basement didn't appeal, but what choice did we have?

I flung the door open and stared in surprise. 'Let me in, for God's sake,' said Lou.

I stood aside. 'What are you doing here?'

'Get your gas mask, and hurry,' he snapped. 'Where's your nearest shelter?'

'In the cellar,' I said, running up the stairs ahead of him. I snatched up my mask, a stub of candle and a magazine of Annie's, and rushed back down. Lou was already halfway down the cellar steps.

'Came to see you both, as I was passing,' he said.

I found the matches, and stuck the lit candle onto a little dish. Lou looked exhausted. He'd lost his hat, and his coat was filthy and ripped under the arm.

'She's at work,' I said. 'So it looks as if you're stuck with me.'

I wished I hadn't said that, as it immediately sounded as though I was waiting for him to say, 'Oh, my dear, it's a delight!'

He didn't. 'Looks like it,' he said instead, settling into Mr Benson's chair. There was no sign of our landlord. 'Why didn't you say?' said Lou, when I mentioned this. 'He's probably deaf. I'm going up.'

'No, don't...' I began, as the house shook above us. The bombing had started again in earnest. Lou was already leaping up the stairs. Two minutes later, he returned.

'No sign,' he said. 'I banged on the door, but he's probably out. Is he a drinker?'

'I don't think so,' I said. 'Why?'

'Because he could either be at the pub or passed out,' Lou said irritably. 'Looks like Fritz has set in for the night. God knows how things will look in the morning.'

With a cold sense of dread, I realised that Lou and I might be stuck together for the entire night. 'Was it very bad today?' I ventured.

'It was a joy, if you like pulling bodies out of a basement while a burst water main mixes with plaster dust, and the city burns,' he said. 'By the end of it, it was like being buried in clay.'

He reached into his coat pocket and pulled out a small metal flask. 'I suppose you were busy reporting on looting amid the chaos, were you?' He took a swig and offered it to me. It seemed unhygienic, but otherwise, I thought, I might die of thirst.

It turned out to be whisky, and I winced.

'No,' I said. 'I was writing an obituary.'

'You've got your work cut out there then.'

'It had to be a specific one.' Another huge crump and boom sounded somewhere, and the ceiling shuddered. What did it matter? I thought. We were going to be killed soon enough anyway, if this carried on.

I told him about Mr Gorringe, and the obituary I'd written, and why it wasn't the one he'd asked me to write. 'Mrs Novak wouldn't talk to me,' I said, taking another drink of whisky. It was going down nicely now, and he held his hand out for it.

'This is the fellow you were asking me about?' said Lou.

I nodded and my head swam. 'I don't know why it's so important,' I said. 'I found another subject and that should be just as good.'

'Because one dead person is just like another,' said Lou, raising an eyebrow.

'No! I don't mean it like that. Just that she was interesting too. I thought Mr Novak might have something to do with Turnbull, the teacher who was killed, but now I don't think he did, really...'

'Whatever are you talking about, York?' said Lou, his face disconcertingly satanic in the candlelight.

I tried to explain how I'd visited Mrs Turnbull and then Arnold, and I'd tried to interview Mrs Novak despite her terrifying dog, but she'd shut the door on me...

'Well, she's just been widowed,' he said. 'What can you expect?'

'Dorothy had lost her mum,' I said, 'but she wanted to talk about Professor Morley-Pratt at great length.'

'Not everyone is a relentless chatterbox,' he said. 'So I'm not sure that's very peculiar.'

I sighed. 'I just think it's odd.'

'We're all odd,' said Lou. He passed me the flask again. In the candlelight, I saw it had an inscription: To L.E.B., With Thanks and Admiration. May, 1937.

I wondered if it was from a girlfriend and was about to ask him, when there was a slow whistle, followed a second later by an explosion so huge a chunk of plaster fell from the ceiling and dust rained down.

'Christ alive,' said Lou. He blew the candle out. 'Get in the Morrison.'

'But what about you?' I asked. My teeth were chattering with fright.

'You'll have to squash up,' he said grimly. 'They seem to have sent the entire Luftwaffe to Violet Bank Terrace.'

There was nothing for it but to move over and let him in. He arranged himself with his head at my feet, so we were top to tail. Suki and I had shared a bed like this at the home, when we couldn't sleep, and she'd crawl in with me. We'd whisper stories to each other until we were too tired to speak. Now, I had Lou's filthy brogues two inches from my nose, but it was just another of the privations of war.

'Do you think we're going to die?' I asked him, as the street took another direct hit, and more plaster showered down.

'If we are, there'll be nobody left to write our obituaries,' he said. 'Or pull the bodies out, for that matter.'

I smiled. He dug in his pocket for his cigarette case and a lighter, wiggling to extract them, so I jostled uncomfortably against the wire cage.

'What about gas?' I said, shocked.

He groaned. 'Can't a bugger even have a fag when he's about to die?'

'If we go up in a ball of fire, it's your fault,' I said sternly, and he lit two cigarettes and gave me one. If it was my last cigarette, I was determined to appreciate it. We lay silently in the dark, smoking, listening to the cracks and blasts above us. It was strangely intimate.

'I think that was town,' he said. 'Maybe Central Library.'

'Oh, not the library!' I cried. Next to the art gallery, it was the place I loved the most in Manchester, the great, circular repository of knowledge and calm. The idea of that temple to wisdom being crushed by some thoughtless Jerry's flung bomb, the venerable old books strewn and ruined...

'Might have been the hospital,' he said. 'Let's hope not.'

'Let's talk about something else,' I said. 'Annie was all right last night, so I'm going to believe she'll be all right tonight. They'll get them all to the shelter, I'm sure.'

Lou said nothing. The tip of his cigarette glowed orange.

'What would you want in your obituary?' I asked him. 'In case I survive and you don't?'

He snorted. 'Unlikely either of us will, in this contraption. I suppose I'd want it to say *A good man who did his best*.'

It was unexpectedly sincere. 'I'll put that in,' I said. 'What about your life story, though?'

'Brief and uninteresting. Grew up in Manchester, joined the police, fought in Spain, died in a festive raid on Fallowfield alongside a pretty but nosy woman.'

I ignored that. 'You fought in Spain?'

'Mm.'

'Against Franco?'

'I can't believe you even asked that,' said Lou. 'If I wasn't trapped in a cage with you, I'd walk out.'

'Sorry.'

'Yes, against the fascist Franco. Ambulance driver, International Brigade, had one lung half destroyed in a blast, and that's why I'm stuck here instead of on the front line. Happy now?'

'Should you be smoking then?' I asked gaily, but he didn't reply. In truth, I was both impressed and shocked.

'That's why I've been promoted,' he said bitterly. 'Because there was nobody left to do the job but little, injured Lou.'

'It's not your fault you were...'

'Yes, it is,' he said. He reached for the flask as another bomb exploded horribly nearby. 'I was driving an ambulance, and they told me there might be an ambush, but I wanted to get the injured bloke behind the front line to give him a chance. He was going to die anyway, I was an idiot. And there was indeed an ambush and we were thrown clear of the vehicle. He was killed instantly, and so was Lorna. I woke up in the scrub by the road and I'm only here because some lad whose name I never discovered checked if I was breathing and got me to a hospital. He's probably dead now too.'

'My God,' I said. 'How awful. Who was Lorna?'

Lou sucked hard on the cigarette before pinching it out between his fingers.

'My fiancée,' he said. 'Another bloody reporter.'

He wouldn't say any more, so I asked what cases he was working on.

'Rescuing people from bombs,' he said. 'That enough?'

'What about Edward Turnbull?' I asked boldly. It was easier to be brave in the dark. 'A Webley revolver? It wasn't suicide, was it? Maybe not even an accident.'

'I can't tell you anything about ongoing investigations,' said Lou. 'As you well know.'

'Have you spoken to that lad, Pocock?' I asked. 'He said he saw someone in the trees. I did too.'

'Someone in the trees, in a training exercise involving a

hundred people running amongst trees, is hardly surprising,' said Lou. 'And yes, we have, and he's about as reliable as a three-bob note. His brilliant suggestion was that a German sniper had joined the training exercise undercover.' He snorted.

'All right, but...'

'Look, Edie, it's late and I need a kip,' he said. 'So kindly shush.'

We fell asleep eventually, my cheek pressed against Lou's wool trouser leg. It smelled of woodsmoke and was oddly comforting. I blinked awake in the dark, and for a moment wondered why I was in prison, then I remembered. The cellar was still standing, and there was no noise of aeroplanes or bombing. As I tried to move without waking him, the sound of the all-clear penetrated.

'Thank God for that,' I whispered, and he stirred.

'All over then?' he asked.

'Seems like it.'

I had a whisky headache and my right leg had gone to sleep. We crawled out in a thoroughly ungainly fashion.

'Annie should be back soon,' he said.

'God, I hope so.'

I didn't dare consider the alternative. I lit the candle again. 'Nearly one,' said Lou, looking at his watch. 'I'm back on duty in six hours.

'Look,' he added, tucking the flask into his pocket. 'I'll give you a hand with the Novak feller. See what I can find out. In return, you keep quiet about my life story.'

'All right,' I said. 'But why? You were quite heroic.'

'Hardly. And you might want to get some pillows in there. My neck feels like a bent coat hanger.'

We made our way up the steps, and I hesitated again before opening the door, afraid of what I might find. The lights came on at the switch, but the glass lamp in the hall was smashed, and the banister was leaning at a strange, drunken angle. There were cracks and holes in the ceiling that hadn't been there before.

'Watch yourself on those stairs,' said Lou.

As he spoke, the front door opened and Mr Benson lurched in. 'Evening,' he said. 'Been at the public shelter. Stinks. Full of shouting kiddies and crying mums. Going to bed.'

I almost laughed with relief that he wasn't dead.

'I'm off too,' said Lou.

'Oh!' I said, 'Don't you want a cup of tea first?'

I'd somehow got used to his big, irritable presence and I was fearful of the damage I'd find in the flat.

'I need to sleep in a bed for ten minutes before I'm up again,' he said. 'Get the feeling back in my neck. I'll be in touch about what we discussed. Tell Annie I said hello.'

He disappeared into the rubble, and I trudged up the wobbling stairs. I pushed open the door and surveyed. A window had been blown out in the living room, and there was glass all over the couch. The blackout curtain hung down, ripped and useless. A table holding Annie's sewing box had tipped over and her pin cushion had rolled under an armchair. Her glass animal ornaments on the sideboard had been smashed to dust, and in the kitchen, a full shelf of pans had collapsed. Our bedrooms seemed unscathed, and the rusting, white-tiled bathroom looked as unwelcoming as ever. We had got away lightly, really.

I thought of all the people who hadn't, as I swept the glass away and patched up the window with card, and by the time Annie came in half an hour later, exhausted, blood-stained from treating casualties, and some way beyond forming coherent sentences, I'd decided that I really did have to do something about joining the war effort.

. . .

When I opened my bedroom window the next morning, the air reeked of burning, and down Wilmslow Road towards town, great plumes of black smoke rose steadily in the distance. There were no buses or trams running at all. Every so often, a shrieking fire engine rattled past on the main road, and all around me, various houses had disappeared like cavities in a row of teeth. I couldn't see any dead bodies, but the streets were full of wardens and ARP, moving passers-by along and discouraging staring as they dragged bedding and mattresses out into brick and glass-strewn front gardens.

I was prepared to walk to work, but would work even be there now, I wondered? Or would our desks and papers and typewriters all be piled onto Deansgate, being hosed down?

There was no sign of Lou today, of course; he'd have been out hours ago, working like a demon to help and organise. Annie was still in bed, but she deserved it after yesterday. I'd taken her a cup of tea, though all I'd seen of her was a puff of blonde hair on the pillow.

I made a sudden decision. Mr Gorringe knew I was keen to get the Novak obituary done, and my absence from the office, if it still existed, would be easily explained. I'd go along to the canteen this morning to help out, I decided, then if I had time, perhaps I could make it to Withington later this afternoon to beg Mrs Novak to reconsider. I scribbled a note for Annie, and set off, feeling determined and patriotic.

At the hall, there was no sign of Mrs Pelham, but there was a long queue of shabby-looking people stretching as far as the postbox on the corner. Nobody was crying, but they all looked as though they'd been robbed of the power of speech. There were children clutching tiny gas masks, a hatless baby rolled into a blanket over its mother's shoulder, and a motley collection of dogs attached to their owners with belts and woollen neckties. I bent to say hello to a little black spaniel who sniffed my hand. I stroked her head, and her owner, an elderly man, said, 'Do you work here?'

'Sort of,' I said. 'I'm a volunteer here to make tea, that's all.'

'Do you know where we're to go?' he asked. 'The house has gone, and we've heard nothing about anything. They took my wife to the hospital, she's hurt her arm. I don't know which one...' He stopped and swallowed, then rubbed the lower half of his face. 'I don't know,' he repeated.

'My friend works at the infirmary,' I said. 'I can try to find out.'

But he was swept away by a sudden gaggle of people firing questions at me.

'Do we need a ration book for the tea?' called one woman, and another shouted, 'Give us some useful information!'

Panic rose in me. 'I'm just a tea maker!' I shouted back. One wag called out, 'Blessed are the tea-makers!' and a few people groaned. I shoved my way to the front and through the open door, where the queue had bloomed into a large crowd. There was now a hubbub of voices and shrieking babies, and a loose dog was barking wildly at the Ewbank carpet sweeper propped in the corner. I took a deep breath and realised I'd forgotten to bring my own pinny.

Over at the back, trestle tables were laid out, with giant urns spitting and clattering streams of hot water into metal pots. There were plates of lumpy rock buns, and a stack of information leaflets entitled: *Have You Been 'Bombed Out'?*

I thought it might be more use if somebody handed them out to the queue, but a hearty-looking girl of around my age in a floral apron grabbed my arm.

'Thank goodness!' she said. 'It's been like this since we opened at six, I haven't stopped. I'm Moira, you must be...?'

'Edie,' I supplied. 'I told Mrs Pelham I'd be here on Christmas Day, as I'm new and it was supposed to be quiet, but I thought you might need me...'

'Well, quite,' she said. 'I'm not sure I got a wink of sleep. I was in the shelter half the night sitting next to the most awful old man – he complained incessantly about the crying kiddies, as if it's their fault, poor little mites—' she broke off. 'Yes madam, leaflets there, Sheila's on tea, I'm afraid we've no sugar left, but we do have lemonade for children, on the far table... And, of course, there's no sign of Mrs Pelham,' she went on. 'She's here every day, without fail, so I'm beginning to worry rather – it's odd, don't you think?'

'I suppose so,' I said, as Moira thrust a spare apron into my hand.

'Can I stick you on tea and free Sheila for another bun-run?' she asked. 'We didn't bring enough.'

Sheila had frizzy hair and freckles, and already looked exhausted. I tied on the apron and was immediately inundated with hordes of people thrusting cups and saucers at me and wanting to know why there was no sugar. Once I'd got the hang of the monstrous urns and ten-ton milk jugs, I felt quite efficient as the hours went by, though I tired quickly of saying, 'I'm so sorry, I'm afraid I don't know, but here's a leaflet.'

Sheila seemed to have disappeared altogether and Moira was wrangling sticky children at the lemonade table and clearing up rock-bun crumbs, when the crowd parted slightly to allow a woman through.

She was tall and very slim. Her black hair was coiled on her head like ropes fixed with invisible pins, she wore a pale wool suit that looked as though it had come from the sort of boutique that offers spindly gold chairs and champagne to its customers, and she dripped and glistened with jewellery. I saw diamonds in her ears, sapphires on her fingers, and some thumping great stones that could have been emeralds in her brooch. She had an alligator handbag, polished to a mirror-like sheen, and her face was astonishing – beautiful, but carved like granite into sharp angles and planes, her features outlined by brushes and powders. She must have been at least forty-five.

'Ah,' she said. 'Here you are.'

I gaped at her, holding a milk jug. I felt like a milkmaid contemplating a queen.

'Lillian Emerson,' she said. 'How do you do?' She was well spoken, and she looked me in the eye. I put down the jug, aware of the restive queue behind her.

'Edie York,' I said, reaching to shake her hand. Her nails were crimson, like shellacked chrysanthemum petals.

'I know,' she said. 'I was told I'd find you here.'

Sheila staggered in, carrying a stack of bun trays. 'Hold your horses,' she yelled at the surging crowd. 'Give me two minutes to get these out.'

Moira looked over. 'Need a minute?' she mouthed. I shrugged and nodded. She jerked her head towards the store room behind us. 'Go on, we'll hold the fort – but don't be too long,' she said, wiping her hands on a tea-towel. 'Those kiddies are like locusts, we'll need reinforcements soon.'

I ushered Mrs Emerson into the small room. The walls were lined with shelves of tinned chicory coffee, tea canisters, elderly enamel kettles and a large tub reading DRIED EGG FOR THE VICAR ONLY. I wished I wasn't wearing a stained apron.

'How may I help you, Mrs Emerson?' I asked. I felt convinced it was a case of mistaken identity.

She leaned against a stack of rubber mats and tapped a cigarette from a gold case.

'Well,' she said. 'First of all, my house was bombed and I do rather need a cup of tea, failing a stiff brandy. Secondly, I've been all over looking for you. First I went to the *Chronicle* and they sent me to your house, then a tiny little woman in a dressing gown sent me down here.'

I assumed she meant Annie.

'Is the *Chronicle* still there?' I asked rather desperately.

'Apparently so,' she said. 'Unlike my home. Anyway, my question is, can you write an obituary of a particular man, without saying where you got the information?'

I stared at her.

'Why would I need to not say?' I asked.

'It's pretty obvious, isn't it?' she said. 'I was his mistress.'

I was startled, but I tried not to show it.

'Wouldn't that be something for... his wife to suggest?' I asked delicately.

She shrugged. 'Look, his wife's hopeless. She'd never think of it. I want Joseph to be celebrated. I want everyone to know about him. Can't you just tell people it was an anonymous friend?' she went on. 'He had a lot of business contacts.'

'Joseph?'

'Novak. He was a refugee, remarkable story.'

My heart was thudding. 'Joseph Novak from Withington?' I said. 'I went to see his wife. She said she wasn't interested.'

'Yes, that's him. She wasn't interested in much,' said Lillian Emerson. She gave a little laugh. 'Very plain tastes. Unlike some.'

I ignored that. I really did not wish to know about the moribund love life of Mr and Mrs Novak, and how this Lillian had improved the situation.

But at the same time, this was a gift from God. If I made friends with Lillian, I could not only write the obituary and keep my job, I could even find out all about Joseph and why he had given Edward Turnbull the painting, and then I could finally produce my in-depth crime report. I had a sudden vision of a front-page story, my name in inky black type alongside: *By Edie York, Chief Crime Reporter*.

'I would love to write Joseph's obituary,' I said. 'Would you like to do the interview now?'

Her face softened slightly. 'I would very much like to,' she said, 'but I'm expected at my son's for luncheon shortly. He's having to put me up, I'm afraid. I don't know what we can salvage from the house yet...'

'Your son?' I asked. She didn't strike me as a motherly type.

'Charles,' she said. 'He's terribly attractive. He'd love to meet you, I'm sure.'

I smiled, uncertain as to what she was implying.

'Come with me and we can do the interview,' she said briskly.

'I'll fetch my coat,' I said.

CHAPTER SIX

As we drove to West Didsbury, via various diversions and fallen joists, I sympathised about her house.

'Well, it's not so much the house, you see,' she said, 'it's my beautiful things.'

'Jewellery?' I asked, imagining vaults of diamond brooches and emerald earrings.

'Not particularly,' Lillian said, swinging the car into a wide, tree-lined street, 'rather, paintings.'

'You're an art collector?'

'Well, not quite, but my late husband was. He adored art, he was such a sensitive man. He died in the Great War, but one keeps it for them, doesn't one? And now, it's all bombed to smithereens.'

'It must have been hard for you,' I ventured, 'when Mr Novak...'

'Yes,' she said. 'It was very sudden and, of course, I didn't find out until he failed to turn up that weekend. There was no sign of him, and he was always so reliable. I had the cocktails ready as usual.' She stopped, and pressed her lips together, perhaps to keep tears at bay.

'I'm so very sorry,' I said. 'So did you tell his wife...?'

'Good Lord, no!' Lillian gave a little shudder. 'I waited till Monday. I thought perhaps Pamela had found out about us, but still, he would have contacted me – I knew something was wrong. And then I made Charles ring up his office and pretend to be a business contact, and they told him.'

No wonder she'd been a good mistress, I thought. Even in the midst of panic, she had the presence of mind to avoid suspicion by ringing his office herself.

Lillian parked the car and led me to the stained-glass front door of a large Edwardian villa. Could Charles really live here? I wondered. He must only be young.

'He rents a flat on the top floor,' she explained, unlocking the door. 'For now, I'm taking his bedroom and he's on the couch.'

I nodded. Inside, a wide, tiled hall led to a sweeping mahogany banister. There were paintings and portraits all over the dark walls, and a huge vase of dried flowers on a polished sideboard.

Upstairs, she opened an unlocked door and led me into the 'flat'. It was more like a cathedral. It spread over the entire top floor, and like the hall, its bone-white walls were almost obscured by paintings and drawings, but here, there were sculptures too – a tiny, bronze dancer on a sideboard, and a lovely little terracotta model of a cat, which looked on the verge of springing to life and winding round my ankles. There were long, low brocade sofas set at right angles to one another, and a real zebra-skin rug.

'There's no fire, I'm afraid,' she said. She threw down her bag on a little button-backed chair. 'Coal savings, I suppose. And Charles's daily woman has disappeared somewhere for the war effort yet again.'

I imagined what it must be like to have a daily woman,

cleaning and cooking for you. Annie would die of excitement, I thought fondly.

'I may bring my own over,' she mused, crossing to a well-stocked, mirrored drinks cabinet and surveying the contents. 'Doris is a treasure. And very discreet. Not that it matters now, of course.'

I said nothing. I should have had all manner of spinning moral compasses – it seemed that Mrs Novak had known nothing about Lillian, and I could only imagine her devastation if it came out. There was every chance she would be both puzzled and angry when she read a glowing tribute to her own husband in print – one which she had already vetoed. Yet, I couldn't help myself. I was desperate to know the story; to understand how Lillian had entered the picture, and to find out why and how Edward Turnbull was involved.

'Would you like a little Christmas drink?' asked Lillian. 'I think I'm going to have a G and T.'

'Just water will be fine,' I said. She looked askance.

'Oh, do join me,' she said. 'These are strange times. I hate drinking alone.'

If she had been Annie, I would have said, 'Don't drink, then,' but Lillian was poised by the cocktail cabinet, her hand on a bottle, and she suddenly looked vulnerable.

'All right then,' I said. 'I'll have a small sherry, please, if you've got it.'

She poured our drinks and settled onto the adjacent sofa. I'd retrieved my notebook and pencil from my bag. 'What would you like to know?' she asked.

What I really wanted to know was all the things I couldn't publish – how she and Joseph had met, who her first husband had been, how her son afforded to live in such a beautiful place, why her lover had once given a painting to grammar school teacher Edward Turnbull.

But I said, 'Tell me about Joseph.'

'Well. He was such a wonderful man. Our affair reminds me of the song...' She began to sing 'Night and Day', in a low, contralto voice that surprised me with its tunefulness. She trailed off. 'Joseph loved Cole Porter,' she said wistfully.

'What was his business before the war?' I asked. 'I don't really know what he did.'

She sighed. 'Oh, it was boring. Something to do with helping businesses that wanted an interest in other European countries. So, you know, a company would want to expand, and he'd find the right firms to contract to help them do it.'

'I see,' I said, though I didn't really. 'Like a sort of broker.'

She shrugged. 'I suppose so. But all that was left behind when he fled the Nazis in '33. Then when he came over here, he met Pamela, and he worked in her father's radio factory. Old Mr Brewer died a couple of years back, and Joseph took over. When the war began, it switched production to aeroplane parts.

'The truth is,' she went on, 'Joseph and I didn't really talk about work. We talked about art and philosophy and music and books. All the things he loved. The things Mrs Novak had no interest in.' She injected venom into the name.

Mr Gorringe popped into my head, owlishly saying, 'in which Mrs Novak had no interest.' I felt a sudden pang of shame. He had given me this job, put all his faith in me, and here I was, drinking at lunchtime while our city burned, interviewing a mistress under false pretences. I'd only done one obituary, and if I carried on like this, I'd soon be writing mine. I needed to steer the conversation more clearly, I decided, and put down my glass.

'How did you meet?' I asked.

'Oh,' she said, 'I was in Germany soon after the last war, visiting an aunt with Charles, and we met in a bookshop on a rainy day. Of course, I spoke almost no German' – she gave a small laugh – 'and he barely spoke English. But I think my umbrella had broken and he offered me his own...'

It was a charmingly romantic tale, the rain teeming down outside, the handsome man and beautiful, widowed young mother in the ruins of war... I wished I could include it.

'Of course, when he fled Berlin, a Jew persecuted in his own country, I helped him to settle here,' she went on. 'And once the war began, he was so patriotic – running the factory in Trafford Park, he would do anything to help Britain, which had been so kind to him, he always said.'

'But when did he marry Pamela then?' I was thoroughly confused.

Lillian sniffed. 'A few months after he arrived here. He wanted to be respectable. I helped him arrange his journey here, you see, and Pamela was one of those people who took in refugees. She had a huge house and was rattling around in there. I think she was delighted. It all happened rather quickly.'

I was increasingly confused.

'But were you still... involved?'

'Well, yes. We had been together on and off for almost twenty years,' she said. 'My aunt died and left me her house in Berlin, so I'd go over there quite often to see him, and in between we'd talk on the telephone. Of course, writing letters was out due to the language problem.'

'Why didn't you...' I began, and she sighed.

'Look, Miss York, I am a widow, yes, but I enjoy my own company. Joseph was charming and handsome, I adored him; but I didn't particularly want to be married again. So it suited me very well to be his mistress.'

'For all that time?'

'Well, he asked me to marry him several times, but' – she shrugged delicately – 'I'm not the marrying kind, really. Not after Captain Emerson died. And Joseph, too, had lost someone in the last war.'

'Who?'

'He never spoke about her,' she said briskly.

'Did Mr Novak have many friends?' I asked. Lillian looked puzzled. 'I mean, was he a sociable type? I'm just trying to get a picture of the whole man,' I added.

'Oh, I see.' She shook her head. 'No. Nobody that I knew of. I imagine he would have dinner with business acquaintances and things like that, when he was abroad. But otherwise, he never mentioned anyone.' That was the tin lid on my dreams of her pouring forth about the Turnbulls.

'What about him and Mrs Novak?' I asked. 'Did they go out as a couple at all? Perhaps with other couples?'

She glared. 'I do wish you'd stop mentioning her,' she said. 'She was just a dead weight he dragged after him because he had no choice. It was me he loved, you know.'

'Of course,' I said, chastened. 'It's just that I met another woman who seemed to know him – well, know of him anyway,' I said. 'A Mrs Winifred Turnbull?'

She shook her head. 'I don't know anyone called Turnbull,' she said. 'I told you, it was just Joseph and me. We didn't need anyone else.'

'Apparently, he was given—'

A peal of bells made me jump. My leg jerked against the coffee table and my abandoned drink rattled alarmingly.

'Oh, that'll be Charles,' she said, getting up. 'He simply will not remember his key, it's infuriating.'

She clicked out of the room in her high heels, and downstairs I heard the front door opening, and exclamations of welcome and delight. I'd been hoping that he would delay his arrival until Lillian had revealed a great deal more. She led him back into the room, saying, 'This is Edie, a young reporter I'm talking to,' ('to whom I am talking,' corrected Mr Gorringe, sotto voce) and I looked round.

I had never laid eyes on such a handsome man in all my life. 'A gale-force ten swooner' Annie would have called him. He was tall, slim, and wearing a nicely cut navy suit – all good signs. But his face... I couldn't get past clichés like 'Greek god', or 'matinee idol'. He had thick, buttery blonde hair in a short back and sides, well-drawn eyebrows, a perfectly straight nose – and his eyes were a pale green, like sea glass, fringed by sooty black lashes. It was almost surprising to me that he wasn't famous, simply for his astonishing looks. I was horribly aware of my crumpled skirt suit and fake pearls.

'Edie York,' I said, standing up and extending my hand.

'Charles Emerson,' he said, shaking it with a dry, firm grip. I whipped mine away as if I'd had an electric shock, in case he thought I was lingering too long. I hated the disadvantage I was at – the sudden feminine need to be found attractive, the worry – was I blushing? Was my lipstick smeared? All because of a man with a face designed by set-square.

'I can't believe you're his mother,' I said to Lillian. 'You really don't look old enough.'

She smiled slightly. 'I was young when Charlie was born, wasn't I, dear?' she said to him. Her gaze was adoring. I wondered whether he had ever set foot in a room where women didn't immediately dissolve and twitter like hedge sparrows in his presence.

'Yes, you were rather,' he said idly, wandering to the drinks cabinet. 'Top up?' he asked. It was hard to remember that last night's raid had happened at all, or that Lillian's home had been destroyed just days ago.

I shook my head, but Lillian lifted her glass. 'One for me, please, Charles,' she said coquettishly.

Charles turned to me. 'So, what brings you to our sylvan hideaway?'

I hoped he wasn't going to keep talking like this. I didn't know how to engage with this sort of drawing-room banter.

'I'm a reporter,' I said. 'I write obituaries.'

'She's going to write about Joseph, darling,' said Lillian, accepting her glass. 'Isn't that lovely?'

Charles's face stiffened, as though a film director had shouted 'Give me furious puzzlement!' through his megaphone.

'Is it?' he said.

'Well, yes!' Lillian sat up. 'She writes obituaries for the *Chronicle*, and of course she won't say where she got the information, but I thought it would be so nice to mark his life publicly.'

'Did you?' Charles sipped his drink, a neat whisky. I wondered if they always drank in the day; whether here, in their little enclave of money and art, cocktail hour stretched from breakfast onwards.

'I did tell you I was going to,' she said, a note of sulkiness entering her voice. He perched on the edge of the button-back chair, removing his mother's bag to the floor.

'Did you?' he said again. 'I hope you know what you're doing, Ma.'

'Perfectly well, thank you,' she said. 'I'm not in my dotage yet.'

'Perhaps I can help,' he said. He looked at me, and I detected no interest in his astonishing eyes. I could as well have been an occasional table. 'Do say, Edie, if you would like to feed my own recollections into this piece of yours.'

'Of course,' I said. 'Though, naturally, I won't say where they came from.'

'Good Lord, no.' He gave an exaggerated shudder. 'The world must never know the truth.'

'Charles,' said Lillian sharply.

'Fine.' He held up his hands. 'Let's do this properly then. I'll take you both out for lunch, and we can have a nice chat about old Joseph.'

'You can't!' I blurted. 'Half of town has been bombed, nowhere will be open!'

'Funnily enough,' he said, 'I passed the Midland Hotel earlier, and it seems to be business as usual, if you don't mind a somewhat limited *carte du jour*. In fact, I saw the bishop wandering in – seems the cathedral's taken a hit, so you can't blame the old boy for wanting a stiffener on Christmas Eve.'

'What about your office, darling?' Lillian asked.

'Oh.' Charles, stood, stretching. 'Took an incendiary. They managed to salvage a lot of it, but the ceiling's not safe, apparently. We're moving somewhere else, but nobody knows where yet. So, lunch.'

'What do you do?' I asked. He seemed profoundly untroubled by it all. I thought of Lou, digging through the rubble for bodies.

'Charles works in intelligence,' said Lillian proudly. 'Awfully hush-hush.'

'Well, not with you around, Mother,' he said irritably.

He drained his glass, handed Lillian her bag, and we trooped out after him. I still had no idea how much he knew about Joseph and his mother's long affair.

He drove us into town in her car – the streets were blocked and flooded from burst water pipes, and it took a long time to follow all the diversions and traffic policemen waving their arms. I found my heart was thudding in anticipation of seeing the assaulted city, and I was battling a sense of terrible guilt. What was I doing, whisking off to Manchester's equivalent of the Ritz, while bodies still lay in the streets, and homes and businesses were in ruins?

I thought of Annie, wearily putting on her uniform for another night at the hospital, and Moira and Sheila tirelessly serving rock buns to the dispossessed. I should be back there with my borrowed apron on.

But, I reminded myself, I had a job to do. It was Christmas Eve and I was back at work on Boxing Day, when Mr Gorringe would be expecting the full uplifting, patriotic obituary on his desk, if it still existed by then. This was my last chance to keep my promotion to obituarist. Otherwise, I'd be on secretarial duties again by New Year, if I was lucky.

On a baser note, too, I had always wanted to go to the restaurant in the Midland Hotel. I'd been in the lobby, but the place itself was hidden away behind long velvet curtains, an enclave of hushed luxury. I once had to deliver a package to someone staying there, and I remembered the scent of roast beef and the tinkle of piano music drifting out when a waiter pulled the curtain back.

Charles parked several streets away. In the distance, I could see huge clots of black smoke – it looked like the Royal Exchange. All of St Peter's Square was covered with a haze of smoke and ash, though I was greatly relieved to see the library still standing. Firemen rushed by, and a crowd was gathered by the town hall, gazing silently down towards Oxford Road. I could see fires by the Palace Theatre and fire engines were parked across the road, to block vehicles. All around, the city burned. There was a heat in the air, despite the chill of the day, and a spiteful wind was carrying the flames ever further.

My eyes stung with tears of shock. I wanted to run to Deansgate, to see if the office still stood, or if our great, red-brick Victorian building had been mortally wounded or destroyed.

'Well, they seem to be making a fair job of it,' said Charles. 'They'll have it cleaned up for Christmas Day, I'm sure.'

We picked our way through glass and rubble, Lillian's kid shoes sliding on the heaps. Eventually, we made our way up the wide steps of the hotel, which had already been swept.

'By Jove,' called a passing man, 'some folks have it all right, don't they?' A few people heard him and muttered agreement. I had never felt so ashamed.

Inside, it was as though the war had never begun, but for the sound of a large children's group having their Christmas party with the luncheon club in a cordoned-off room.

Lillian disappeared off to the 'powder room', as she called it, and Charles lit a cigarette and offered me one as we waited for her in the shining marble lobby. I shook my head.

'I don't trust people who don't smoke,' he said, inhaling sharply. 'How do you pass the time?'

'I do smoke,' I said, thinking of my peculiar night with Lou. 'I just don't want the taste to spoil the food.'

'Take more than that,' he said. 'They know what they're doing here.'

'Do you come here a lot?' I asked, then felt heat rise to my cheeks. I might as well have murmured, 'hullo, sweetheart,' and pressed myself against him.

He ignored my embarrassment. 'Yes, I do,' he said.

I wondered how old he was. His immaculate suit and Grecian looks made it difficult to tell, but he was surely no more than my age or younger.

'What did you do before the war?' I asked.

He turned to look towards the door of the ladies', as Lillian emerged, snapping her crocodile handbag shut.

'This and that,' he said. 'I hadn't been long out of university.'

I immediately felt intimidated.

'What did you study?' I asked, as Lillian beckoned us over to the restaurant entrance, where the maître d' was hurrying towards her, clutching a sheaf of menus. No paper shortage here, it seemed.

'I read history at Oxford,' he said. 'Useless really, unless one wants to work in some stuffy publishing firm or go in for the BBC.'

'And don't you?'

'Charles has a talent for many things,' Lillian said to me.

'Hardly,' he said. 'Just the one, really.'

They both seemed to be using me as an umpire. It reminded me of when I was little and Suki and I had showed off when visitors came, driven and giddy, almost trying to sell each other in the hope that our charming selflessness would be noted. 'She's very clever, you know!' 'But Suki is prettier! Look at her hair, it's so shiny and long!' 'But Edie is very small, she could fit anywhere – she can get inside the roundabout at the park!' The couples would loom above us, in belted wool coat and flowered hat, Sunday visiting clothes, and smile glassily, then Mrs Pugh would come scuttling out – 'Tea is served in the office... run along, you two, stop bothering the lady and gentleman' – and another possible future would roll away, like workmen dismantling a stage set.

The maître d' flourished the menus at us and asked if we'd like 'an aperitif'.

'Would we?' mused Lillian. 'No, perhaps we'll go straight in.'

'*Madame, bien sûr*,' he said, sweeping back the curtain. It was like the set of a ballet – faded, pastoral tapestries on the walls, and tiny, gilded velvet chairs. I'd saved up in my first few months at the *Chronicle* and bought a ticket to see Sadler's Wells dancing *The Sleeping Beauty* at the Palace Theatre. I was so high up in the gods that the dancers looked like tiny, leaping fleas, but just being there was enough.

I had a similar feeling now, as I was ushered to a spindly gilt chair, and the waiter snapped open a starched napkin and placed it over my lap. Another was doing the same for Lillian across the table.

'A bottle of Pauillac, please,' said Charles, and Lillian nodded. I had no idea what it was. I had seldom drunk wine, and the few times I had, it had gone straight to my head and made me feel loose-limbed and giggly, and thoroughly unlike myself. I thought I'd better stick to water.

'And three of the set lunch,' he added.

'*Du pain?*' the waiter asked Charles.

'*Oui, merci bien*,' he said, and I tried not to stare at him. His French accent seemed impeccable to my untutored ears.

'Do you speak French?' I asked.

'Just did,' he said cheerfully, flicking open his gold case and tapping out another cigarette.

'Fluently, I mean,' I said.

'Comme ci, comme ça, cherie,' he said, making a balancing motion with his hand. *'Und ich spreche Deutsch.* That's a pricy education for you.'

I smiled, feeling foolish, and looked up at Lillian. She was shooting a look at Charles – it looked like a warning, for speaking German. I thought she was right, today of all days.

There was a flurry of wine pouring and bread delivery, and I reached into my bag to retrieve my notebook and pencil.

'Oh no, surely not,' said Charles. 'I'll feel rather as though we're in a police interview if you spend lunch scribbling into that thing. And besides, the food will be far too delicious to ignore.'

'But I thought we were going to talk about Mr Novak,' I said, my bag open on my lap.

'We are,' Lillian said. She waved her glass expansively. 'But you'll remember it, won't you? Then you can write it all down afterwards.'

'And as I'm paying,' Charles added, 'I insist that you join in and we have a proper conversation.'

I felt utterly outmanoeuvred and was putting my bag back under my chair when I saw a pair of shining, conker-brown brogues stopping by a nearby table. They looked oddly familiar. I looked up, inexplicable fear rising, and saw Mr Gorringe being seated by an obsequious huddle of waiters. His lunch companion was the Superintendent, who had clearly been up all night, and was handing his dented hat to a coat girl.

'That's my editor,' I whispered in horror.

Lillian tinkled a laugh. 'How lovely,' she said. 'Do you want him to join us?'

'No!' I hissed. 'He wouldn't like me being here.' I could only imagine the shame of being seen at the next table – his most junior reporter, living it up at the Midland in the middle of the day, a full glass of red wine in front of me as our city smouldered just feet away.

'But you're interviewing us!' said Charles. He sounded outraged on my behalf. 'How can the old fellow object to that? It's my treat, it's not as if you're putting it on expenses.'

'It's just... inappropriate, I suppose,' I said. In my fluster, I took a large gulp of wine. Dark, liquid heat poured through me. I thought of thorns and brambles, cigar smoke, something animal and powerful lurking in the forest. 'Gosh, that's terribly nice,' I said, and Charles laughed.

'A Bordeaux lover,' he said. 'What good taste you have, Miss York.'

Mr Gorringe had his back to me, but Charles's patrician voice had carried. I felt, rather than saw, him turn round.

'Miss York?'

Hot with shame, I turned. 'Yes,' I said. 'I'm so sorry, Mr Gorringe. This is Mrs and Mr Emerson. I'm interviewing them for the Novak page, and Charles suggested that we—'

He held up a hand.

'I shall anticipate nothing less than excellence then,' he said. 'And I trust you shan't be troubling Miss Paulson this week.'

He meant with receipts, but was far too canny to seem mean in front of onlookers.

'Of course not,' I said. He nodded, and turned back. I heard him say, 'I see the warehouses on Peter Street have gone up now. Any more dead?'

Briefly, I closed my eyes.

'Oh, come now,' said Lillian. 'It'll do him good to see you enjoying the high life. Perhaps you'll get promoted!'

'I doubt that.'

The waiter appeared, solemnly delivering plates of pâté and melba toast as if he were handing out the Victoria Cross. It was a wonder he didn't touch our shoulders with a sword while he was at it. What had seemed exotic and wonderful a few minutes before now felt pretentious and ridiculous. Who was I to be sitting in a velvet chair at The French, eating brandied chicken liver pâté on tiny triangles of friable toast, when I should be doling out weak lemonade and leaflets?

'Well,' I added loudly, for Mr Gorringe's benefit. 'Let's get back to Mr Novak. Perhaps you could tell me a bit about his early life?'

Lillian balanced a small square of pâté on her toast. She said nothing.

Charles's glass was already empty. He beckoned to the waiter for more.

'Mother and I aren't too sure about that sadly. All we know is that he grew up somewhere in Germany, and worked in the export business.'

The pâté was divine. I wished I could simply forget the interview and the war, and sink into the sensory wonder of wine and food, with Charles to look at. Instead, I was miserably aware of Mr Gorringe ordering – 'just water, please, if you have any' – nearby.

I took another sip of wine, which turned into a gulp. It was like settling a warm, velvet cloak around me, insulating me from the horror of my boss behind me, and the terrible carnage outside.

'How old were you when you met Mr Novak?' I asked Charles. He blew out a stream of smoke. He seemed to have abandoned his pâté, and I wished I could ask to take it home for Annie.

'I don't really remember,' he said. 'Small. He was a big, kindly man. He'd take me out sometimes, in Berlin. The Tiergarten, or the zoo.'

'Then Charles went away to school,' said Lillian. 'So I'd visit him alone.' She took a sip of wine and pushed her plate away. A waiter appeared at her side like an adoring genie and whipped it away.

While the waiters delivered what Charles called 'angels on horseback' – they seemed to be Whitstable oysters on toast, and I made the mistake of chewing them and had to wash away the disturbing, rock-pool tang with wine – Lillian told me what she knew about his life in Manchester, which amounted to very little.

'Well, I helped him, when he fled Germany,' she said. 'The Nazis were on the rise, and clearly, for Jews, it was a very dangerous time. As has been proven,' she added, waving a hand at the windows, out of which I could see the smoke. 'Their shops were being smashed up, windows broken, and the Nazis were already creating Jewish ghettos and making new laws to inconvenience and humiliate them. So at first, Joseph's factory was making radio parts, but it soon became clear that we'd need munitions, and that's when he began to work for the government.'

'Why did he not come and live with you?' I asked.

Lillian looked annoyed. 'Well, that would hardly have been appropriate,' she said. 'Charles was still at school, and besides, I enjoy my own company. Joseph was a wonderful man, as I said, but we were very different.'

Perhaps that was why lonely, lumpen Pamela had been such a perfect choice, with her vast house and a patriotic business ready to go. I wondered if Joseph had enjoyed having a wife and a business and a glamorous mistress, and concluded that like most men, he probably had.

The waiter was back, reverently laying out plates of chicken with cream-baked potatoes, with fussy little dishes of buttered beans and carrots alongside each plate. This was the grandest meal I had ever eaten, and the most delicious, and all I could think about was Mr Gorringe lurking nearby like a disappointed headmaster, while I got slowly drunker in the middle of the working day.

'I wonder if I could have some water,' I said to the waiter, who nodded discreetly.

The obituary wouldn't work so far. I couldn't explain how I knew any of this, and it amounted to nothing – a handsome, cultured Jewish refugee, who had a successful business that I didn't understand. But now I'd accepted Charles's generosity, I could hardly say, 'I don't think this is any good,' and abandon them both amid a sea of crumpled linen napkins and half-eaten chicken. And I was still no closer to discovering the connection between Edward Turnbull and Mr Novak.

'We're not telling you what you need, are we?' said Charles, as if reading my thoughts.

I was taken aback. 'Well, it's difficult, I know, particularly under the circumstances...'

'Look, Mother,' he said to Lillian. 'You know I think this is a loony idea. What are you hoping to gain? No offence meant,' he added, turning to me.

'No, it's perfectly all right...'

'You know what I hope to gain,' Lillian said. 'I want Joseph's life recognised publicly. I want the world to know who he was and what he did. He was a good man, and I just want it recorded.'

I nodded. In my short tenure as obituarist, I had heard this several times already. 'We want a record of his life.' 'We just want people to know about Dad.' It was as though a life only counted if others bore witness, a printed version of a funeral. I had an image of our army of readers, all across Lancashire, slowly removing their hats and gazing silently at black words on white paper. It was as though putting it into print somehow confirmed someone's existence, gave it an unassailable reality. But if I thought like this, I felt utterly unequal to the task.

'What were his favourite things?' I asked. 'What did he enjoy?'

'He liked the wireless,' she said. 'It helped him with his English. He enjoyed *Children's Hour* because it was easy to follow the words.'

I imagined Mr Novak listening solemnly to *A Trip to the Seashore with Larry the Lamb*, and almost laughed.

'What about culture?' I persisted. 'You said he loved art?'

'Oh yes, he did.' She brightened. 'He had a favourite quote. Let me see, how does it go?'

Charles had put his cutlery down, and was still, waiting.

'Yes... by Schumann. The composer. "To send light into the darkness of men's hearts – such is the duty of the artist."' She nodded, pleased. 'It would be lovely if you could include that. He did so love what he called "the life of the mind".'

'So your pictures... the paintings,' I clarified. 'He must have liked those?'

'They were my real father's,' said Charles quickly. 'He came from pretty good stock, you know. They're all inherited.'

I nodded. 'Your father...'

'Died in the war,' he said. 'When I was all of three months old.'

'How awful,' I said. Lillian was lighting a cigarette and I couldn't see her expression. Had she been distraught? It was hard to imagine her unravelling.

'Well, it happened to a lot of people,' she said. 'It was very fortunate for us that he left us rather well off, and we could travel.'

That explained their sense of old money, and the beautiful paintings and sculptures, though it must have been rather like living in a mausoleum, I thought. I suddenly remembered Arnold. Perhaps I should go and see him. Find out if he knew anything about Lou's investigation into Turnbull's death.

I wondered why Lillian wasn't more distraught about her

home having been destroyed overnight. The people I had met earlier were in shock. She seemed as unperturbed as if she'd just stepped out of a beauty salon.

There was a rumble of movement behind us, and I half turned to see Mr Gorringe standing up, and the Superintendent lumbering to his feet to shake hands. The water jug and the remains of their one frugal course each stood on their table, as powerfully symbolic as any Dutch still life.

The waiter hadn't brought my water.

'See you back at the office,' said Mr Gorringe as he passed, a waiter already holding out his dust-stiffened gaberdine coat for him.

'I'll be back as soon as I...' I began, but I was speaking to his retreating back.

Lillian gave me a small, complicit smile. 'Pudding, I think,' she said.

It was almost three when we left. A full ten minutes, it seemed, were devoted to French exchanges of delight and gratitude with the gaggle of waiters who had appeared to see us off, and by the time we were finally waved out of the hotel's great carved doors, I was itching with fear, and the beginnings of what I presumed was a hangover.

I was convinced that I'd walk into the office to find Mr Gorringe holding up a giant fob watch, like the white rabbit, and pointing to the exit.

I took my leave of the Emersons on the hotel steps. The smoke was still drifting, and sirens wailed nearby. It would be dark again soon, and I couldn't imagine the city withstanding another vicious bombardment.

Christmas Eve, and thousands of children would wake in a strange place in the morning, all they knew and loved buried in the rubble. At least I had never known my parents, so I'd never known the pain of losing them.

'I can't thank you enough,' I said to Charles. 'It was wonderful.' He waved it away.

'Here' – he rummaged in his pocket and produced a small silver pencil and a little notebook. – 'my number,' he said, scribbling, and presented me with the ripped-off page. 'In case you need to ask anything else.'

'Thank you,' I said. 'It's just – I'm not sure what else—'

'There's bound to be something you'll wish you'd asked,' he said.

Lillian held out a gloved hand. 'Delighted,' she said. 'Will you let us know when it's in? Oh, and here,' – she whipped the notebook and pen from Charles's hand and wrote quickly – 'this is the exact quote he loved that I mentioned. It would mean so much if you would include it. Please don't forget.'

I nodded, and folded it into my bag.

I picked my way to the office, through backstreets full of grit and sandbags, a sick headache thudding between my eyebrows, and dread in my heart.

CHAPTER SEVEN

It was a great relief to find that the office was still standing, though at the end of Deansgate, I could see the great spines of Manchester Cathedral still in flames. It looked like an apocalyptic Turner painting.

I turned away with a shudder and went inside. The office was unnervingly quiet when I finally crept to my desk. Presumably, the reporters were all out reporting on the bombardment. There was no sign of Mr Gorringe, and everyone else seemed to have their heads down, as though an inspection had just taken place.

'Part-time now, are you?' said Pat, appearing out of nowhere.

'I was out on an interview,' I said. 'Was everything all right at home last night? Is everybody accounted for?'

'Far as we know,' she said. 'Though I barely slept and my sister's house took a battering. She's bunking down with the chickens in the Anderson shelter for Christmas – we've no room.'

'Chickens?'

'Oh, she won't be parted from them,' said Pat, heaving

herself into her chair. 'Gloria Swanson and Greta Garbo. She sings to them, she says it makes for bigger eggs.'

I took my notebook out and tried to remember everything Charles and Lillian had told me, but it was impossibly difficult, through the haze of wine, to recall what I was and wasn't able to make public, and after a fruitless half hour, with one ear cocked like a police dog for the sound of Mr Gorringe tacking across the parquet to dismiss me, I realised that it would be impossible to do this at all without speaking to Mrs Novak again. Lillian wouldn't like it, but I was not Lillian's lapdog, and the more I scribbled notes, the more I realised that most of it would read as the recollections of an intimate lover, not the cheerful anecdotes of a beneficent colleague, as I had hoped to angle it. It was hardly likely that Joseph Novak would have shared his beloved artistic quotations with some businessman over dinner in Lille or Düsseldorf, let alone the fact that he listened to *Children's Hour* in his spare time.

Besides, the more I tried to recall, the clearer it became that Lillian and Charles had hardly told me anything. What Joseph did between the wars was still vague, Charles had contributed very little, and Lillian had somehow contrived to make it seem as though she was being guilelessly open while in reality, all I had were nuggets of gossip and unprintable secrets.

In the depressive fug of my afternoon hangover, I decided that I had allowed my burning desire to solve the mystery of Edward Turnbull to lead me into a ridiculous and unprofessional situation.

My sigh was so extravagant, Pat looked over. 'Blowing a gale in here today,' she said. 'What's the matter, royal coach not available to take you home?' A passing secretary giggled and turned it into a cough.

It seemed I had two choices: admit the truth to Mr Gorringe, or visit Mrs Novak again and beg her to give me more details. The first would probably end my tenure at the *Chronicle*, while the second was just frightening and embarrassing.

I would go on Boxing Day morning, I decided, and have it all written by that afternoon.

And when I spoke to Mrs Novak, I would try to get to the bottom of the Edward Turnbull business too – because something about it felt very odd.

When I stood to leave the office, it was already dark outside, and the firemen and wardens were working with torches and arc lights in the blackout. Oxford Road was still blocked, according to the typing pool, who always knew everything first. My sense of direction was not my greatest trait, and I had no idea how to find my way home through a series of dead ends and backstreets. As I pondered, a secretary appeared.

'Young man for you in reception,' she said. 'He says he'll wait.'

My heart leapt. Had Charles gallantly returned to drive me home? *Surely not.* I imagined slipping into the passenger seat, Lillian safely at home, and going back to the Midland for a drink...

I almost skipped down the stone stairs, and was sorely disappointed when my waiting saviour turned out not to be Charles at all, but Arnold.

'Hullo!' he said cheerfully. 'How d'you do? Rum do, more likely. What a mess it all is!'

'Arnold!' I said. 'Whatever are you doing here?'

'I was up at Salford, helping with the bodies,' he said. 'They needed people to clean them up a bit, so relations could identify them. Of course, some were far beyond that, poor things. In those cases, we just put the various parts into a sort of bag, and we... anyway,' he said hastily, seeing my face. 'Pretty gruelling stuff, but needs must. I expect you've been out in it all day? You look very clean, mind you, if you don't mind my saying. Quite a rest for the eyes.'

He smiled. 'Anyway, what with all of this, I thought I'd see if you needed a lift home. I've got the morgue van, but if you don't mind squashing up in the front...'

'Are there... bodies?' I asked.

'No, no,' he said, 'All safely delivered to the morgue. A terrible business. A warehouse with shift workers on overnight. A few didn't make it to the shelter. A young woman... by jingo, that bothered me, I can tell you.'

'Oh, how awful,' I said uselessly. Having Arnold here before me, covered in dust and God only knew what else, it was as though the curtain I'd hidden behind all day had suddenly lifted. I felt a fresh wave of shame about my debonair lunch. I might as well be a collaborator.

'Anyway, on we go,' he said. 'It's Christmas, so no point grumbling.'

He ushered me out and switched on his torch. Outside, the air still blew warm with smoke and ash, falling like snow on the broken beams and jagged shards.

Arnold led me to the discreet black van, its headlights half taped over, and I climbed in gratefully. I felt I'd had no sleep for weeks and the lunch was taking on the quality of a lurid dream, one I was glad to wake from.

'Heard about you and Lou,' Arnold said, pulling out and away.

'Me and...?'

'Your Morrison shelter trouble.' He smiled again. 'Very cosy.'

'It was not!' I said. 'It was horrible, we thought we'd be killed any minute, and I had his great feet in my face.'

'Ah well,' Arnold said. 'He seemed quite happy about it when I bumped into him earlier.'

'Well, I've no idea why,' I said crossly. 'And besides,' I said, in a rush of annoyance, 'I might have my own young man.'

'Might you?' said Arnold, surprised; with horror, I realised he thought I was talking about him. 'Oh, I... just someone I'm – I've only met him once, he's in intelligence,' I stammered. 'It may come to nothing.'

Arnold raised his eyebrows and nodded. I was relieved he hadn't questioned me further on this figment of my imagination.

'Look here,' I said. 'We haven't got much in, but would you like to come for a bit of lunch tomorrow? It's just Annie and me, but I'm sure we can stretch to three. Unless you're having a family lunch, of course.'

He seemed delighted. 'No, no. Mum likes to spend most of the day at church, praying for our dad's soul, and my brother's in the Air Force, so Lord knows where he is. I had no plans, though it looks as though I'll be working for at least some of the day. Here's hoping Jerry doesn't go again tonight.'

I couldn't bear another night in the cellar. In fact, the idea of a grim Christmas Eve alone, while Annie worked at the hospital and I wondered if I'd ever see Charles again didn't appeal in any way.

'Arnold,' I said, 'could you possibly drop me at the church hall?'

We arranged that he'd come at noon the following day. 'I may find a treat or two I can bring,' he said, and he drove off, cheerfully wishing me a merry Christmas. For the second time that day, I went into the hall, expecting to find Mrs Pelham manning an urn.

Instead, I saw Moira, who had apparently put in a twelve-hour shift so far, and another harassed-looking woman. There were groups of people sitting in small encampments of blankets and borrowed mattresses across the hall, and several more dogs and babies. The steam from all the bodies, some of which smelled rather unwashed, hit me like a wall.

'Edie!' shouted Moira, beckoning me over. 'Thank goodness you're here.'

'What's happened?' I asked. A vast pan of lentil soup had

appeared, and the harassed woman was ladling it into pale green pot bowls, saying, 'Mind, it's hot' to every person.

I noticed that Moira's brown eyes were red-rimmed.

'It's Mrs Pelham,' she said. 'We only found out an hour ago.'

'What?'

'Her house.' Moira's voice wobbled. 'The bomb went right through and made a crater, they said.' Tears ran down her pink cheeks. 'She didn't know anything about it. She was asleep in a Morrison in the cellar, but...'

'But she has another grandchild on the way,' I said stupidly.

'Yes.' Moira nodded. 'Her daughter must be so upset. Well, we all are.'

Mrs Pelham had been so full of life and purpose, eyes shining with determination to do her bit. It could as easily have been Lou and me, or Annie. It still could be. A wave of cold sickness passed through me.

'What can I do?' I said. Moira laughed hopelessly.

'Everything,' she said. 'It all needs doing.'

I tied on another borrowed apron and began.

I didn't see Annie until Christmas morning. I'd crept in at one o'clock, so tired I could hardly move. I lay in bed and all I could see when I closed my eyes were giant, spitting urns and grimy hands holding out teacups.

When I woke, she had left a cup of now-lukewarm tea and a small present, wrapped in brown paper, on the bedside table. I drank the tea, and struggled into my dressing gown. I had forgotten to wrap the red hat I'd knitted for her.

In the living room, the old armchairs and oilcloth-covered table were dramatically improved by the addition of a small Christmas tree, draped with silver tinsel and glass balls. On the mantelpiece were cards from Annie's mum, the grocer (who had enclosed his bill, somewhat less festively) and Mr Benson –

'Tidings of the Season' over a snowy scene. Inside he'd simply written 'Mr B'. Nobody could accuse him of being overgenerous with words.

I could hear Annie in the kitchen, clanking about, and singing 'Hark! The Herald Angels Sing' to a syncopated jazz beat she'd invented.

'Annie!' I called. 'What's this tree doing? However did you get one?'

'Oh!' She popped her head out. 'Isn't it lovely? They had them for the wards, then they were all evacuated in the raid, and they just left the trees behind. So David and I liberated it.'

'Did you like your present?' she added, stirring a pot of porridge.

I extracted it from my dressing gown pocket and carefully prised away the wrapping paper to preserve it. It was a gold powder compact with an enamelled swan on the lid.

'Oh, Annie, it's beautiful!' I said. 'But you shouldn't have.'

'Well, you're my dearest friend, so why not?'

I ran to fetch mine, and apologised profusely for the lack of wrapping.

'Use mine,' she said, so giggling, I turned my back and wrapped my present to her in the brown paper.

'What charmingly witty paper!' she said, opening it carefully. 'However did you choose it?'

We were laughing, and for a moment I forgot all about the horror of yesterday, and Mrs Pelham and all the terrible chaos of the world outside, as Annie modelled her red hat and we shared another cup of tea.

The ring of the doorbell made us both jump, and I suddenly remembered, with horror, my invitation to Arnold. I'd completely forgotten to tell Annie.

'Oh, blimey,' she said. 'That'll be Lou. He's early.'

'Lou?' I repeated blankly.

'I forgot to say,' she called, running downstairs. 'He said he'd drop in for a Christmas drink.'

'It's half ten in the morning!' I said.

'Merry Christmas,' he greeted Annie, then came his heavy tread on the stairs.

'Merry Christmas, Edie.' He was carrying a bottle of brandy and a battered box of crackers.

'Both stolen and impounded yesterday,' he said. 'But it's a bit late to find the owner, so we might as well make use.'

Annie clasped her hands together with delight, as though Lou had single-handedly solved the paper shortage. 'Oh, stay for lunch!' she said. My heart sank.

I hoped now that Arnold would turn up, otherwise it would all be rather awkward. As it was, Lou followed us into the kitchen and pulled up a chair while Annie made stuffing and I chopped carrots. It was all for the very small chicken we'd managed to bag, via her flirting with Mr Straggan, the butcher, who was at least sixty and constantly bright red in the face. It would only stretch to four if we padded it out with a lot of potatoes. They were my job, too, but now Lou was blocking up our tiny kitchen, there was no possibility of my shoving in with a giant pan of spuds and blinding clouds of steam without braining somebody.

Instead, I put the wireless on, and listened to carols float through the living room, thinking about Mrs Novak and what I would say to her tomorrow. I wondered, too, what the king would say in his speech later, now that London had been so heavily bombed, and whether he'd mention Manchester at all.

When it was all prepared, we returned to the living room and had a tot of brandy and a mince pie each.

'I can't believe I've got to work tonight,' grumbled Annie. 'There'd best not be another raid, our nerves are all shredded to hat ribbons as it is.'

'Over five hundred dead now,' said Lou. 'I don't think there will be. They'll have used up all their ammo now, and flown home for a nice German Christmas.'

'I hope so,' I said. I told them about Mrs Pelham, and Annie paled.

'Oh, dear heaven,' she said. 'That's terrible. I was only speaking to her the other day!' She blinked away tears. 'I s'pose we'll have to get used to it.'

'No call for that sort of talk,' said Lou briskly. 'Our lads will see them off soon.'

'Have you heard anything from Pete?' I asked. It had occurred to me that she hadn't mentioned him for ages.

'No,' she said. 'I think he's fed up with me. I've not heard a thing since November.'

'He's probably somewhere they can't send post,' Lou told her. 'I shouldn't worry.'

'I'm not,' Annie said. I wondered if Pete was really all right, having a soldier's Christmas in his barracks, wherever they may be, or if something had happened to him. That was the awful thing now – nothing felt safe, everything could change in a moment. I thought of Charles, and wished with all my heart that he was coming for lunch instead of Arnold. If we were going to be imminently blown up by the Hun, I'd rather it all ended in the arms of someone I could at least kiss, as fire rained from the sky.

'Oh, by the way, Edie,' Lou said, topping up his brandy, 'I heard something about your Mr Novak, might be useful.'

I sat bolt upright and mince pie crumbs scattered over the bosom of my wool dress.

'What?'

'Why thank you, DI Brennan, I'm so grateful,' he said. I was about to roll my eyes, but he was smiling. Christmas must have softened his usual bark.

'Not much,' he went on, 'but it was when we were sorting out the bodies, and I heard from a pal of Arnold's – you know these funeral sorts, they stick together – that when Novak's Trafford Park munitions factory went up the other night, there was a German passport found in all the rubble.'

'Novak's?' I asked. 'He was German, he was a German Jew. That's why he escaped a few years ago, when the Nazis were on the rise. They'd started looting Jewish shops and businesses, and...'

'No, a Herr Hörst Thomas Müller,' said Lou. 'There was nobody of that name listed working there, though.'

'What does that mean?' asked Annie.

'Well, obviously, it's raised some rather worrying questions.'

'You can't possibly think he was a Nazi?' I demanded.

'Good Lord, calm down,' said Lou, taking a large bite of – I noted – our last mince pie. 'No, it was probably another refugee Novak brought in under a false British name, a friend of his from Germany, perhaps, who needed work. It happened a lot, but with all the anti-Semitism and now anti-German sentiment, he'd have had to change his name. Why he had his passport with him at work, I don't know.'

'So he's dead, whoever he is?'

Lou sighed and replaced the mince pie on the dish.

'There were no survivors. As I know all too well.'

Annie leaned forward. 'I know why,' she said. 'Why he'd have his passport, I mean. We had a Jewish refugee on the ward back in the summer, and he had everything with him. He wouldn't even go to do his' – she glanced at Lou and changed 'business' to 'ablutions' – 'without his little valise. He said he took the things he left with everywhere – his documents and special keepsakes. He said you never knew when the Nazis would come, and it was better to be able to run, without ever worrying about what you'd had to leave behind.'

Lou nodded. 'Sounds about right.'

'I don't know where he went when he left hospital. I think

about him sometimes. He was quite handsome, actually,' she added thoughtfully, and I rolled my eyes.

'I just hope he's still alive after the last couple of nights,' said Lou darkly.

We subsided, sunk into sudden gloom, when the bell went again.

'Arnold!' I exclaimed.

'Arnold?' Annie repeated, as Lou said, 'Belting!' and clapped his hands together.

I flew down the still-rocking stairs to the door, as she shouted, 'But how will I stretch the pudding? It's already the size of a marble!'

'Merry Christmas!' Arnold came in, beaming with goodwill. He was carrying a large muslin bag containing what looked like a football, and a bunch of holly. Under his arm, he had wedged four bottles of beer. I found I was delighted to see him.

He put all his items down, like a beardless Father Christmas, gave his hat to Annie, and looked about. 'I say, this is something like,' he said, lifting his head at the waft of roasting chicken.

Lou lifted the muslin experimentally and gave it a swing.

'Is this a pud or a trebuchet?' he asked. Annie shot me an anguished glance. She had saved rations for weeks to make our little treacly ball with a sixpence stuffed inside.

'Oh yes!' Arnold said. 'I hope you don't mind, Mum always makes one extra and the relations are very generous, you see – we always have ingredients about.'

I realised he meant 'the relations of the dead'. I didn't like the notion of taking a bereaved person's rations, but here the pudding was.

'Mum said to boil over a low heat for three hours.' I thought of the gas meter, and I felt certain Annie was too. Her face was rather set as she carried it into the kitchen.

'It's awfully kind of you,' I said. I'd take the no-doubt copious leftovers to the WVS canteen later on.

Lunch was surprisingly cheerful. We managed to get everything ready on the three tiny gas rings by shoving it all into the oven as soon as it was ready, to 'keep warm' (my words) or 'incinerate to a blackened crisp' (Annie's). The kitchen was full of steam and pans and jugs, as Lou and Arnold sat wreathed in cigarette smoke, drinking the beer and occasionally breaking into guffaws. It was strange to have two large men in our little flat, like a pair of buffalo suddenly stamping into the llama enclosure at the zoo.

We pulled Lou's crackers, which contained dreadful jokes ('When is a boat just like snow?' I asked. 'When it's adrift.' Everyone groaned with genuine misery) and very small paper hats, though we wore them anyway, and rather useless things like cardboard lipstick-holders and a flimsy paper tape measure. Arnold won a small pocket mirror with a flower on the back, and pretended to roll his hair in it with Annie's borrowed hairpins, which had us all falling about.

It struck me that he was good fun, and not nearly as shy as I'd thought at first. We had another brandy after the pudding – it was an excellent one, though I knew it cost Annie to say so – and then we listened to the king's speech in a solemn silence.

'*Time and again during these last few months, I have seen for myself the battered towns and cities of England, and I have seen the British people facing their ordeal,*' he said, in his soft, hesitant voice, over the static crackle of our old wireless.

'*I can say to them that they may be justly proud...*' I felt tears sting my eyes and glanced at Annie, who was also rigid in her chair, and trying not to cry. I thought of us all, across the whole country and beyond, listening to him, all hoping for better days.

When it ended, we sat in silence for a moment before Annie sprang up to get ready for work. I hoped she wouldn't breathe fumes over the patients, though perhaps the men shouldn't mind too much.

Lou and Arnold helped us clear away, and I did the washing-up while Arnold dried and Lou gave Annie a lift to the hospital – or as near as they could get, with most of the roads into town still closed. So far, the day had been peaceful, but I dreaded another raid this evening.

Once everything was put away, Arnold and I settled down for a last cup of tea and I added a bit more coal to the fire. It was Christmas, I reasoned. We could always wear extra jumpers next week.

It was rather odd – I barely knew this man but here he was, sitting in our armchair on Christmas Day. War and crime made strange lunch-fellows, I thought to myself, and smiled.

'What are your plans this week, Edie?' Arnold asked politely. I was full of his mum's lovely pudding and a bit squiffy on brandy, and I felt I owed him something interesting, so I told him what I'd discovered about Joseph Novak, without mentioning Charles, or Lillian, and explained that he was somehow linked to the Turnbulls and had given them a missing painting.

'But I've hardly got any information, and Mr Gorringe wants a full page,' I said.

'Can't you pad it out with a bit of general refugee stuff?' Arnold asked. 'There must be loads of books about it.'

'I don't think that would be very ethical,' I said. 'I'm trekking off to fifteen Alfreton Avenue first thing tomorrow to talk to Mrs Novak again. I want to know all about this German passport that was found too.'

I realised what I'd said too late, damn brandy. Then again, if Lou had happily told me and Annie, would he mind Arnold knowing? I decided he wouldn't, and filled him in.

'How peculiar. How did you get the story about Mr Novak?' Arnold asked.

'A business contact of his got in touch,' I said. It sounded enormously unlikely, but Arnold nodded and sipped his tea. I longed to sit by the fire reading my detective story, drinking more brandy, but I thought of Moira slaving away by herself and all the poor bombed-out people with no Christmas at all, and I stood up to find my coat and hat.

Arnold was so profuse in his thanks, I felt he must be about to produce a bouquet from behind his back to the roar of a crowd.

'It really has been wonderful, Edie,' he said, clasping my arm. I rather wished he wouldn't use my name all the time, like a vicar.

'Perhaps... if you're not too busy,' he said, 'I could take you out for a drink soon? I'd like some advice...'

He saw my face. I must have looked like the very boat adrift in snow.

'As a friend,' he added hastily. 'Wouldn't presume on another chap's lady!'

I smiled weakly. 'Of course,' I said. 'As I said, I may be going out with someone, you see. In a way. It's very early on, so it may not be...'

'Of course!' Arnold spoke over me. 'I understand completely. Well, I shall be in touch! Merry Christmas!'

In his fluster, he had apparently completely forgotten that he was going to drive me to the canteen. It was getting dark, and the lights in nearby houses were snuffing out as blinds and curtains were drawn. I watched as he scuttled off to his van, feeling dreadful about my silly lie – as if Charles Emerson would look twice at me – and set off on foot, remembering halfway that I'd forgotten my gas mask again and would have to go back. The brandy had thoroughly worn off by the time I reached the hall.

CHAPTER EIGHT

Inside, Moira was wielding a vast teapot. She had a small green party hat perched on her curls, and had dabbed on scarlet lipstick, which had bled somewhat in the steamy atmosphere.

She greeted me like a lost jungle explorer, with festive wishes and exclamations of gratitude as I handed over the remains of the pudding, then put it aside and thrust a tray of mince pies into my arms. 'I must go,' she said. 'I promised Dad I'd be back by five and, lawks a mercy, I'm late.'

'You're off already?' I said foolishly.

She laughed. 'Don't fret! Sheila's coming later, but her boy's home and she's been mad to see him, he's an officer, and terribly handsome!' She winked at me, and rammed her brown felt hat over the party hat she'd evidently forgotten about.

'I'm cycling home, wish me luck!' she called, as she dodged through knots of people to the door.

I had never dreamed I might have to man the entire operation single-handedly, but already a queue was snaking to the back of the hall and the bad-tempered urn was spitting and in need of fresh gallons of water. I rolled up my sleeves.

Two hours later, there was no sign of Sheila, and I was

damp with perspiration as I fetched and carried and poured and handed out the new Ministry of Information pamphlets that had finally turned up. I could feel my hair sticking out in all directions like a jester's cap, and my good Christmas dress was covered in crumbs and tea stains, despite the apron. As for my feet, I didn't dare think about putting them through a long walk tomorrow. They'd revolt, all on their own.

The door at the back of the hall slammed and I murmured 'at last', expecting to see wispy-haired Sheila rushing in, full of apologies. Instead, it was a man – tall, in a hat and well-cut coat, who looked as out of place in this hall of the dispossessed and soot-stained as a thoroughbred in a stable of pit ponies.

'Compliments of the season,' he called, and I saw with an electric shock that it was Charles.

'Thought I'd come and wish you a merry Christmas,' he added. 'It struck me that you'd said you'd be doling out tea and buns like the excellent citizen you are.'

I couldn't bear to think about what I must look like. 'Merry Christmas,' I said weakly. 'How's your mother?'

'Oh, as bomb-proof as ever. Listening to the wireless with her feet up, and her clothes all over my living room.'

I laughed. 'But she must be so upset about her house, and the paintings...'

'Yes,' he agreed. 'I think we've hatched a plan to go back tomorrow and see if anything can be salvaged. Rather grim, but needs must.'

I almost offered to go with them and help, imagining myself unearthing a Renoir covered in brick dust, and Charles embracing me in delight. Then I remembered my plans.

'I wish I could come with you and be useful,' I said, 'but I'm afraid I'm going to have to trek to Withington to see Mrs Novak. My editor will insist on her permission for the obituary, you see.'

'I assume Mother was a little too delightfully vague yesterday,' he said. 'I did warn her this might happen.'

Another queue was forming, hoping for soup, but I didn't want to stop speaking to Charles. As I opened my mouth to apologise – for what, I wasn't quite sure – the door banged again, and Sheila flew in.

'Sorry! Sorry!' she called, tying an apron on as she ran. 'Hello,' she said to Charles. 'You must be Edie's young man.'

'Oh gosh, no!' I shrieked, horrified, but Charles was laughing.

'Well, perhaps, in time,' he said, shaking her hand. 'Charles Emerson.'

Charmed, she blushed and said, 'Go on, Edie, have a break – I'll start the soup.'

I had no idea where to take Charles – in the end, we dragged two chairs into a corner, and I brought over cups of tea and a mince pie each.

'How perfectly lovely,' he said.

'Makes a change from the Midland,' I said. 'I should apologise,' I added, before my nerve went altogether. 'It wasn't professional of me to enjoy such a lovely lunch and drink wine when I was on work time. I'm so sorry...'

'I was delighted that you did,' he said. Now that Lillian was out of the picture, his whole manner had changed. 'I was only sorry myself that I didn't get the chance to talk to you properly. Once Mother gets the bit between her teeth, she can gallop to the top field without looking back.'

I smirked, then thought I should be more circumspect.

'What brings you here, really?' I asked.

He smiled at me. 'Well, I really did want to say merry Christmas,' he said. 'I've been at work all day, in the catacombs, and it's lovely to see a face that doesn't have a moustache.'

I laughed.

'I also wondered if you might need a bit more from me, on

old Joe. Make sure you had enough to go at. And mother's worried about her special quote.' He rolled his eyes. 'It "means so much to her", apparently.'

'I will include it,' I promised. 'It's clear that art meant a great deal to both of them.'

He nodded. 'I think it's what brought them together in the first place.'

'Did you know him very well?' I asked. It was a strange place to conduct an interview. A ragged chorus of 'Ding Dong Merrily on High' had broken out across the hall, and a small, grubby boy was repeatedly banging a toy dog on wheels into a nearby chair.

'Well, I was mostly away at school, you see.' Charles looked at the tea-stained Formica table as if studying it for clues. 'Then I went up to New College.'

'Oh,' I said. 'I thought you went to Oxford.'

He looked amused.

'It's an Oxford college,' he said gently. 'No reason why you should know, of course.'

I suddenly wished I was drinking a glass of sherry or another brandy. Perhaps it would have taken the edge off the hot flush of embarrassment I felt.

'Really,' he went on, noticing, 'I imagine you're a modern sort of girl, who left straight after school cert, and did something useful. Look at you now – you can't be much older than me, and you're a reporter.'

He was so kind, I felt like weeping. I had left at fifteen, while most of my friends stayed on at the girls' grammar. 'Edie, you are a very capable girl,' Miss Pinner had said, as I stood in her office. 'I cannot imagine why you think that getting "a job" is preferable to working hard, even going to university. We are a modern school, with modern ideas, and we don't like to see our brightest girls simply wandering off because they can't be bothered.'

I didn't want to tell her the truth. Everyone was thrown out of the children's home at sixteen, and it would be my birthday in September. We were expected to find work, and support ourselves, having burdened the state for long enough. They didn't care if I was at a grammar school or fishing bodies out of the Irwell, they just wanted to see the back of me. Miss Pinner was a kind woman, and if I'd told her, she would have probably found a teacher to take me in as an unpaid lodger – 'Pay us back when you have a job' – but I'd had enough of creeping about, trying not to annoy anyone, having cold baths because someone more important had used the hot water, and going to bed at the time stipulated by somebody else. I already felt weary and grown up, and I couldn't imagine what I'd do at university, when I simply wanted to be a crime reporter.

Perhaps at eleven, I'd had some fantastical idea of using my dazzling journalistic skills to trace my parents, but that idea had long since died – or so I told myself. I just wanted to get a job on a newspaper, join the adult world, breathe in ink and paper and talk to people about something other than husbands and babies – the only things the girls I knew were interested in.

'I feel it's rather a shame that you ever passed the eleven-plus,' Miss Pinner had said. 'There are many girls who would have given a good deal for your opportunities.' I'd shrugged, and she dismissed me, her lips in a thin line.

Now, how I wished I had stayed and worked hard, and gone to Oxford instead of working for the council until the *Chronicle* took me on; been one of the girls in Charles's shining orbit, crouching down to change the gramophone record, laughing at some obscure joke from a tutorial, him reaching over to light my cigarette...

'Anyway,' he said now, taking my silence as acknowledgement. 'Back to Joseph.'

He settled back on the wooden chair. 'I suppose he seemed sad,' he offered. 'I knew he was married these last few years, of course, but he seemed rather lonely after he arrived in Manchester. He had many friends in Berlin, of course – he was a big, handsome, charismatic man, but here, it was as if Mother was his only friend. He never mentioned anyone else.'

'What did you talk about when you saw him? Even if it was only once or twice?'

'Well, perhaps rather more than that – Mother used to drag me over to Germany to see him, and we'd go about a bit. They'd go out a lot, to cabaret clubs and restaurants and parties, and, of course, we'd go to art galleries.'

He smiled. 'There was an old Berlin lady, Frau Schneider, who used to look after me when they went out together – hundreds of terrible little dogs, relieving themselves on the furniture and yapping. She always served this ghastly, nutty torte, and I had to be polite about it. I think I concealed half of it in a pot of ferns; it's probably still there.'

I laughed. 'But did they really never want to marry, or at least... be together?'

He shook his head and pulled a face. 'As she said, Mumsie wasn't the marrying kind. Joseph asked, several times I believe, but... well, we were perfectly well off, and it suited her as it was, for years. But of course, when things went wrong in Germany, and he needed a plan, she helped him. And it sort of brought them closer, I suppose.'

He sighed. 'That's why I don't really see the point of chatting to Pamela, Edie. She barely knew him – they both needed respectability and she had good connections, that's all. I doubt she really loved him. Not like Mother did.'

'I do understand,' I said. 'It's Mr Gorringe, really. I daren't upset him.'

'You'd think he'd have bigger things to worry about, what with Manchester burning down.'

I suddenly remembered the passport.

'Look, was Joseph always called Novak?' I asked. 'I don't suppose he changed his name?'

Charles looked baffled. 'What do you mean?'

I explained what the rescuers had found in the remains of the factory, and he shook his head.

'Not his,' he said. 'I always knew him as Mr Novak. It must have been an old friend of his, perhaps, a fellow refugee he gave work to. He was a kind man, you know.'

I felt a strange wash of relief – partly for the integrity of my obituary, and partly because I didn't want to be suspicious. I didn't like things that made no sense, probably because I had so few answers about my birth, and where I came from. I loved crime books – the way the clues eventually clicked together like a Chinese puzzle and offered a solution. Sometimes, I had to remember that real life didn't work like that.

'Well, Edie,' Charles said, turning to me. He put his cigarette in the ashtray, and studied me. 'I've told you about me. Now tell me about you.'

I laughed. 'There's not much to tell.'

He carried on regarding me, the way I imagined a psycho-analyst would. I felt foolish under his gaze.

'I write obituaries.'

'I already know that.'

'All right.' I gulped tepid tea to give myself thinking time. 'I don't have brothers or sisters.'

'Parents?'

'No.' I needed to wrest the conversation back onto safer ground.

'But why don't you have parents? The Great War, like my father?'

It was too hard to explain. 'Yes,' I said, and immediately regretted it, as he went on, 'Then where did you grow up?'

'Various places,' I said. I didn't want to lie, but I hadn't talked about the truth for so long, it was possible to believe it had never happened. As he looked at me, I envisaged an imaginary aunt, someone cultured, kind, someone who cared what happened to me and made sure I had clean pinafores and pocket money and presents on my birthday.

'It wasn't so bad,' I added.

'Children's home?' he said. I felt light-headed, as if all the brandy I'd drunk earlier had suddenly released its poison at once.

He saw my face. 'Sorry. I just thought you had that wariness – I recognise it from some of the scholarship chaps at school. They had nowhere to go in the hols, preferred to stay on at an empty school.'

I stared fixedly at the table, wishing I had a cigarette. I didn't like to ask.

'Edie,' he said. He reached out and touched my knee with his elegant hand. 'I'm sorry. You seem so bold and brave, I didn't know I'd upset you.'

'Bold and brave?' I spluttered a little laugh. 'Hardly.'

'You're delightful,' he said seriously. I looked at him, and suddenly we were gazing into each other's eyes and my heart was galloping.

'Let me take you out,' he said. 'If the Grosvenor Picture Palace is still standing, they were showing *Rebecca* with Joan Fontaine – what about Saturday? Can you get away?'

I thought I'd happily abandon Moira and her rock bun formations for an evening with Charles, and nodded.

'Top hole,' he said. 'As the fellows at school used to say. I'll pick you up at six and we can track down some supper afterwards. Air raids allowing, of course.'

I had a sudden vision of sharing the cramped Morrison shelter with Charles, rather than Lou, and blushed.

He bent and kissed me on my flaming cheek. 'Merry Christmas,' he said quietly. 'Better get back to Mother before she sends an ARP warden out. "Don't you know there's a war on?"'

he snapped, in perfect imitation. '"Why no, goodness me, is there really?"'

I laughed and waved as he left, and Sheila came bustling over. 'My heavens,' she said. 'You've done all right for yourself there.'

On Boxing Day morning, I woke up feeling I'd taken part in one of the Depression dance contests, where couples jigged till they collapsed with exhaustion. My whole body ached from carrying great trays of weighty teapots, and all the cooking and washing-up and serving.

All the same, I knew I'd have to get over to see Mrs Novak before I was sacked by Mr Gorringe, and I washed and dressed in my tweed skirt and a jumper, feeling like a woman going to the gallows.

A light snow was falling on the street, and a few children were rushing up and down shrieking and sliding, damp gas-mask boxes banging on their backs. Others were climbing on the unstable remains of a fallen house, over lethal-looking struts and glass panes. I thought about calling a warning, but they didn't look as though they'd listen.

Of course, there were no trams or buses, but I'd had an idea – Mr Benson kept an ancient bicycle in the scrubby back garden of our house, and ages ago he'd said I could borrow it. It didn't have the white blackout stripe painted on the mudguard, and it weighed more than a car, so until now I'd never felt the urge. Today, however, it might save me.

I pumped up the flat tyre and polished the rusty bell so it now made a sort of dull grinding noise. It was unfortunate that the roads were dusted with ice crystals, concealed rubble and tyre-piercing glass, and that my legs already ached as though I had influenza, but I mounted the old machine, and wobbled off down the road.

It was a journey of around two miles, and gritty sleet and snow blew into my exposed face as I pedalled doggedly along, keeping to the centre of the roads. There were few people about, and the shelters had stood mostly empty overnight. I saw various wardens stumping along, and a gaggle of WAAFs, who looked as if they hadn't been to bed at all, slithering along and laughing.

I passed the blackened skeletons of bombed-out houses looming through the seething white air, and shuttered, sand-bagged shops with taped-up windows. Yesterday's jolly Christmas dinner seemed a memory from another lifetime.

In Alfreton Avenue, however, the large houses remained unsullied, front gardens pristine under their light blanket of snow. It seemed even the Luftwaffe wouldn't dare disturb their winter calm.

I left the bike propped against the garden wall, gave myself a quick brush down and tucked my hair into my damp woollen hat.

'Here goes nothing,' I whispered. Mrs Novak's milk was still on the step; the cold had burst the top, and created a strange ice formation. I picked up the bottle to offer her and rang the bell.

I expected to hear the dog again, hurling its muscled body against a door somewhere, booming its protective fury through the house, but there was no sound as I stood on the step.

The car was still outside, a huge and stately maroon Wolseley dusted with snow, so she must have taken the beast for a walk, I thought. I would wait, grateful to have a few more minutes to think of ways to charm her.

Fifteen minutes passed, then half an hour, and I began to wonder if she was really the sort of person who would go for a long walk in the snow. I had assumed she wouldn't celebrate Christmas, as a Jew (or was she?), but that didn't mean she couldn't go away to see friends or relations. She could be away for weeks, I had no way of knowing. The only clue that she hadn't left for long was the fact that the blackout curtains had been drawn back, so she had clearly been here this morning.

After half an hour had crawled glacially by, and my fingers had gone numb, I decided I'd have to think of something else – a letter, perhaps. I dug in my bag for my notebook and pencil, when it occurred to me that perhaps she was at the back of the house with the wireless on. I didn't know where the dog might be, but I could just go and check before I committed any more unseemly begging to paper.

I unlatched the side gate, tensed for a volley of barking and scrabbling claws, but there was nothing. The wintry garden was as tidy as a sewing box, beds of snow-dusted shrubs, little paths tracing a square round the clipped lawn, with its iced-over stone bird bath in the centre. The kitchen window overlooked the garden. At the top, it was cracked open slightly, but it was too high for any burglar to take a chance. It was too high for me to see into as well, but there was a metal boot scraper by the back door. Before my courage failed, I dragged it beneath the window and pulled myself up, holding onto the sill so I could peer in. If she was there, I thought, I could say I'd been worried about her not answering the door.

Inside, the kitchen was pristine. There was a large dresser holding white china, and a big, polished kitchen table with nothing on it. I thought of ours, with its piles of library books and old ration cards, scribbled notes to each other and milk jugs, and felt a pang of homesickness.

There was a flowered cup upside down by the sink, but that was the only thing out of place. It was clear there was nobody here – even the two huge dog bowls for food and water were empty and gleaming. I was about to lower myself back to the ground, write my hopeless begging letter, and set off on the chilly pedal home, when I heard muffled barking and whining coming from inside the house. I stood on the boot scraper again, and climbed onto the freezing outside downpipe to pull myself up higher, so I was at waist-height to the windowsill, trembling with the effort of holding myself up.

Closer to the open window, I could hear the noise properly. It sounded as though the dog was shut in somewhere, and it was frantic. I strained to see beyond the open kitchen door, and as my eyes adjusted to the murk inside, I could faintly make out the shape of something smashed on the hall floor – it looked like a plant pot. Perhaps the dog had been left on its own, I thought, and knocked it over, hurt itself... but if that was the case, where was Mrs Novak, whose handbag was also visible, hooked neatly over the mahogany banister's newel post opposite the front door?

I was beginning to feel horribly uneasy, but equally, I really didn't want to create a great, melodramatic fuss as if I were in an Agatha Christie, and have it all turn out to be nothing. I contemplated traipsing down the road to the public phone – perhaps Lou would know whether this was worthy of a police visit. Though, imagining the conversation – 'I sneaked round the back and thought I heard a dog that sounded upset...' and his likely response – I thought better of it.

Perhaps the thing to do, I thought, would be to try and find a way in, and check what was going on before I raised the alarm. The whining was carrying on, accompanied by distant scrabbling noises – if the dog had just been shut in a room, having heard its normal response, I thought it would be barking itself silly.

'Hello?' I called tentatively. There was no reply.

I scrambled down and tried the back door. It was the kind with two frosted glass panels. I could just make out the shapes of hanging mackintoshes and dog leads. It was locked, and my violent rattling didn't make the slightest difference. I had seen men in films wrapping a cloth over their hand and punching through glass, but I had a feeling it wasn't that easy when all I had as wrapping was my coat, and the glass looked painfully tough. Besides, I also didn't fancy finding myself in Willert Street station on a charge of breaking and entering, having lost my job as a result.

I scanned the garden. At the gate, where I'd entered, was a metal bin for ashes. The side return wasn't overlooked – these big houses were protected by bushy hedges, and all I could see of next door was the small bathroom window. I dragged the metal dustbin round to the area below the kitchen window with a roaring, scraping sound, but nobody appeared over the hedge.

I was truly worried now – the whining had become a sort of choking whimper. I pulled myself onto the sill, grasping the icy drainpipe. It was just wide enough to stand on, and if I fell off, I calculated, I'd be winded but not seriously damaged. I pushed the upper window, which grudgingly opened an inch or so before sticking fast.

'Hello?' I called cautiously. 'Is there anyone in there?'

There was silence. I could smell the cleaning powder that Mrs Novak, or her maid, used in the kitchen. I peered at the hall again, and saw, beside the plant pot, a dark and glossy splash.

My heart began to pound, and my legs shook. I was like an animal that had wandered into the path of a threat it didn't yet understand.

'Hold on!' I yelled. I'd been afraid before, in the raids and at the home, but not like this. I was barely sentient at all, my actions seemed to be coming from some deep, ancient place, a simple directive that one did not leave another human in trouble; this drove me on to thrust at the wooden part of the upper window with all my strength, so it splintered inwards and swung free. I put one foot on the drainpipe and kicked against it, until my upper body was through the small window frame, then I dangled headfirst till my hands were on the draining board. The flowered cup slid off and smashed on the floor as I scrambled through and lowered myself like an ungainly schoolgirl gymnast into the sink, nearly overshooting the edge. I was sweating, my hat had snagged on a splinter, and I dropped to the floor, taking a great breath and letting it out slowly before I went further.

'Hello? Can you hear me?' I called again. 'It's all right, I'm going to get help...'

The silence of the house pressed in.

I opened the nearest kitchen drawer, hoping for a knife, and found a large pair of scissors amongst the serving spoons and carving forks. Holding them open, I edged towards the entrance hall. The broken pot was an ornamental Chinese urn, and earth was scattered across the polished parquet floor, with some flaccid palm fronds. The whining was coming from upstairs, but downstairs was entirely silent. I braced myself to look again, and realised that the splash was the start of a shining, crimson trail that led to the front parlour.

Its panelled door was half pulled-to, and terror surged through me. There was no point creeping – I'd made more noise getting in than a travelling circus. 'Are you in here?' I called, and imagined I heard a faint, answering whimper.

I pushed at the door and a smell rose to meet me. It reminded me of the butcher's shop before the war when they'd had a delivery; big, aproned men hefting pig carcasses, and housewives in their headscarves queuing outside for the best cuts.

The door was sticking, and I had to put my shoulder against it and shove, so I half fell into the room. It was the sort of parlour where ladies took tea, wearing hats, but a mist of blood was sprayed across the pale Chinese rug, and pooled like spilled tea on the yellow silk brocade sofa.

'Oh God,' I whispered – or I tried to, but what came out was a high-pitched noise that bore no relationship to actual words. 'Is there...' I began again, and then I noticed the foot sticking out from behind the sofa.

There was a gap between its high, cushioned back and the

pale wall. I blinked, hard, and clutching the scissors, I walked towards it, sick with fright at what I'd find. 'Come along, Edie,' I said to myself, 'don't be feeble-minded. Imagine Lou Brennan's mockery.'

Holding my breath against the blood, the fear, my own urge to cry out, I peered over the back of the sofa.

CHAPTER NINE

Mrs Novak lay face down. I'd heard the expression 'in a pool of blood', but that wasn't quite right. It was a lake, a welter. The blood was everywhere, covering the wall, the couch, the floor and her. I couldn't see a weapon, but then, I could barely see at all for shock.

'Oh, dear God,' I said again, though my teeth were chattering. 'It's all right, Mrs Novak, I'm here, I'm going to telephone for an ambulance.' I reached down and tried to turn her face, so I could feel for a pulse on her neck. But her hair was sticky with blood, and I snatched back my hand, revolted and afraid. She was making no noise at all.

There was a telephone on an occasional table near the door, and shaking with horror and shock, I connected to the operator and said, 'Manchester City Police, please', her warm blood still on my hand.

By the time the police arrived, I suppose I was in shock. I couldn't stop shaking and my head was tingling, as though my scalp had been compressed by the straw hat they used to make us wear for church. Sometimes, I'd have a red band printed round my forehead afterwards. I had barely moved since I'd put the phone down and edged out into the hall, away from the terrible scene in the living room. The dog was still squealing upstairs, but I didn't dare let it out – I had a vague notion about fingerprints on the door handles, and besides, I couldn't let him see his mistress like that. I called, 'It's all right, Major, somebody's coming,' and he seemed to calm slightly.

'Don't move, please,' the police telephonist had said. 'Just stay where you are, miss, somebody will be with you very shortly.' It had felt like an hour, though the grandfather clock in the hall, with its loud, crunching tick, showed that only about ten minutes had passed before I heard the sirens in the distance, their mechanical two-note wail bursting into the quiet street. I felt embarrassed, somehow, that I'd launched all this fuss, that neighbours would soon be hurrying out and exchanging shocked words over the festively snowy hedges.

When the men finally arrived, I saw the tall constable's hat beyond the window, and tears of relief sprang to my eyes. I was so overwhelmed that I hadn't thought of the two greatest dangers – that the murderer might still be in the house, or that the police might think I'd killed her. I felt a wave of sickness, as if I was on a pitching ship, and I must have turned pale because the policeman on the step, who didn't look much older than me, grabbed my arm and said, 'Steady on, miss.'

'Sorry,' I said, though I didn't know what I was apologising for. Being there? Dragging them out of their cosy station on Boxing Day when they could have been eating mince pies and filing reports?

'Miss Edie York?' he said.

I nodded.

'Where's the victim?' asked the older one, who had come up behind him. 'We'll need you to leave the premises now.' I noticed he didn't say 'miss.'

'I picked up these in the kitchen... just in case,' I said. I handed him the scissors.

He took them as if they too were covered in blood. 'These will have to be bagged and fingerprinted,' he said.

I pointed to the front parlour. 'And the dog. It's upstairs. It's upset.'

I'd once met a girl who told me she'd chatted to a pleasant man at a party who revealed, after a couple of hours, that he was a psychoanalyst. 'And after that, nothing I said or did seemed normal,' she told me. 'I felt he was assessing everything for signs of madness.'

I probably had guilt written all over my face, purely because I was now so afraid they were looking for it.

And now, walking down the path with the younger policeman, past the frozen milk bottle still on the step, and being put into the back of the police car like a naughty child, I realised that it might not look too good, once they found the broken window and the smashed cup, the bin I'd used to climb on... my heart began to race unpleasantly, the way I'd felt as a child when I'd been called to Mr Pugh's study.

'Shut the door, Edie,' he would say, in his dark, chapel voice, and I'd have to take an extra breath because suddenly the air was made of thick, black fog, and I couldn't gather enough into my lungs. Only then, it was a vicious spanking. Now, the idea that I could be arrested for murder almost made me laugh, as I climbed, trembling and light-headed, into the freezing black car.

'I'm Sergeant O'Carroll,' said the younger one. 'We need to take a statement, so we'll take you down the station when we've finished here.' He slammed the door and locked me in the back.

The older one had already walked into the house, in his big, polished shoes, the door swinging open behind him. I wanted to shout out and warn him of the horror, but perhaps he'd seen it all before.

They must have called for more officers because after a few

minutes, another car swung into the road and two more men, this time in plain clothes, jumped out and ran towards the Novaks' house. One was dark and tall, and for a brief moment I thought it was Lou, and almost called out to him. But of course, this wasn't his patch; these would be coppers from the local station. I imagined what they might be doing inside, based on the vast number of detective books I'd read. If they were American cops, they'd be chewing gum and calling Mrs Novak an 'old dame' and drawing round the body with chalk. And if they were Agatha Christie detectives, they'd be pacing before the fire, saying, 'You see, Mrs Novak cannot have known her killer, or else why would she not simply have let him in and prepared tea for him? Yet, there was only one cup on the draining board and a broken window catch...'

The awareness that I was probably the prime suspect washed over me. A thunderous trial, with Annie in the public gallery, weeping. Years in prison, or perhaps the gallows. I'd never get to be a crime reporter, or go out again with Charles, or help Moira and Sheila win the war with giant pots of tea. I'd be in a cell, surrounded by real murderers.

I sat there, my life unspooling, trying to breathe slowly, while around me, just as I'd imagined, neighbours began to emerge like rabbits from their burrows, sniffing the air, pricking up their ears. My watch had stopped – perhaps I'd banged it in my ungainly descent from the sink – but I guessed I'd been there a good half hour by the time the ambulance came and the uniformed men trotted up the path, carrying a stretcher, as if somehow she might still be brought out alive.

I closed my eyes, though I knew they'd cover the body. But every time the image loomed before me, I had to clench my fists and dig my nails in to distract myself, stop myself sobbing wildly or being sick. Anything to remove the sight and smell of the matted, thick blood, and the feeling of my own pulse pounding through me like high waves on a sea wall. I had never seen a dead body before, but normally, I imagined, they would be laid out as they are on tombstones, calm and prone, folded hands and a blank expression, a peaceful indication that life was now extinguished. Mrs Novak had been utterly desecrated and abandoned amid chaos. It struck me that perhaps the killer hadn't dumped her body behind the couch – perhaps she'd been hiding and he'd found her there, which was an even worse thought. But no, the blood suggested a struggle in the hall, and then he must have dragged the dog upstairs – or perhaps Mrs Novak had shut Major in before answering the door. For all I knew, the killer could still be lurking upstairs, caressing his shining, silver knife.

'Oh God,' I said out loud, and looked up to see the middle of O'Carroll's torso outside the window, his silver buttons level with my gaze. The ambulance had left some time ago, but I hadn't opened my eyes.

He unlocked the door.

'Righto, we've done all we can for now,' he said. The other two men were still on the path, conferring with the older policeman. One held a little bag in his hand, which contained the scissors. I wished I'd never picked them up. A neighbour in a headscarf and gumboots, dragging a small girl, trotted up to the gate.

'Officer,' she called, 'can you tell us what's happened?' Suddenly, it was 'us', as though the whole street had conferred, and elected her the spokesperson. Perhaps they had.

'I'm afraid not,' said the older man. 'I'm sure you'll be informed in due course.'

'Is Pamela quite all right?' the woman went on. 'Where is she? I saw the ambulance.'

'I cannot divulge any information at this moment in time,' he said, and the other two men hurried past without speaking to her at all. I longed to climb out of the car and ask her what she knew. Had she heard anything?

That thought finally occurred to O'Carroll as well because he said, 'Wait here,' as if I had a choice, and got back out. He went over to her and took out his notebook, jotting down details, so presumably he intended to question her gently at some point. When they'd finished with me and thrown me into a cell, probably.

'Right,' said the older bobby. 'Terrible business. We'll take you down to the station, take a statement, and see where we get to.'

I nodded. 'Can I just explain...' I began, and he held up a meaty hand, as if he was showing off his armband. 'Any explaining can be done at the station,' he said. 'I am Inspector Beeston, so any concerns you have, you may address to me when we're in a more formal situation.'

I had a sudden image of us in evening clothes, sitting opposite each other at a white-clothed table, while a violinist played.

'But I'm not being arrested?' My voice squeaked pitifully.

'Nobody is being arrested or even cautioned at this stage,' he said heavily. 'We are currently working on the assumption that if you had seen a suspect of any kind on or about the premises, you would have alerted us. And that you did not move or touch anything, other than the telephone.'

'I don't know,' I said. 'I came in through the window and I broke a cup. And I went into the front parlour to see if...' I took a deep breath, and dug in my nails again. I couldn't speak. 'Sorry,' I managed.

'We won't take that as a confession. Yet.' O'Carroll grinned. 'Most of our suspects aren't pretty young ladies.'

'That'll do,' said Beeston, and O'Carroll subsided as we drove away from the house. Its memory had assumed a dark pall now; it was impossible to remember anything about it without the smell of blood in my nostrils, and shock and fear coursing through me.

They drove me back to town, Mr Benson's ancient bicycle

left abandoned outside Mrs Novak's house. I wondered if the police station had survived, as we crawled over debris on Corporation Street. There were groups of civilian men with rolled-up sleeves, helping to shovel wreckage into trucks in the snow, and members of the Home Guard, standing outside the ruined shells of buildings, moving people along. The old marketplace had gone, the great glass dome a smashed toy, and the medieval buildings of the Shambles stood defiantly in a wasteland of tumbled masonry. Great walls of broken bricks and beams were piled so high it was impossible to see over them. Under normal circumstances, I might have wept at the wholesale destruction of my city, but all I could see was Mrs Novak's bloodied body.

I shuddered convulsively, and the sergeant said, 'Nearly there,' as we took another detour past the crumbled remains of shops, and a soldier from the Pioneer Corps lifted a hand in acknowledgement of fellow service. O'Carroll waved back, and gave him a thumbs up, and I suddenly saw how reassuring it was to be on the inside in life, and how cold and lonely to be banished.

At the station, a grimy Victorian building that appeared unharmed, the desk clerk's face was the shining red of a Dutch cheese.

'What've we got then?' he said wearily, then he looked up and saw me.

'Blimey,' he said. 'They're making the criminals better looking these days.' O'Carroll smirked, and Beeston said reprovingly, 'She's a possible witness to a murder at this stage, she's here to make a statement.'

'Not to worry then, love,' said the desk clerk. 'You'll be back with your bloke by teatime. Tell him all about it.'

I didn't speak as O'Carroll went off to find a free room, and Beeston filled in the desk clerk on the murder. 'Nasty,' he said. 'It'll be big news, this. We'll have the BBC and the *Chronicle* breathing down our necks.'

'I work for the *Chronicle*,' I said.

'You what, love?'

'That's what I was doing there – trying to speak to Mrs Novak about an article I was writing...'

The clerk lit his pipe and raised his eyebrows wryly at Beeston, who looked furious.

'Well, be certain that you're in no position to be passing on tittle-tattle to your colleagues,' he said. 'This is a police investigation, not some hold-the-front-page nonsense.'

That was exactly what this was – I was yearning for a phone, to dictate my copy to the paper's telephonists, and finally see Mr Gorringe shake his head in awe at my daring and professionalism. Aside from the horror of it all, there was a significant part of me that was already constructing the opening paragraph.

'Righto.' Sergeant O'Carroll was back. 'Shall I do the honours, Inspector?'

'Go on,' said Beeston. 'But if you need to issue a caution, or worse, I want to know about it.'

'A caution?'

'We'll get to that if it's necessary,' said O'Carroll infuriatingly. He had a baby face: glassy blue eyes, the sort of skin that flushes bright pink, and red lips like a doll. He may have been attractive to a certain type of woman, but not me. For the first time since finding the body, I thought of cool, elegant Charles and felt a stab of longing, as O'Carroll ushered me into a little grey room with a wooden table and two chairs and closed the door.

'Take a seat,' he said. 'Must have been a shock.'

He stuck his head out and asked a secretary to bring tea, and when he returned, he set his pencil down and said, 'Right, Miss York. Can you explain how you came to be at the scene of a murder on the morning of December 26, 1940?'

'I'll do my best,' I said.

I tried to explain what had led me there. There was a lot of back and forth, where I'd say, 'So I went to see Lillian,' and he would say, 'Right, so Lillian is Mrs Novak?' and I'd have to explain that Lillian had been the woman having an affair with Mrs Novak's husband, who had approached me about an obituary, and that I'd been going to see Mrs Novak to beg her to tell me more, to add to the mistress's fond recollections. When I said it all out loud, it sounded not only unlikely and suspicious, but deeply morally questionable.

Of course, I had thought about whether I should mention Lillian at all. But I wasn't cut out to be a spy; I was a believer in facts and in reporting them as accurately as possible.

My tea had gone cold, but I drank some anyway. It tasted of scorched milk and there were still tea leaves floating it in.

'We do need to make some sense of all this, miss,' said Sergeant O'Carroll. He looked at me. 'You've still not explained to our satisfaction why you were climbing through the window in the first place.'

It was now after two, according to the clock on the wall above his head, and I hadn't had any lunch. I thought of yesterday's long-ago roast potatoes, then I remembered Mrs Novak again, and all trace of hunger left me.

'I heard something,' I said.

'What sort of thing?'

'The dog was whining. It sounded upset – trapped, maybe. I thought she might be listening to the wireless, so I'd gone round the back. And the window was open a bit – shall I slow down?'

He was laboriously transcribing all this in a careful copperplate.

'No, go on,' he said. 'You say you went round the back. Did anyone see you?'

'Well, I don't know,' I said. 'I didn't see anyone, it all seemed quiet and it was snowing.'

'Covers prints. Murderer could have been in the house

already,' he said, nodding. 'Or have already exited the premises. But you didn't see anyone on the street as you arrived?'

We had already been through this several times. I shook my head. 'It was all quiet.'

'And who else knew you were attending the address?' he asked, and I blanched.

'Annie,' I said. 'My best friend. I share rooms with her. And Arnold Whiting, another friend, who works in a funeral parlour.'

'Oh, Whiting's, yes,' murmured O'Carroll. 'We know Arnold. Nice chap.'

I nodded. 'And Charles Emerson,' I added.

'Another young man, is it?'

'He's a friend, that's all,' I said, embarrassed. 'I met him through work, I've just told you all about his mother...'

'Ah. Nice to see you befriend your interviewees so readily,' said O'Carroll. 'And did any of them put you up to this?'

'Put me up to... no! I told you, I needed some quotes for her husband's obituary.'

O'Carroll took his details and said, 'We'll need to speak to this so-called mistress, of course.' Then he placed his hands on the table and sighed.

'I want to help you here, Edie,' he said. 'You seem like a nice girl, it's Boxing Day and we all want our tea break. But here's the problem,' he went on. 'Your story's a bit flimsy. I still don't really know what all this business about Lillian' – he consulted his notes – 'Emerson adds up to. It sounds a bit cock and bull, excuse my French. You heard a dog. You found the body, after breaking into her kitchen—'

'I broke in because I heard the dog, and then I saw the blood!' I interrupted. 'I wasn't trying to burgle her!'

'Now we have some bloke popping up called Charles, and what's your relation to him?'

'Nothing!'

'You just happened to see this Mrs Emerson's son before setting off and finding a body.'

'Yes!' I said. 'I was chatting to him yesterday at the WVS canteen where I work. For the article,' I added lamely. I didn't think the fact that I'd thought about him all day could be considered remotely relevant.

'On Christmas Day,' he said. 'I see. Do you mind if I ask how you go about finding your information for these' – he paused – 'obituaries? Sounds a depressing job for a young lady.'

'No, I find it fascinating,' I said. 'Actually, I hope to become a crime reporter one day.'

He pulled a disbelieving face.

'They don't all have to wear brown macs and trilbies,' I said. 'I have contacts, and sometimes people get in touch with me, like Mrs Emerson. And I know a police...' I stopped. 'I have a friend who's a DI,' I amended. 'Louis Brennan, do you know him?'

O'Carroll looked surprised. 'Yes, I know DI Brennan. We trained together for a bit.'

'Do you think I could ring him up?' I said. 'He might be able to confirm what I do, and why I was at Mrs Novak's. It's something I talked to him about.'

'I can't see how DI Brennan...' he began, as I said, 'Please.'

There must have been something desperate enough there to make him soften because he said, 'Fine. But I'll telephone him, not you.'

He was back five minutes later.

'You're in luck,' he said. 'The guv'nor was just leaving, but I caught him.' It was odd to hear Lou referred to as 'the guv'nor' by adoring underlings.

'He's verified your version of events. But if we do take the decision to caution and release you, based on your statement, I have to say that it won't hold much water unless you can prove where you were at the time of death—'

He broke off as someone knocked at the door.

'Right, we've got developments,' said Beeston, stepping inside. He filled the small room like a lugubrious Alice in Wonderland, looming over us in his navy serge. 'Can I have a word, Sergeant?'

I was sitting at the table with my head in my hands when they eventually came back. I had a poisonous headache throbbing behind my eyes; Annie would be wondering where I was; it was almost certain that the *Chronicle* was at the scene, interviewing the nosy woman in the gumboots; Charles would probably never speak to me again for dragging him into all this; and, of course, there was the small matter that I was still potentially the main suspect in a murder case.

'Seems the time of death was well before you broke in,' said Beeston, marching back in.

I sat up. 'When?'

'Not your concern. Mrs Novak was already long dead by the time you got there – your footprints were still visible, according to Constable Barker, who had the sense to check.'

I was shocked that Mrs Novak had already been poked and prodded over. Somehow, I had expected it to take much longer.

'Is the dog safe?' I asked.

'I'm quite sure the correct animal husbandry procedures have been followed,' said Beeston in quelling tones.

'I think we've got all we need for now then,' said O'Carroll, getting to his feet. 'We'll be in touch.'

I gathered my coat. I was stranded miles from home, with no buses or trams running.

'Oh yes,' O'Carroll said, when I tentatively mentioned this. 'I meant to say, DCI Brennan's on his way. He said he'd pick you up and give you a lift home. Friends in high places, eh?'

Beeston snorted. 'I trust none of this will be finding its way into your newspaper,' he said. How could he think a murder wouldn't be on the front page?

'I hope my statement is useful,' I said rather haughtily. 'And I hope you find out who did such a terrible thing.'

'Oh, we intend to,' said Beeston. I didn't believe he had a clue what was going on, but I nodded sagely. I was so relieved to be out of there, I'd have kissed him, if he'd asked.

I waited outside for Lou. It had stopped snowing and there was the ghost of a moon already hovering above the ruined city.

'Hop in,' he said, drawing up in his big black car. I was too exhausted to hop anywhere, but I collapsed into the seat.

'You're quite the girl detective, aren't you?' he said. He wasn't smiling. 'Two bodies within a week.'

'I just went to interview her!' I said. 'How could I know I'd find her...' The image reared up again, the blood and the matted hair, and the smell that I didn't think I'd ever be able to get rid of, no matter how many handfuls of Annie's precious bath salts I used.

'For God's sake, though, Edie!' he said tightly. It was hard to square this professional Lou, in his dark coat and hat, driving this big, serious car, with the funny, relaxed man of yesterday, who had distributed crackers and brandy and bonhomie.

'Whoever did her in could still have been in the house, you know that, don't you?'

I had known it, but I didn't want to think about it for long.

'Who'd kill her, though?' I asked. 'She was just an ordinary woman – a widow, for God's sake. Do you think it was a burglary?'

'Not many burglars are going to break in with a dog that size barking itself stupid,' said Lou. 'Shut in or not.'

'So it might have been someone she knew?'

'Edie,' – he fumbled for his cigarettes as we pulled up at the traffic lights, and didn't offer me one – 'let me make it clear that this lift is a favour, not an interview. You're the chief witness. I can't tell you anything.'

'All right,' I said haughtily. 'Is it your case?'

'Seems to be,' he said. 'I'm already working on Turnbull and a black-market warehouse burglary in Cheetham Hill. With half the boys gone, we're stretched in all directions as it is. What wouldn't I give to be piloting a Spitfire over the Channel, giving Fritz a hard time. Instead, here I am.' He gestured hopelessly to both of us, the car, the falling light outside.

I felt rather insulted.

'Will anyone tell me what's happened?' I tried. 'Seeing as I found her.'

'If we need any further information, I'm sure someone will be in touch,' said Lou. 'But for now, you're back to being a helpful member of the general public, my dear.'

I suddenly felt hopeless. I wanted to have a bath, and crawl into my blankets and sleep for a week. It occurred to me that I hadn't rung up the office to let them know what had happened either.

'Thanks for the lift,' I said, and he raised his hand.

'I might nip round later, raids allowing,' he said.

I was on our landing when I heard the voices.

Annie's giddy rattle, the way she talks when she's excited, and a deeper, more measured tone that was familiar.

I pushed open the door. Annie was on the couch, holding a cup of tea. Opposite her was a man. I could only see his back, but my body knew who it was before my brain caught up.

'Here she is!' said Annie.

Charles turned round and smiled. 'Thank heavens,' he said. 'We were getting quite worried about you.'

He'd been interviewed already. 'Pair of eager bobbies

turned up at my door,' he said. 'I'd just had a bath, and honestly, my first thought was that I'd flooded something.'

Annie shrieked with laughter.

'But they told you what had happened?'

'Yes. I'm so sorry, what a dreadful shock it must have been.' He laid a hand on my arm, and a little rush went through me. 'They knew that you'd told me where you were going, and wanted me to prove I hadn't decided to nip round and bump her off. It was like some ludicrous Agatha Christie.' He adopted a ponderous voice. 'We need to ascertain, sir, your movements at an earlier time of this day, wheretofore you may or may not have terminated the existence of an unnamed individual...'

Annie snorted, the little sycophant, but it was all so awful I couldn't laugh.

'I'm so sorry,' I muttered. 'I had to tell them about Lillian and then they asked about you. I didn't want to lie...'

'Entirely understood,' said Charles. 'Seriously, of course you had to tell them. Luckily, I had at least two alibis and so has Mother. Though if she'd wanted to see off poor Pamela, I imagine she'd have done it before now.'

A nasty thought struck me, but I didn't want to sound jealous. I tried to think of a way to ask, when Annie said, 'Not another woman, I hope, Charlie?'

Charlie? I thought.

'Only if you count my mother and my landlady,' said Charles. 'Old Thelma saw me whacking the boiler on first thing for my bath, and buttonholed me for twenty minutes about the Christmas paper salvage collection. Mother dropped down to say hullo too. And, of course, one saw the neighbours this morning, in the snow – I had a word with one or two, merry Christmas, all that. Then we went off to see what we could save from the house.'

'So you're in the clear?' I asked.

'Of course.' He looked puzzled. 'Edie, I do understand, you

know. It must have been appalling for you this afternoon. I suppose we're just joking because it's so shocking. I came round to see you straight afterwards, and Annie kindly let me in to wait.'

I nodded. 'It was the worst thing I've ever seen,' I said. 'The blood...'

My voice came out in an embarrassing quavering whoop, and I felt a surge of heat behind my eyes. I screwed up my face to stop the tears, but it was too late. I dropped my head down and sobbed.

'Oh, love.' Annie was beside me, fishing for a hanky behind the cushion where she usually stuffed it, but Charles had already whisked a clean handkerchief from his jacket and placed it gently in my hand, his other arm around me. I felt like a hysterical child, being comforted by her parents. It was an unfamiliar but surprisingly pleasant sensation.

I let myself cry, and when Charles pulled my head onto his shoulder, I didn't resist. Annie whispered, 'I'll make a cup of tea with a splash of brandy,' and crept out.

'It was so horrible,' I wailed. 'There was blood everywhere, and she... she...'

'Shh,' he said, stroking my hair.

Annie brought the tea, and we all three sat huddled up on the couch while I drank it. She had lit a fire and drawn the blackout curtains, and the little Christmas tree glowed in the flickering light. It couldn't have been cosier, but there was an icicle through my heart. I couldn't stop reliving the moment of finding Mrs Novak, the sprayed blood. Why, at least, could whoever did it not have strangled her? I wondered. At least it would have been clean. Why be so brutally visceral – to leave a message? And after Turnbull...

With a sickening lurch, I wondered, for the first time, if that warning had been for me.

CHAPTER TEN

'Edie!' said Annie, 'you've gone quite white! Put your head between your knees, quickly.'

I bent forward. The room spun and settled, and the seething beat of blood in my ears eased. Charles rubbed my back lightly, and when I sat up, Annie thrust another generous measure of Lou's brandy under my nose. 'Drink it,' she ordered, and I did.

'Lou's coming round later on,' I remembered, when I felt better. 'Or at least unless this... murder' – I filled my lungs as the room swam again – 'doesn't mean he's working all night.'

Annie looked thrilled. 'Is Arnold coming too?' she asked.

'I doubt it,' I said, and her face fell.

'I'd better smarten myself up a bit, either way,' she said, and stood up. 'I was writing a farewell letter to Pete anyway. Seeing as he seems to have thrown me over.'

'Oh, Annie. You don't know that. He might be on a top secret mission, or...'

'Or found another sweetheart, more like,' she said grimly. 'No, it's all over and done. I may as well step out with someone who's actually here, don't you think?'

'Well, you do have a point,' said Charles. He smiled at me. 'And here I am.'

I laughed, and when Annie disappeared into her bedroom, Charles put his arm round me properly, and then he leaned in and kissed me.

At first, it was just a way of immersing myself in something other than the memories of my terrible day, but as I felt his hands on my back, his mouth on mine, the physical sensations replaced my thoughts.

Everything about him was practised, smooth, thoughtful. He was so far from men like Lou and Pete and Tom Harwood, he was like a different species. When Annie's door clicked, we broke apart, and he said, 'Well, I know you've had a dreadful time, but should you still like a visit to the pictures tomorrow?'

I said I would, of course, and we sat and chatted a while longer, as he stroked my hair. He seemed so sophisticated, it was hard to remember that he was only my age.

If Lou did join us, I thought, perhaps I could get a bit more out of him about the murder. A few drinks might loosen him up, then I could go to Mr Gorringe with the full story tomorrow, and get my front-page scoop: I WAS THERE: THE *CHRONICLE'S* EDIE YORK ON THE MANCHESTER MURDER.

I was never going to get closer to being a crime reporter than actually discovering the victim. Again, I thought with a shudder. I remembered when I'd been to see Mrs Novak the first time, how the dog had been shut in the kitchen while she opened the door. So that was something she usually did before she knew who it was, I thought, and if she'd been upstairs when the doorbell had rung, the dog would have been locked away up there. So, I concluded, my brain hurting with the effort, it all pointed to the fact that the killer had rung the bell, and she didn't know him. It could have been a woman, of course, but I couldn't imagine any female killing someone with a knife. It was too visceral and brutal.

Or had he come in the same way I had? Was that why the window was open? But I was small, and nobody my size could have done that. And no one could have climbed up there alone, without dragging the bins about, as I had, and making an unholy racket, then putting them back. I needed to find out about the will. If all Joseph's money went to Pamela, perhaps Lillian had snapped. But no, she had an alibi and besides, as Charles said, they were perfectly well off.

What if, though, it was somehow related to Edward Turnbull and his mysterious connection to Novak? My brain hurt from thinking.

'Edie?' Annie was staring at me.

'What?'

'You haven't said a word. Are you in shock? Do you need a doctor?'

I shook my head. 'Some more brandy might be medicinal, though.'

She poured me an enormous measure. 'Thank heavens for Brennan's Best Brandy,' she joked. 'That man seems to be everywhere at the moment.'

Of course, Lou came round, as I had known he would. He disturbed the air wherever he went. We'd been talking quietly, the three of us, I was outlining my dog theory, and then there was a sputtering of car engine outside and a violent ringing of the bell.

'Thought you'd be working late,' I said, when Annie ushered him in. 'Under the circumstances.'

'Under the circumstances,' he said. 'I've been at work for over twelve hours, convened a murder team from the useless rabble available, had a lengthy briefing with forensics, taken a good look at the mutilated corpse down at Newton Street, done the paperwork for the Home Office pathologist's report, and written up extensive notes. So given that it's Boxing Day and the city's in ruins and nobody's at work, I think I deserve a drink.'

'Course you do,' said Annie. I could tell she was rather impressed by his showing off. I knew he was young for a DI, but did he really need to swank quite so much about his important job?

'What are you drinking?' Charles asked him politely. 'Charles Emerson.' He offered his hand.

'Ah, Charles "off the hook" Emerson, no thanks to this one,' said Lou, glancing at me.

'We're all drinking brandy,' I said pointedly. 'For the shock.'

'I'm more of a beer man,' said Lou. 'But tea will do.'

Annie went to make it, and I asked, 'Any news?'

'None that won't be gone over in the briefing for the press at Willert Street tomorrow,' he said, blowing out blue smoke in a cloud that hung in the warm air and obscured his face.

'Oh, come, DI Brennan,' I said. Shock and brandy had made me bolder, and I hadn't eaten anything. 'There must be something you can tell us.'

He shrugged. 'Fair do's. I'll tell you what I'd tell anyone. Looks like a bloke did it – angle of the arm, and all that. Right-handed. We're not sure how he got in, but thanks to a certain person, we know the window was already open, so it could have been through there if he was a little fella, though we think more likely Mrs Novak let him in. No weapon found yet. Forensics have been over it, the murder box has been truly utilised, and apart from yours and Mrs N's, there weren't any fingerprints, so the bastard wore gloves. Pardon my French,' he added to Annie.

'The murder box?' she said, screwing up her nose like Shirley Temple.

'The bag forensics use for evidence,' he said. 'Gloves, vials, bags, tweezers. You can't just go charging all over a murder scene. Unless you're called Edie York,' he added, raising his eyebrow.

Hot rage rushed through me. 'You wouldn't have known there'd even been a murder without me,' I snapped. 'Excuse me.'

I stamped to the bathroom and locked the door, even though it had a horrible tendency to stick in cold weather. Lou really was insufferable.

'She's had a horrid day, you shouldn't tease her,' I heard Annie saying.

It was only Charles kissing me goodbye on the front step that saved my evening. The snow clouds had cleared and stars were out in the inky sky. 'Hope there's not a bomber's moon,' I said, and he looked worried.

'You do have a shelter here, don't you?' he asked. 'I don't like to think of you having to run to the public one. You never know who's about.'

I wondered if he thought I might be in danger too – from a murderer, rather than the Germans.

'I haven't seen anyone following me,' I said, joking, but as the words left my mouth, I thought of the person who kept turning up out of the blue, my unexpected helper, our new friend, someone I'd brushed off only yesterday – Arnold Whiting.

After Charles had left, I went back upstairs. Annie said, 'Shall we go to the dance next week?'

'There won't be one, surely,' I said. 'Half the neighbourhood has been bombed out.'

'They're holding it in the function room at the Friendship Inn,' Annie said. I had no idea how she knew these things. 'It'll be a new year and we should celebrate.'

'Whatever is there to celebrate?' I said. 'I've been at the

scene of two deaths in a week, and Manchester's been smashed to bits around us. I don't feel very jolly.'

'Being alive,' said Annie shortly. 'Ask Charles on your jaunt to the pictures tomorrow.'

'I can't ask hi—'

'Oh, for goodness sake,' she said. 'Just mention it, and he'll leap at the chance to take you. He's thoroughly smitten.'

'Do you really think so?' I asked, unable to stop a foolish smile breaking out.

She rolled her eyes. 'A black cat in a locked cupboard in a dark room could see it, you idiot.'

I went back to work the following day. It was a Saturday, but a few buses were running the length of Oxford Road, and I managed to squash onto the back of one, while the female clippie kept up a cheery stream of comment. One man was reading a morning newspaper, headlined BRUTAL MURDER IN LEAFY AVENUE – POLICE QUESTION SUSPECTS, and I realised with a horrible plummet of the stomach that I was one of them. 'Dreadful, isn't it?' she said chirpily, looking over his shoulder. 'So nearby too!'

'Should hang the bugger,' said the man, turning the page.

I remembered again what I'd seen, and for a moment, I had to shut my eyes until the sickness passed.

The city still looked like a Victorian etching, the old Co-operative building a stark, black frame as I trudged through the rubble-lined streets, but inside the office, though some were still off for the Christmas weekend, all was almost normal. Ada rattled through with the tea trolley, and Desmond appeared shortly afterwards, holding his dog-eared notepad.

'May I speak with you, Miss York?' he said heavily. 'I believe you were first on the scene yesterday at the very upsetting death of a local widow...'

'You don't need to talk like an Edwardian chaperone, Des.' I sighed. 'You know I was, and if I can't write about it myself, I'll happily tell you. But I want to ask Mr Gorringe if I can...'

'Ah,' he said. 'The boss was in earlier. He asked me to do the splash.'

'So I'm not allowed to write about it?'

'Not when you might be the chief witness in court,' said Des.

That hadn't occurred to me. My heart sank.

'Then I suppose we can chat, if you'll buy me a ham sandwich at the Cona Café. If it's still standing.'

'Cheap at the price,' he said. 'You poor old dear.'

As it seemed ludicrous to write about Joseph without any answers on what had happened to Pamela, I spent the morning working on the next obituary, of a man who had worked his way up from ten-year-old shoe-polisher in St Ann's Passage to business owner. He had owned a chain of grocer's shops, and his widowed wife described him affectionately as 'a man of simple tastes. He liked egg and bacon for breakfast every day, and a meat pie for lunch.'

I thought of Lillian's very different tone, describing Mrs Novak's plain tastes. Then I thought about the silk couch, and the sticky, crimson carpet, and felt suddenly faint.

'Bad oyster?' said Desmond cheerfully, appearing by my desk again.

'No. Any news?'

He shrugged. 'Not found a weapon. A neighbour thought she might have seen a car, but then again, she might not. No tracks because of the snow. No screams or anything.'

'So I'm not the chief suspect?'

'Seems not. I will, though, have your golden memories of the murder scene in the paper later.'

'Marvellous.'

I returned to the grocer's obituary, trying to blot out the images from my mind. I remembered that tonight I was going to the cinema with Charles. Perhaps we'd go out for supper afterwards.

Would Joseph's death have an effect on his income? I wondered. It seemed unlikely. I had no idea how he funded his life, but I assumed it was all inherited from his father, the late, art-loving Captain Emerson.

I was in the lobby, waiting for Desmond to stand me the promised ham sandwich and pump me for information, when a familiar figure appeared.

'Edie!' said Arnold. 'I'm back on duty, was just passing. Have you got a moment?'

'Of course.' I felt like a Judas.

'It's just... some police fellers have been round. Mum was a bit upset,' he added, 'but I wanted to let you know it's OK, I'd have done the same.'

'The same...?'

'Oh, come now,' he said. 'I know it was you who told them because you'd told me you were going to see Mrs Novak. Let's face it, you don't know me all that well – how would you know I didn't shut the dog away upstairs and stab her to death?'

'I'm so sorry,' I said. 'I just thought I should mention anyone who—'

'Honestly, it's fine,' he said. 'No hard feelings. I was at work all morning, as it happened, so – there's plenty of dead bodies that can vouch for me.' He laughed uneasily.

I smiled, and in a rush of apology, said, 'Look, perhaps we could all go dancing again next weekend – you and Lou, and me and Annie... as friends,' I added lamely. I regretted it as soon as I'd said it.

'Yes, why not,' said Arnold. 'I'll check my packed social diary and let you know.' I waved him off, far too enthusiastically, as Desmond huffed into the lobby, ramming his hat on. He was smoking his pipe and looked rather like Winston Churchill in shape.

I imagined the comparison would please him.

We walked to the café, which had brown paper over the windows and sandbags piled outside. It was packed and steamy, full of recovery workers, ARP wardens, fire wardens – it seemed the city had been taken over entirely by the emergency services.

We settled at a table at the back, and a waitress took our order. 'No ham,' she said. 'Cheese or tinned sardines only today. Blame Hitler.'

We ordered two rounds of cheese sandwiches, and a rather dense-looking bun each with our tea.

'Des,' I said. 'The police briefing you had this morning – I need to know something.'

'Go on.'

'Did they mention a dog?' I asked.

He stared at me through curls of smoke. 'What dog?'

'Mrs Novak's dog,' I said. 'It was shut away upstairs.'

He whistled through his teeth. 'What a nutter,' he said. 'A woman's one thing, but shutting away a defenceless pet...'

I ignored that. 'Why wouldn't they tell you that?' I asked.

'Oh, they often keep a detail back,' he said knowledgeably. 'There was one murder when I was over in Yorkshire, the lass's teeth had all been...' he trailed off as our sandwiches arrived. 'Anyway, they didn't refer to it. So if they get a confession, or a suspect mentions it, they know they've got the right man.'

'Did I tell you about the dog this morning?' I couldn't remember.

'Nope. This is news to me.'

But, I thought, it hadn't been news to Arnold.

'Thanks,' I said, and put my sandwich down, cold and afraid.

. . .

Back at the office, Mr Gorringe beckoned me aside. He looked exhausted, and I wondered what sort of Christmas he'd managed to have, or if he'd been in the office, sleeping under the desk.

'This development rather alters matters, Miss York,' he said, pushing his glasses up his nose with one long finger. 'We can hardly run a glowing obituary which ignores the subsequent crime.'

I felt my career slipping away as he spoke. I was braced for him to say, 'So I feel you'd be of greater use returning to your secretarial post.'

Instead, he went on, 'And, of course, until your own status is formally resolved, we cannot run anything. However, I'd like you to speak to Mrs Emerson again. Not only can you perhaps uncover more useful information about Mr Novak, it would also be salutary to find out more about this woman. Alibi or no alibi.'

'You don't think she's a suspect?'

He regarded me. 'In times of war, Edie, the normal rules do not apply. Innocent until proven guilty is a luxury of belief limited to peacetime.'

This was as close to crime reporting as I'd get, I decided – and it meant I'd be able to see Lillian again.

The switchboard found the number for me, and she answered on the first ring, as if she were waiting for a call.

'Didsbury five-six-three,' she said. 'Oh, it's you.' I felt a dart of fear. Had Charles told her that we were seeing each other? Perhaps she thought I was much too common for him – and, of course, she'd be right.

'I believe Charles told you about what happened to Mrs Novak?' I said. The first evening papers would be rolling off the presses now, with further details and my quotes, and I wanted to speak to her before she saw them, and realised that she might be the next victim.

'Oh yes,' she said. 'Good job I'd had a sociable morning, or they'd have put me in the frame, I expect. The black widow strikes again.' She laughed rather grimly.

'So you're definitely not a suspect?'

'Apparently not,' she said haughtily.

'It must have been a shock,' I ventured.

'Of course it was. The worry, of course, is that the killer's someone with a grudge against Joseph. In which case...' She left the sentence hanging in the air.

'Oh, I'm sure not,' I said feebly, given that I'd had the very same thought.

'Could I nip along and see you again?' I asked. 'I've no idea what's going on, but I'd like to hear what you think.'

'I'm not a detective, darling. To tell you the truth, though, I'm rather rattled staying here by myself today, waiting for a grudge-bearing killer to turn up, so I'm sure I could stand you a coffee.'

An hour later, I walked into the Palm Court at the Midland to find her already sitting at a table, examining her face in a gold compact. She had ordered coffee in a silver pot with a tiny jug of cream and a bowl of sugar lumps. The contrast between the hushed elegance here and the crashing cutlery and chipped pottery cups at the Cona made me wonder if I should tell Lou that I'd had a conversation about the dog with Arnold. Perhaps, I thought ghoulishly, he had developed an obsession with death through working in the morgue.

'Shall you be joining me at any stage?' asked Lillian. I'd been staring into space, but it must have looked as though I was admiring myself in the big curved wall mirrors.

She was smiling. She had a very pretty face when she smiled; it was easy to see that she would have been exquisite as a young woman, with her dark eyes and sleek black hair.

Charles's fair colouring must have come from his war-hero father. I imagined a straight-backed captain, hair slicked back under his cap, being waved onto the train, unaware that he'd never see his little boy again.

'I'm so sorry,' I said. 'I was thinking about yesterday. It was such a shock...'

'I can imagine,' said Lillian. 'The poor woman. I never really thought about her, and now she's dead, like some horrible warning.'

'Warning?' I said. I took a sip of the coffee. It was delicious. How lovely to be Lillian, drifting through the nicest restaurants, able to drink the best coffee, surrounded by beauty. I felt like a matted, feral kitten beside a tiger in its prime.

'Look, Edie,' she said. 'Joseph was an awfully rich man once he took over the factory. Mrs Novak would have inherited a lot of money. I wonder if there's anyone else named in the will.' She looked at my blank face.

'Keep up, darling. If she's out of the picture, then maybe the money goes to them, do you see?'

'Weren't you in the will then?' I asked.

She shook her head and pushed a little almond biscuit away from her. I was desperate to eat it.

'No,' she said. 'I was left more than enough by Captain Emerson. He was from a very good family, so...' She spread her hands out as if to say 'there we are'.

'Joseph had to leave behind everything he owned in Germany when he fled,' she added. 'But I helped him, of course, when he arrived, until he was back on his feet.'

She took a sip of coffee. 'Money was never a quarrel between us. Our connection was of the mind, it was nothing to do with finances. He would buy me trinkets sometimes, but I never thought of the cost.'

Of course, Lou was probably knee-deep in the will already, interviewing solicitors and shouting at underlings. It hadn't seemed as if Joseph had anyone else in his life, though, I thought – who would he leave his money to, other than his wife, his mistress or Charles?

Then I thought of Edward Turnbull. The man who needed money more than anyone, who had been thwarted by Joseph's death. Suppose his wife, Winifred, believed Edward's death was Mrs Novak's fault, for not giving them the money they needed? What if she'd sent her thug of a brother round to demand the money and Mrs Novak had refused... I thought again of his cold, assessing eyes on me, and imagined him standing over Pamela, a knife in his meaty hand.

'Edie, are you quite all right?' Lillian asked. 'You look rather pale.'

'I've just had a thought,' I said, absently picking up the almond biscuit and eating it.

I told her about Edward Turnbull.

'Heavens,' she said. 'As I told you before, I really can't imagine how he would be connected to Joseph – you say he gave him a little painting?'

'Apparently. Lillian...' I was unsure how to frame the question.

'Yes?' She filled her coffee cup again. I noticed she didn't refill mine.

'I know this is probably ridiculous, but do you think there's any chance at all that Joseph... well, could he have been seeing someone else? I mean, would it be possible that he'd had an affair with Winifred Turnbull, and Edward Turnbull was demanding money to keep quiet, and send her away to America?' Even as I said it, I saw an image of wispy, unhappy Winifred Turnbull beside Lillian, like a ghost beside the living, and the words died on my lips.

Lillian smiled tightly. 'That's rather "cheap novelette", isn't it?' she said. 'I think I would have known if Joseph had romantic interests elsewhere. Besides, he only arrived here a few years ago and married Pamela.'

'I'm sorry,' I said. 'You're right, it's very far-fetched.'

She shrugged, and the pin on her brooch must have loosened, because it clattered to the floor. I scrambled beneath the table, banging my head, to retrieve it for her.

I'd never held diamonds before. It was in the shape of a flower, but as it caught the light, it glittered like something alive, ancient crystals of frozen light trapped inside the stone.

'It's so beautiful,' I said, handing it back to her to pin on her green silk suit jacket.

'A present from Joseph, of course,' she said. 'Mrs Novak didn't like diamonds. A plain pearl strand was more her style,' she said scornfully.

I wondered how she would manage now her house was gone, her paintings and furs – I was stabbed with pity for all she'd lost, and here I was, quizzing her about my ludicrous theories.

'How will you cope?' I blurted. I didn't know why I cared about Lillian so much; I barely knew her. But she was potentially my future mother-in-law, and there was something about her that I found mesmerising – her confidence, perhaps, or her determination.

'Cope?'

The waitress loomed, proffering menus. I was starving, but Lillian waved them away.

'I just mean... will you be able to rebuild your house? It's so dreadful that you've lost so much...'

'I'm perfectly all right, thank you,' she said, as if a door-step gypsy was trying to foist clothes pegs on her. She softened. 'Look, I'm fine. I have my ways,' she added. 'Edie, is the obituary still going ahead?'

I nodded. 'Of course – but it's been delayed, in case there are developments in the murder investigation.'

'Oh,' she said irritably. 'Well, when it does go in, you will include everything we discussed, won't you?'

'Oh yes,' I began. 'I want to make sure of that...' I found myself reassuring her, when I was meant to be finding out where she'd been yesterday.

'Mrs Emerson,' I said, 'I'm so sorry to ask, but my editor needs me to be perfectly certain of my sources. Could I just ask about where you were yesterday morning?'

'I believe Charles has already told you that,' she said coldly. 'I was chatting to him, as I'm staying there thanks to my own house being bombed to smithereens, then I spoke with Thelma, who lives downstairs – it was Boxing Day, and Charles and I went to try and salvage anything we could from my house. I'm certain somebody would have seen the car there. Oh, and there was an ARP warden later, silly little man, hectoring away about curtains like a clockwork toy...'

I nodded. 'Did the police speak to you?'

'Oh well, I don't count that,' she said. 'Yes, I suppose they asked a few questions, but of course, Charles and Thelma and the neighbours were able to back me up, so who cares whether I was in the bath or waltzing with the King of Persia?'

She threw three shillings on the table. 'Look, darling, I have to rush. Let me know when it goes in, won't you? And I believe you're seeing Charles tonight? He's taking you to the pictures, isn't he?'

I felt obscurely flattered that he'd told Lillian about our plans.

'Yes,' I said. 'We're going to see Joan Fontaine in—'

'How lovely,' she said. 'Have fun.' She strode out of the restaurant. The waitress came back with her pen poised.

'Nothing, thank you,' I said, and she wandered off. I hurried back to the office, feeling as if I'd just been given the elbow.

. . .

I rang Lou. I couldn't concentrate without knowing if there'd been any developments, and Desmond hadn't returned. He was probably in the pub, blowing clouds of smoke in the centre of a clutch of policemen.

'Brennan,' Lou said briskly. 'Oh, it's you.' He was the second person to say that in one day. It would have been nice to hear someone say, 'Edie! How lovely!'

'If you're ringing up to ask who the murderer is, I'm afraid that's not been magically revealed to me yet,' he said.

'No, actually, I'm not,' I snapped. He had an exceptional ability to turn me into a bad-tempered fourteen-year-old.

'Then while a flirtatious chit-chat leading to a *cinq à sept* Parisian liaison at the Midland would be delightful, I'm extremely bloody busy.'

'Lou!' I shouted. 'I have something I should tell you. It might be useful.'

'Go on,' he said. He clearly had a cigarette clamped between his teeth.

I explained my theory about Winifred Turnbull.

'Winifred Turnbull?' he said. 'The one Arnold knows, who was meant to go to America before Edward was...'

'Yes, but perhaps her brother wanted to try and get the money...' I trailed off. Lillian was right – it did sound ridiculous. And besides, if Edward's death wasn't an accident, why would he kill his own brother-in-law?

'I'll look into it,' he said, in a tone which meant he wouldn't. 'Cheerio.'

'Hold on!' I said.

'Yes?' he asked with exaggerated patience.

'It's – this sounds silly,' I said. 'But the only other person who knew I was going to see Mrs Novak yesterday was Arnold.'

'Arnold?'

'Our Arnold. Mortuary Arnold.'

'What...' There was a pause. 'He's already been questioned,

thanks to you. And besides, are you really suggesting that my funny, kindly pal Arnold has a mysterious, long-standing grudge against Pamela Novak, so he relentlessly pumped you for information and then crept round there and stabbed her to death? What with, his nail clippers?'

Now Lou was annoyed with me too. *Add him to the list*, I thought.

'You may as well write the obit, though,' he added. 'With no sign of a suspect, I can't see it being used as evidence as long as you don't mention the murder in it.'

I was relieved for myself, of course – and almost more so for Lillian. Now, at least, I could write the obituary, although facts were still thin on the ground.

I didn't stop thinking about the murder until I was at the cinema with Charles, and Joan Fontaine had moved to Manderley with Maxim de Winter, feeling haunted by Rebecca. The idea of his lost wife reminded me a little of Lillian – bewitching and imperious, in equal measure.

I greatly enjoyed it, but the vast majority of my attention was focussed on the shadowy presence beside me of Charles, who was gently holding my hand. I felt that he would never say, 'Oh, it's you.'

Afterwards, Charles said, 'Look, would you like a spot of supper? I've plenty of bacon and eggs in – not quite the Midland, I know, but it might fill a hole. And, of course, Mother will be there.'

I was concerned that I'd burned my bridges with Lillian, but I couldn't bear to turn him down. Besides, bacon had just been rationed, and I didn't know when I'd next see a slice.

CHAPTER ELEVEN

Charles let us in, and I thought I'd better keep my voice down in case his formidable landlady was already in bed, but as we climbed the stairs leading from the polished hall, a voice called 'Charles? Is that you?'

A woman poked her head over the banister and looked down. She had long red hair in a victory roll bigger than a Bath bun, crimson lips, and her face was like a very pretty Pekinese dog – squashed and petulant.

'Oh hullo, Thelma,' said Charles, stopping on the stair above me. 'I thought you were out.'

'I thought you weren't in tonight,' she said. There was a pause.

'This is Edie,' he said. 'My new girlfriend.'

I tried to suppress the glow of pride.

'Do you live here too?' I asked her, from my awkward spot on the stairs.

'Yes,' she said. 'On the first floor. It's my house.' I thought she must mean it belonged to her parents, but Charles interrupted.

'Thel's a glittering society heiress, aren't you, dear?'

Slowly, it dawned on me that this was the landlady he'd casually referred to. An attractive woman in her mid-twenties, slinking about in cocktail dresses, emerging from the bathroom in a silk negligee. I'd assumed she was a dumpy type in her fifties, with a headscarf firmly tied under her chin and warning notices everywhere.

'Since I was tragically orphaned, yes,' she said. 'I say, I'm listening to the gramophone, do you want to join?'

It was clearly an invitation aimed at Charles, rather than me. To my relief, he shook his head. 'I think we'll just go to my quarters and drink fine wines,' he said. 'Not desperately in the mood for music after all that cinematic bother.'

'Suit yourself,' she said. 'Nice to meet you, Sadie,' and we carried on up the stairs to the top floor.

There was no sign of Lillian. 'Mother?' he called experimentally, but there was no reply, and it struck me that I might have given Charles the wrong idea by coming back to his flat alone.

'Sorry about old Hell's Thels,' he said, clinking about in the drinks cabinet once I was safely on the couch. I could hear the distant sound of Louis Jordan And His Tympany Five drifting up the stairs. 'She's a bit of a Cerberus.'

'A...?'

'Where's your Greek, child? Three-headed dog, mouth of hell. Surely you did your myths at school?'

'Not really,' I said. 'It wasn't that kind of school.'

'What kind was it?'

'Oh, you know... corporation, everything painted that murky municipal green, lads fighting in the playground; everyone left at fourteen to get a job...' I was uncomfortable, outlining exactly how different our lives had been. 'Look, are you hungry?' I said. 'Shall I make a sandwich for us?' I went towards the kitchen, wondering if he had any of the bacon he'd mentioned.

'No, don't,' he said, standing up with two glasses in his hands. 'Sorry, darling, let's just have a drink and a smooch. I don't feel like eating now.'

I wondered if anyone in Charles's family ever did. But I subsided onto the couch beside him and took the glass of whisky he offered. And as he reached for me, I tried not to think about the fury I'd seen in Thelma's eyes when she saw me coming up the stairs behind him.

By ten, we had kissed, chatted, and he'd finally fried some bacon and eggs. I tried not to wolf it down, but it was tricky – I hadn't tasted anything so wonderfully normal in months.

'However did you—' I began.

'Oh, the daily sorts all the food out,' he said vaguely. 'She's awfully good.'

Charles offered to drive me home, but I insisted on getting the bus. I didn't want to be a nuisance, and I was worried about his petrol ration.

'Shouldn't your mother be back by now?' I asked him.

'Oh, she'll be all right,' he said. 'She's probably back at her house again, seeing what she can salvage.'

'But it's dark.'

'Mother is like a cockroach,' Charles said. 'She survives. You don't need to worry, dear Edie.'

I was pleasantly distracted by the 'dear', and the frantic jitterbugging from Thelma's floor seemed to have stopped. Charles saw me onto the bus with a brief kiss, and I rattled off through the blackout, thinking moonily about him. I got off at Daisy Bank road, round the corner – it was only a short walk home, but I'd forgotten my torch and after yesterday, I felt strangely jumpy. I edged along walls, palming gateposts as I passed to reassure myself, when I heard footsteps behind me.

I assumed they would pass by, so I stopped and cleared my throat to let whoever it was know I was there, but they stopped too. I thought perhaps they'd misunderstood, or were checking the time, and I carried on again – and so did they.

My heart sped up. Home was another long street away, and I cursed my anxious politeness. I could have simply got a lift, and now I was stranded in the dark with a stranger. I could tell by the steady tread that it was a man, and I hoped it was an ARP warden, trying to teach me a lesson about being out after dark. I'd give him a piece of my mind if so.

I risked a glance behind me, but the man's torch was pointed downwards. I could make out a medium build, a coat and hat, but that was all. It was not a uniform, I could tell that much.

I scuttled on, the cold striking through my shoe soles, and I heard his steps speed up too. My breath came in brief gasps. I turned into our road, wondering if I should scream, anticipating a leather palm slapped across my mouth, a struggle – and then I realised that it could be Mrs Novak's killer who was following me, about to dispatch me in the same way.

Fear coursed through me, a prickling rush over my skin. I clamped my hand onto the next gatepost and turned up the path. Whoever lived there, I thought, they were unlikely to be a murderer. I knocked on the door, aware of a bulky shadow hovering at the garden wall.

I was getting someone out of bed, I thought, sick with panic, but then someone shouted, 'I'm coming, Cecil!' The door opened a crack and a young woman's face appeared. She was dressed in her neat grey WVS uniform.

'Oh!' she said. 'I thought you were the warden.'

'I'm so sorry,' I gabbled, 'I think I'm being followed – I only live down the road, but he was behind me and I thought...'

'Oh, my dear child,' she said. 'Come on in, do. I'm Clara. I was just getting ready for my shift. Mum and Dad are upstairs, but we shan't disturb them in the snug.' She led me through to a warmly lit little room with a flowered couch and a radiogram.

There were framed family photographs on the walls and piles of dog-eared books about Egypt on the desk. My heart began to slow.

'Thank you so much,' I said. 'You may have saved my life. Perhaps I'm just being silly, but he kept stopping whenever I did.'

'I must say, you're out alone awfully late,' said Clara. 'Were you at work?'

'I was with my... young man,' I said.

'Golly,' she said. 'He could have seen you home, surely!' I wondered if she was right. Perhaps Charles should have insisted. I had no idea what was normal.

'Look, I need to set off,' she said. Clara whisked about, gathering keys and her gas mask.

'I'll walk you home, and he won't dare try anything with two of us.'

My heart sped up again as we set off, this time with our way illuminated by Clara's torch.

She tucked my hand comfortingly into the crook of her elbow. There was nobody by the wall as we turned onto the pavement.

'He was here,' I said. 'He was watching. I promise I'm not making it up.'

'Why on earth would you make it up?' she asked briskly. 'Look, pretty horrid things have happened to women in the blackout, you know. You need to take better care. Men aren't always... chivalrous.'

I appreciated her warning, and though she was right, I couldn't think how to explain that I had genuine cause to worry about being murdered. I would tell Lou, I thought, though what good would that do, with my description of 'a medium-sized man in a hat and coat'? I could hear him now, saying, 'I'll keep an eye out for all the men in Manchester, shall I?'

'This is my house,' I told her, and she walked me right to the door, sweeping her torch into the shrubs by the steps.

'Is there somebody in?' she asked.

'Yes, my flatmate, Annie.'

'Oh, I know Annie!' Clara said. 'Awfully pretty, the little nurse?'

'Yes! She's my oldest friend,' I added proudly.

'Good,' said Clara. 'You'll need one, with your hopeless boyfriend.'

I laughed. 'Will you be all right on your own?'

'I'd jolly well better be,' she said. 'Otherwise we'll be walking each other to and fro forever.'

I thanked her profusely, and she brushed away my gratitude. 'Just take care in future,' she said gruffly. 'I expect I shall see you anon.'

I locked the door behind me and ran upstairs, desperate to see Annie. I didn't expect to find her bent over a letter, her shoulders shaking.

'Oh God, what's wrong?' I thought of her kind mum, her funny, teasing brothers.

'It's Pete,' she wailed. 'He's finally written and it's taken ages to get here, and he says...' She was shaken by a fresh storm of tears. 'He says that "under the circumstances" we should "reconsider" and... an...' She thrust the blue airmail letter at me and collapsed sideways, holding a hanky to her face.

With one arm round her shoulders, I scanned what he'd written: *...understand you have cooled towards me... a lovely girl such as yourself deserves a fellow who's certain of his future... if there is someone else, I shall endeavour to understand...*

'Annie! You told him it was over! He thinks you've gone off him!'

'Well, I have,' she said, scrubbing at her eyes. 'But now I've got nobody!'

I felt laughter building inside me, and struggled desperately to contain it.

'What about Lou?' I said, trying to cheer her up. 'He's good-looking if you like that sort of thing.'

'Oh no.' She shook her head, sniffing. 'He's not my type, too tall and bossy and reminds me of Pete. And he's not the type to be keen on me.'

'Why would he not be keen?' I asked, surprised. Generally, Annie cut a swathe through any gathering that included men. One toss of her flaxen curls and they were all competing to light her cigarettes and buy her drinks, while I was trampled underfoot in the rush. To her credit, she barely noticed.

'Oh,' Annie said, 'I have the impression he likes someone else.' She perked up a little. 'But there *is* Arnold...'

'Arnold?' I was staggered. In all the years I'd known Annie, I should never have imagined her with a quiet mortician. Pete had been cocky, the life and soul, full of certainty about himself and his opinions. I hadn't taken to him, but Annie was dazzled by his blue eyes, his uniform and his height. If I was being entirely honest with myself, I was quite pleased at this turn of events – I had long dreaded being Annie's lumpen bridesmaid while she floated down the aisle towards a man who didn't deserve her, who dismissed her opinions because she was 'a silly hen' and 'playing the giddy goat' when she was simply happy. But Arnold – the man who was now high on my 'possible suspects' list?

'I didn't think he'd be your sort,' I said.

'Oh, I've never been out with a redhead!' she said. 'They're supposed to be quite passionate, aren't they? All fire and fury!' She laughed, and I was glad she'd cheered up. 'Besides, he's quite a good dancer,' she added, 'and they're pretty thin on the ground, I can tell you. At the hospital dance, I had my toes stepped on so many times I felt like admitting myself to the acute ward.'

'I'd be careful with Arnold,' I said awkwardly. I didn't want to share my fears with her, they sounded so overwrought. 'We don't know him very well...'

'All the more reason to get to know him better then,' she said. 'He makes me laugh, and that's worth something these days.'

She crumpled Pete's letter and threw it into the fire, where it flamed and disintegrated to ash. 'Good riddance to you, mister,' she muttered. 'Anyway, Edie, my New Year's resolution is to have fun. I'm not marrying anyone, so I may as well enjoy myself before we're all blown up in our beds.'

'I know,' I said. 'But just be sensible, don't get carried away...'

'In what way do I appear to be carried away?' she asked quite reasonably. 'I'm sitting on the couch with a cup of tea – I'm hardly dancing the Lindy Hop on the town hall steps.'

'Sorry,' I said. 'I just don't want you to get hurt...'

'By Arnold?' She laughed. 'He wouldn't harm a caterpillar. Lou, on the other hand... there's dark depths in that one.'

'Why do you say that?' I stretched my feet out towards the grate and took a sip of her tea. Sometimes, I thought, I enjoyed chatting to Annie about men much more than I enjoyed actually meeting them.

'Troubled,' she said. 'I can sense it. My mum's a bit psychic, you know. She had a cold prickle down her spine when Auntie Pearl took ill, and I think I've inherited a bit of it.'

I snorted. 'Come on. "*A dark stranger has news from overseas...*" You don't believe in all that, surely?'

'You sound just like Lou sometimes,' she said crossly. 'Anyway,' – she stretched and rotated her ankles – 'work calls. Again. Off I go, a spinster of this parish, dedicated only to aiding the sick and injured.'

I threw a cushion at her. 'Better invite Arnold to the dance then,' I said.

I ignored my doubts. Lou would surely never be friends with someone who could kill – and he seemed to trust Arnold. As for me, I would only ever be the aunt type, I had long thought, wedded to my career, turning up at Annie's house occasionally to make awkward small talk with adorable five-year-olds. Though perhaps now I'd met Charles, I'd be looking at a different sort of future altogether.

I did another shift at the canteen on Sunday, making sure I took my torch and walked home as fast as possible afterwards. One woman cried on my shoulder. She said her house had been bombed, but she couldn't get a reply from anyone – she had even sent a telegram to the town hall. She and her three children were sleeping on a neighbour's floor, and her husband was 'serving away' in the navy, and had no idea what had happened. 'And you see, miss, if he writes, I shan't get his letters – and he won't get mine for an age, and I don't know what to do.'

I felt utterly helpless, and wondered if I should be doing something more useful. Later, I saw her over by the cakes, reading a newspaper with a thick, pot mug of tea before her, and told myself that news still mattered. How else could we get through the war, unless we all knew what was happening in our city and beyond? Or so I had to believe, at least.

There was no news from Lou about the murder investigation. That evening, Annie and I were at home when the siren wailed, and we rushed down to the cellar, with knitting and torches. 'I can't face getting in that thing,' said Annie, pointing at the Morrison. 'Can you? It's like being a guinea pig in a cage.'

I thought of Mrs Pelham. 'Perhaps we might start going to the public shelter,' I said. 'It may be better protection.'

'Oh Lord, no,' said Annie. 'All the people, and the dreadful smells – I get enough unwashed bodies at the hospital, thanks, I don't need to spend the night with them.'

The all-clear sounded after two alarming hours of distant whistling and banging, and we returned to our beds. It wasn't until the next morning, when I arrived at the office, that the news broke.

'Heard the latest?' asked Des, smoking his way through the office like an express train as usual. He stopped by my desk. 'That woman of yours was badly hurt in the raid. She's in hospital.'

For a moment I thought he meant Lillian, and I felt light-headed.

'Good heavens, you've gone quite white, my dear,' he said. 'I thought you'd only met Mrs Turnbull the once.'

'Mrs Turnbull?'

'On her way to the shelter,' he said. 'Couple of others killed on the street too. Irony is, the house is fine, apparently. If she'd just stayed at home...' He shook his head. 'An incendiary in a front garden. She's in Withington Hospital, I heard, but I don't know what her chances are.'

Edward had been right, after all. His beloved Winifred had been hurt, trying to stay safe. I'd intended to go back and see her anyway. Perhaps this was providence. The trams still weren't running, of course, but there was a bus every hour. I picked my way through the rubble and waited.

The bus arrived too early for visiting time, so I hung about outside the hospital, like a stage-door Johnny, watching people coming and going. It was profoundly depressing – all these lives, people who had fallen in love and had affairs that seemed like the end of the world when they ended, and longed for promotion and gave birth and celebrated and sat by other sick beds praying for good news, and it all came down to an iron truckle bed and a nurse saying, 'It won't be long now.' It made me wonder what the point was of all the thrusting and hoping, the clambering up the ant heap, when on the other side it was just a slow decline towards decay and forgetting.

'Cheery sort, aren't you?' Suki used to say to me at the home, when I gave voice to this sort of thing. 'Well, it isn't ever going to be worse than this. So that's something to look forward to, at least.'

I tried not to think about Suki too often. She was lost to me, ever since we'd gone our separate ways at sixteen. I remembered her saying, 'It's all right for you, Edie,' as she picked up her cardboard suitcase, and I remembered the stiffness of her back as she walked away down the wet street, off to get married to a cruel and ignorant man, though she still seemed like a child. If only I had replied, or gone after her, or shouted that I loved her and had meant well. *Too late*, I thought. The saddest two words in the English language.

Finally, just before noon, I went inside and located Ward Four. At the door, a harassed nurse was arguing with a very old man who looked like a deflated balloon inside his hospital gown.

'You can't go home, Mister Hughes,' she kept saying. 'You need to be looked after, and your house was bombed.'

He was mumbling confusedly about his wife, and he looked desperately sad. I wondered if it would be easier in some ways to go out young, in a blaze of glory, than endure that sort of miserable withering.

So by the time I found Winifred's bed, I was already feeling utterly depressed. I'd never have known it was her. One broken leg was in a cast and she was wrapped in bandages. Only her eyes, nose and mouth were visible, and the hand lying on the sheet was badly burned.

'Who are you?' she said. Her voice came out in a rasp, nails on sandpaper. I felt a terrible urge to run, skittering down the polished parquet and out through the doors, away from the hospital smell and the miasma of imminent death that hung over everything. I made myself stay, hovering by the bed, clutching my handbag like a duchess on an official visit.

'I'm Edie York,' I said. 'You probably don't remember, but I came to see you—'

'Oh, I remember,' she creaked. I looked round for a nurse, wondering about getting her some water. Her breathing was like a rusty gate swinging in a breeze.

'Mrs Turnbull,' I said. 'I'm so very sorry about what's happened.'

'Maybe best,' she wheezed. 'Be with Ed.'

'No, no,' I insisted, a jolly idiot. 'You'll recover, of course you will!'

'No,' she breathed. 'Too much pain.'

There was a pause. 'What you want?' she managed.

I wanted to vanish, and take my shame somewhere dark and forgiving, but I steeled myself.

'I just wanted to see if you could possibly remember anything at all about Joseph Novak. Because, you see, his wife Pamela was killed. And I'm trying to find out who' – my British sensibilities were urging me to say something gentle and unthreatening like 'caused the trouble', but I ignored them – 'murdered her.'

'I saw,' Winifred croaked. 'In the paper. Why'd I know?'

I subsided into the chair by her bed, laying my handbag on the metal cabinet.

A women coughed violently in the next bed, a demonic, sulphurous spluttering, and I waited for it to abate before I said, 'I believe your husband knew Mr Novak. Pamela's husband.'

She turned watery eyes to me. 'Edward fought in Spain, you know.' Her breath sawed and whistled.

'I didn't know.'

'Yes. Against Franco, of course... he was... good man.' She trailed off wistfully.

'Was Mr Novak in Spain too?'

'No, no.' She shook her head, and it set off a burst of coughing. She gasped and choked, her reddened eyes bulging, and I was convinced she was about to die in front of me. I didn't want to be the only witness to another death within the week.

I scanned the ward, frantically, for a nurse. A girl in uniform eventually strolled up in response to my wild beckoning and calling. She looked about twelve.

'I think visiting time is over,' she said to me. 'Mrs Turnbull is very badly injured.'

'I can see,' I said. I felt desperate. 'Look, Winifred, very quickly – you were talking about Spain,' I said. 'Who did Edward know there?'

She finally recovered her breath. 'Nobody...' she breathed. Her eyes were closed.

'I did say, miss, visiting hours are over,' said the nurse, her words drowned by the ringing bell. 'See,' she added rather triumphantly. 'I'll have to ask you to leave.'

'Did Edward teach Joseph English?' I asked in a rush. 'Is that how they met?'

Winifred did not reply. The nurse was preparing an injection. 'I won't tell you again without calling Matron,' she said.

As she spoke, I heard heavy footsteps behind me and turned, feeling a sense of dread.

Dennis stood at the foot of the iron bed.

'You,' he said in a low hiss. 'Why are you always here? What do you want with our Winifred? She's at death's door and you're hovering like a ghoul at the bloody feast.'

'I was just leaving...' I began. I felt queasy with fright as he glared at me.

'Never mind bloody leaving,' he said. 'You shouldn't be here at all. Trying to get money out of her, is that it? You reporters, you disgust me,' he spat.

'Money? No!' I cried. 'I just want to try and find out who killed Mrs Nov—'

'And that has nothing to do with my sister!' he growled. 'Out! Before I throw you out. And don't let me see your bloody face again.'

The nurse stood by impassively, her cap streamers down her back like the wings of an avenging angel.

'I'm going,' I said quietly. 'I'm sorry.'

I left, feeling his furious gaze on me all the way down the ward. When the double doors swung closed behind me, sealing all the stale, ill, hospital air inside, I took a breath so huge I thought my lungs would burst. There were benches in the chilly hospital garden opposite, and people in wheelchairs, their faces turned towards the weak sun like grateful turtles. One was being pushed by a girl around my own age, who was wearing an WAAF uniform and looking bored. Perhaps after flying planes to their bases, trudging round a barren hospital garden was not very exciting.

Looking at her, it occurred to me that Winifred had a daughter, Sylvia – and that there was a slim chance she'd be on her way home.

Intruding on yet another person's grief and worry was becoming second nature by now, and the following morning I set off on the long walk to the Turnbulls' house again, determined to find an answer that would begin to unravel the entire mystery.

As I approached the step, it occurred to me that Dennis might be there, which was an alarming thought as I rang the bell. I expected that within ten seconds I'd be on my way, with a vicious flea in my ear. I looked upwards, in the direction from which I expected Dennis's angry, bereaved face to appear. Though perhaps I could slip in a couple of revealing questions, find out where he'd been on Boxing Day…

The woman who answered the door was smaller than me, about my age I guessed, with long, fair hair. She wore a flowered cotton dress with a Shetland jumper, thick lisle stockings and lace-up shoes, and she looked exhausted.

'Afternoon. Who are you?' she asked. Her accent was still Mancunian, but posher than her mother's.

'I'm...' I paused, wondering whether to come clean. 'Look, I'm a journalist,' I said. 'I write obituaries.'

'Oh, from the *Chronicle*?' she said. 'You'd better come in. I'm Sylvia, Winifred's daughter.'

I was so surprised by her welcoming tone that it wasn't until I was sitting on the couch in the stark little parlour that it became clear why she was so accepting.

'Mum died last night,' she said, and though it wasn't so surprising, a jolt of shock fizzed through me. 'Her injuries...' Sylvia added.

'I'm so very sorry,' I said.

'I assume you want to do an obituary of Mum,' she said. 'I still can't believe it. Uncle Dennis was here, but he's gone to see the vicar about the funeral. I'm not sure when I last slept,' she went on. 'Or ate.'

'You poor thing,' I said. 'Can I fetch something for you? I could make you some toast.' My culinary abilities petered out after that. 'I'm so sorry about your mother,' I added feebly.

'No, it's all right,' she said. I wasn't sure which of my comments she was answering.

'I just... I thought there'd be time to sort things out between us,' she said, as if she were talking to herself. 'I'm so busy in London, then we were evacuated to bloody Dorset the other week and I didn't imagine that living here, in the boring old suburbs, she'd be in danger.'

'Your dad, Edward...' I began.

'Oh no.' She shook her head. 'My dad isn't Edward.'

I looked blank.

'My real dad was a soldier,' she said. 'Corporal Freddie Brown. He was going to take us to live in the country, roses round the door, chickens on the farm... then he was shot two months before the end of the bloody war. And that was that,' she added bitterly. 'No more lovely life in the countryside with her real parents for Sylvia. Shy Edward Turnbull, who's held a candle for Winifred since they were little, steps in all noble, and marries her instead. And so I grew up here,' she said, indicating the small living room with its ticking clock, and the hectically coloured print of *The Hay Wain* over the fireplace.

'That's why I went to be a nanny,' she added. 'I love little children, and London, and it got me away from here. But now we've all just been evacuated to Dorset, it took me hours and hours to get back on the trains, and I had to leave Teddy and Jeannie with Mrs Harper, who runs the farm. I'll have to go straight back after the funeral. I feel bad enough as it is, and I promised Jeannie we'd help with the milking...'

She seemed far more troubled by the prospect of Jeannie missing dawn in the milking shed than by her mum's death.

'Didn't your mum miss you?' I asked.

She looked at the rug as if whole worlds were swirling inside its ordinary pattern.

'More that I didn't miss her,' she said quietly. 'Of course, I'm sorry she's died. I set off as soon as I got Uncle's telegram saying she'd been injured. But we weren't close.'

'Did you know about Edward?' I asked. 'About how he...?'

'Oh yes,' she said. 'Awful luck. I think they're trying to find out what happened – it was a horrible accident, of course.'

I didn't want to tell her that I'd been there. Or that I was beginning to think it hadn't been an accident at all. Lou was being cagey, but I knew that by now they must have looked at every gun in the platoon – and seemingly, none were a match.

'Look, would you like a whisky?' she asked. 'I hate drinking alone, and it seems the only sensible way to get through this. Then you can tell me what you need to know.'

I agreed, to be convivial. Despite her hardness, or perhaps

because of it, there was something about her that I liked. She seemed truthful.

She gave me a glass, filled with a tot so generous even Lou would have struggled to down it.

'So,' she said, folding herself into the chair opposite the couch, 'what do you want to know?'

I thought about Mr Gorringe, the obituary page waiting for me to fill it, Lillian, Mrs Novak, lying with her blood all over the carpet.

'I don't know exactly,' I said. 'I'm trying to solve a small mystery. It may have to do with your fa– I mean, with Edward Turnbull.'

She pulled a disgusted face. 'Him again,' she said.

'Was he unkind to you?'

I thought of Mr Pugh at the home.

'No, nothing terrible. He was all right, as wicked step-parents go.' She shrugged. 'But I was always in the way. He was besotted with my mother. I think she was his first and only love. How terribly romantic,' she added, gulping whisky.

'Your mother mentioned he went to Spain,' I said.

'Oh yes. He was very left-wing, believed in social justice, alms for the dispossessed, all that. He wanted to help, which I suppose was decent of him. But all I really remember of my childhood is him adoring her, like a lovesick swain.'

'That must have been odd for you,' I said.

She nodded. 'No one wants to play the gooseberry in their own home.'

'Did they have friends?'

'Well, neighbours, I suppose. Occasional drinks parties and that sort of thing. Edward had a society he went to every week after Spain.'

'A society?'

'Something to do with refugees. He taught them English, helped them with paperwork, that sort of thing. They used to come to the house sometimes, and Edward would see them in the front room. I was a bit scared of some of them. I'd have to answer the door and take their hat and coat.'

'Did you know their names?'

She thought for a moment. 'I didn't really know any of them. They were sad people, who didn't have anything. Edward always wanted to help people, always going on about oppressive governments and fascism.'

She drained her whisky. 'Top-up?' she said, but mine was still half-full. She went to the kitchen and came back waving the bottle. 'May as well,' she said. 'Can't do this on nanny duty.'

She splashed more into her glass. She must be getting quite drunk, I thought.

'Sylvia,' I said, 'do you remember a German Jewish man called Joseph Novak? Tall, blonde, quite handsome, in his late forties when you would have met him?'

'Novak,' she said, considering. 'It was mainly Spanish people or Russians who came, but hang on,' she closed her eyes. 'There was a tall man, I think – blonde and about that age. He was handsome. I thought he was Russian.'

'Did he become friends with Edward?' I asked. 'I wonder, because before Joseph died, recently, Edward wrote to him about the money he needed to send you and your mum to America.'

She looked startled. 'Money?' Sylvia said. 'I don't think there was any money, other than Edward's teaching wages. It would have been impossible to send us, even if I'd wanted to go.'

'That's why I wonder what you remember. Whether they had any business dealings. Or a friendship. No one else seems to know anything about him. Apparently, he gave Edward a painting...'

My heart was pounding so loudly I felt she must be able to hear it. She looked into her whisky, then lifted it to her nose and inhaled it. 'What a comfort drink can be,' she said. 'There might have been one thing, actually,' she added. 'I do remember something about a painting.'

'Go on.'

'It's just... I might have got this all wrong – it was quite a while ago.'

I nodded. 'It doesn't matter. Please, tell me what you remember.'

'Well, I think that after the lessons, this man said he wanted to pay. And Edward said no, it was free, to help him, but the man didn't want charity. I remember now, because most of them were so grateful to have something for nothing, but I suppose this one must have been very proud, or pig-headed. And he came back, the next day, with a little painting. He told Edward he could sell it if he ever needed money.'

The kaleidoscope had turned round by a single notch, and all the chaotic, coloured glass within was suddenly, finally falling into a pattern.

CHAPTER TWELVE

'What was the painting of?' I asked. 'Why didn't he sell it?'

'Oh, Edward knew nothing about art,' she said. 'Who would he have sold it to? And I remember it was quite modern and abstract. Mum must have hated it. She liked classical paintings – things like that daub.' She gestured vaguely at *The Hay Wain*. 'I think it must have been shoved away into the attic – they probably didn't believe it was really worth anything.'

'So do you think when Edward really needed the money, he tried to find it?' I asked her. 'That maybe he thought it was worth something, after all?'

'It's possible,' said Sylvia. 'As far as I know, nobody else ever offered him anything. We're not a well-off family, just normal – a teacher and a housewife and a nanny. Or at least, we were a family.' Tears finally appeared in her blue eyes. Perhaps the whisky had unleashed them.

'Do you think it's still there?' I asked. It was impossible to disguise my excitement. I wondered if there was a note with it, a signature – or had Joseph painted it himself?

'I imagine so,' she said. 'Unless Mum had a clear-out while I was gone.'

'Look,' I said. 'I know this sounds ridiculous, but do you think we could possibly go up and have a look? It might be important.'

I saw Edward's body lying on the wet grass, the neat bullet wound. Had somebody wanted him out of the way – or was I once again turning a tragic coincidence into a plot, making the facts fit my theories like a second-rate detective?

'For heaven's sake,' she said. 'The last three days have been so peculiar, things couldn't get any more strange. I'm so tired you're probably a figment of my imagination, so we might as well. Then you can tell me why you're so fascinated by my deceased parents and some old charity case of Edward's.'

'I promise I will,' I said, and we put down our glasses and shook hands, like men in some historic club.

We went upstairs to the small landing, Sylvia dragging a wooden stepladder, which she put up underneath the square door in the ceiling. 'We'll need a torch,' she said. She disappeared into the bedroom; I heard her rummaging around, then she emerged with a small blue and white Bakelite reading torch. 'This will have to do,' she said. 'I left my blackout torch in Dorset. Golly, you know there's a blackout in the countryside – you can't see your hand in front of your' – she swung herself onto the ladder. It rocked violently, and she lurched sideways, towards the banister and the drop.

'Sylvia!' I shrieked.

'I'm a bit tight,' she said. 'Maybe you'd better do it.'

I felt none too steady myself, but I wasn't going to risk her breaking her neck. I took her place and climbed up, while she held the ladder.

'There's only rafters up there, from memory,' she said. 'So you'll have to be careful you don't go through the ceiling.'

I undid the bolt and pushed up the door. The loft was pitch dark, and smelled of dust and cardboard. The thin torch beam lit up a stack of boxes and, around them, tumbled bags, stuffed willy-nilly with clothes and toys, and strewn paper. It seemed someone had already been up here, searching, increasingly frantically.

Around the walls, further boxes were piled, labelled 'baby Sylvia's clothes', 'wedding dress', 'textbooks'. I waved the torch, trying to see further back.

'What can you see?' called Sylvia. 'Are there rats?'

I nearly dropped the torch on her head. 'I hope not,' I said. The bar of light fell on a series of tea chests that had been stacked in the corner. There were old pans, a Victorian mincing machine and something that looked like a cricket stump sticking out of the top.

'Hang on,' I called. 'I'd better go in.'

It hurt, yanking myself over the edge of the gap, and climbing onto the splintered rafters. I felt my woollen stocking ladder, and a nail pressed agonisingly into my knee. If there were rats, I was going to scream, and almost certainly plunge through the ceiling plaster into the bath below. I wasn't prepared to think about the spiders that might be lurking.

I inched my way over to the chests and gingerly pulled out the bits of mincing machine with the hand that wasn't holding the torch. It looked like some dreadful torture apparatus. Deeper down there was a blunt bread knife, and then under that, a biscuit tin with ladies in Victorian dress on the lid. It felt heavy, so I set it aside to investigate, and dug further, hoping that Winifred hadn't decided to stuff her old carving knives down there.

'What are you doing?' shouted Sylvia.

'I'm looking in a box,' I called. I pulled out a teddy bear with one ear, and a knitted pink mouse, but beneath them, the box yielded nothing but old baby books of Sylvia's: *The Dear Little Rabbit* and *Fairy Tales for Good Children*. I started on the next, which turned out to be carefully folded blankets layered with reeking mothballs.

'I'm getting another drink, will you be all right?' called Sylvia. I said I would, thinking how peculiar my life had become – crouching in a bereaved family's loft on a workday, covered in dust.

The next box was labelled 'family pictures'. A few were scattered about the rafters, so Edward had evidently had a good rummage through already. Nevertheless, I had a surge of hope, but when I lifted the lid, it was just a collection of old, framed sepia photographs – soldiers in long-forgotten uniforms, women in feathered hats on a Whitsun outing at the seaside, two rather toad-like women in round spectacles, sitting in deckchairs with a picnic. Other people's families were always fascinating to me, and I spent some minutes speculating on who they all were, which one was Winifred's mother – or were they relations of Edward's, generations of Turnbulls going back decades, to Victorian times?

I dug further and pulled out two more. One showed a small boy, perhaps Edward himself, in a sailor suit, looking awed and slightly frightened. The second frame was smaller, about the size of my notepad, and when I shone the torch onto it, I was surprised to find a much more recent photograph of Sylvia smiling out. She looked several years younger, fifteen or sixteen, and it was obviously a professional shot as she'd had her hair curled and was half turned to the camera, looking over her shoulder. I thought of the framed pictures downstairs, and realised there were none of Sylvia on the piano. 'Mum was furious when I left home,' she'd said. Furious enough to hide her picture, banished to the attic with all the dead relatives, I thought. No wonder Sylvia wasn't devastated by her death.

I turned it over, wondering if there was any note on the back to say what year it had been taken. The torch beam was weakening, and I could hear Sylvia coming back up the stairs. There was nothing written on it, but the brown paper backing was torn and broken, as though someone had taken the back off and replaced it rather carelessly.

Slowly, I levered out the loose picture nails and pulled it away.

Inside, I didn't see the back of a recent photograph, but a much older, thin wooden board. I used my fingernail to hook it away from the glass. The photograph fluttered down. *To Mum and Edward, with best wishes from Sylvia, 1936* was written in ink on the back. I left it there, pulled out the board and turned it over, using the last of the torch beam to examine it.

The painting showed trees by a river, a hint of a bridge. On it stood a man, wearing a hat. There was something in the set of his shoulders that suggested weariness, despondency. It was a painting about age, and time, and enduring.

But the colours... they seemed to have been stolen directly from nature: damp jungle greens and slashes of pure, sunlit yellow, reflecting in the deep, earth browns of the river. It was almost impressionist but not quite, as if the artist was moving too fast to linger over clouds, or leaves, and wanted to present the scene right away, as he saw and felt it.

I had a strange sense that I'd seen something like it before. A distant chime sounded in my mind, but then it was gone, like a vivid dream that drifts to scraps of nothingness when you wake.

When I was younger, I'd take the bus to town on a Saturday and wander round the city art gallery. I'd drift through Impressionists and Pre-Raphaelites in the high Victorian rooms, where nobody shouted or pushed, and nobody called you a 'stupid cow' for wanting to be on your own, or stole your petticoat or pretended they were 'just messing about' when they and their huge, sixteen-year-old pals had locked you in an airing cupboard to amuse themselves.

Like my books, I'd learnt the paintings as if they were love letters, poring over the memory of them, so that I could bring them out like hoarded treasure when I needed comfort.

I didn't know a great deal about the artists, but I knew how great art could make you feel. Lifted and encouraged, and moved, all at once; and reminded that other people had felt what you had felt, and would do so again. This painting was not some amateur attempt at a pastoral scene. It had greatness within it.

'Any luck?' shouted Sylvia from beneath me.

'I might have got it,' I called. I fastened the back on again, throwing the photograph into the chest, and then realised I couldn't carry the framed painting, the biscuit tin and the torch and crawl back. I stuffed the torch down my girdle, and clamped the painting and tin under my arms. It was dark, apart from the pale square of light from the landing, and the unearthly glow emanating from my waistband. I still felt drunk from the whisky, and I had a brief moment of hysteria at the absurdity of it all, and the euphoria of finding the painting. But if Edward had only done so...

'Are you all right?' Sylvia shouted. Apart from the fact that I was breathing in a miasma of dust and my knees were ripped to shreds, I claimed that I was. I leaned down and handed her the framed picture, threw the tin onto the floor, then slithered down the ladder, breathless, hair askew, and streaked with grey dust balls.

'Do you recognise it?' I asked. I didn't like her holding it. It felt as though I'd dug up a hoard of treasure on the beach, and a grown-up had taken it from me.

'Gosh, that's it!' she said. 'I remember it now – Mum said it looked like a child's finger painting.'

'She used the frame for something else,' I said.

'My photo?' asked Sylvia, and I wished I hadn't said it. 'Perhaps I'll get it out again,' said Sylvia. 'Put it up there, instead of the bloody *Hay Wain*.'

Back in the sitting room, we laid the painting carefully on the table, where it glowed like a religious relic.

'I think this genuinely might be worth something,' I said. 'It might even be by a famous artist.'

'You ARE joking?' Sylvia said. She sounded irritated. 'How could it be? If it's the right one, he was some penniless Jewish refugee. It's not possible.'

'Maybe it was all he had at the time that was worth money,' I suggested.

'Maybe,' she said. 'Mum did say something, actually, in one of her rare letters, about Edward needing the money – she said something like, "even if we could sell the thing, nobody can remember what happened to it. It probably got thrown away." I didn't know what she was on about. Look, I still don't even know what the point of all this is,' she said. 'Why are you so interested?'

I wondered whether to explain. It seemed complicated and unlikely, and exhausting.

'I'm writing an obituary,' I said. 'But it's of Joseph. The man who I think gave you the painting. He became a successful businessman, and I'm trying to find out more about him.'

'Not of Edward? Or Winifred?'

Embarrassed, I shook my head. 'Sorry.'

She made a dismissive gesture. 'Ah, who cares? It's not as if she ever did much. I wish I could help.'

I realised the biscuit tin still sat, untouched, on the table. 'Can I...?' I asked.

'Go ahead,' said Sylvia. 'I'm going to make toast. There's nothing else in.'

The lid of the tin was rusted and tight, and I broke a nail as I struggled to prise it off. Finally, it jerked loose. I had feared buttons, or dull house deeds, but it was filled with letters and notes, some tied together, others loose and furred at the edges with age.

Darling Winnie, began one notelet. It was from Edward, and as I sorted through, increasingly disappointed, it transpired that this was simply a collection of their dull missives to one another. *Can't wait to see you and the little one on Saturday.* And *Lovely sunny day today, but the beach at Porthmadog is disappointing, very muddy. Had potted shrimps in a nice café.*

I was about to throw them all back in when a small bundle of old bills fell out of another pile of boring sentiments.

I rifled through, just to be thorough. Shoe mending, a new stove for the Turnbulls in 1929 – and then a piece of blue writing paper. I pulled it out.

Thank you for so much lessons, it read in a spidery, sloping hand. *Much appresiate. I hope you like and sell if in need. J.N.*

So it was him. I had assumed, of course, but now there was no doubt. I tucked the paper into my bag.

Sylvia came back bearing a plate of toast, her eyes pink from whisky and exhaustion. 'There's no butter, but I found some beef paste,' she said.

To be polite, I ate a piece. 'You can take it if you want,' she added.

I thought she meant the biscuit tin.

'The painting,' she clarified. 'You can get it valued for me. God knows, there's no inheritance for me except this horrid little house, so if it turns out to be a Renoir or something, I'd be happy.'

More importantly, if I could find an art expert to look at it, they might be able to tell me who had painted it and I'd find out why Joseph Novak had given it to a teacher who had no interest in art.

Before I left, I wrapped it in some newspaper, tucked it under my arm, and said goodbye to Sylvia.

'I'll write as soon as I know,' I said. 'Or if it's worth lots, I'll send a telegram.'

She laughed. 'It could be a piece of happy news amid all the sadness,' she said. 'You might be doing me a good turn.'

But, as it turned out, I was doing nothing of the kind.

It was still not quite New Year, but it felt as though winter had lasted forever. Manchester was in tatters, and the reports were only just beginning to creep into the paper because everything had to be checked by the Ministry to make sure we weren't accidentally encouraging the Germans to bomb us further. The newspaper itself was down to eight pages thanks to paper shortages. My obituary column was still a part of it, and I knew I should think myself bloody lucky, even if it was tucked away in a corner.

Nobody was doing anything at New Year itself, as Annie was working, and Lou was no doubt tracking down murderers, while Charles was 'likely to be slaving away in my bunker,' he'd said regretfully. On that basis, it occurred to me that perhaps we should have a little get-together beforehand, and make a toast to better times in 1941. Annie sounded keen when I suggested it. 'We can go to the saloon bar in the Friendship,' she said. 'They don't seem to mind women, as long as the lads order for us. And we need a bit of fun before January ruins everything again.'

Annie ran to the public telephone box to ring Lou up at the station, and he said he'd round up Arnold. I didn't much like the idea of making a cosy foursome, so I went out straight afterwards and phoned Charles. Lillian answered and I asked her to pass on the message.

'I shall tell him you called, dear,' she said.

I didn't have any coppers left, but I asked, 'Did you manage to save any of your things?'

'A few,' she said. 'It's been heartbreaking. There's so little left. Edie, when will the obituary—' Then the pips went.

Annie and I put on our good wool dresses. 'Though I'd get

more free drinks in uniform than in mufti,' she said. 'I know a girl who actually puts on her nurse's outfit to go out, and men never stop asking her to dance. And more,' she added darkly. 'I'd rather not smell of carbolic soap on my night off, though, thanks very much.'

I wondered whether I should invite Clara. 'Oh, I know her,' said Annie. 'She's always grinning at me like a loon when we pass in the street. Yes, why not, she seems a decent sort.'

I nipped to Clara's house, and her mother, who looked exactly like her, answered the door. 'Clara is on duty from nine,' she said formally. 'But I shall pass on the message, and she may be able to join you earlier on.'

At seven, Annie and I set off with our gas masks, torches and handbags banging against our hips, slithering in unaccustomed heels.

'How can it be only five days since Christmas?' she grumbled. 'It feels like a lifetime ago. I hope Lou turns up. If none of the boys come, it'll be us and Clara talking awkwardly about WVS duty for three hours.'

I laughed. 'I think she's nice,' I said, as we pushed open the pub's door onto a roaring, steamy, smoky fug. The Victorian windows dripped with condensation. The saloon bar was packed with uniformed men and women, with a few, like us, dressed in ordinary clothes. Annie spotted a small table at the back and dragged extra stools over, while I scanned the crowd and failed to spot any of our friends.

'Might just be us, after all,' she sighed, as the door swung open again to admit Arnold and, just behind him, Clara.

There was a flurry of introductions and drink orders, and Arnold went to the bar. Clara asked for a half of mild, which raised eyebrows. 'Oh, I can't be bothered with those silly little glasses like an elf's flower vase,' she snorted, and Annie laughed, surprised. Clara was wearing twill slacks and a white shirt and looked as though she'd be perfectly capable of fixing an engine if a mechanic was suddenly required.

'Do you have a young man, Clara?' I asked, and she smiled.

'Goodness no,' she said. 'I find life's rather easier without one, I'm afraid.' She deftly rolled a cigarette and stuck it behind her ear, and I suddenly wished I could be as certain of myself as she seemed.

Lately, I felt, I'd done nothing but blunder about, stumbling on murders and ranging through strangers' attics. The picture was wrapped up in my dressing table drawer, waiting for me to take it to be valued – if the valuers hadn't been bombed, of course.

Thinking about Mr Novak led me to think about Mrs Novak again, and the terrible scene I'd discovered just a few days ago. I wondered why Lou had agreed to join us for a drink, instead of doing everything in his power to find Mrs Novak's killer. And I wondered what had happened to the dog – it was rather terrifying, but I didn't wish it ill.

Clara leaned forward. 'Cat got your tongue?' she said. I explained what had happened. 'My goodness!' she said. 'What a shock that must have been. So, who d'you think did it?'

'I don't know,' I said, admiring her ability to get straight to the point. 'Someone with a grudge against refugees, perhaps?'

'Well, why wait till the refugee in question was dead?' Clara asked. 'I mean, if you had a grudge, or were horrible and anti-Semitic, you'd kill him before her, surely? And besides, if he's been here for years, why wait till now?'

They were all excellent questions. I was wondering whether to explain the connection to Edward Turnbull, or if it would all sound too mad, when Lou barrelled through the door, dragging something behind him.

With a spark of shock, I realised it was Major. The huge dog trotted into the saloon bar on a leather lead that looked frankly inadequate for keeping him under control. He lifted his muzzle, sniffed the smoke and beer, and seemed to approve, glancing at Lou for further direction.

'Good grief,' said Annie. 'He's brought a bloody wolf with him.'

Lou made his way over, the crowd parting like the Red Sea to avoid the huge dog. I heard a woman say shrilly, 'Is that beast allowed in here?' and a large man in uniform leapt nimbly out of the way as Major padded by.

'Evening,' said Lou, drawing up a stool. 'This is Marple. He's had a slight name change.'

'In honour of Agatha Christie's Miss Marple?' I asked.

'No.' said Lou. 'In honour of my Auntie Vera who lived in Marple.'

I shrank back as Marple sniffed my hand. His hot breath felt like the gust of wind before a summer storm. Then he laid his head on my knee and gazed upwards.

'Give him some attention,' ordered Lou. 'He likes a good scratch between his ears.'

'Is this your new room-mate?' asked Annie. I noticed she'd gathered her skirt out of jaw-range.

'For now,' said Lou. 'Nobody else to take him. Mrs Novak has no surviving relations, it seems. So he's going to help me solve crimes till we can find him a new place.'

'Is his food terribly expensive?' asked Clara. 'I mean, he must eat rather a lot.'

'We'll manage,' said Lou. 'Turns out the butcher down my way is a dog lover, so he's been putting scraps aside.'

I was torn between admiration for Lou taking on this enormous creature who had lost its mistress, and my own nervousness. I'd never had a dog, or known anyone with a large dog – I didn't count lapdogs – and to me, they were unpredictable, alien creatures. Marple heaved a great sigh and drooled lightly on my skirt. I dared to scratch his head, and he responded by licking my hand with his enormous pink tongue.

I wondered if we were now allowed to know that he had been locked away during the murder.

'Lou,' I said, 'Was he all right after being lo—'

'Shh,' Lou said. 'Edie, any details about the murder scene are classified information. I must ask that you keep them to yourself.'

'Sorry,' I muttered.

My heart lifted as the door opened again and Charles came in, looking as if he'd stepped out of a newspaper menswear advert. Under his beautifully cut tweed overcoat he wore a brown suit and he carried a furled umbrella. Heads turned – mainly female ones, I noticed, with a flush of pride – as he made his way over, placing his trilby carefully on the hatstand. Marple currently had one vast, furry haunch squashing Lou's hat, but he didn't appear to have noticed.

'How d'you do,' said Lou briskly, gripping Charles's fingers in an iron clasp. I saw Charles wince, and felt for him. Marple slid his ten-ton head off my lap and went to sniff the newcomer's polished shoes.

Charles stepped back irritably. 'Who's this great fiend?' he asked.

'He belonged to the Novaks,' I said. 'Don't you recognise him?'

'This is Joseph's dog?' Charles looked startled. 'No. I never visited. Mother mentioned him, of course, but... my God, he's enormous.'

He sat down on my other side, away from Lou and Marple. The dog lifted his head and stared at Arnold, who had appeared with a tray of drinks. As he set it down, Marple growled, low and threatening.

'Hello, old boy,' said Arnold peaceably. 'Not keen on my trousers?' Marple was sniffing his hems violently. He barked, a thunderous echo around the bar, and several people jumped and spilled their drinks.

'Quiet,' said Lou firmly. 'Don't you bark at my old pal Arnold.'

'Oh, I know what it'll be,' said Arnold suddenly. 'I went to feed our neighbour's cat. They're away for Christmas, so I'm looking after Nanette. She's a dear thing, a huge tabby like a cushion. She was all round my ankles.' He smiled at Annie and she twinkled back.

'I've always wanted a tabby kitten,' she said.

The moment was gone; Marple heaved a sigh and flopped under the table, making it rock alarmingly. But I felt a chill running through me that had nothing to do with the weather outside.

Charles fetched a Scotch for himself and settled beside me again.

'Any news on the murder?' I asked Lou.

Charles leaned in. 'I'm sure you're doing a marvellous job,' he said. 'My mother... well. You know the story, I'm afraid.'

Lou nodded. 'No judgement here,' he said brusquely. 'We're just interested in finding whoever killed Mrs Novak, and Edward Turnbull.'

'So it was murder?' I asked. 'Not an accident?'

Lou looked at me. 'You are relentless,' he said wearily. 'Yes, it looks deliberate. But I don't want that in the paper yet. We're at a delicate stage of enquiries. Don't ask anything else, please. I won't answer.'

I wondered what 'delicate' meant, and why anyone would have wanted to shoot poor, kindly Edward. I thought again of Dennis, and his pale, furious eyes.

Lou offered Annie a Woodbine, and I leaned over and took one too. 'Anything interesting?' I asked.

'None that won't be gone over in the press conference at Willert Street tomorrow,' he said, blowing out blue smoke in a cloud that hung in the warm air and obscured his face.

'Oh, come on,' I said. The sherry had made me bold, and I

hadn't eaten anything since my toast with Sylvia. 'You know Desmond Barry will go to that. You wouldn't even know about the body yet if it weren't for me.'

'I can't tell you anything, Edie,' he said. 'But we don't know if he's still out there, so if I were you, I'd be extremely careful. I'm not happy about you and Annie walking to the pub on your own.'

'Yes, she thought she was being followed on Saturday,' said Clara, suddenly tuning back in as Arnold droned to Annie about ancient funeral rites. I could hardly blame her, but the last thing I needed was Lou leaping in.

'When was this?' he asked sharply. I told him. 'I see,' he said. 'That's worrying. You need to be much more careful, Edie. We don't need another body on our hands.'

'My God, Edie,' Charles said quietly, as Lou turned to give Marple a reassuring scratch. 'I had no idea. I feel dreadful for letting you get the bus. What did he look like?'

'Normal,' I said. 'Medium-sized, coat, hat... I couldn't really see.'

Charles glanced at Arnold. 'I'll have to look after you,' he said, and put a hand on my knee.

I downed my sherry. Charles bought me another, and I chatted to Clara about her ambition to join the Women's Auxiliary Air Force. 'I'd jolly well love that,' she said. 'Imagine being up in the air, all alone, in the clouds...' I couldn't think of anything worse. I was enjoying talking to her, but Charles was warm at my side, and I felt every second not immersed in his sea-green eyes was a second wasted.

Yet, I needed to ask Arnold a crucial question before he and Annie got any closer. It was so important, I felt rather sick, and kept fluffing my chance to ask him quietly. It had been on my mind for days, and I had tried to push it away. But now, with Marple's reaction to him... I couldn't say nothing.

Clara left for duty, in a flurry of thanks and hat-searching

(Marple was using it as a pillow), but Arnold talked to Lou about football and Annie about her nursing, and somehow, I couldn't find a moment to ask him.

'Arnold,' I began, as the bell rang for last orders and the others ordered their drinks. 'Did anyone tell you about Marple?'

He blinked at me pleasantly. I thought perhaps he was a bit drunk. 'Marple?' he repeated. I glanced at Lou, but he was talking to Charles.

'Where he was... during the murder?'

'No,' he said. 'I think it was in the paper. Must have been. Awful business.'

I nodded and sipped my sherry.

'Why do you ask?'

'I just wondered. How you knew he was locked in, I mean.'

He took a long drink, a sign I'd always recognised in men as a chance to consider what they were going to say next.

'Well, that must be how,' he said, pushing his stool back. 'I'm just nipping to the gents.' As he went, I saw him fumble for a cigarette and take a deep drag. Unease swirled inside me like falling snow. When he came back, Annie had decided to toast the new year early. She was standing on a chair, and half the bar was swaying and singing 'Auld Lang Syne.'

By closing time, we were all drunk except Lou. He had only drunk half a pint. 'I don't drink much when I'm driving,' he said. 'Seen too many nasty car accidents.'

'I'm afraid I do, rather too often,' said Charles. 'I'm sure you're right, though.'

'You might want to watch that tendency,' said Lou.

Annie winced, and I caught Charles's eye. I tried to apologise without speaking, but I could see he was irritated. It was an enormous relief to know that I wasn't the only one.

Marple leapt into the passenger seat as if he'd been doing it all his life, and Lou drove off into the night. Arnold and Charles walked us home, and I left Annie and Arnold chatting on the step while Charles said goodbye to me at the gate.

I said awkwardly, 'It was lovely to see you.'

'And you,' he said, kissing my cold cheek. 'I'll be in touch soon, m'dear.'

Arnold left too, and I stood in the doorway listening to his footsteps die away, until Annie shouted, 'There's a draught like a hurricane coming up those stairs,' and I reluctantly went inside, feeling frustrated, irritated and, much as I hated to admit it, somewhat afraid.

CHAPTER THIRTEEN

The following morning, I arrived at work via the usual rubble-strewn apocalypse – I was getting used to it – and went straight to my typewriter. It was time to write the obituary, I had decided, and if Mr Gorringe felt it was in bad taste, that was up to him. I tried to put aside the murder and all my seething fears around who was responsible, and I wrote. I included the quote Lillian had given me, about Joseph's love of art, but a few paragraphs in, I realised it wasn't working. My attempts felt feeble, as though I was making up a character in a play, the noble refugee who had been a successful businessman and much-loved husband. As I once again ripped the page out, and Pat audibly tutted at my profligate wasting of precious paper, it occurred to me that I could structure the whole thing around the mysterious painting.

I needn't say it might be worth money. I could simply write about how vital art was to Joseph's spirit as he suffered; how, even as a penniless, desperate refugee who barely spoke English, he had repaid a kindness with something far more nourishing to his soul than just notes and coins.

From then on, it flowed.

Joseph Novak believed in the power of art, I wrote. *His love of colour and beauty sustained him throughout his life, and even as a ragged, alien refugee, he understood that a painting could be worth a thousand words.* I went on to tell the anecdote, referring to Edward as *a local language teacher*, and recounting how the family *had hung on to the painting – it may not have been worth money in their eyes, but it was a symbol of gratitude that outlasted Mr Novak himself, whose life was cut short by sudden illness just days before his workplace was bombed to smithereens.* I included the quote Lillian loved so much, and finished with a line extolling the British welcome to refugees and how Novak's hard work exemplified what they brought to our country.

Admittedly, it was rather flowery with a hefty dose of propaganda. But by the time I'd finished editing and polishing, it seemed a touching and charming tribute to a man who nobody except perhaps Lillian had really known.

I knew that the subs would add some awful line about Pamela's murder, with *See page 3 for details*, but I couldn't help that. I ripped the paper out, set it in the editor's in-tray, watched beadily by Parrot Paulson, and returned to my desk feeling unburdened.

'It is regrettable that the police appear to have made little progress,' Mr Gorringe commented as he passed my desk later on, 'but I much prefer the tone of this piece, Miss York. It shall run in this evening's edition.'

I was pinning up mental bunting when he added, 'Where is this painting of which you speak? It may be advisable to include an image.'

It was at that moment wrapped in three layers of newspaper and stuffed into the handbag on my chair.

I could see that Mr Gorringe had a point. The only picture

we had of Joseph was one Lillian had provided of him in a hat and coat looking Edwardian and pale-eyed, sitting formally on a bench. It would be lovely to show the painting with which, I'd rather whimsically argued, Mr Novak had paid his dues into British citizenship.

But something was stopping me. I felt that it wouldn't be fair to Sylvia – because if it was worth money, and someone saw it and realised, they might try and insist it should go to a gallery and then she may never get her inheritance. Besides, it wasn't mine to offer up.

I tried to explain that it belonged to someone else, and that they may not give permission, but he waved his hand irritably. 'Well, ask. And if they say no, then so be it,' he said, and swept off to his office, while Parrot Paulson smirked at me from her perch outside.

As I was putting my coat on to go and send a telegram to Sylvia, the desk telephone rang.

'Morning, my dear,' said Charles. I loved his voice, it was so elegant and well-spoken. Lillian's voice was flatter somehow, as though she'd been taught to speak by an elocution teacher.

'Charles,' I whispered, 'I can't talk, I'm at work.'

'Just a quick question from dearest Mother,' he said. 'She's agitating about whether the obit's going in this week. Lord knows why.'

I was relieved that I could bring this little gift and lay it at Lillian's kid-shod feet. 'Oh, yes. Tonight.'

'Marvellous,' he said. 'I may come and see you later, if you're available.'

I knew I should not be available. I should be working at the canteen, or mending the rip in my coat lining, or doing useful war work, knitting for the troops. And I certainly shouldn't sound overly keen, accordingly to everything I'd ever learnt about men.

'That would be super,' I said.

. . .

Charles arrived at eleven, after his late shift, and we saw in New Year with a kiss and a glass of the champagne he'd somehow found, before he drove off. 'Better not leave Mother alone,' he said. 'She's had a lot to cope with.'

I arrived at work on the morning of New Year's Day feeling remarkably cheerful. I had bought a copy of the paper at the kiosk in St Ann's Square last night, and there it was, my obituary of Joseph Novak, almost unchanged from how I'd written it. My byline, *Miss Edie York*, shone from the page like a neon sign.

As I hung up my unmended coat, hoping for praise and comments on its success, I heard a commotion in the news section.

'It's true,' I heard Des say. 'Just came in on the wires.'

Gloria cried, 'Oh, that's terrible!' amid a hubbub of concerned voices and ringing telephones. Immediately I was overcome with a sense of doom.

'Edie,' Desmond called. 'Can I have a word?'

I turned towards him, thinking about another bombing, somewhere else, many dead.

'What's happened?'

'There's been another murder,' he said. A dark stone sank in my stomach.

'Who?'

'A girl in Burnage. They found her this morning,' called Pat, rummaging in her desk drawer for the biscuit tin. 'Only young, she was. Strangled.'

Black spots seethed at the edges of my vision.

'What was her name?' I asked faintly.

'Sylvia Brown,' said Desmond, as I had known he would. 'They don't know much yet. The postman saw her body through the letterbox, so I've got my headline: THE LETTERBOX

Killer. Or maybe The New Year Murder,' he mused, puffing on his pipe.

But I knew. That it was my fault. That someone had read the obituary I'd written – I'd thought I was so clever – and wanted to get their hands on the painting. The painting that was now stuffed inside my handbag, hanging on the back of my chair, like a parcel from the butcher's, dripping blood.

And sad, willing Sylvia had been the victim, just because she'd wanted to help me out and didn't want to drink alone, the day after her mother died. I felt a great sob building in my chest. ''Scuse me,' I said to Pat, and ran to the ladies' toilets, where I threw myself into the ornate, tiled cubicle, sank down onto the seat, and heaved silent tears, sick with guilt and confusion.

When I'd finally shuddered to a halt, and felt limp and empty, I splashed water onto my face and re-pinned my hair in the old Edwardian mirror above the sinks. The next thing was to ring Lou, and hope he'd understand that my accidental involvement in another murder didn't mean I was responsible for any of them.

'Where's the bloody painting now?' Lou asked.

Once again, I was in an interview room at Willert Street and Lou Brennan was glaring at me as if I'd stolen his last shilling. I almost wished Marple were there – another living presence would have been reassuring.

'At the office,' I lied. 'It's safe, it's locked in my desk.' After this, I was intending to go to Payne and Son valuers, who still seemed to be in business when I passed earlier, so the painting was in the handbag which I was clutching. I didn't want it impounded by the police – I felt I'd made a promise to Sylvia and I was determined to keep it.

I wasn't palmed off on a junior constable this time; Lou interviewed me himself. I told him everything.

'Look,' he said, when I finally drew breath. 'I still can't understand why you're so convinced there's some vital connection between all three deaths. All right, Novak gave Turnbull the painting years ago, but so what? It seems clear to me that Miss Brown was murdered because somebody read about it and wanted to get their hands on it, but Mrs Novak never had it. He hadn't even met her when he gave the painting away. And Edward didn't know he still had it. There's a lot of people desperate for a few shillings at the moment,' he added. 'We had a bloke kill his wife for the gas money a few months ago. Knocked her clean across the kitchen and she hit her head on the stove, all because he wanted to go drinking. He'd just got back from the front and he wasn't right in the head. In Strangeways now.'

'So I suppose you think it's my fault.' I was so tired of it all, the murders and mysteries. Surely the war and keeping my job was enough to worry about, without all this on top. I didn't want to acknowledge that if I'd just left things well alone, I could be peacefully writing about the likes of the academic botanist and her faded bequest of sixteenth-century prints, and I wouldn't be sitting in a police interview room again, watching Lou frown a deep V between his neat black eyebrows.

'No,' he said. 'But you've already been followed, and I think you need to start looking out for yourself before whoever they are decides to come after this interfering lady journalist.'

I felt a little glow at the word 'journalist.' I couldn't help it, even if he was talking about my potential murder.

I stepped over icy puddles and past rubble and glass that had now been roughly shoved to the side of the pavement as I headed to King Street. The bones of buildings loomed overhead, and men in metal helmets and filthy boots toiled like insect colonies to make them safe, dismantling and shifting, trudging up and down great heaps of plaster dust and broken bricks. Nothing felt solid any more – even the painting in my bag felt like a stupid frippery. Who could begin to care about a bright little daub when Sylvia was dead, when so many people's lives had ended, when we could still lose the war? It all felt hopeless, and I was wondering if I should just chuck the picture in the back of a truck and forget the whole thing when I heard somebody calling my name.

I turned and saw Charles at the wheel of his sports car, leaning from the open window. 'Need a lift?' he called.

I hurried over. 'What are you doing here?' I asked.

'Oh, the panjandrums of intelligence decided they could spare me briefly,' he said. 'I was hurtling off for a lonely lunch, then I saw you. I thought, "I know that walk", and I was right. Care to join me?'

After two hours of Lou's abrasive dressing-downs, I felt I'd like nothing better. Sylvia's guileless face suddenly popped into my head, and I remembered her saying, 'Maybe you'll be doing me a good turn.'

'I'd love to, but I need to do an errand first,' I said. 'Something awful has happened.'

'Oh, not again!' said Charles. He sounded like a schoolboy being denied tuck, and I smiled, despite everything.

'Jump in and tell me everything,' he said. 'Where are we going?'

I sank back against the leather seats, wishing with all my heart that this could be my life permanently.

'Payne and Son,' I said. 'The art valuers. Look, I don't suppose... I mean, I've never been to a valuer, and I've got the painting here, but I don't really know what to ask...'

'Come along and smooth the path?' said Charles. 'Of course. Delighted. So what was the awful thing?'

'Someone else has been killed.'

'At the front?' he said sympathetically. 'Awful when it's a pal.'

'Another murder,' I said, wondering why there should be any difference in deaths. 'Sylvia, the Turnbulls' daughter.' I outlined my visit and the connection to Joseph that I was sure I'd discovered.

'Good Lord,' said Charles quietly, 'How utterly ghastly for you. And her, of course. It's funny, now you mention it, I think Mother did say something about Joseph learning English. She'd taught him a bit, of course, but he needed a professional, really. I was away at school, though, so I missed all this.'

'Couldn't Pamela have taught him?'

'Pamela?' he said. 'He'd only just arrived here at that point – they weren't married. Besides, she was too useless even to teach her dog to calm down. Mother said the brute was impossible, so I don't know how Brennan's managed to train him so quickly.'

'She used to go to the house?'

'Occasionally – when Pamela was staying with her awful cousin, Trudy. Ma would drive over and she and Joseph would have a lovely, civilised evening, talking about art and life, apparently. As long as old Fang was shut away.'

Could Lillian... I wondered. But again, it all came back to lack of motive. I couldn't imagine that charming, elegant woman stabbing another woman and wrangling the dog, leaving a welter of blood, not caring whether the dog died of starvation before the body was found. I couldn't imagine anyone doing it – and of course, I remembered, Lou had said it was a man.

I thought of Dennis again. Was he angry enough to kill Pamela, or even his own niece? Thinking about his menacing glower at the hospital, perhaps he was.

'Sweet dreams?' Charles asked, as I gazed sightlessly ahead. 'We're here, Sleeping Beauty.'

The Gothically arched doorway of Payne and Son was lined with sandbags, and a cracked window was taped, waiting for the overworked glaziers, but inside, it seemed that nothing else had changed since 1902.

The mahogany-panelled lobby still had the old gas lamps set into the walls, and a dark green, leaf-patterned wallpaper that reminded me of Mr Pugh's study. A clock ticked sonorously on the mantelpiece. I had seldom felt so out of place. It was only Charles's patrician, reassuring presence beside me that stopped me bolting.

Mr Payne was out for a New Year lunch. His tweedy secretary was so dazzled by Charles she could barely speak. 'I shall inform him as soon as he gets back,' she said.

Charles smiled. 'I expect he'll see us before you have a chance to,' he said. 'Seeing as we're in the lobby and he'll be walking past us.'

She blushed and giggled, and I felt a shameful stab of pride at being with him. It was astonishing how quickly I'd embraced the sybaritic lifestyle that Charles offered: French wine at lunch and sports cars. And aside from all that, I was totally gone over him. Not just his looks, but his manner, his kindness, his wit. Most men tried to squash me, but not Charles. He seemed genuinely interested in what I thought about things. Unlike Lou Brennan, I thought crossly.

'Ah, good afternoon, Mr and Miss...?'

Mr Payne, immaculately monochrome as a penguin, had returned. Charles introduced us, and we were ushered through to his office.

It beat in my mind that if the painting really was worth a fortune, then Sylvia's death was all my fault. I knew I'd have to hand it over, and now, in Mr Payne's dim office, which smelled of linseed oil and cigars, I felt almost relieved that I was about to pass over the burden. Since I'd heard about Sylvia, the painting had felt poisonous, as if I were carrying her last wishes about with me like a vengeful eighteenth-century ghost.

'Let's have a look then, m'dear,' he said, moving aside a huge cut-glass ashtray. I thought how easily one could pick it up and smash it into someone's temple. I was feeling hopelessly nervy; there was no reason for anyone to want me dead. It was a ridiculous thought, like a silly film, but perhaps the fact that I now kept seeing murder weapons everywhere wasn't surprising.

I pulled the package out, unwrapped it and was about to place it on his desk when he said, 'No, no, allow me,' and pulled on some white cotton gloves before he reached for it. He switched on the desk lamp and studied it for a moment.

'And its provenance is...?' he said flatly. I had hoped for a tremor of excitement, a barely concealed hint that this was something worthwhile.

I told him. 'I'm worried,' I explained, 'that whoever killed Sylvia wanted this. The police wanted to get it valued, so I said I'd bring it in.'

Mr Payne was peering at the painting's corners, perhaps looking for a signature, though I'd been unable to find one.

Charles was quite still, and I glanced at him, but he, too, was mesmerised.

'Do you have any idea who could have painted this?' asked Mr Payne. He lifted a tortoiseshell magnifying glass to study a section. 'It has certain qualities that one might attribute to a Cézanne, or one of his better imitators.'

Heat suffused me. 'Do you think it's worth money?'

'I have no idea at this juncture,' he said disapprovingly. 'Our own area of initial interest is provenance and authentication.'

I nodded, abashed.

'And you say the poor girl who gave it to you has been...' He looked faintly repulsed.

'I'm afraid so,' said Charles.

'Then I strongly advise that you contact her family, and return it to them, to decide whether it will go to auction, assuming it is authenticated as a Cézanne,' he added.

'There's Dennis,' I said. 'Mrs Turnbull's brother.'

'Do you have an address?'

I shook my head. 'Somewhere near Withington, I think.'

'What happens to the painting in the meantime?' asked Charles.

'Well,' – Mr Payne winced slightly – 'we would happily keep it secured until such time as the true owner can be traced.'

'And if he can't?' asked Charles.

Of course Dennis was traceable, I thought. It couldn't be that hard to track down Winifred's maiden name and find him.

'Then it would revert to the next of kin. Or failing that, Miss York would theoretically have a claim in a court of law.'

'Well, perhaps you can ask your experts to look at it very swiftly,' said Charles. 'We can pick it up tomorrow, then track down the uncle and come back when he's seen it, to organise the auction.'

'As you wish,' said Mr Payne. 'We shall take great care of it.'

Outside, I realised I was hours late back to work. Pat was probably on the phone to Bootle Street, trying to trace me.

'Let's meet later, for a debrief,' said Charles. 'We can try and trace this brother fellow.'

He kissed me goodbye, and I hurried back into the office, thinking about the painting. I wondered why Joseph had loved art so much, and whether that love was what had brought him and Lillian together. I couldn't understand why Lillian hadn't simply married him. Was she really so wedded to her independence? As I trudged up the stairs and back to my desk, it struck me that I'd forgotten all about Sylvia.

I spent the afternoon trying to catch up on other obituaries, including someone who had done something terrifically sporting to do with yacht racing in 1912. I wasn't enormously looking forward to that interview.

After hours of grubbing about in the dusty cuttings library, all I wanted to do was have a good wash and a sleep, in the hope that Charles might want to take me out later on for our 'debrief'. I wasn't expecting that when I emerged from the office into the blackout, Annie would be leaning against the door frame, crying.

My first thought was that something had happened to Lou – the plucky detective, mown down in the course of duty – or that she'd discovered something awful about Arnold. I had intended to share my doubts that evening, before things went any further between them, but as I reached her, she gripped my arm and said, 'Edie, it's my mum.'

Dead, I thought, with a flash of panic.

'A telegram came this afternoon, to the hospital,' she sobbed. 'I was so scared, I thought it was Will, or Norman...' She took a shuddering breath. 'And I opened it and there was an air raid in Barrow, and Mum was badly hurt, and she's in the cottage hospital. I'm getting the train now, there's one from Manchester Central in ten minutes, so I must rush...'

'Oh, Annie!' I cried. 'Your poor mum. Is she...'

'Conscious? Yes, it's her legs,' she said. 'I don't know if she'll be able to walk, and if she can't, I'll have to move back home, and I may need to anyway, to help... There's no chance of me getting hold of my brothers, they're away fighting God knows where... Oh, the bloody, bloody Germans!' she finished on a sob. 'They ruin everything!'

'You haven't got anything with you,' I said.

'There'll be some of my bits and bobs at Mum's,' she said frantically. 'Look, I've got to go. I've told work. If I have to stay for long, can you send me some things?'

'Of course.' I gave her an awkward hug. We weren't huggers, Annie and I – or rather, I wasn't. 'Tell Arnold,' she shouted, breaking into a trot.

'Send a telegram with news!' I cried, but her answer was muffled by a bus roaring past, and then she was gone.

Back home, things felt flat and cold. I was worried about Annie, of course, but equally prevalent was the fear that the killer of Mrs Novak and Sylvia had some plan to off me as well. I didn't like the idea of being on my own that evening, with just the pinging of the gas pipes, and Mr Benson's wireless yakking downstairs. I had few female friends, apart from Annie. It wasn't through choice, but most women my age were a mystery to me, and though I liked Clara greatly, I didn't feel we were on 'popping round' terms yet.

I sat on the sofa, thinking about Annie and her mum, and desperately hoping that Charles would make good on his promise to visit.

I also needed to see Lou. Could I perhaps meet up with him out of work hours, to try and find out more about Sylvia's death? It wasn't exactly that I thought the police might have overlooked the crucial clue; more that it didn't make any sense. I felt sure the painting somehow linked the deaths of Edward, Pamela and Sylvia, but I couldn't see why – motives and meanings were lost in a fog of confusion. Was the painting stolen, I wondered, and someone wanted it back – but why now? And why kill Pamela when it was never hers? Why murder Edward in broad daylight, when he'd already given up looking? And as for Sylvia – she must have simply been in the way. Killed downstairs, as the murderer searched frantically for something that now lay on Mr Payne's desk, safe from harm.

I thought again about Dennis and his rage at my interference. He would have known about the English lessons, and known that Edward wanted money. He may well have heard about the painting, and seen his chance to step in, the protective brother. I remembered him saying, 'If it's about the mortgage...' as I stood on the step. Money was the first thing on his mind.

Worse, I still wasn't convinced that Arnold was innocent. He had lied over how he knew about the dog, and though I'd planned to warn Annie, she was gone for now, and out of harm's way.

A plan, which in some ways may have been rather reckless, began to form. If I called on Arnold to let him know about Annie, I could try to establish whether I should really be suspicious. Of course, I'd meet him somewhere public, I wasn't that stupid. And part of me struggled with the idea that Arnold could ever be a murderer. There was something so guileless and friendly about him. Then again, he worked with dead bodies – and I'd read enough Agatha Christies to know it was always the least likely suspect.

I ate some toast with the dripping that Annie had left in the tiny pantry, and wastefully poured my tea down the sink. I wanted to get on with it quickly, which suggested that I already knew this was a bad idea.

I was putting on my coat and hat when the doorbell rang. I ran down the rest of the flight, nearly turning over on my ankle, and flung it open to find Charles standing on the step.

'Evening,' he said. 'Thought I'd come courting, like a Victorian gent.'

I laughed – my mood had transformed at the sight of him.

'Shall we go for some supper?'

In my life, supper meant a dry biscuit and Ovaltine before bed, but Charles was several social strata ahead, and I presumed he meant the sort of thing that rich people ate before the theatre, at pink-shaded tables.

'That would be lovely,' I said. 'If you're sure you can afford—'

'That's not for you to worry about,' he said. He caught hold of me in the doorway and stroked a bit of stray hair away from my left eyebrow.

'I like you so much, Edie,' he said. I looked into his eyes, their strange, astral green, and felt like a girl in a comic strip, swooning in the arms of her handsome beau.

'I like you very much too,' I said. I was utterly hopeless at this. What was one supposed to say? My heart was thudding appropriately, but my brain was wading through wet sand to catch up. It was as though I had missed some crucial page of the romance manual.

He gently put his arms around me, and tears sprang to my eyes.

'My dear,' he said. 'What is it? Is it because of Sylvia?'

'Oh, Annie's mum's been hurt in a raid,' I quavered, 'and yes, Sylvia, and...' I took a deep breath. 'I feel certain that somebody wants to kill me. And I was going to go and see Arnold to tell him about Annie going home. And also because I don't trust him. And then you arrived.'

'Then let's go together,' he said. 'I hate the idea that the man could be a lunatic, and you were going on your own. Not that I doubt your capabilities,' he added, kissing my temple. 'But still.'

I wondered what Arnold would think about us roaring up outside the funeral parlour in Charles's sports car, but still, we had the excuse of passing on news.

'And afterwards,' Charles said, 'it might be too late for a restaurant, so come back to mine and I shall cook you a proper supper. Or at least, I'll see what the housekeeper's left for us in the larder. She makes a very good rabbit pie; I think the butcher must have a *tendresse* for her.'

'That sounds marvellous,' I told him. Perhaps, too, I could see Lillian and get her own expert view on whether Joseph had known the painting's true value.

'Edie!' Arnold said. He looked shocked. From the stairs behind him, there came a scent of mutton stew, and I realised we'd interrupted his evening meal. He noticed Charles emerging from the car, and his face changed, the way a membrane comes over a snake's eyes when it blinks. It was already apparent that this visit was a mistake. Charles and I had spent the short journey joking about me being a glamorous lady spy, but we hadn't managed to define a strategy to find out anything. I had thought we'd invite Arnold for a drink at the pub, but clearly his mum was up there, ladling out stew and chatting about bodies.

'What brings you here?' Arnold said. He glanced helplessly behind him. 'We're just having tea. Do you want to come up?'

'No, no,' I said, as Charles joined me and shook Arnold's hand. 'We just thought we'd come over for a drink, see if you were free...' I added feebly.

'Look, old man,' said Charles, 'We'll just repair to the pub, and if you'd like to join us for one, please do.'

Arnold nodded. He pointed down the street to the Bull, the pub where I'd asked for directions the first time I'd visited him. 'See you there in about half an hour,' he said, disappearing back upstairs. I was relieved he hadn't refused, particularly as I'd forgotten to pass on Annie's message.

This time, it was a miserable-looking barmaid pulling pints, and I felt disgustingly pleased with myself for being here with such a handsome man, even if the pub itself was hardly the Savoy.

Charles handed me a gin and tonic, and I must have looked surprised. 'Oh Lord, sorry,' he said. 'It's what mother always has. Force of habit.'

'I don't mind,' I said. Its bitter, botanical tang felt exotic to me. It made me feel closer to Lillian, and I realised that I missed her. There was something secure about her, a sense that she knew exactly who she was, which I envied deeply.

'How is your mother?' I asked.

He shrugged. 'It's still not long since Joseph died and her house was bombed. Good job she's stoical. But she definitely liked the obit – she saw it this morning.'

I was hoping she would be in later so I could check on her. As this killer was seemingly picking off anyone with a connection to Joseph Novak, my darkest fears now involved Lillian's sudden death, as well as my own. I thought of her, lying in a pool of blood by the cocktail cabinet, and shuddered.

'Goose walk over your grave?'

Charles lit two cigarettes and gave one to me. I wondered where he'd picked up his smooth ways. At Oxford, perhaps, sharing a punt with some languid female student, smoking and talking about poetry. I had a sudden image of his landlady, Thelma. I didn't like her, pouting little cat that she was.

'I'm perfectly fine,' I lied. Charles was so ludicrously good-looking that it was sometimes hard to think of something intelligent to say when I was with him. I longed for him to take my hand, or say something affectionate, while despising myself for being so feeble.

'So,' he said, eventually, tapping out his cigarette in the rusty ashtray which read POTTER'S BEST MILK STOUT: ASK FOR IT BY NAME! 'Arnold Whiting. What do we think? Murderer?'

'Shh!' I said, shocked. The girl behind the bar raised her head. She must have known about Sylvia, it was only down the road.

'Oh, don't be so bourgeois,' said Charles. 'We may as well be honest. You do wonder about him, don't you?'

'It's a bit odd, that's all,' I said, and was telling him what Arnold had said about the dog, when the door opened and Arnold himself came in, flustered, raising a hand in greeting and setting the overhead bell jangling. I felt an awful stab of pity for him, and wished we hadn't come. But of course, for all I knew, he was planning to garrotte me with the curtain pull before the night was out.

I smiled at him as he returned from the bar, and patted the

stool next to me as he turned with his tankard of beer, splashing some on the floor.

'Hear about Sylvia?' he asked, sitting down. I nodded.

'Awful business,' said Charles.

'She was such a sweet kid,' Arnold said. 'We used to play in a go-kart made from orange boxes. She always wanted to go faster. And her mum too. All three of them, gone in a month.'

A silence fell and we sipped our drinks, unable to think of a suitable epitaph. Instead, I launched into the story of Annie and her own mum, and he expressed concern and asked for the address. 'I'll send her a card,' he added.

I didn't want to let him know where Annie would be, but, I reasoned, he'd been to our rooms and hadn't tried to murder us. Then I remembered that I'd been followed in the blackout. I couldn't think of a way to refuse, so I scribbled the address down on a bit of cardboard from his battered packet of Craven A. Charles smoked Rothmans Pall Mall, and kept them in a monogrammed case.

'Rum thing, another murder so nearby, isn't it?' Charles said. I froze. I had expected that we'd chat for a bit and I'd slip a few subtle questions in somehow. I was the journalist, not Charles, and he'd played his entire hand before the foam had subsided on Arnold's pint.

Arnold looked up, a little moustache of froth clinging to his lip.

'Very,' he agreed. 'Poor girl. We didn't deal with it – her body went straight to Central.'

'Is that what always happens with a murder?'

I closed my eyes and swigged the last of my G and T.

'Yes, of course,' Arnold said. 'Sometimes, I've been down there to lend a hand, but it's always the Home Office pathologist who does the post mortem. Look, this isn't very nice to be discussing with a lady present.'

'I'm a journalist, not a lady!' I said. I was profoundly wishing I'd stayed at home with Charles.

'What do you make of it?' Charles persisted. 'So soon after Pamela Novak. Think it's the same lunatic?'

'I've no idea,' said Arnold. 'I suppose it must be.'

'Did you know the Turnbulls well?' Charles went on. 'Or the Novaks? You must have dealt with Joseph's body?' I tried to catch his eye. Arnold looked puzzled and annoyed, and I was desperate for Charles to stop.

'Yes, I did,' he said coolly. 'It was just a heart attack, nothing to do with his wife's horrible death.'

'Yes, that's what my mother was told,' Charles said, sipping his drink. 'Interesting about the dog being locked away, don't you think?'

Arnold gazed steadily at him as Charles lit another cigarette. The look on his pale face, I realised, was contempt.

No answer was forthcoming, and Charles said, 'Drink?'

I waved my empty glass and nodded. I didn't want to antagonise him, regardless of how insensitive he was being.

There was a huddle of beefy, khaki backs at the bar, ARP wardens gathering before the night shift like a herd of Aberdeen Angus, and Charles joined the noisy queue. As soon as he was out of earshot, Arnold leaned forward.

'Edie, I don't think he's good for you,' he said in a low, urgent voice. 'Where's he from really? And all these peculiar questions he's asking me. I don't trust him.'

I laughed awkwardly. 'He's from Didsbury!' I said. 'He's just trying to help me get to the bottom of things.' I stopped. If Arnold was a killer, he didn't need any more information to encourage him.

'I read your obituary of Mr Novak,' he said quickly.

Charles was saying something to the barmaid. I saw her laugh.

'I thought it was brilliant,' Arnold went on. 'It made him a human being.'

I wished Charles had said the same.

Arnold continued, 'But don't you think it's odd that he'd give a painting potentially worth thousands to...'

Charles put his hand on my shoulder and squeezed as he put another gin in front of me, and I was ashamed at the wave of relief I felt that he still liked me.

'Have I missed anything?' he asked.

'No, we're just talking about... ow!' Arnold had kicked my ankle with a sharp tap of his brogue.

I didn't continue. I had no idea what was going on with Arnold and while I'd always thought it might be fun to be a femme fatale with men fighting over me, in truth it was just embarrassing. Not that Charles was fighting very hard.

I still half hoped that I could rescue the conversation, and find out how Arnold had really known about Mrs Novak's dog. Or I did until Charles opened his mouth again.

'So, do you get to know many details about these murders,' he said conversationally, 'what with being mates with the DI?'

Arnold stared at him. 'I only know what the public knows,' he said.

'Right.' I tried to kick Charles in turn, but his legs were on the other side of the stool, as if he were riding side-saddle, and I couldn't reach without tipping mine over.

'So you didn't know about Mrs Novak's dog being locked up and left to starve then?'

An icy claw gripped my insides.

Arnold pushed his stool back and stood up. He looked paler than ever, as if there were no blood left in his body, and in the dim light of the Saloon bar his hair was a quivering vermilion flame.

'I don't like your tone,' he said. 'Are you suggesting that I'm somehow involved in all this?'

Charles shrugged an elegant shoulder. 'That rather depends,' he said. He held up a hand and ticked off on his fingers. 'You're an undertaker, you're used to dead bodies. You're not away fighting, though you certainly seem strong enough to stab or strangle someone. You knew Sylvia as a child. You knew about the painting. Perhaps you found out about it and thought it was at Joseph's house, and that's why you killed Pamela, so you could get your hands on it. And there's the dog, which you also mysteriously knew about. You're right-handed, judging by the way you wrote that number down. And now, you've developed a peculiarly strong interest in Edie and her friend. Am I getting close, Whiting?'

'Charles!' I said, snapping out of my state of frozen horror and extending a useless hand to stop him saying any more, but he was still looking at Arnold.

'I've nothing to be afraid of,' said Arnold. 'But maybe you do, you jumped-up bastard.'

He lunged forward, and shoved Charles hard in the shoulder. His stool topped sideways, and Charles staggered and righted himself, knocking into the table. Glasses fell and smashed on the floor, and a uniformed man at the bar shouted, 'Oi!'

'Don't!' I cried, but it came out high and wavering, a child's voice. I had seen fights at the home, but that was just boys, grappling. Arnold swung his fist at Charles's cheek, and Charles wheeled backwards into the next table. A woman shrieked as beer soaked her dress, and the barmaid shouted, 'Outside!'

But now Charles was coming at Arnold, who was standing like a bull, his head thrust forward, his balled hands at his sides. Charles made an ineffectual push at him, and Arnold grabbed his arm, and punched him in the stomach.

I screamed as Charles fell, closed eyes and open mouth, onto a stool, bounced off and lay still on the sticky floor amongst the broken glass. People were exclaiming and milling, someone was yelling about calling the police.

'What have you done?' I shouted. Arnold was breathing heavily, his eyes dark with rage. I sank onto the floor beside Charles. He was choking, trying to get his breath. Finally, he took a shuddering, warbling gulp of air and whispered, 'Bloody madman.'

'Sorry about that,' Arnold said to the room at large. 'But he flaming well deserved it.' He kicked half a broken tankard towards Charles's legs, then shouldered through the blacked-out door. The air in his wake was toxic with spilled beer and adrenaline.

'Jesus.' Charles was struggling upwards, and I gave him my arm. 'What a damn lunatic. If that doesn't prove...'

I righted the stool, and he heaved himself back onto it. Around us, people were shaking their heads, and the barmaid looked undecided about throwing us out. 'We're going in a sec,' I called to her. 'He's just getting his breath back.'

'Come on,' he said after a moment. 'Let's get out of this hell-hole.' He was still a little stooped, after such a painful winding, and I put my arm around his waist.

'I'm fine,' he said, and shook me off as we left. He clearly no longer felt like going for supper, and when he said, 'Look, would you mind if we just left it for this evening? I could do with a hot bath after that,' I didn't suggest he could have it at ours. The hot water wasn't on anyway.

I said, 'Of course.' He drove me home in heavy silence, and told me he'd see me soon.

Then I went upstairs and sat in the half-dark on the couch thinking about Annie and Lou, and Arnold, and Marple, and wondering why Charles had turned so viciously on Arnold – and whether he was, in fact, right to do so.

CHAPTER FOURTEEN

At work the following day, I was still beset by troubled thoughts. I gazed out of the window beyond Pat's desk, and tried to wrestle them into order.

I knew that Edward Turnbull had taught Joseph, and that Sylvia had almost certainly been killed for the painting, but then, I reminded myself, it may have been worth nothing at all. Perhaps Joseph was just a decent artist, and had knocked it up himself. In which case, why did it matter so much to someone?

In detective stories I'd read, the killer always had a signature style, a way of strangling, or stabbing, that meant he was easily traceable. But here, we were dealing with a shooting, a stabbing and a strangling. What if they weren't related at all? It seemed unlikely, but the war had unleashed strange and desperate reactions. And then there was Lou's observation, which haunted me. What if I was getting in the way, and the killer was already considering how best to do me in? With Annie gone, was I safe at home alone?

Arnold had known about the Turnbulls, he'd known where Mrs Novak lived, he'd known about the dog, he had opportunity... but despite Charles's list of likely events, I couldn't find a decent motive for him. I racked my brains – was he in love with Sylvia and she'd rejected him? Did he want to sell the painting and escape his mother and his sombre career? Perhaps Edward stood in their way... but Sylvia lived in London, and as far as I knew, he hadn't seen her for years.

Lillian wasn't in the will. So if she'd wanted to bump Mrs Novak off, surely it would have been when Joseph was alive, not after he'd died? Could she have been enraged at finding out she'd been overlooked? But no, I thought, she must have known, and though she had no affection for Pamela, I couldn't envisage elegant Lillian hating that ordinary little woman enough to pay someone to stab her to death.

Charles? He had alibis, but he had also known about the will. What if he'd tried to persuade Mrs Novak to hand over some money for his mother, and it had gone wrong? But that didn't explain Sylvia's death. He and Lillian already had plenty of money, and walls full of paintings – and besides, he was my boyfriend, a man who was intensely protective of me, and sweet despite his sophistication. The idea of his stabbing a defenceless woman seemed ludicrous.

Perhaps Dennis, Winifred's brother, then? He could have known about the painting. He had been full of rage. Maybe he had gone to see Pamela Novak to argue that she should hand over the money for Winifred's airfares, and she'd refused – so in a rage, he'd killed her. Though Edward was already dead by then, and he surely wouldn't kill his own niece – unless, of course, he had no feelings for her, or was furious with her on his sister's behalf. After all, Sylvia had defied her mother to go to London, then defied Edward to stay there. Perhaps once Dennis knew she was standing between him and a valuable painting, he no longer cared. But he'd only had to ask her, and she'd simply have said, 'I gave it to that Edie girl.'

Unless she was trying to protect me, I thought with horror.

Perhaps she'd refused to tell him where it was, and he'd lost his temper, and fixed his meaty hands round her throat.

'Penny for them,' said Pat, passing my desk. 'Or judging by your face, a farthing.'

'Not even worth that,' I said, and I turned back to my typewriter.

I came home to a note on the door. *So sorry about last night. I feel such a fool! I came by to apologise in person, but missed you – see you soon for that supper, C.E. x*

Relief washed over me, though he hadn't suggested he'd return today. In the larder we only had an unpleasant scrag-end of mutton, leaking into its paper wrapping, and a wizened onion. It was not inspiring. It occurred to me that I could pop round to Charles's, check on Lillian, and make sure everything was all right between us. On a deeper level, which I didn't want to think about, it also meant I'd be less vulnerable to a murderer creeping up the stairs.

Going out in the blackout was being severely discouraged – other than Knowing the Fastest Route to Your Local Shelter, and Volunteering as a Warden – but I was tired of being afraid, and sick of feeling like a sitting duck every night. There had been no raids for the last two nights, and I suspected the Germans felt they'd destroyed enough of Manchester (or, 'a large North West industrial city') and had moved on to new targets.

Before my boldness ebbed away and left me staring at a watery stew, I gathered my gas mask, bag and dying torch and headed out into the night. It was a good forty-minute walk to Charles's, and the torch was emitting only a feeble glint by the time I arrived. Once on his wide, tree-lined road, I felt less courageous, but I thought of Lillian and cocktails and Charles's welcoming kiss, and braced myself.

. . .

Of course, he wasn't in. His car had gone, and I felt a pang of dread. Was he out with some other sweetheart, laughing gently at her jokes, placing his warm hand on her knee as he drove? I felt sick with jealousy imagining someone much more suited to Charles's sophistication and looks.

All I'd done was moan and shudder about murderers, and get him punched for his trouble. I wondered why he liked me at all.

Of course, the car could be in for fixing, I decided. Or perhaps he'd be back any minute. Now I'd come, it seemed defeatist and silly to turn and go home again, to the empty flat.

I rang the bell and heard it echo through the house. The click of a door, skittering footsteps on the stairs. I thought of Sylvia again, and how guileless she'd been.

Thelma opened the door. Her hair was set to tumble over one eye, and she had on a chic black dress with diamante shoulder buttons, and high suede heels with real nylons. She looked much less like a Pekinese now, with her eyes made up, and she wore scarlet lipstick. She reminded me of the elegant drawing on a dress pattern packet.

'Oh!' she said. 'I thought you were Charlie.' I didn't like her calling him 'Charlie'. 'Charles' or 'my lodger, Mr Emerson' would have been fine.

'I've come to see him,' I said. 'Do you know how long he'll be?'

She affected surprise. 'You're Sadie, aren't you? I hadn't realised...'

I wanted to shout, 'Hadn't realised what?' Hadn't realised he was still seeing someone as hopeless as me? Hadn't realised I cared enough to come and see him of my own accord?

She shrugged. 'He's taken Lillian back to her house to look through some things they've salvaged. I was about to cook dinner for us.'

'For whom?'

She gave a little laugh that made me want to slap her. I felt like an evacuee, standing on her step in my wool coat and sensible shoes, clutching my torch and gas mask box.

'For Charles and I.'

Charles and me, I heard Mr Gorringe say in my head. Thinking of him reminded me why I was here in the first place.

'I need to ask him about something,' I said, 'So if it's quite all right, I'll just wait till he gets back.'

'Suit yourself,' she said, turning away rudely. 'But I'm afraid there's only enough steak for two.'

I felt a brief flare of rage. What did Charles think he was doing, encouraging his landlady's crush on him? Perhaps we'd laugh about it later, but as I followed her like an obedient terrier up the stairs to her rooms, I felt less sure. The small table was laid for two, with a white cloth and polished silver. There was a fire flickering in the grate, and a record on the gramophone, warbling, '*...you walk by... December feels like May...*' in a crooning tenor.

'Do you often have dinner together?' I asked, miserably aware that I was failing to sound even slightly casual.

'When he's about,' she said. 'He's rather good company, and we both like art, and politics. He's a very good conversationalist.'

As she spoke, there was the sound of the front door banging and feet on the stairs. 'Sorry, darling,' Charles shouted. 'Just getting my cigs.'

Darling? Now I felt like smacking him.

I heard his flat door open and shut, and Thelma smirked. 'I'll give you a moment,' she said, 'but our dinner will be ready in ten minutes, so...'

Charles appeared. He didn't knock on the door, he just wandered in. He leaned forward to kiss her, and saw me.

'Edie!' he cried. To give him credit, it was an impressive recovery.

I smiled tightly. 'Sorry to interrupt,' I said. I wished bitterly that I was the sort of girl who threw plates and made a fuss. But embarrassment was worse than hurt feelings to me, so I stayed standing there, stiff as a Buckingham Palace guard, while he bypassed Thelma and came over to me.

'Darling,' he said, 'whatever are you doing here? Thelma's kindly offered to knock up some supper for me, I had nothing in, so... I was going to come back and see you later, as it happens.'

I wanted to believe him. 'I needed to ask you something,' I said.

'Don't mind me,' said Thelma, and skipped off to the kitchen. She was all sweetness now Charles had arrived, though no doubt she'd be stewing furiously over the pans.

'Look, I'm sorry if this looks a bit rum,' Charles said in a low voice. 'Thelma is rather lonely, I think. Let's just say she makes the most of a bit of male company.'

He studied my face. 'I was just going to have a bite to eat, then come over to you. I've missed you,' he added, taking my hand. His palm was warm and dry against mine, and I felt my treacherous body yearn towards him.

Charles was wearing a white shirt and black trousers. Most men would have looked like a waiter, but somehow, he contrived to look like some bright young thing in a Noël Coward play. 'Here,' he said, flipping open his cigarette case and offering it to me. 'I'm delighted to see you, but what's prompted the visit?'

I took one, aware that time was passing. I could smell butter sizzling in the kitchen. I was starving. I thought I'd better pretend it was to do with the murders.

'It's just a quick thing,' I said.

He squeezed my hand. 'Cough it up then.'

Thelma banged skillets and clanked plates, like a terribly obvious theatre production where a character is trying to imply impatience.

'It's simply...' I stopped. I had been mulling it all over for days, but suddenly, a question occurred to me from nowhere.

'Charles, did you know your father?'

He coughed. 'My father? No, he died just after I was born. I told you. Why?'

'But Lillian never told you his full name? Or where he died? You don't remember him at all?'

Charles shook his head. 'Nope. Never asked. I imagine if she'd felt the need to tell me, she would have done.'

'But there are no photographs...?'

'Bloody hell, Edie,' – he drew on his cigarette irritably – 'do you want fingerprints? There aren't any photographs because they'd only been married for five minutes before he died. They were married in the last war, and there weren't too many photographers lounging about waiting to take snaps.'

'That seems sad. That you never knew what he looked like.'

He shrugged. 'Like me, I suppose. Considering I look nothing like my mother. Anyway, why are you asking?'

'It's...' It was impossible to answer without embarking on a long explanation, as Thelma's mysteriously off-the-ration steaks cooled and her temper rose.

'Look,' I said, 'I'll get off now, you have your dinner. You could come round later, and we can talk about it then.'

'Certainly,' he said. 'I shall.'

On my way down the stairs, I tried to rein in my jealousy. It seemed wrong that he should see me off and sit down to a cosy supper with Thelma. He could have shared a bit of his steak... so perhaps I wasn't his girl at all. And I was nervous about his visit later. Now the question had occurred to me, there was something making me oddly uneasy about Charles's answer.

I needed to know whether handsome Captain Emerson had ever existed. Or if Charles was, in fact, Joseph Novak's son and Lillian had never told him the truth. If he was, then technically, the painting would belong to him. And presumably, the Novak's family home would too.

But if that were the case, why would Lillian keep his parentage a secret? Shame? She didn't seem the type, though a baby born out of wedlock during the last war would certainly have caused some judgement. Most ended up in orphanages, just like me, not being raised by rich, artistic, Bohemians, shuttling between England and Berlin. Surely now, though, it would be in her interest to come clean, as there were no other Novak children and Charles would inherit.

The sensible thing would have been to ask Lillian herself, but I didn't have the courage to go barging in, demanding answers. She intimidated me still. And Charles was my boyfriend, or so I'd imagined, and I'd assumed he might be more forthcoming.

I got the bus home, torturing myself by imagining the two of them in the candlelight, Thelma reaching over to pour brandy, Charles taking her hand... I considered what Annie would say. Worse, I imagined what Lou would say. And I resolved to tell Charles that if I was really going to be his girl, the cosy suppers with his landlady would have to stop.

Back home, after ignoring Lou's instructions about walking alone in the blackout – really, it wasn't as if I had any choice – I waited on the couch, blinds drawn tightly, and the wireless firmly off in case I didn't hear the doorbell. I couldn't bear the miserable mutton, thinking of Charles and Thelma over their meal, so I made myself a sandwich with the hardening bit of mousetrap cheese Annie had left, and sat, chomping miserably, while I thought about it all.

If Joseph was Charles's father, he must surely have known – particularly if Captain Emerson was a figment of Lillian's imagination, designed to confer respectability. It might also explain why Joseph had been so committed to their safety and security. But then, where did the money come from – and the art? Joseph? Why would he marry Pamela, though, if that were the case? There would have been nothing to stop him and Lillian marrying. Everywhere I turned, there was another blind alley.

I waited until past ten o'clock for Charles to arrive, but there was no sound of an engine purring to a halt outside, no slamming car door or hurrying steps. A couple of WVS girls went by, chatting, and a dog had a long, barked conversation with its friend across several frosty gardens, but other than that, the street remained silent.

At a quarter to eleven, I gave up and went to bed. I'd forgotten to lay the fire, so I lay with the blanket pulled up over my head, thinking about blood and strangulation and Annie's mum, and air raids. I tried hard not to think about Charles taking Thelma in his arms, pushing away her drooping hair so he could kiss her scarlet lips. It wasn't a peaceful night's sleep.

I spent the weekend working at the canteen again, trying to take my mind off all my problems. It was certainly busy enough to distract me, with streams of soldiers on leave joining the usual crowd for a free cup of tea. I poured and distributed and wiped and smiled, but every time there was a brief lull, I found myself thinking again about the murders and – less nobly – about why Charles hadn't been back to see me. Perhaps he had simply decided Thelma was the one for him, and had no more use for me. I tried not to feel hurt – he had made me no promises, after all, but for a few kisses and a claim that he 'liked' me. I had only known him a couple of weeks. But a world of colour and culture had opened up before me, and I longed to step into it. I didn't want the door to the Emersons' gilded lives snapped shut in my face – particularly if Thelma was the lucky recipient instead.

My thoughts gave additional verve to my scrubbing of trestle tables and hefting of pots, and by Sunday night, I was exhausted.

I came home to a telegram from Annie. *Mum home. Back soon. A.*

Relieved and cheered, I pulled the blackout curtains shut, made myself a tea of potato pancake with a rather tired sausage, and went to bed with the library copy of *One, Two, Buckle My Shoe* that I'd finally borrowed. There were no more raids, but I slept badly – every creak of the old house sounded like a murderer on the stairs, and by dawn, I was glad to get out of bed and scuttle across the freezing landing for a wash.

I arrived at my desk to find an envelope laid on the blotter. It was a thick cream weave, addressed in a swooping hand with raven-black ink, the sort of letter I used to dream of receiving during my interminable childhood. *Dearest Edie, I am your rich, long-lost uncle...* Of course, it was always lost in the post.

But this one was addressed to me, and had arrived by the first post.

'Ooh, is that an invitation?' said Pat, bustling back to her desk. 'Queen's garden party again, is it?'

I slit the envelope and withdrew an equally heavy sheet of paper.

Of course, it was from the valuers. With all my worry over Charles, I'd forgotten about this crucial factor in the whole mess.

Dear Miss York... a most interesting example... rare... cause to believe...

The word that leapt out didn't quite make sense at first. I read it again, and then a third time.

A Cézanne.

It went on to remind me that the utmost care must be taken of this great work – *an early piece, our expert suggests* – and to request a meeting at my earliest convenience, to discuss the ownership, auction value, and the future of this *quite remarkable, previously unknown piece.*

I sank into my desk chair.

'What?' said Pat. 'You look like you've had a turn. Is it bad news?'

I had no idea. But it seemed almost certain that I was now responsible for Sylvia's death, if not Mrs Novak's. If it hadn't been for me, nobody would know about the painting. As it was, half of Manchester was in the frame.

'Frame. Hah.' I said out loud.

Pat shook her head. 'Get yourself to Boots and get some aspirins,' she said. 'Have a cup of sweet tea while you're at it. Then you might deign to tell us what's sent you funny.'

I did as she said. I needed air.

'What's going on with Arnold?'

'What do you mean?' I said. I'd answered my desk telephone as I came back in, hoping it might be Charles, but when the operator put through the caller, it was Lou Brennan. He certainly didn't bother with niceties.

'Don't play the innocent,' he said. 'I've heard all about you and your smarmy sweetheart, accusing my pal of being a murderer. I'd like to know your game, Miss York, because quite frankly, I've had enough of your unasked-for involvement in my job. Everywhere I look, you're there, finding bodies, giving statements, asking questions, flinging accusations. It's unacceptable, and as a Detective Inspector, I'm telling you...'

My cheeks were flaming. 'Lou, listen,' I said urgently, aware of Pat slowing her typing, so she could earwig more effectively. 'Arnold knew about Marple being shut in the bedroom. I knew you hadn't told the press, and I didn't tell him, so how did he know?'

'And nobody thought to mention this to me?' Lou said, just

as Parrot Paulson passed my desk, mouthing 'I hope that's a work call.'

'Look, I've got to go,' I said.

'I'll drop round later to sort this out,' said Lou. It sounded like a warning. 'Will you be in?'

'Yes. Any advance on the investigations?' I asked quickly.

'What do you think?' he said, and rang off. He was always so bad-tempered.

I forgot all about Lou when I left the building at lunchtime to buy a bun from the kiosk. Charles was sitting on a bench in the cold, wrapped in an expensive-looking coat and wearing a trilby. He was smoking elegantly, and drawing glances from office girls as they passed.

'So sorry, darling,' he said, at my boot-faced greeting. 'Been at mother's house, cleaning dust off salvaged ornaments all weekend. Look, whatever silly idea you've got, I fell asleep on Thelma's couch, that's all. She put a blanket over me, and I was out like a light. Mother came in at midnight and woke me, and that's where I found myself the following morning – with a whisky hangover and a large serving of regret.'

'Really,' I said tightly. 'I see.'

'Oh, come on, Edie,' he said. 'I really am sorry – but Thelma's just a pal. She's got a young man in the RAF, and they're getting married after the war. Besides, I'm here now, begging forgiveness. And if you won't go out with me, I'll have to ask Mr Benson.'

I smiled grudgingly. 'That's my girl,' said Charles, and put his arm round my waist. I wanted to be angry, but I was with him again, which meant he wasn't with Thelma, and I was desperate to tell him about the painting.

'Lunch at The French, to make it up to you?' he asked. 'I know the maître d', he'll squeeze us in.'

'I've got an interview to do this afternoon,' I began. It was the woman in Northenden, whose brother had lost a leg at

Ctesiphon in 1915 and become a swimming instructor at Victoria Baths for the next twenty-five years. I imagined Lou saying, 'Swam in circles, did he?'

'We'll make it quick,' said Charles. 'Beats a kiosk bun.'

I couldn't argue. Once again, I slid into his car feeling I'd somehow been outfoxed.

When we were installed at a discreet little table for two and had ordered, I told him what the valuers had said.

'Good Lord,' he said. 'Are you sure?'

I had refused wine this time, but I would have loved a glass. My greatest fear, however, was that Mr Gorringe would walk in again, and I'd positioned myself facing the door, so I could dive under the table if necessary.

'I'm not sure at all, but I need to see them as soon as possible.'

'Well, eat up,' said Charles. 'This is quite incredible, we'll go straight there after this.'

Somehow, the explaining about Thelma, and my intrusive questions about his paternity, had fallen off the agenda. In the soft light of day, amongst the linen cloths and sparkling glasses of The French, my night of dread seemed rather overwrought.

'Well, you don't have to come...' I began.

'Of course I do!' he exclaimed. 'I know a little about art because of Mother. And Joseph, of course. I can help you discuss things, if you'd like.'

I knew a little too, but I had no experience whatsoever of dealing with valuers and auctioneers, and working out the legal nightmare of to whom the painting belonged.

'All right then,' I said. 'I know Joseph loved art, but do you think he really had any idea how much it was worth? Or what it was?'

'Well, he can't have done,' said Charles. 'I don't know how he came to have it – he was a refugee for goodness' sake. Mother wouldn't know either, I'm sure, but we must tell her. She'll be agog.'

'Does she have anything like that?' I asked. 'Or, did she, I mean?'

'Well, hardly a Cézanne, no,' he said. 'Some decent minor pieces. But that was mostly due to my father's interest.'

'Your father...' I began, just as a waiter flourished alongside the table, proffering the bill to Charles as if it were a shameful written confession.

'So sorry, sir,' he murmured regretfully. 'May I leave this here...?'

By the time it was all sorted out, another waiter was holding my coat, and Charles was saying, 'To the valuers!'

This time, there was no sign of Mr Gorringe.

Mr Payne was much more welcoming this time. He rang for tea, and his secretary returned with a plate of small, shop-bought biscuits and a full set of jugs and pots and tea strainers and began a silent ballet of pouring and stirring, which was somewhat distracting.

'This is quite remarkable,' he kept saying. 'Quite remarkable.'

He addressed all his remarks to Charles, as though I'd just wandered in off the street, hoping for a free cup of tea.

'I suppose the police will need to be informed,' I said, 'given that the picture may have been the cause of the murder.'

Mr Payne withdrew slightly at the word 'murder'. It probably wasn't often spoken in his serene suite of mahogany rooms.

'Leave that to me, my dear,' Charles said. 'I'm afraid you've had far too many unpleasant dealings with the police lately – I can't let you get tangled up in all the dismal whys and wherefores again.'

'But I was given the picture,' I began, and he shot me a quelling glance.

'We'll certainly make them aware,' Charles said firmly.

'In terms of ownership,' Mr Payne said, ponderously, packing his tortoiseshell pipe with tobacco, 'I believe there was an uncle you mentioned?'

'Yes, indeed,' Charles said. 'A Mr Dennis Donnelly. We intend to visit him this evening.'

This was news to me.

'And may I assume you'd prefer us to retain the picture in question until its future is determined? At which point, the wheels of commerce may be permitted to creak forth' – he allowed himself a small smile – 'as we prepare for a, frankly, unprecedented auction. This will put Payne and Son firmly upon the map,' he added, drawing on his pipe and gazing at the dark oil paintings hung around his office. They were mostly of crofters' cottages with smoking chimneys, or dead deer, with huntsmen standing over them. My light-filled Cézanne was clearly a very different prospect.

'Actually, I think we might prefer to take it with us,' Charles said. 'We'll need to show Mr Donnelly, after all, so he can decide what to do.'

'Of course, the fellow is welcome to come and study it here,' Mr Payne said worriedly. 'But I do fear that, with such a valuable piece, it may fall into the wrong hands. Not to mention the air raids – we have a secure vault downstairs, with a lead-lined door. It can withstand any blast.'

'Even when it's coming from the wife!' said Charles, and they chuckled together, to my fury.

'Mr Payne,' Charles said, amusement still lingering in his tone, 'I assure you, I shall take the utmost care of this precious piece. I have my car outside, and it shall not leave my sight. Then tomorrow, we'll return it first thing, and if Mr Donnelly is willing, we can press ahead with the auction.'

The painting was repacked, this time in a crate of tissue and straw, and reverently handed over.

'Thank you for...' I began, as Mr Payne shook Charles's hand and murmured, 'Absolute pleasure... no, indeed, the thanks is all mine...' to him, before handing back our hats and ushering us out onto the cold street.

I was already late for the interview with the swimming instructor's sister, but I was bursting to speak.

'What was that all about?' I demanded. 'I barely spoke! It was me who found the bloody picture...'

'Darling, men like Mr Payne don't listen to young women with Manchester accents, I'm afraid,' said Charles. 'What exactly did you object to? You're off the hook when it comes to being back in the police station, we've got the painting, now off we go to reveal its wonders to the discerning Mr Donnelly.'

'Manchester accent?'

'Well, darling, you're hardly Ellen Terry, are you?' he said fondly. 'My scrappy little cat.'

'And how do you know he's called Dennis Donnelly?'

He tapped his nose. 'I'm not in intelligence for nothing.'

Charles could see I was cross. 'Come on, sweetheart,' he said. 'Hop in the car, and I'll give you a lift to your old swimming woman.'

I was tempted to refuse, but it was very cold and I was going to be extremely late otherwise. I wondered why Charles wasn't at work.

'Working all day and all night tomorrow,' he said. 'Even intelligence types get a day off occasionally.'

I longed to ask him what he was doing in his bunker, but of course, he was sworn to secrecy. I imagined him plotting cardboard planes onto complex graphs, and intercepting coded messages, crouched over a crackling receiver, but perhaps my ideas of intelligence work were too heavily rooted in the adventure comics the boys used to smuggle into the home.

'The other thing is,' I said, 'we don't know where Dennis Donnelly lives.'

'Oh, don't we?' he said. 'Mother has a telephone book to aid her many social calls. I shall return home, read the entire D section, and return to collect you, furnished with the information.'

'All right,' I said. 'But I'm keeping hold of the painting.'

'Of course,' Charles said. 'It's yours, after all.'

The bereaved sister was sweet and eager, and had made a very dry, eggless cake with caraway seeds. They always felt like perfumed grit in my mouth, but I forced two slices down to be polite. After the lunch with Charles, I felt like a stuffed goose.

I emerged into the winter dusk to find him waiting outside, as he'd promised.

'I've found a Mr Dennis Anthony Donnelly living in the right area,' he said. 'So we have our man.'

I hadn't expected it to be so easy, somehow. I'd seen us knocking on doors like a pair of coppers, with barking dogs slithering up the hall to throw themselves against the panels, and angry householders warning us off.

'So what do we do?' I asked. It wasn't like me to hand things over to Charles, but he had such natural authority, I found myself deferring to him. I wondered if it was to do with education. He just seemed to assume he'd be welcome everywhere.

'We go and see him,' he said, shrugging.

'But he might be dangerous,' I said. 'It might have been him who killed Sylvia. And a man who'd kill his own niece to get a painting...'

'As opposed to a man who'd kill his own niece for a perfectly valid reason?'

I laughed. 'But what can we say to him?' I asked. 'Maybe I

should tell Lou. I do want to know if there've been any developments in the case.'

Charles raised an eyebrow and blew smoke through his elegant nostrils, like a racehorse on a cold morning. 'Well, we can be there and back before you tell that great lummock and he impounds your Cézanne,' he said. 'We'll go and tell this Mr Donnelly about the painting, gauge his reaction, and if it seems odd, we'll pass the whole thing over to Brennan.'

'Dennis was very bad-tempered when I met him.'

Charles patted my arm. 'We'll be charm itself,' he said. 'Come on, you want to be a crime reporter, don't you? I'll keep him chatting, and you can ask to use the outside loo and have a snoop.'

I felt thoroughly unnerved by this plan. At the back of my mind, some missing piece of information scratched like a cat in a locked room, but I ignored it. I couldn't make sense of it, and it was probably irrelevant anyway. Much more concerning was the prospect of Dennis Donnelly, grieving brother and possible murderer, clapping eyes on me again.

CHAPTER FIFTEEN

We found the street hidden away at the back of Burnage Lane, a cul-de-sac of semi-detached houses, like Winifred's. 'It's number six,' said Charles, peering at the doors. Dennis's house was set back from the road with a slightly unkempt front garden, a huge laurel bush spilling over the path, and a sign on the rusted green gate reading BEWARE OF THE DOGS.

'Marvellous,' I said, getting out of the car with the cumbersome crate, and pointing at it.

Charles sighed. 'Dogs. They always want to leap at you, they've no social graces. Give me a cat any time.' I thought of Thelma and her little squashed face, and determined to be brave and bold, to show her up for the rich idiot she was.

'Come on then,' I said. 'I'm game if you are.'

He joined me by the gate, and I unlatched it. I had a horrible momentary feeling we'd find another murder scene, that Dennis would be hanging from the banisters, his face blue, or lying in a pool of blood in the living room.

'I'll do the talking, you show the painting,' Charles said, and he rang the bell.

There was no wild volley of barking, or scrabble of claws, and I relaxed marginally.

Footsteps came from the back of the house, and the door was opened by a blonde woman in a flowered housecoat, with two elderly Dandie Dinmont terriers weaving about her ankles. Cooking smells drifted out. They seemed to be having something with mince.

'I'm terribly sorry to bother you,' said Charles. 'Mr Charles Emerson and Miss Edie York. Is Mr Donnelly available?'

She looked at Charles, puzzled. 'Are you canvassing? There's no election, is there?'

'No, no.' He smiled, 'We have some news for him, to do with the estate of your late... is it sister-in-law? Winifred Turnbull. And the greatest of sympathy for your recent losses.'

He was laying it on a bit thick with 'estate', I thought. But she turned and shouted, 'Dennis! People here to see you! I can't leave the mince, it'll catch,' she added and shuffled off. Dennis appeared in her place. He looked less intimidating this time, in shirtsleeves, braces and work trousers, but I looked into his pale eyes, chilly and assessing, and I thought of what his large hands might have done.

'How can I help?' he said. 'Bloody hell, it's you.' He shook his head. 'Look, whatever story you're after, as a so-called journalist, you can just—'

'No, no, we don't want a story,' Charles interrupted. 'We have some very interesting information for you.'

'It had better be good,' he said. 'I'm sure you're aware that my little niece was murdered in cold blood the other day. Haven't even buried her mother yet. Come in then, and you've got five minutes. My tea's on.'

'Charm school,' Charles whispered behind his back, as Dennis led us to a living room with a worn brown and green carpet and a brown horsehair-stuffed couch. There was a dressmaker's dummy with a skirt half-pinned in the corner, and over the fire was a framed print of a greenish horse, against pale green wallpaper that had been stained darker by nicotine. The overall effect was like being trapped down a well.

'Spit it out then,' he said, clamping his hands on his knees. He gestured to Charles and me to sit down. I held the crate on my lap.

'We have something that may be yours,' said Charles. I had hoped for fussing with cups of tea, a gentle preamble, but no, we were straight in.

'Mine?' Donnelly looked nonplussed. 'Nothing's missing.'

'No, it belonged to your sister Winifred, you see. Or perhaps Edward, strictly speaking. But given the circumstances...' he trailed off delicately.

Dennis gazed at us, clearly hoping for good news, a windfall.

'It's a Céz—' I began, and Charles cut across me.

'It's a painting,' he said. 'Your niece, Sylvia – I'm so dreadfully sorry, by the way.'

Dennis nodded. 'Bloody tragedy,' he said. 'I hope they get the bastard soon.'

Charles lowered his eyes respectfully. 'Well, she gave it to Edie here for safe keeping, but I'm afraid it was all rather a muddle, and she may have thought it worth more than it is.'

I stared at Charles. What on earth was he doing?

'What painting? I don't know what you're talking about,' Dennis said.

'Edward gave English lessons to a refugee and he repaid him with a little picture,' said Charles, as if charmed by this innocent foreign gesture.

I lifted the lid and cleared away the tissue to show Dennis. I felt so attached to it; the painting glowed like fire from its bed of straw.

Dennis stared, uncomprehending.

'But we took the liberty of having it valued,' Charles went

on, 'and it seems that it's not really worth anything, I'm afraid. I wondered what you'd like us to do with it.'

I was paralysed with shock. This must, I thought, be some cunning plan of Charles's, to draw Dennis into admitting he'd been at Sylvia's that night, that he'd killed her – did he really expect him to blurt 'I did it!' and be led away in leg irons like Magwitch?

'You've come and interrupted my teatime, in a period of mourning, to tell me about some painting that's not worth anything?'

'Well, the sentimental value...' Charles said chidingly.

Dennis looked revolted. 'I've no need of it,' he said. 'It looks like a child's painting. Do what you like with it.'

'Of course.' Charles nodded. 'If you could just sign here.' He drew a small leather-bound notebook from his pocket and indicated. Dennis took the silver pencil and signed his name.

We said goodbye, the smell of mince intensifying as we left.

'Why on earth...' I began, but Charles gripped my elbow and bundled me into the car.

'Why do you think?' he said, hurling himself into the driving seat and gunning the engine.

'Because you wanted to keep the picture?'

'No, Edie.' He sighed. 'Because if he'd said he wanted it, it would have proved he knew it was real and that he killed Sylvia for it.'

'But it is real, and it's probably his.'

'Such a pedant,' he said. 'Look, Edie, that painting is worth a fortune. Do you really want those idiots banging it up over the fireplace next to that bloody mouldy horse?'

'That's not the point,' I said. I didn't want to argue with

Charles, but my heart was racing and my voice was spiralling upwards, as it always did when I felt faced with injustice. I would have been a terrible barrister, squeaking away like Minnie Mouse.

'What will happen to it if the Donnellys don't have it? And besides, Mr Payne will tell them anyway...'

'Oh yes, the venerable, all-seeing Mr Payne,' Charles mocked. I realised he'd be a terrifying adversary in a fight, as glacial as I was hectic. Lou in a rage, I thought, would chuck ashtrays and bellow, and it'd all be over in five minutes. Charles would be a slow burner, punishing and contemptuous. I didn't want to experience any more of it.

We sped through the streets. 'Where are we going?' I demanded.

'Back to mine, where I am going to write a letter in an ill-formed, workmanlike hand, explaining to Mr Payne' – he put inverted commas round the name – 'that I, Dennis Donnelly, have no need of the painting and that it shall therefore revert to Edie York, its finder.'

'That's illegal,' I cried. 'It's stealing! And besides, why would he give it to me when it's worth so much?'

'Why, hark at the lady crime reporter,' said Charles. 'It's all right, you can give it straight to me, if you're worried about fencing stolen goods. Even though it's not stolen and it almost certainly now belongs to you.'

'Only because Dennis didn't know!'

He turned the wheel abruptly and the car swerved. 'Be quiet, will you! For God's sake, Edie, I'm doing you a favour here!'

'I don't want illegal favours!'

'Well, good luck being a journalist, darling,' he said, cannoning down Didsbury Road.

He put his hand on my knee. 'Let's not row,' he said. 'I

thought you'd be pleased. Dennis is off the hook for murder, and you're in the money.'

'I can't be, when it's not mine.'

'Oh, save it,' he said. 'Let's see what Payne says when he gets the letter.'

'It's a crime.'

'You took it from the house,' he said. 'You withheld its true provenance. You revealed its existence to most of Lancashire, which almost certainly resulted in a murder. So, good luck arguing your case, dear.'

We were at his flat. He skidded to a halt outside and got out. 'Coming?' he said.

I thought perhaps I'd better, if only on the basis that I could tell Lou a fuller story when I saw him later. I already knew it was over between Charles and me, and a dull passivity overcame me. What was the point of arguing? He was going to write the letter, and I was going to tell Mr Payne and Lou Brennan the truth, and then I had no idea what would happen. I didn't want Charles to be arrested on fraud charges, but I couldn't stand by and let him appropriate the Donnellys' inheritance, even if he thought he was doing it for me.

'It's not as if you need the money,' I said, following him upstairs.

'It's not for me, is it?' he said. 'And keep your voice down, you great foghorn – Thelma's in.'

'Why do you even care?' I asked. 'What's it to you?'

He ushered me in. There was no sign of Lillian.

'I care because I care about art,' he said. 'And I'm not letting that idiot get his hands on something that's beautiful and worth thousands. Not when I could keep it.'

'I thought you said it was for me.'

'Well, I'm your boyfriend, aren't I?' He was by the cocktail cabinet, sloshing whisky into glasses. 'Christ, Edie, I don't understand you.'

'It's not even as if we could keep it a secret!' I said. 'It'd have to go to auction, and the Donnellys would see it in the paper and know.'

'Why would it have to go to auction?'

'Because... what else would you do with it?'

'Sell it,' he said.

'Who to? You can't just sell a Cézanne as if it's a second-hand coat! If it doesn't go to Dennis, it must go to a gallery.'

'Darling.' Charles crossed the room, and put a hand on my arm. 'We have to sell it. Don't you see? Mother has lost almost all her art, all her precious things. We're going to need the money, once the war is over – and that could be soon. Hitler's making great strides.'

A wave of revulsion ran through me.

'You say that almost admiringly.'

'I'm saying it factually,' he said. 'We can sing "Roll Out the Barrel" and gather in shelters and say "mustn't grumble" and live off bits of scrag-end and dried egg all we like, but it's all propaganda, you must know that. He's going to win.'

'You can't say that!' I said. 'He isn't, he isn't at all!'

Charles sighed. 'Look, the truth is, we need money, and you will too if you stick with us. You're not going to get it from that little job of yours. We could have a lovely life, you and me. What do you say, hmm?'

I couldn't speak. Thoughts were speeding round my mind like the motorcycle riders on the Belle Vue Wall of Death, and any second, there'd be an almighty crash. I shook my head convulsively.

'You can't sell it,' I said again. 'It's not yours.'

'Oh, Edie,' – he pushed the glass of whisky into my hand – 'I'm afraid you're behind the times, my dear. That painting is worth a fortune, it's no use stuck on the wall. We're selling it – but not at auction.'

'What do you mean?'

'Contacts,' he said. 'Mother and I...'

It hit me like a physical slap.

'That's what you do,' I said. 'You sell art. Illegally. You sell it to... people in Europe.' I couldn't quite make the leap, but I knew. Deep down, I knew. 'That's why you're in financial trouble, now her collection's gone.'

'What if we do?' he asked. 'It's doing no harm. We didn't steal anything. We rather hoped, in fact, that you might like to come in with us, for a cut, of course. You're good at research, no family or personal ties, quite brave,' he mused, as if he were selling a horse to a doubtful buyer. 'And a couple of the same age is always more reassuring to buyers than a single man and an older woman. You'd have to learn some German, of course, but we were going to...'

'How did you get it?' I asked, my fingers gripping the glass so hard I thought it might shatter. I didn't care. 'How did you and your mother get all this art to sell?'

'Ah well, you see, she and Joseph – and yes, he was my father – they met in Berlin towards the end of the last war. He had lost his fiancée. Tragic,' he added mockingly. 'She was a rich Jewish girl, and she and her family fled and left Joseph to look after their art collection for them. Of course, they never came back.' He shrugged lightly as if their disappearance was an irritation, somehow their own fault.

'Mother took him up, and came up with a brilliant idea to make some money – they'd sell the pieces to her contacts. Not illegal, and worked like a dream. Joseph knew business and Mother knew charm.'

'Contacts?' I said.

'She was no stranger to a hotel bar,' he said. 'A lot of top brass used to drink there, and she'd dress up and go and... delight them. They'd tell her things she shouldn't know, and then she'd sell them paintings in return for her silence. Or buy them at a very affordable price.'

'Blackmail,' I said. I wondered why he was telling me all this now. Surely he couldn't think I'd keep quiet?

'Not blackmail,' said Charles scathingly. 'Business. And when Joseph left Germany and came here, Mother brought the collection over, and was helping Germany to retain its cultural assets...'

'But Joseph was a Jewish refugee,' I said blankly. 'He was running away from the Nazis.'

'Oh, Edie.' Charles gave a gasp of laughter and inhaled sharply on his cigarette. 'You poor little idiot.'

I stared at him. 'He was a Nazi,' I said, my voice wavering. 'He came to make sure the pictures were safe if there was to be a war. And your mother...'

'Looked after them, yes. And made sure to send them to the right people. Look,' – he ground out his cigarette in the silver ashtray at his elbow – 'we make a lot of money. Of course, we lost so much in the raid – it was earlier than we thought, we were taking it down to the basement, but we'd barely begun moving it when it happened. We ended up, Mother and me, crushed into the Morrison shelter.' He gave a short laugh. 'Just like being a little boy when I used to climb into bed with her. When she was alone, at least.'

I was dumb with shock and self-recrimination. How could I have failed to see it? I'd been so ready to accept Charles and Lillian into my life, so happy to help them. Simply because, I now realised, they were rich, and beautiful and represented exactly the sort of cultured, rarefied life I'd longed for, growing up. Now, that life had been exposed as a pretty stage set concealing a dirty, treasonous criminal enterprise – and I as a pathetic social climber.

'You could still join us, you know,' Charles said. 'We need a third wheel, and Thelma's proved herself pretty useless. Well, pretty, but useless. You may be an idiot, but you've got pluck.'

'No!' It burst from me. 'You must be mad if you think I'd do that! Selling art that isn't yours to Nazis!'

'You may call us Nazis,' he said calmly. 'We'd say people who don't want their beloved country to lose its assets, that's all. Who are willing to reinvest, to ensure their homeland isn't stripped bare of all its own cultural artefacts, should Hitler lose. Which he won't, of course, but times are tricky and...'

'You bloody well are a Nazi,' I whispered. I looked at his blonde hair, his strange, light eyes and I saw the gleam of fanaticism in them.

'Mother and I simply know the country well,' he said, 'and it desperately needed change. Hitler understands that. You have no idea what the German economy was like before, Jews siphoning off profits everywhere you went, good people afraid for their livelihoods because they'd simply invaded decent neighbourhoods like parasites and undercut the true Germans, and the same is happening all over Europe. Why shouldn't we have a regime which puts national interests ahead of interlopers, where the hard workers who care for their own country aren't cast aside?

'You've no idea how much prices have gone up since the war began, how well we were doing, until that bloody air raid took almost all our stock. Edie,' he went on, his eyes blazing with righteousness, 'that painting belonged to Joseph, and I'm his son. So it doesn't belong to you, or the Donnellys, or the nation, or whatever cock-eyed ideas about social justice you have in your woolly little head. It belongs to me, and it belongs to my mother, and we need the money.'

I thought of Mrs Novak, slashed and sprayed with her own blood, and of trusting, sad Sylvia, his gloved hands gripping her throat and squeezing until her small body was limp and lifeless. I thought of Edward Turnbull.

'How did you know Edward wanted the painting?' I asked. 'How did you know it existed?'

'Well, if it's all coming out...' Charles sipped his whisky, and sat down, crossing his legs as if about to recount an amusing story.

'Joseph told Mother,' he said. 'Simple as that. Turnbull tracked him down, wrote him a letter, explaining he needed money, he'd lost the painting, if it was indeed worth anything, was there any chance of a loan till it turned up... Of course, my father said no. He'd handed it over in a moment of weakness – they had so many paintings, so many beautiful things, he thought it wasn't worth much compared to some. And he didn't have his own money till he married Pamela... But Mother was furious, of course, when she heard. She wanted it back, but we couldn't risk exposure.'

'Hang on,' I said. My voice seemed to be coming from somewhere far away. I wondered if I was in shock. 'How could he not have money? I thought...'

'Oh, it was all Mother,' said Charles with satisfaction. 'She was the planner, you see, she kept track of everything. And when Joseph came over, he had to appear penniless, so she kept the money until things were settled. She couldn't have him swanking about looking well off; for the plan to work, he had to convince as a poverty-stricken refugee.'

'And then he married Pamela,' I put in.

'Indeed. Good old Pam,' said Charles. 'Madly in love with him, and with a rich father happy to leave them everything. You have to admit, it was rather a brilliant scheme. Anyway, when Joseph died – probably nagged to death by Pamela – it became vital to recover the painting. We needed to contain all our assets, and that meant getting bloody Edward Turnbull out of the way so we could look for it. I must say, Winifred dying was a stroke of luck. That, we didn't plan.'

'My God, Charles,' I said. 'You killed them all.'

He shrugged modestly. 'In war, there are always civilian casualties,' he said. 'I see no difference between my actions and those of the soldiers on the front line. We are, first and foremost, Germans. We want our Fatherland to triumph, and if people get in the way of a battle campaign, well... it's pure bad luck.'

'Why Pamela?' I asked. 'Why couldn't she live?'

'Oh, darling,' he said, 'we couldn't risk her finding Turnbull's letter and claiming the painting for herself, could we? Besides, with Joseph gone, what did she have to live for? She was a dim old thing, rootling round that great house with her bloody dog – so I popped round, explained who I was, and she was, shall we say, less than accommodating. She had to go, I'm afraid.'

He said it as though he'd sold an item of heavy furniture that was no longer required. A wardrobe that was in the way.

'Shame about Sylvia,' he added. 'She was rather pretty. But I thought she still had the picture, you see. That was all your doing.'

'No,' I said. I had blamed myself since I'd heard of her death. But I wasn't having this. My throat felt too dry to speak, and I took another large gulp of whisky.

'You're mad,' I said. 'You're a murderer. You've killed three people for a painting!'

'I'd kill three hundred if I had to,' said Charles. 'Art outlasts us all, Edie. This is a war,' he said again, 'and I intend the Fatherland to win it. Collateral damage, that's all.'

I tried to speak, but he interrupted.

'Before you mount your moral high horse again, I've killed far fewer people than your British bombs have. The ones you and your rag of a paper celebrate, raining down on Berlin, indiscriminately killing innocent children. But they don't count, do they?

'Oh dear,' he said, looking at my horrified expression with affectionate pity. 'You're going to tell that pet copper of yours, aren't you?'

'Of course I am,' I shouted. 'You can't just pretend three murders meant nothing! You can't...'

I felt very strange. There was no record on the gramophone, but it was spinning, somehow, and as I looked up, the fireplace buckled and swerved.

'I don't feel...' I started. Somewhere far away, a glass fell out of my hand with a small thud. I thought for a second I was going to be sick, and then everything zoomed inwards to a point of white light, and blackness descended, like a cloth thrown over a cage.

I was in bed, but my body wouldn't move when I tried to turn over, and the material under my cheek wasn't my flowered pillowslip but something hard and scratchy. It felt as though I was lying on coconut matting. Panic shot through me like an arrow, and I tried to sit up, but my limbs wouldn't move and there was something in the way, something that made a metallic rattle in contact with my foot.

'Hello?' I said, and my voice emerged in a half-whisper, as though I was in one of those dreams where you scream and nothing comes out.

I was wide awake now, and my wrists were bound somehow... it was impossible to remember. I had a flash of a horse picture and a journey, a gramophone, of feeling angry... it swam into place.

'Charles!' I called, my voice croaking and feeble. 'Charles!'

The Morrison shelter, I assumed, in the basement of Charles and Lillian's house.

I was folded up like a deckchair, my knees at my chest, and everything hurt. There was no light, but I knew the damp, coal-dust scent of a cellar. I understood that this was very bad – I could die, and probably would. The air was frigid with cold, and

I couldn't see my watch to tell what time of night it was, or how long I'd been unconscious.

I manoeuvred my wrists to my mouth and felt the bindings with my lips. They were tied tightly with string, rather than rope, so I told myself I still had a chance. I edged and writhed into a half-sitting position and drew my fingers up and down the bars until I found the lock. I prayed there wasn't a padlock. If not, it was a case of freeing my hands, then finding the clasp to silently inch it open.

A cold sweat bloomed on my forehead and under my arms, and the tight bindings felt increasingly like a saw cutting into my flesh. It was probably all he had to bind an unconscious woman at short notice. What had he given me, I wondered – phenobarbital? Perhaps he had done the same to Sylvia. I hoped she was at least unconscious before he killed her. The thought beat in my mind that he was coming back at any moment to kill me too. Perhaps he didn't want the mess of a body and was deciding what to do with me.

Nobody, he assumed, would come looking.

But they would, I told myself. *They would.* Annie, and Lou, and my colleagues, and maybe even Arnold. Arnold, who I had so wrongly suspected, who had tried to warn me. They would wonder where I was, and – with a plummeting stomach – I remembered that Annie was still away, and may not be back for days. Lou would doubtless be relieved if he didn't hear from me, and Arnold had probably washed his hands of me after the scene in the pub. If I didn't arrive at work tomorrow, they'd think I'd taken a day off and grumble a bit, and when there was still no sign of me, they'd assume there'd been an emergency and I'd rushed off to see distant family, and gradually, as the weeks went by, my desk would be covered in other people's folders and pens, and in the end, someone else would sit there and I'd be forgotten altogether.

My breath was coming in gasps, my ears straining for the

sound of purposeful footsteps. I frantically rubbed the string against my teeth, nibbling and sawing. I had a pounding headache, from whatever Charles had slipped into my drink, and a residual nausea that came in waves.

It may have taken ten minutes to chew through it, but eventually the final coil frayed and gave.

I reached down, my wrists on fire, and spent another eon picking apart the knots at my ankles. It was like trying to weave a basket in pitch darkness. I almost cried several times, as my nails broke, and the knots remained firm, but finally a little space opened up by my heel, then grudgingly widened. I used both hands to wrench at the ties till a piece snapped and I could flex my crippled ankles. Thank heavens he had been in a hurry and left my tightly laced-up shoes on, probably exhausted after wrestling my inert body down three flights of stairs. I wondered where Thelma was – perhaps she was in on it all. Now, I only had to work out how to get the cage open and escape from the house.

When I was younger, I'd sometimes thought about my own death, and wondered how it would come. In my fantasies, it was usually in some noble and heroic fashion – saving a child from a runaway horse, or sprinting into a burning building as firemen bellowed at me to stand back. I had never considered the possibility that I might die trapped in a wire cage in a cellar because I'd been a stupid, trusting idiot. I tried to breathe slowly and think, despite the excruciating pain.

I could feel the clasp of the shelter's side, which should easily push open, but while Charles may have been in a hurry, he wasn't slapdash.

As I ran my fingers up and down again, I felt a cold, smooth shape the size of a child's fist. A padlock. There was no chewing through that. I pushed the heels of my hands against my eyes. Crying was pointless. As I pressed my eyes, my fingers in my hair, I touched metal.

I had read enough detective stories to know that if anyone was picking a lock, a pin of some kind was a useful item. In books, locks always sprang open almost immediately, and the detective burst into the room, but I didn't expect to have any luck. It was my last hope. I made an inventory of what I had on me – hairpins, buttons, shoelaces – and I pulled the pin from my hair.

Finding the tiny keyhole was like writing on the head of a pin with my eyes shut. I swore and sweated, all my concentration funnelled into locating the minuscule gap. When I finally got one end of the hairpin in, I couldn't persuade it to undo the lock. I thought of Lou saying, 'Come on, Edie, you can bloody well do this,' and Annie saying, 'Don't let him win!', willing me on. I thought of Arnold saying, 'Well, this is a right old show, isn't it?' and briefly felt less alone. I thought of all the things I wanted to do in my life, and how much I wanted to help us all win the war, and how I needed to have Charles and his bloody mother arrested, so they didn't get away with it. I thought of Edward and Sylvia again, and Mrs Novak, and I poked and jiggled and pressed, so carefully, so gently. Nothing.

I hissed a fervent 'please!' and gave the pin a hopeless last wiggle, and I heard the catch click and the lock spring free.

As quietly as I could, I pushed open the side of the cage and crawled out onto the dank stone floor. The cellar was entirely in darkness, but I inched forward, feeling my way round a corner, and saw the faintly lit outline of an interior door at the top of the stone steps.

My whole body was seized with cramp; it could have been an hour or a day since I'd been thrown down there, but I was desperately thirsty, so I guessed at least a few hours had gone by.

I had no idea how I was going to get out. And then I realised. Of course. I wanted to howl. The cellar door would be locked.

. . .

At the home, we used to like watching the coal delivery, as the huge men tipped sacks into the coal hole with a grating roar. Or we did, at least, until it began to be used as a punishment. Suki spent a whole night in there once. She came out blowing black snot from her nose, pink streaks from her tears snailing through the soot on her face.

I crept up the steps, already sensing the resistance of the jammed door, the lock that would never yield to a hair pin. I was going to die. As I neared it, reaching out towards the latch, I heard voices, distant but getting closer.

'...still in there,' I heard Charles say.

'There's no point dealing with it now,' said Lillian, and my heart almost lifted at the sound of her familiar voice until I remembered what had happened and why I was here.

They must have been satisfied that I was still lying unconscious in the shelter, trussed like a Christmas goose.

'I didn't mean to let her in on it at all,' Charles said. There was a clink of glass bottles.

'...silly,' said Lillian. 'If she'd agreed, it would have been easier, of course, but it was always a gamble.'

'Could have told her anything,' he said. 'If things went ahead with Krall, I'd have just said it all went in taxes.'

Lillian's laughter. 'Need to move pretty fast with this one, now they've seen the code in the paper...' Her voice drifted away into another room, and Charles's footsteps followed.

I couldn't quite imagine what they were doing, but it was now clear, without a shadow of doubt, that they weren't intending to release me alive and send me off to DI Brennan clutching my bravery badge.

Hot fury coursed through me as I remembered how I'd felt about Charles, my eagerness, how easily I'd gone along with whatever he suggested, just because he had a posh voice and a nose like a statue in the art gallery. The artistic quote she'd been so keen on – it was a message, to tell her contacts that she was ready to carry on without Joseph.

I'd been so dazzled by both the Emersons, a silly picture-goer mooning at the silver screen. They had betrayed me from the moment I looked up and saw Lillian standing incongruously in the canteen. They had been betraying my country for far longer.

I heard their steps moving away, Charles saying something and the higher register of Lillian's reply. Nazis. Murderers. Spies? His job in 'intelligence', her ability to insert herself into society, listening and reporting, hard and inscrutable as a glittering insect.

No wonder her house being bombed had proved so devastating. The handlers who bought their stolen art would be waiting for more, and the Emersons – was that even their name? – would be keeping most of their vast wealth in a Swiss bank account, waiting for Hitler to win, so they could go back to Germany and join him. The painting I'd found was worth everything to them now.

I had no idea where it was. I couldn't imagine how they got the goods to the buyers. But I thought about the factory Joseph ran, how feasible it might be to pay somebody to pack up paintings hidden in crates of radio parts and have them shipped to Europe, and smuggled over the border by sympathisers... no wonder his business before the war had been 'export'. They'd been doing this for years, and when Novak left Germany it wasn't because he was a refugee – it was because war was imminent, and they needed to get into position in Britain, ready to spy for their paymasters.

That was why they'd targeted Pamela, and handsome Joseph had seduced and married her. Because her father ran a factory.

He had come, hiding in plain sight as a persecuted Jew in

need of shelter, his path smoothed by Lillian and her money and contacts. Pamela gave him respectability, but of course, feelings towards German-speakers with strong accents were not positive. He had found Edward Turnbull – harmless, suburban, kind – and Joseph Novak had given him the little painting in a moment of gratitude, perhaps even guilt.

Novak. It meant 'new'. It wasn't his name at all. It was one he – or Lillian – had chosen for his new life as a German spy.

CHAPTER SIXTEEN

I heard their steps going upstairs – perhaps only to fetch something to kill me with – and knew I had to act. I grasped the metal latch, pressed down, and was so shocked when the door swung inwards, I almost fell backwards down the steps.

I was looking into a large yellow kitchen, with drawn blackout blinds over the long windows, a well-stocked larder, with its door ajar, and a lit range. The remains of a dinner lay on the white-clothed table – they had been eating while I was tied up and unconscious, and according to the clock on the wall, it was just after ten.

I froze as I heard their voices draw nearer again. They were coming downstairs. I pulled the cellar door shut behind me, dived into the larder, and pressed myself into the far corner behind the door. If they opened the door, they would see me, and I would be killed. I wanted to scream with fear, but I pressed my remaining nails into my palms, making agonising dents, like I used to at the home when the boys cornered me, or when Kenneth died. I had so little chance of escape.

'Pack it up and get it sent as soon as we can...' Charles came into the kitchen again. I could smell his tobacco.

'Krall's been complaining about the delay, he wanted it as soon as I told him about it,' Lillian said, following. 'It's not too big, is it?'

'No, it's rather small,' said Charles. There was the sound of paper being unwrapped.

'How ridiculous that it was in some tea chest.'

'If I'd known she bloody had it all along, I wouldn't have needed to...' The next bit was inaudible.

'Good old Joseph, to the rescue even after death,' said Lillian with a little laugh. She sounded as if she was concentrating on something.

'Thelma's out for the count till morning. And what shall become of our little reporter?' asked Charles, as idly as if he were speculating about a goldfish.

'We wait till just after the raid begins, then before the all-clear, you'll have to get her to the nearest bombed-out building. Shame we can't dump her there beforehand – looks more authentic if she's genuinely got rubble all over her – but the trouble is, as we know, one can't be absolutely certain of which they'll hit.'

'She won't wake up?'

'Well, one hopes not, darling,' said Lillian irritably. 'I assume you gave her a decent dose.' I heard the scratch of a flame and her sharp intake of smoke.

'What about identifying her?'

'Already burned her ID card and ration book in the kitchen range,' said Lillian. 'I doubt the ARP idiots will even notice her if you do it properly. It's going to be a big one, should be starting at just after midnight.'

'Happy New Year,' said Charles.

'Well, it should be, at last,' said Lillian. 'We're on the up. And we have a Cézanne for our favourite buyer. It's quite a little beauty, isn't it?' she murmured. 'Who could ever have guessed he'd just handed it over?'

'It was when he had no money of his own, though,' said Charles. 'Before Pamela. I imagine he did it to punish you for not marrying him.'

'Well,' Lillian said. She snapped her cigarette case shut. 'I certainly couldn't let him have that sort of power. Besides, as he knew perfectly well, if one of us got caught, we'd both go down. This way, we were safer.'

'Should I check on her?' Charles asked, and I convulsed with dread. There was a pause.

'No need,' said Lillian, 'best do it all in one later, Karl. I'll bring the car round to the side. It's all rather unpleasant, but you've not given us much alternative.'

'I had no choice!' Charles – Karl – sounded angry. 'She was mad about me. I thought she'd go along with it. I didn't expect her to get on her moral high horse, she's a journalist, for God's sake.'

'Shame, really,' said Lillian. 'I rather liked her.'

I wondered if anyone would send a wreath for me. *Condolences from all at the* Chronicle. *RIP.* But I may never be found, of course, if Charles was going to bury me in rubble. I'd just be another statistic. INCENDIARIES KILL 34 CIVILIANS IN RAID ON INDUSTRIAL CITY. Or 99. Or 1000. They knew about the timing of the air raids. Charles was passing on secrets as well as paintings, and getting tipped off in return. I thought of Mrs Pelham, and Annie's patients who didn't survive, and her mother, lying in hospital. Winifred Turnbull. All the still, silent children, waxen faces caked in grey dust, and the beloved homes, and the precious things, all gone. I would have killed them both if I could.

I had to get out. I had to warn people that on this cold, ordinary Monday night, German bombers were assembling to soar over our city again, dropping death on us all.

I could have single-handedly solved every mystery that had

ever baffled mankind, and I'd still be the stupidest person in the world for trusting Charles and his mother.

I remembered his 'alibi'. Thelma. 'My landlady will vouch for me.' Of course she would. Spoilt, lonely Thelma, desperate for the attention of her handsome, charismatic landlord – for now, it was perfectly clear that this was not her house at all, but Charles's.

I stood behind the door of the larder, shaking like a dog in a thunderstorm. I was not brave, I was not intrepid. I was terrified of dying, and I had no clever plans other than to find a way out.

The most terrible yearning seized me; for Annie, for Arnold – even for Lou. Just not being a deranged murderer was enough to recommend him. And he'd hated Charles from the outset. How annoying that after I was dead, he'd probably say so and everyone would shake their heads at my stupidity.

'I need to contact Krall and give the signal,' Lillian said now. 'Can you package it up?'

'All right,' said Charles irritably. He was closer to the larder now. One glance in and he'd see my wide, terrified eyes staring back at him like a trapped cat.

'Who's taking it now Hörst has gone?'

'Me,' said Lillian. 'While you sort out madam downstairs. The packaging is all in the drawing room, darling. May as well take the painting up there.'

The door closed behind them and I heaved a vast, shuddering sigh as their footsteps retreated upstairs.

This was my only chance. I dashed to the door after them and peered into the empty hallway, with its shining red and black tiles, an archway from which hung a large glass lampshade, a polished sideboard holding a vase of silk flowers, and the vast, black front door, impenetrable as a prison wall.

Upstairs, I heard Lillian on the telephone.

'Herr Krall,' she said. Then, 'Yes. We have it ready for you. To send light into the darkness of men's hearts – such is the duty of the artist,' she said carefully. '*Ja, wir werden*. By Thursday.'

The telephone clicked back into its cradle with a muffled ding, and I squeezed my eyes shut and held my breath. No wonder she had bloody diamond brooches – selling Sylvia's painting, stealing art from God knows where else, flogging it to her Nazi contacts, while her son passed vital information to them, gleaned from his 'intelligence' job. And I'd been their willing patsy, nodding and grinning like some wheedling plantation slave while my owners led me to the creek to drown.

Fury gave me strength. I drew a great breath, silently pushed the door open, and made a dash for the foot of the stairs, where I paused to assess the front door. If it was locked, I was enduring the last few moments of my life. There was no sound from upstairs. In one movement, I ran, twisted the handle, and wrenched. The door opened, and I was outside, facing the lightless street.

I had no handbag, no money, no keys. As soon as they found me gone, Charles would follow me – he knew where I lived. I had to get to the police, warn them about the air raid, and tell them all I knew. If only I had a number for Lou. If I rang the desk sergeant babbling about spies and murders, they'd assume I'd had too much leftover New Year whisky.

I dashed down the steps and into the road – with no torch, I was in grave danger of tripping over something, but I had to get to the nearest telephone box. I knew there was one on Barlow Moor Road, and I'd have to run, but there was every chance Charles would find me first. My breath was coming in short huffs of panic as I sprinted, tensed for the beam of his torch to sweep over me, his gloved hands to clamp me to him.

As I turned the corner, I went headlong into something hard and metallic, which clanged to the ground, landing painfully on my foot. A bicycle, which someone had propped against the wall. It was a man's, and my feet didn't reach the road, but that didn't matter. I leapt onto the seat and wobbled off with no lights on, pedalling as hard as I could manage, until my knees burned and my chest was tight with the effort. I kept glancing behind me, wavering dangerously, expecting the swoop of dipped headlights, the purr of the MG engine.

I kept Lou's face in my mind as I cycled, focussed only on letting him know. For all his annoyances, I trusted him. And I should have trusted Arnold too. Midnight was drawing closer, soon the sky would be on fire again, and when Charles and Lillian realised I was gone, they'd do their utmost to hunt me down and get rid of me for good.

I swerved into Barlow Moor Road, past the closed shops, and there was the phone box. As I put on an extra burst of speed, I heard it behind me – the sound of an engine, gunning and sputtering. Someone was driving too fast, heading for the corner, and was getting closer.

I swung into the driveway of a large house, flung the bike into the laurel bushes, and hurled myself after it. I heard the car slow, crawling along now, searching. He must have known I'd head for a telephone. The only thing in my favour was that they didn't know how long a head start I'd had – I could be long gone by now.

I lay, my face pressed against cold leaf mould, sharp twigs in my hair, the sound of the still-spinning back wheel a strange, humming lullaby beside me. I heard the engine roar again, and fade into the distance. He hadn't seen me. I left the bike where it was, and dashed to the phone box where I snatched up the receiver and demanded the Manchester City Police. I was so thirsty, my voice sounded like a creaking door.

'Putting you through,' said the operator in a bored tone.

'May I speak to DI Brennan?' I asked the sergeant who answered. 'It's urgent.'

'Not here,' he said. 'Probably at the pub.'

'Then I need to warn you, there's going to be an air raid,' I said. 'I've had intelligence from somebody, a spy, and you need to arrest Lillian and Charles Emerson – they're planning to kill me, and they murdered Pamela Novak and Edward Turnbull and Sylvia Brown.'

There was a heavy pause on the line.

'I know it sounds ridiculous,' I said, 'but it's true. I'm a reporter at the *Chronicle*, they just drugged me and tied me up and I've escaped, but they're coming after me.'

I could hear him breathing. 'Is this a joke?' he said. 'Spies? Murderers? We take wasting police time very seriously, madam. I've no doubt you and your friends think it's very humorous to—'

'I'm telling the truth!' I shouted. 'I'm a reporter with the *Manchester Chronicle*, and Charles Emerson is chasing me and he's going to kill me. And there's an air raid starting at midnight!'

'You'd better give me the address, and I'll send someone out,' said the sergeant. 'But I warn you, if this is some drunken New Year prank...'

I told him the address, and he laboriously repeated it back to me. It was pointless, I thought, because Charles was already after me, and Lillian would be halfway to a safe house with the Cézanne in the passenger seat. The police would find nothing but a bent hairpin in the cellar.

'Please,' I said, 'let the wardens know, let them know to start the sirens early.'

'On your say-so?' He scoffed. 'I think you'll find that's...'

I put the phone down, and ran back to the bicycle. I had to get home, in case Annie was already back; I had to warn Mr Benson, and Clara and her parents about the air raid. I cycled as if the hounds of hell were at my back, passing groups of pub-goers with torches, some in uniform, one group spilling out of the Railway Inn, singing a ragged chorus of 'We'll Meet Again'. 'Have a drink with us!' one called out as I flew past.

'Air raid at midnight, get to a shelter,' I shouted back, and heard their tuts of annoyance and surprise that anyone would joke about such things.

I was terrified that Charles – or Karl, as I would now think of him – would drive back the other way and see me hurtling towards him. And there was an outside chance that Lillian was also out looking. They'd been so sure I was unconscious, they must have been furious. Finally, just after eleven, I reached our road. It seemed so innocent: blackout blinds drawn, people inside, gathered round their fires, or getting ready for bed and hoping for victory to come this new year.

I didn't have my key any more, so I scanned the dark road for Charles's car. I couldn't see anything but the dark shapes of a couple of parked cars further down, probably belonging to the neighbours. I dumped the bike by the gate, ran up the steps and banged on the door. Once inside, I would check whether Annie was back, then I could run to Clara's and beg for help.

I heard Mr Benson's door click, and his slow tread down the hall. 'Hurry,' I muttered. 'Hurry!'

He fiddled with the lock, and finally, the door opened.

'There's going to be an air raid. Get to the shelter,' I shouted. I ran past him, upstairs, hoping to God I hadn't locked the flat door. I didn't usually bother.

'What?' he said, cupping a hand to his ear. 'Your young man's up there, waiting for you. I let him in, but no consorting please, this is a respectable house.'

I skidded to a halt just outside our door, about to spin and rush back downstairs, when it opened, and an arm shot out and pulled me inside.

The door closed behind us. We were standing in the dark living room, and his leather-gloved fingers were biting into my arm.

'Took your time,' he said. 'Serves me right for giving you a low dose. You were supposed to be unconscious – you wouldn't have felt a thing, darling.'

'How could you?' I had nothing left to lose. 'You vile, depraved Nazi murderer!'

'What a lot of big words,' he said. He dragged me to the sofa. 'You were all for me earlier, quite keen, as I recall.'

'You should hang,' I spat, wrestling against his iron grip. 'Killing women for a picture! And your insane whore of a mother with her stolen diamond brooches! She's no better!'

'Don't you insult my mother, you little bitch.' He smelled acrid, he was sweating and his breath was pure whisky and the foul tobacco I'd once thought so sophisticated.

He threw me onto the couch. I thought of all the evenings Annie and I had sat moaning about our jobs, listening to the wireless, chatting about rationing, or Pete's intentions, how pleased she'd been for me about Charles.

He loomed above me, holding me down, one knee agonisingly across my thighs.

'You stupid girl,' he said. 'We could all three have done it together. You would have been an asset. You'd have been rich. I don't want to do this, but you've given me no choice.'

He removed his hand from my left shoulder and thrust his forearm across my neck, with all his weight behind it. Immediately, I was choking. There was no more air entering my lungs, my world shrank to the darkness around us, the leaden heaviness crushing me. I was dying, and when I was dead, he'd come back when the all-clear sounded and drag me into his car and bury me in rubble along with all the other bodies. They wanted us all dead, they wanted Hitler to win.

Rage sent a spasm to my legs, and I bucked violently beneath him. He swore, but the pressure on my windpipe didn't ease. I was beginning to see spots in the darkness, pulses of light like stars on a frosty night.

My lungs burned, and my heart was still galloping away, trying to send signals – Run! Escape! Fight! A magic lantern of bright pictures spun in my mind: Mr Gorringe's face, when he read my first piece. Suki, whispering, 'We'll always be friends, you and me.' Now I'd never be able to find her. Annie, doubled over with mirth. Arnold's tentative smile. Lou's weary, reluctant grin. Would they miss me? The darkness was everywhere now, in my mind, and outside. From far away, I heard a noise cutting the blackness in two – a piercing wail. For a moment I thought it was me, that I'd found enough air to scream, but Charles was still lying on me, squeezing the air from my body, his muscular arm locked across my neck.

The siren. It was true then. It was nearly over. Nothing could be done now. There were bursts of rays like sunlight in my brain, and I heard Annie's voice calling my name, a last reassuring sound from my short life, to send me over the edge into an eternal nothingness.

Except she was shouting.

There was banging and scuffling somewhere, the siren was still sending its eerie whooping across the city, but I didn't care, I was floating away, my body left behind me – and the pressure lifted, and I sucked in a vast, choking, rattling breath, and I could see again. In the darkness, bodies were rolling and shouting, a dog was barking wildly, Annie was screaming, 'Kill him!', and as I choked, she ran to me and clutched me to her. I was gasping against her shoulder, tears soaking her best wool coat.

She smelled of her Blue Grass scent, and I had never breathed in anything so wonderful. 'Oh, Edie. Oh, love,' she was saying, rocking me against her.

She leaned and switched the lamp on, and then I saw them, Lou and Arnold, wrestling with Charles, hitting and punching, pulling and kicking, and Marple, a blur of teeth and fur, snarling and lunging at Charles's legs. For a moment, he broke free, and I saw him scan the illuminated room, then sprint to the kitchen, Lou and Arnold scrambling after him.

Marple raced after him to guard the door. How could he hide there? It led nowhere. My body was shaking convulsively; I felt there could never be enough air in the world for my deflated lungs, and we all four had to reach the cellar before the raid began in earnest.

'I am arresting you,' shouted Lou. 'Murder, attempted murder, attempted murder of a police officer...'

'No!' Annie screamed in my ear, and I turned to see Charles brandishing the carving knife, just as he had done to Pamela Novak. He sliced it through the air.

'Marple!' yelled Lou, and the dog retreated slightly. Charles lunged at Lou, who threw himself sideways, sending the wireless toppling to the floor. Arnold charged at Charles's chest, head down, and Charles arced the knife above his head, ready to bring down into Arnold's back.

Annie screamed again and leapt to her feet, as Lou roared, 'Stay back!'

I knew I should get up and help, but my legs wouldn't move. Lou was back on his feet and in one movement he kicked out at the back of Charles's knees, and brought him crashing to the floor, Marple seized his trouser leg, and Annie stamped her heel on the hand holding the knife. Charles screamed in pain and let go, and Arnold dived to snatch it up.

'The air raid,' shouted Annie. 'We have to go.'

Arnold was sitting on Charles's back, a hand forcing his

head into our dusty Persian rug, and Lou was tying his hands with – was that our kitchen apron? It was only a couple of hours since I'd been equally tightly tied.

'Go!' Lou shouted at Annie and me. 'I'll ring for reinforcements, you get down to the cellar!' He and Arnold dragged Charles to his feet. He was screaming insults, kicking out, jerking his body, but Lou had him in a rough headlock, and Arnold was holding the knife to his back.

Annie flung open the door, and as Marple streaked down the stairs, barking, they manhandled him down ahead of us. I'd have to wake Mr Benson too, I thought madly, and where was the torch?

We stepped onto the small landing, and I realised the sirens had stopped. The air shimmered and held its breath – I heard Charles screaming 'Mother!' and then the stairs fell away.

I came round again. I was half buried under plaster dust and bricks, and a short beam, pocked with nails, had fallen across my legs. Everything was dark, but for a white glow somewhere to my left. I couldn't hear anything, it was as if my ears had been stuffed with cotton wool. I wondered if I was dying, if I would leave my body again, if these were my final seconds on earth. Above me, moonlight shone through the skylight, and where the stairs had led to our flat, there was nothing, just empty air swirling with choking dust.

I must be lying in the hall, I realised, and the front door was open. I could feel the draught playing over my face. Perhaps I was bleeding, I couldn't tell. Slowly, I turned my bruised neck and saw that Mr Benson's flat was no longer behind a door. The wall had vanished, and it wasn't a skylight above me – we didn't have one. It was the roof that had gone.

I could see a splintered sideboard and an armchair half-buried under bricks. I could see a hand, limp and lost, dangling beneath.

It came to me all at once – my friends. If I was lying here, where were they? Whimpering, I tried to move, and with a vast adrenaline surge of relief, I felt my arms and legs obey my instructions. Like a factory machine, I cleared away brick and plaster until I had enough room to sit up, and then I lifted away the beam – it was the newel post from the bottom of the stairs – and found I could move my legs. My ears still seemed to be underwater.

'Annie,' I called, and choked on the dust. 'Annie!'

Please don't be dead. Please, please. It beat like a chant with the racing of my heart.

I saw movement beside me and flinched. Charles. But then the figure appeared, covered in grey plaster dust like a terrible ghost, only his teeth and eyes gleaming in the moonlight. 'Lou,' I said. I wanted to cry with relief.

'Thank God,' Lou said. His voice sounded a long way away. 'Thank God, Edie.' He put his arms round me and hugged, and I clung back.

'But Annie,' I began. 'Arnold...'

'Arnold's in the cellar, he's all right,' Lou said. 'He made it down. We were holding that bastard Emerson too, but I don't know if he...'

There was a muffled bark. Lou sprang away to locate the sound.

'Annie!' I cried. The noise was coming from a heap of fabric – Mr Benson's curtains must have been blown into the back of the hall, and shielded her from the deluge of roof tiles and plaster.

'Help,' a small voice called. Lou and I climbed over the rubble and wrenched the filthy, torn cloth away, and there was Annie, clutching on to Marple's dusty fur, alive, and blinking, and trying to sit up.

'What the heck,' she said. 'What the heck happened? My God, where are the stairs?'

Marple shook himself violently and licked her hand. Lou rubbed dust from his eyes. His hair was sticking up like a cartoon chimney sweep's.

'Hi?' It was Arnold's voice. 'The door's wedged, is there anyone there? Hullo?'

There was a scrape and a bang and the cellar door fell forwards, revealing Arnold. He looked far better, and cleaner, than the rest of us.

'Thank heaven,' he said. 'Thought you were all goners.' Annie was sitting where the stairs should have been, clutching her bleeding wrist. She had a cut on her forehead and her blonde hair was now dark grey in the half-light. She looked as frightened as a child, and a hundred years old.

'Where's that bastard?' Lou asked Arnold.

'Under there.' Arnold pointed at the broken tiles and debris beneath our feet.

It took Lou, Arnold and me a good ten minutes of shifting it gradually before Charles's ear appeared. Then his hair, an eye. I thought he was dead.

'He blinked!' shouted Lou. 'We need to get the ARP blokes in, they know how to do this properly.'

I cleared away the remaining chunks of plaster, and Charles's mouth moved, his one visible eye fixed on mine.

'Mother,' he was trying to say. 'Mother.'

'What?' I asked. 'What about her?'

'In the car. Waiting. We were...' His voice faded and his eyes closed, then flicked open again. 'We were going to take you together. Didn't know... know raid... be here.' He breathed, a rattling gasp. 'She's... the painting.'

'Don't talk,' I said. 'The wardens are coming.' Through the hole that had been the doorway, I could see Lou talking to men in tin helmets, pointing at us. They were trying to lead him away, but he wasn't having it. A fire flickered in the street, and fire wardens were uncoiling hoses, shouting instructions. My hearing was returning.

'No,' Charles murmured. 'Tell her... tell her how I love her. Tell her she'll be all right. Tell her I'll see her soon...' His voice drifted into silence.

'Come on,' I said urgently. 'Come on, don't die.' I knew he was going to hang for what he'd done. But to see him slipping away... he was still a person, still someone I'd cared for, though that felt long ago.

'Good riddance,' said Arnold behind me. 'He's gone, Edie. Let's get out.'

He was right. Charles's pale eyes would see nothing more. I held out my hand to Annie, and she staggered to her feet. We stood on the doorstep, amongst the roof tiles and sagging joists, and a warden came and gave us itchy wool blankets and ushered us into the street. 'We'll check you over in a minute,' said one burly man. 'There's someone still inside?'

Arnold was now talking to a fire warden, telling him what had happened, and Lou had gone back in, Marple trotting at his heels.

'We need to—' I began, when Annie said, 'Look,' and I turned to see the remains of a sports car. It had been parked further up, beyond our garden wall, and in the dark, I had thought it was somebody visiting neighbours. In the white glow of the arc lights it was clear that it had taken a direct hit from an incendiary. The mangled car was half sunk into a blackened crater in the road, the front seats obliterated. Like someone hypnotised, I walked towards it.

'Don't, Edie,' shouted Annie. 'Come back, you don't want to see...'

I went closer. A high, pale suede shoe had been thrown onto the pavement, soaking in water from the running hoses. Inside the crater was only a black, tangled mass of metal and wire, sending spirals of acrid smoke into the still air.

As the white light shone down, I made out a small scrap, stuck to part of the bonnet. Carefully, I peeled it off, and saw the colours – jungle green, rose madder, slashes of yellow and thick sweeps of blue.

Slowly, I pushed it into my pocket and walked back to Annie.

'She's not there,' I said.

'And now they'll never face justice,' said Annie bitterly.

I thought of Charles's final words.

'He really loved you,' I said towards the crater, and turned away.

CHAPTER SEVENTEEN

We were in the pub again. Annie and I were staying at Clara's, and her wrist was now properly bandaged, though she'd teased her hair over one eye to hide the bruise from the rubble. 'It'll scar, you know,' she told me.

'I'm just glad you're here,' I said, and tears sprang to my eyes.

'Daft girl,' said Annie. 'I'm going nowhere.' She had told me that as her mum had been discharged, and was now walking with sticks, and a prognosis of full recovery, she had come back home to work. She had expected to find me there and went to the pub to look for me, but instead, bumped into Lou and Arnold, who were having a pint. They'd walked Annie home and heard Charles's voice – and luckily, Annie did have a key.

Lou was still at the bar, and Arnold was coming over with the drinks. It was a much more subdued atmosphere tonight. The worst of it had been cleared from the street, but most of our things were gone.

'Stay as long as you like,' Clara had said. 'Golly, if one can't help friends in need, what's the point of it all?'

Her parents were equally solicitous and kind, but Annie and I had plans to move as soon as we could scrape the next month's rent together, and find a suitable place.

'One on the ground floor,' she said. 'No stairs, no cellars, ideally. No murderers.'

'And not in Didsbury,' I added. 'I can never look at it again.'

I had apologised so much for bringing Charles – or Karl – into her life, she had become quite irritated. 'You couldn't have known, Edie, love!' she kept saying. 'It wasn't your fault!'

But I felt I would carry that particular guilt for a long time.

'Here we go.' Arnold set the pints and sherries down before us. 'Here's to better times.' He was being particularly solicitous, and had confessed, in an agony of shame, that he'd been the man following me home that night.

'I didn't trust him, Edie,' he said. 'I just wanted to be sure he wasn't going to hurt you or Annie, so I waited on your street to keep an eye on you. But then you were alone, and I didn't want to frighten you... I'm such a fool.'

I fingered the patterned silk scarf round my neck – Clara had insisted on giving it to me. 'At least you can cover up what that bloody beastly man did till it heals,' she'd said. 'Excuse my French.'

Lou returned, handing out cigarettes, and threw himself into a chair. He looked exactly the same as usual, jaunty hat and smart, double-breasted suit with a gold tie pin tonight. I wouldn't forget the look of horror I'd seen in his eyes, though.

'Right then.' Annie leaned in. 'Have you found out all the details?'

'Not that it's any of your business,' said Lou, and we all groaned. I was relying on the extra information he could provide for the front-page scoop I was writing. Mr Gorringe had been extremely encouraging, but agreed it needed more explanation.

Double Raid Death of Mother and Son Murder Nazi Spies was the working headline. 'We'll certainly sell papers with that,' my editor had said approvingly. So at least something good had come of it.

'Look here,' said Lou. 'I'll tell you what we found out – but don't go thinking it will always be this easy to get me to crack.'

'Easy!' I said. 'I almost got murdered.'

Lou ignored me. 'Well, Lillian was born in Germany. She had an English mother, which explains her command of the language. Joseph fought against Britain in the last war, and he was down on his luck in Berlin when she picked him up in a hotel bar. We think she was... well...'

'Was what?' asked Annie. We were all leaning in, our drinks forgotten.

'A lady of the night,' said Lou uncomfortably. 'But Joseph had been entrusted with looking after his fiancée's art collection. Lillian knew about art from her high-up clients, and she recognised that it was worth something.'

'So she stole it?'

'No,' Lou said. 'The family didn't come back – they were killed in the war, and so it belonged to Joseph. She wheedled her way in with him, and with her contacts, they found a buyer who would pass it on to rich people who didn't care too much about the provenance.'

'Why did they come over here?' I asked.

He shook his head. 'Because by the mid-thirties, Lillian was very strongly linked with the higher-up Nazis and they could see the way things were going. He posed as a refugee, and she came over on the basis that Charles was at boarding school here – which he was.'

'So he really was Joseph's son?' Annie asked.

I had heard all this from Charles. It was odd to hear it confirmed, though. 'Yes,' I said. 'He was.'

'Though, with her, who knows?' added Lou. 'She certainly claimed he was. Obviously, that was a gift to her contacts – three German spies for the price of one.

'A little Nazi sympathiser, Müller was working for him too – though he got killed,' he added with satisfaction. 'They didn't know about all the raids, it seems. And with dear old Charles's Oxford degree, he slid straight into an intelligence role. With Lillian to facilitate it all.'

We were silent for a moment.

'Lillian must have been furious about the painting,' I said.

'Furious enough to get her evil son to murder three people,' Lou said. 'More, if you count all the people killed in the raid.'

'What about Thelma?' Annie asked. 'If it was their house, why did they need a lodger?'

'They were going to use her as another spy,' said Arnold. 'I assume. She was in love with Charles, wasn't she? Keep an eye on her, and all that. Then he met you, and you were a better bet.'

'Exactly,' Lou said.

I put my head in my hands. 'I'm an idiot,' I said. 'A stupid, selfish, thoughtless idiot who nearly got you all killed.'

'And yet we still think you're all right,' said Lou, to my surprise. He smiled at me.

'The church hall dance is still on tonight, you know. If anyone fancies it. Marple enjoys a jitterbug.'

Couples were foxtrotting round the hall when we arrived and paid our 3*d* entry. The band was different tonight: a banner read MALCOLM TENNANT AND THE TENORS, and a man with greased-back hair and a loud suit was crooning away while cymbals crashed behind him.

'Would you like a drink?' Arnold shouted in my ear – they still weren't quite back to normal. 'Just a lemonade,' I shouted back, and he saluted. A sudden thought struck me.

'Arnold,' I said, 'I need to ask you something.'

He looked nervous. 'Fire away,' he said.

'Marple. How did you... well, I've kept wondering. How did you know about him being trapped?'

Arnold heaved a sigh. Couples danced past, laughing and clutching each other, and the door swung open again to let in a gust of chill January air behind Clara, still in uniform, who was with a woman I didn't know. She waved frantically.

'I should have said,' he admitted. 'But Lou would have court-martialled me. He told me about it right away because he was so upset it had been trapped with no food or water. He knows I'm fond of animals – even if they're not fond of me.' He lifted his wrist and showed me a livid, scarlet scratch. 'Nanette did that,' he said. 'I was only trying to stroke her. Anyway, Lou wanted to know if I could take Marple, but Mum's not keen on dogs,' he went on. 'So I said he should keep him. He's a lovely dog, really. But Lou said I wasn't to tell the press any details, and well, you're a journalist. Sorry, Edie – I knew I'd slipped up, as soon as I said it.'

I laughed. I looked at Arnold's puzzled, kindly face, and I couldn't stop. 'I thought you were the murderer,' I said eventually. 'I'm so sorry.'

He pulled a face. 'Haven't got the Latin,' he said, and then we both laughed.

'Let's get that drink, shall we?' he said, and I was about to follow him when Lou arrived at my side. The band were striking up a new song, faster and less formal.

'Dance?' he asked me.

I looked over at Annie, to see if she'd mind me abandoning her, but she was waving at Arnold, and he was going over to ask her too.

'Go on then,' I said. Lou took my hand and we whirled into the sea of bobbing couples. He was a good dancer, he knew when to pull and when to release, and how to hold me so I wasn't buffeted by all the passing traffic. I looked over at Annie and saw her head resting on Arnold's shoulder as they drifted round the floor. They looked happy.

For that brief dance, I forgot about Charles and Lillian and murders and paintings. The song reached its crescendo and we swirled on, dipping and swaying, moving in rhythm, glad to be here, to be alive, on this cold January Saturday evening, in a warm church hall with the war happening somewhere in the distance, somewhere that couldn't reach us here, tonight, as we danced on and on to the irresistible music of the band.

A LETTER FROM F.L. EVERETT

Hello,

Thank you so much for deciding to read *A Report of Murder*. Every reader has my eternal gratitude, because reading a book is an investment of hours and money and optimism that you'll enjoy it – and I so hope you enjoyed spending your valuable time with Edie, Annie and the others.

I'd love to know what you thought of the book – it would be wonderful to hear your views. The good news is, Edie and co will be back soon in a new novel, so to keep up-to-date with my latest releases, just sign up at the following link. Your email address will never be shared and you can unsubscribe at any time.

www.bookouture.com/f-l-everett

I've always been interested in the Second World War. At school, we used to watch a television programme called *How We Used to Live*, about housewives and ration books and brave men going off to fight. I always felt there must be more to it all than just courage and queuing, and I loved hearing my late grandparents talk about the war in Manchester, where I grew up. My grandpa was in the Home Guard and was once so cold he lit a fire on a freezing hillside to keep warm. Unwise. My grandma worked in intelligence, plotting planes on maps, and remembered crunching to work over broken glass during the

Blitz, and it was lovely to be able to incorporate some of their recollections into the book. It wasn't really so long ago, and yet it was another world, one now fading from living memory.

When it comes to Edie's ambitions, I started my own career as a columnist on the *Manchester Evening News*, and I wanted to explore what it felt like to be a local journalist back then, what happened when a terrible crime took place in a city that was already under bombardment, and what kept people going and cheered them up.

Thank you again for reading Edie's story. I hope you enjoyed it and, if so, I would be extremely grateful if you could write a review. It makes a huge difference in helping new readers to discover my books. I love hearing from my readers, wherever in the world you may be – you can get in touch through Twitter, Goodreads or my website.

Thanks again for reading,

Flic x

fliceverett.com

ACKNOWLEDGEMENTS

I'm always amazed by how many people get thanked in acknowledgements, and I feel a bit embarrassed that I hardly have any. That's probably because, much like Edie, I'm not a 'joiner-inner', so I shrink from helpful things like writers' groups and reading circles.

That said, there are some who must be thanked properly.

Firstly, Susannah and the wonderful Bookouture team, who believed in me and offered brilliant suggestions and so much support throughout. I'm endlessly grateful and feel extremely lucky to have landed here.

Thanks to the retired coppers of the Manchester Police Museum, who were so helpful (and much less sarcastic than Lou) and to the Imperial War Museum North, a fount of useful information.

I'm also grateful to my lovely friends, who listened to me banging on about my novel for years, and I offer a witchy sacrifice to the coven, who get me though the working day, every day.

Thank you most of all to my wonderful son, Wolf, who has had a lifetime of his mum staring into space and not listening properly because she's just had an idea; to my mum and dad, who made me want to write in the first place and actively encouraged reading novels at the dinner table; and to my relentlessly enthusiastic dogs, who drag me outside even when I don't want to go.

And to Andy, my beloved husband, who doesn't necessarily read my books immediately because they're not about breaking news or fluvial eco-systems, but is always entirely supportive of me writing them, and who also makes a lovely cup of tea.

Printed in Great Britain
by Amazon